Birth Under a Crescent Moon

Birth Under a Crescent Moon

JENNA WARD BRENNAN

Contents

For Julyett.

I am sorry. Sometimes growing doesn't always mean together.

I miss you my catfish friend. If you taught me anything,
it was how to dance.

"And Ossie, don't forget what happened to the man who suddenly got everything he ever wanted," said Wonka.
"What?" Charlie responded.
"He lived happily ever after."
"There is no life I know like your imagination. Living there, you'll be free like you truly wish to be."

Willie Wonka & The Chocolate Factory

My Life in the Year 2,010 A.D.

*T*here is a town that lives in the right side of my brain. The name of the town is Right Side, BR (BR is the postal abbreviation for "brain"). For some reason, in this town, the locals speak with a Southern drawl, like they do in N'Awlins, Lose-ee-anna.

To me, Right Side's Main Street looks suspiciously like St. Charles Avenue. Wandering the cypress lined sidewalks, I notice immediately that there are peanut shells where the pavement should be.

Blinded by thirst, I remember a time in 2,010 A.D. when I closed my bedroom door and walked alone down Right Side's Main Street.

I strolled for a bit and caught glimpse of a girl who sat rocking on a wooden swing that dangled from the posts of a decrepit looking porch. The girl's name was Claudia. As I passed by her, she smiled at the thought of my face. She held a book in her hand but I could not see its title.

This girl, Claudia, had red hair. She had red, curly, thick hair. You couldn't run your fingers through it if you tried. She had clean white skin too. It was pure as snow. Soft, flawless, pale, and Irish are all words that come to my mind when I think of her. She was very quiet, with a gentle soft-spokedness surrounding her. But Claudia, looked sad. She looked very sad.

I stopped to gaze lackadaisically at Claudia. Suddenly, a man with an unshapely goatee cried out to me. The man was leaning out of the second story window of a tall brick building, which was positioned to my left. I turned to walk toward him and kept stepping on the peanut shells that covered the ground where Main Street's pavement should have been.

I remember it being very hot as I walked. The street kept getting longer and longer. The shells kept multiplying and multiplying until I was surrounded by this sea of brown, wrinkly, pock-marked, broken shells.

When I grew tired of walking, I looked up and saw some other buildings and some more people. There were happy people. There were sad people. There were apathetic people. There were all sorts of people.

I spied another man sitting on a rocking chair in the middle of the shells. This man told me to sit down next to him and have a beer, so I did. It was good beer. It made me want to swim in the shells on the street. It made me imagine all of the shells being in neat horizontal lines like an army. None of the soldier shells in the image were broken and they all held nice, ripe peanuts inside of them.

I think the beer gave me a buzz. When I sobered up, I got scared. I stood up straight and ran. I ran faster and faster until I couldn't feel my breath any longer. All I remember was the sound of shells crackling and crunching underneath my feet.

Suddenly, Main Street stopped. It just stopped.

I was standing on an edge. When I looked down, it was dark. When I looked to my left, it was dark. When I looked to my right, it was dark. When I looked up, it was dark.

I bent at my waist and picked up a shell. I put it in my mouth. The shell was empty. I couldn't find the peanut. Then, I got the blues. I got the blues as if the blues were like the flu, or like a paper cut, or like something that needed nothing more than time to heal.

I closed my eyes and jumped off the edge.

Part One
Love

Gingko Berries

I am alive. I breathe. I move. I read. I think. I touch. I see. I drink. I eat. I fuck. I walk. I write.

For the past three years of my life, I have worked happily as a store clerk in Oz and Endz, a used bookdealership in Olde City. Today is my last day of work. I am moving far away and leaving many of the things I have loved dearly in Philadelphia behind me.

I want to leave here, yet I am home.

As I finish my last remaining tasks at Oz and Endz, I try to fight the uncomfortable feeling that has been churning in my stomach for the past week. It reminds me of the feeling I had when I jumped off the car the first time I rode Space Mountain when I was eight years old and visiting Disney World with my parents. Excitement born of fear is the strongest motivational force I have ever known.

When I graduated from Bryn Mawr in 1992, I had high hopes of capturing a glamorous job in New York City writing for "Spin," or "Rolling Stone," or some other ultra-hip, trendy magazine. If I didn't get that I figured I'd meet a modern day Gertrude Stein and hole up somewhere in the French Quarter of New Orleans writing my great American novel or some mind numbing poetry filled with all the tormented angst of Sylvia Plath or Dorothy Parker.

As I waited patiently for these events to happen to me, I stumbled across my position at Oz and Endz. I believed that, within no time, I would be able to save up enough money to create my own destiny. No time turned into three years, however, and three years of my life have escaped me as if three years lasted the length of yesterday.

Needless to say, I am now not a world renowned journalist and I have yet to pen my first novel. But I have learned great things here and I have loved great loves. And it will all come with me because there is nothing that I can leave behind.

Two days ago, I hired a girl named Audrey to replace me at the shop. Today is her first day on the job; I am training her.

I met Audrey before, on two prior occasions. Both times, she was dressed in black from head to toe, with the exception of her white Doc Martens. She'd spray painted fluorescent flowers on the leather boots in a haphazard pattern. Audrey's ears were pierced four times on each lobe and her right eyebrow once. At first glance, I almost dismissed her as nothing more than a fashion obsessed punk. She won me over though when she commiserated with me over the fact that she'd been reading Joyce's *Ulysses* for over a year and a half and was only on page three hundred and twenty-two.

I was ahead of her by forty pages.

I laughed when Gus, my boss, asked me to train Audrey. I thought he was joking. Running the cash register behind the big brown desk at Oz and Endz is a rite of passage, not a text book lesson.

In the end, Gus convinced me to give in. Although secretly wishing I were alone in the bookstore on my last day in Philadelphia, I now sit training Audrey.

It is late in my shift and I have grown fidgety. I move from behind the register and walk toward a glass enclosed bookcase on my right that houses our more expensive first editions. I stretch on my tippiest, tippy toe to reach the clock radio, which looks as if it has perched on the top of the bookcase since the beginning of time. Its reception is terrible. It only gets a handful of AM frequencies and two FM. On a clear day, I can tune in five or six different stations at best.

I fumble with the dial as Audrey interrupts me. She states my name matter-of-factly and then asks where she can find the Biography section. I muster up some polite cheer and point Audrey toward the biographies. She leads a frail-looking elderly man in the offered direction, chatting with him all the way. Watching her forces me to realize that I am in between worlds-the one in which my old life has ended and the next in which my new life is waiting.

I turn my attention back to the radio. I capture a steady strain of jazz crackling from 90.1 FM. I pause for a moment to let my hand rest lightly on the dusty wood of the bookcase. I am startled by the sickly clank of our silver metal "Ring for Service" bell and turn back to the register. I accept a handful of Harlequins from the grasp of a heavy set, red haired woman. On a clean white tablet, I begin to tally the prices that are penciled inside the front cover of each book. When finished, I wrap the paperbacks in a plastic grocery bag and hand it to the woman.

Harlequins. My mom always called them beach books—as if beach books were a literary genre. My mom loved beach books because they were a quick read. They always told the same story—a beautiful heroine falls in love, overcomes adversity to be passionately seduced by an even more beautiful hero, and then lives happily ever after.

I think that was the life my mom wanted for me. She wanted a quick read.

My mom only came to visit me once after graduation. It was a year ago, during early December. She called me out of the blue and said she was going to be in town for the weekend. She would be visiting my grandmother in the suburbs to take her to a doctor's appointment downtown. She suggested that we grab breakfast beforehand to catch up on things.

My mom knew that Remy and I had moved in together a few weeks before. We were living in the Devil's Pocket. Our apartment was small and not unpacked at the time of my mom's visit. Rather than subject mom to cockroaches, the corner drunk, rolling dust bunnies, and the edge of West Philly, I offered to meet her at Little Pete's on 17th Street. I told her that Remy had to work but that he'd try to come later if he could get someone to cover his shift at Third Street Jazz & Rock.

My life habitually runs fifteen minutes later than the rest of the world.

So that morning, I set the alarm twenty minutes early to ensure that I arrived at Little Pete's before my mother. I burst through the front door of the diner with the pages of the "City Paper" rustling through my left hand. I followed the rainy Sunday morning feeling of Philadelphia as it enveloped the restaurant's foggy windows, swirled about the shop, and lingered over the piping hot cups of coffee that wafted under the noses of regular customers.

I wiped the soles of my Doc Martens across the brown welcome mat, which read "Go Away." Then, I crossed the hard faux marble floor to the right side of Little Pete's "u" shaped counter top. I spun the red pleather cushioned seat of one of the three available stools and began to peel off the outer layers of my winter clothing. I scampered into a comfortable position and knotted my legs together underneath me. I did not have a straight view of the doorway.

Being early heightened the anticipation I had in seeing my mother again. I tried to calm myself by flipping through the smooth pages of the newspaper. I gulped long sips of my coffee and listened nervously to the tinkling bell, which rang each time the front door opened. The first few times I heard the jingle, I turned to see who was walking in. After awhile though, I stopped turning around and concentrated instead on the inside of my stained white mug.

I looked up instantly when my mother opened the door. It was as if her presence commanded my immediate attention. She wore a bothered, aloof look across her face. It was a look that revealed too much. I could tell she was thinking that this was the last place on earth she would ever want to be seen by whomever it was that mattered.

I watched my mother scan the room feverishly, until she recognized me sitting patiently awaiting her discovery. When she saw me, she tried a slightly forced smile strictly for my benefit. She moved toward me and leaned over to peck an insincere kiss on my cheek. As she did this, she draped her arms loosely over my shoulders in a weak attempt to hug me.

She greeted me in a high-pitched, sing-songy voice, which made her touch all the more surreal, "Hello, Claudia."

"Mother," I replied without hesitation, "It's good to see you."

There was an awkward pause between us. I began to worry if asking her to brunch had been a mistake. My worry slowly began to dissipate, however, when her lips erupted into a fragile grin.

She surveyed my outfit without comment. It was rare that she did not remark about my appearance—"you're too thin," "you really shouldn't tan," "that dress, it does nothing for you." I took her silence as a good sign. I felt it may have been her attempt at coming to terms with her daughter, the anomaly.

I fidgeted uncomfortably under her familiar stare. I was so accustomed to gazing into her blue eyes with child-like innocence that now my separation into womanhood forced me to feel foreign to her. My dependency on her, which had for so long felt like a burden to both of us, had disintegrated because I was strong enough to make my *own* decisions. In no longer needing her, I believed I had earned the respect one should gain in becoming equal to those under whom one had once been subservient.

My mother didn't agree.

My mother writhed free from the warmth of her coat. I hung it for her on the brass coat rack, which stood an arm's length from the doorway. Before we sat down, I asked her if she would rather move to a booth. She insisted she would be more than comfortable sitting at the counter where I had already strewn my coffee house persona. Instinctively, I knew by her tone that I should have selected a booth when I walked in earlier; counter's were far too bourgeois for a woman of my mother's stature.

The waitress returned to top off my coffee. My mother ordered coffee too and loaded it up with sugar and cream. I eyed her carefully as she poured cream from the white plastic containers given to her by the waitress. I laughed to myself remembering an old friend of mine who used to chug creamers in one gulp and then slam them with his fist as if he were crushing an empty beer can.

"So how are you, dear?" my mom asked.

"I'm doing great, mom. How's Nana?" I returned, in an attempt to divert her attention from me.

"She's responding better to the treatment. But I don't think that's saying much," she answered. "I have to watch the time so we're not late for her appointment," she forewarned me, in a droll tone.

"Yes," I agreed. "You have to watch the time. Traffic on a rainy day is always worse than you expect it to be."

"How long do you think it will take me to get out to pick her up?" my mother asked.

"'Bout half an hour," I said.

"Half an hour doesn't seem so long. Maybe you could get out to see her soon," baited my mother. "She'd love to see you," she added.

I cringed at the suggestion and tried to formulate a brilliant excuse in order to mask my apparent disinterest. I was relieved of the onus by our waitress who approached us and deposited long, laminated, diner menus into our hands. The menus were crammed with so many words that they were difficult to read. I smiled at the waitress and told her that we were expecting a third person to join us.

My mother tried to engage the waitress in conversation by making an off-handed remark about the rainy weather. Not to my surprise, the waitress grunted a monosyllabic response and wiped off the counter top beside me to set a place for Remy. She walked away to remove a cheese cake from a glass enclosed turn stile and left another menu behind in her wake. I watched as she carefully proceeded to cut off a huge chunk of the cake and serve it to a suspicious looking man who was sitting across from me.

My mother and I sat alone awkwardly and sipped coffee for longer than I would have liked. Then, she began to fill me in on all of the parties that she and my father had attended recently. With painstaking detail, she described who they hob-knobbed with, why they hob-knobbed with them, and what they hoped to gain tomorrow from hob-knobbing today. She rounded out her gossip column by rambling on about who in town was getting married to whom, who was going back to grad school, and who was pregnant in or out of wedlock.

I wasn't interested in anything my mother was saying but nonetheless tried to look enthusiastic, if only for her sake. I continued to smile at her mordacious comments. I diverted my attention toward the view of both Barton & Donaldson's, the custom shirt-maker across the alleyway from Little Pete's, and the neatly aligned ketchup bottles, which were stacked in rows underneath the counter top facing us.

I perked up slightly when my mother told me that her best friend's son, Ethan, would be in Philly soon. Ethan and I had grown up together and maintained sporadic contact during our college days. He played in an indie rock band named Don Carlos that toured the club circuit regularly. Last I'd heard, they'd wrapped up a string of European dates.

"Any idea when they're playing?" I asked my mom.

"No, no," she began. "I'm not sure Sarah told me. I think they're at some place called The Pass," she added, crinkling her nose in uncertainty.

"The Pass?" I repeated sounding perplexed. "Oh, you mean the Khyber Pass," I exclaimed.

"Something like that," my mother agreed. "Sarah's concerned that Ethan isn't eating. Apparently he lost his job at the newspaper and is living on donuts collected from a friend who's working the night shift at a local donut shop."

I chuckled as I pictured Ethan standing alone behind a dumpster, waiting for donuts. My mother shot me an annoyed look.

"What about you, Claudia?" she attacked. "Have you had any better luck lately looking for a new job?" she asked hopefully.

"Mom, I'm very happy at the bookstore. I'm not *looking* for another job," I scolded her. "I'm learning some great stuff about collecting—I'm hitting the auctions and talking to dealers from all over the country," I continued as politely as I could muster.

"Oh," she muttered almost dejected. She remained silent for a moment as if she were carefully calculating her next thought.

Then, she pushed with another sword, "What about grad school? Daddy could make some calls if you wanted to look into programs at Penn."

"I know, mom," I sighed. I closed my eyes and rolled my head along the back of my shirt collar.

"I thought about it but I'd like to do some traveling first," I told her. "Remy's trying to book dates for a Spring tour. I may take some time off to go with him," I added.

My mother digested my words slowly. After a long pause, she spoke again, "What does this boy do, Claudia?"

"He's a choreographer," I responded.

"A choreographer? How does he afford to *live*?" she dug.

"We're making ends meet just fine," I said harshly.

"I want you to do better than that, dear," she informed me, rubbing her fingertips across the knuckles of my right hand.

"Mom, Remy is wonderful. You're really gonna like him—you just have to get to know him," I started, trying to build up to my point. "There's something I've been meaning to tell you about him," I said cautiously.

"What is it dear?" she asked as she moved nearly to the edge of her chair.

I swallowed the growing lump in my throat. I opened my mouth to answer her but was interrupted by the sound of the bell dangling above the front door of the restaurant. I stole another sip from my dirty white mug. As a tiny stream of piping hot coffee dribbled down my chin, I turned to see Remy walking in from the rain.

I wiped the coffee from my face with the back of my hand and smiled slightly as I watched him shake his head like a wet puppy dog. Tiny droplets of water flew from his dreadlocks and broke into the air around him.

I spoke softly to my mother as if she were a fragile china doll who would break at the sound of my voice. I whispered, "Mother, Remy is here."

She didn't seem to hear me the first time I said it. I repeated myself again, waiting for a response from her that didn't come.

I sat quietly for somewhere near eternity and waited for my mother to say something. She remained silent.

"Sorry I'm late," Remy offered apologetically. He draped his wool plaid jacket over one of the hooks of the brass coat rack, next to my mother's.

He walked toward us at the counter and delicately placed a kiss on my cheek. I could feel my mother cringe. She started to fumble through her purse pretending to look for something like a lost tube of lipstick or a stale pack of bubble gum.

"Hi Mrs. Dubois," Remy said, trying to introduce himself in an upbeat tone. He extended his hand in my mother's direction for her to shake. She did not accept it.

"It's great to meet you. Claude's told me alot about you," Remy added sincerely. I could tell that he was nervous by the way he was chewing on the inside of his cheek. I guessed that the skin there was already raw.

I glanced at my mother. She deliberately avoided my eyes. She responded to Remy with composure so remarkable that she made me quiver, "You must be Remy. It's good to meet you too."

In the same breath, she continued, "Sit down. Here's a menu."

My mother's hand was shaking as she leaned over me and thrust the menu lying at Remy's place into his hands. She motioned for him to take the seat on the other side of me so that I was positioned steadfastly in between the two of them.

Suddenly, she changed the direction of her voice and addressed me coldly, "Claudia, I'm ready to order now."

My mom managed to quickly attract the attention of our waitress, flagging the unwilling woman over in our direction. Once in front of us, the waitress stared blankly over our heads with an annoyed look. She grasped a black pen tightly in one hand and a palm-sized note pad in the other. She cracked her gum loudly while she waited for my mother to speak.

My mother turned to me and said, "Go ahead, Claudia."

I blinked, startled by the attention. I had known what I wanted since I walked in earlier. I had been obsessing about one of Little Pete's tuna melts all morning. I never ordered anything but at the diner. The greasy, grilled sandwich tasted like nectar from the gods.

I closed my menu and flopped it back into shape with the jerk of my wrists. I hungrily ordered my usual, "I'll have the tuna melt with fries and a chocolate milkshake, please."

The unpleasant waitress scribbled something illegible onto her pad and turned to Remy. I was sure that my mother would be bothered by the fact that the waitress had neglected to take the ladies' orders first.

Remy wasn't sure what he wanted, so he motioned for the waitress to attend to my mother. My mom was quick to respond with a low fat request of fresh fruit and plain yogurt with granola. She also suggested that it would be nice if her coffee were topped off. Her tone was biting and seemed to irritate the waitress.

After Remy ordered, fresh coffee was poured for each of us. Remy opted to tempt fate further by requesting extra Sweet & Low. I was sure his audacity would result in someone in the kitchen doing something horrific to our food. I only hoped the waitress remembered that I was the one in the bunch who had kept her mouth shut.

I closed my eyes and inhaled deeply. Without the waitress, an awkward silence developed between my mother, Remy, and me.

Remy took it upon himself to break the deafening stillness, which hung in the air with the diner's stale cigarette smoke. His eyes darted between my mother and me as if he were watching a tennis match.

"I'm drenched. I didn't expect it to be raining so hard when I left the shop," he laughed. He brushed his jeans in an exaggerated motion, pretending to wipe water off the denim.

Remy stroked his neatly trimmed goatee with the index finger and thumb of his right hand and politely continued, "You guys been here long?"

Not expecting my mother to respond, I answered him, "No, Remy. We've only been here about fifteen minutes." My hollow voice sounded devoid of emotion.

Remy bobbed his head up and down in acknowledgment of my statement. I flinched as I felt his hand lightly massage my knee underneath the countertop. Although it was out of my mother's view, his gesture made me nervous. I ran the fingertips of my left hand across my lips.

Our waitress returned carrying the Sweet & Low and my chocolate milkshake, which she had just finished making. Remy sifted two of the pink packets of sweetener into his mug. I turned my attention to my milkshake and slowly poured the frothy liquid from its frosty metal pint container into a small glass. I unwrapped the straw I had been given and began to sip at the luscious concoction. Meanwhile, my mother watched both of us with a curious eye. She was ready to strike.

"So Remy, Claudia mentioned you had to *work* earlier," my mother said condescendingly. "Where do you *work*?"

Remy sensed what she was trying to do and handled her well. "I work at Third Street Jazz and Rock," he responded politely. "It's just my day job though."

"Starving artists have to eat too, you know," he added wistfully, tilting his head slightly in my direction.

"It's a CD shop that's close to the bookstore, mom," I interjected. "That's where Remy and I met," I told her.

My mother ignored my comment. I took her cue and buried my head in the copy of the "City Paper," which I had drug in with me earlier. I began to flip mindlessly through the pages and waited for the next word of the conversation in which I was clearly not welcome.

"Hmmm, interesting," my mother muttered to Remy.

She ignored his starving artist comment and continued, "Does your shop specialize in any particular type of music?" she asked, almost sounding genuine.

"Mostly Jazz," Remy answered. "We've got a great space in Olde City. It's two floors," he explained. "We've got the most expansive collection of Jazz and Blues anywhere in Philly. That stuff's my specialty. We also carry enough modern rock and other Billboard money makers to keep the ship afloat," he added.

"I rather enjoy New Age myself. My husband and I recently saw George Winston perform at the college theater in town," my mother said.

Remy listened intently, eyeing my mother curiously as she paused to pick tenderly at a French fry plucked from the plate the waitress had just delivered to her.

"You should check out Temple's jazz station while you're in town, Mrs. Dubois. I think you'd really get into it," Remy told her.

"One of my buddy's hosts the Sunday night historical show. Plays alot of the old school stuff. I stop in to see him any chance I get when I'm up at school," Remy continued.

"Oh, do you go to Temple?" my mother asked.

Intrigued, I looked up from the paper. Remy was self-taught and street smart. He shunned formal schooling and kept his artistic projects personal. Unadulterated creativity comes only from the heart. Remy had been gravitating more and more often toward the Academe as a source of financial support; grants and fellowships were emerging as the key to his survival.

"Sort of. I'm a candidate for Tyler's Artist in Residence program," Remy explained.

"Really," my mother remarked. "Artist in Residence," she repeated. "What exactly does that entail?" she pressed again.

"It's a mutually beneficial relationship. For me, it helps out financially to free up my time," Remy responded as he shook his head. "It lets me devote more effort to my dance company and choreography," he continued.

"Really?" my mother exclaimed with slight interest. "Claudia hadn't mentioned anything about your creative work," she added, patting my hand.

I shot her an annoyed look and jerked my hand away. Angrily, I turned my head down toward my food. I listened half-heartedly as Remy began to tell my mother about his dance company, Pure Motion. I began mindlessly pulling the excess tuna chunks from my sandwich. The crust was tough and chewy but the soggy parts of the bread melted in my mouth.

My mother listened to Remy politely but seemed to be growing restless. Remy sensed her disinterest and turned to concentrate on his food. My mother finished her granola and signaled the waitress for our check. Then, she nudged me softly in my ribs and whispered in my ear requesting directions to the bathroom.

I wished that I hadn't suggested we eat at Little Pete's. I avoided their bathroom at all costs. It was cramped and dirty. To get to it, you were forced to wriggle behind the counter and traipse through the greasy kitchen where you were ogled by foul mouthed line cooks. I thought about lying to my mother for a moment by saying that they didn't have a bathroom. I figured things couldn't get much worse for me though and pointed her in the right direction.

My mother patted my shoulder and got up to walk to the back. I slouched forward, closed my eyes, and sighed to myself in defeat.

I could feel Remy lean closer toward me. He rubbed my neck with his strong hand. He shook me forward and back a few times with the weight of his arm.

"How ya' hangin' in there kiddo?" he asked.

I looked up at him and let loose a half-hearted smile.

"Don't worry," Remy said. "We'll bail right after we pay the check. I'll take ya' home and give you a *real* back rub," he promised.

Remy always knew just what to say to make me feel better. I put my hand over his and spoke with a far off stare, "I know. I know."

My voice sounded defeated.

My mother made no remark about the bathroom when she returned to the counter. She snatched the bill from beneath the metal napkin dispenser. Remy and I hadn't noticed it was there; I guessed that the waitress must have folded it and dropped it off when we weren't looking. My mother carefully examined the tiny slip of white paper for errors. Once satisfied, she tossed down a few crumpled bills from her wallet for a tip.

She chugged a long, last slurp from her coffee cup and announced abruptly, "I'm stuffed. Are you two ready to get out of here?"

Although we didn't ask for an explanation, she continued, "I've really got to get going to your grandmother's. Her appointment is at 3:00PM."

The listless cashier took the bill from my mother's hand. She paid him without a word. Remy tried to split it with her but my mother would not accept his offer. I plucked a mint toothpick from the plastic dispenser near the register and gazed at the autographed black and white photos of famous people who had eaten at Little Pete's before.

Remy and I applauded the tuna melts, omelets, and French fries and thanked my mother far too many times to prove sincere. I pretended to clutch my stomach to show how full I was. Remy held the glass doors for us as we stepped outside into the misty drizzle. I could feel the dampness penetrate my skin. The humidity was high and I remember wondering if it were raining in New Orleans too.

My mother and I fumbled to open our umbrellas. Remy crawled under mine to shield himself from the sky. He took the umbrella from my hands and raised it comfortably above his head so that he was no longer forced to crouch to my height. We all avoided each other's eyes. I turned back to steal a glance inside Little Pete's windows. The diner looked warm and inviting. It reminded me of something you'd see on a television show.

The three of us walked slowly through the raindrops down 17th Street, turning left onto Locust. Amidst the fallen and slippery autumn leaves, tiny gingko berries splattered on the sidewalk under the pressure of our feet. The bicycle tires and skateboard wheels treading and turning on the asphalt street squished them too.

I watched my mother's nose upturn, as she exclaimed in disgust, "What is that smell, Claudia? It's awful."

"It's just the berries from the gingko trees," I answered, as I kicked one of the yellowish-green fruits from the curb.

"The history behind the trees is that the city imported them directly from Japan years ago to enhance our fall foliage display. Supposedly they dropped a pretty penny on them before anyone discovered the smell," I continued, offering a feeble explanation.

"The berries should only be around for another two weeks at the most," I concluded.

"Regardless Claudia, I don't want you guys tracking them into my car," my mother advised me in one of her most aristocratic voices.

I shook my head in disgust. In the distance, I recognized the outline of my mother's deep blue SAAB parked on the left hand side of Locust Street in front of the red doors a church. From experience, I knew that she was parked illegally. I expected that she would have gotten a parking ticket. As we walked closer to the car, however, I glanced on her windshield and did not see the familiar white slip of paper under the wiper blade. Somehow my mother had miraculously escaped the Philadelphia Parking Authority.

"Mom, you know what?" I asked.

"Hmm?" she answered sounding disinterested.

"I think Remy and I are going to walk back uptown," I said.

"But Claudia, it's raining," my mother said, stating the obvious. "I really don't mind dropping you off. I would love to see your apartment. I wanted to see if there was anything I could send you to make things more comfortable," she added.

"No, that's O.K., mom. I like walking in the rain. I have a few errands to run anyway," I lied.

"Oh Claudia, are you sure?" my mother whined. "It looks like it's going to start pouring soon, and I don't want to see you catch cold," she said.

Remy squeezed my hand tightly. I wondered what he was thinking.

"No really, you head up to see Nana. I'm sure she's waiting for you. We'll be fine," I told her.

Remy stood quietly behind me with a supportive smile on his face. He hadn't said a word since we'd left Little Pete's. He just splashed happily in the puddles and seemed to have slipped into his own little world.

"Oh all right, if you insist. I suppose there isn't much else I can say," said my mother. I thought her voice sounded relieved.

"At least let me take you to your first stop. Where do you need to go?" she offered.

I gulped as I tried to think of a believable answer for her. Remy did not offer any suggestion. He had begun humming to himself. I could tell he did not want to be involved in my self-created foible.

"That would be great, mom," I said. "There's a CVS up a few blocks on Chestnut. Would you mind heading over there?" I asked.

"No, not at all," she responded.

She pushed open the automatic locks of her SAAB and we all piled in. Remy scrambled into the back seat, still without uttering a word. I hung out of the passenger side and tried to shake some of the water droplets from my umbrella. I accidentally splashed the leather interior of the car and brushed the seat wildly with the palm of my hand in an attempt to hide this fact from my mother.

We pulled away from the curb and turned left onto 16th Street, heading toward Chestnut. I gazed out of the foggy window into the side view mirror and watched as our tires spun along the pavement. The tires stopped and started abruptly at traffic lights and screeched through alternating speeds of fast and slow. They forced a gentle mist to swirl up behind their treads. I watched this mist break into smaller and smaller droplets—the water splintered and shattered before my eyes.

We continued with our strained conversation, focusing our discussion on the historical sites that I pointed out around us. My mother appeared disinterested and seemed to concentrate intensely on her driving. I tried to take advantage of the awkward pauses of silence, which occurred between us by slipping into introspection.

I struggled to absorb the distinct feeling of the rain on an unseasonably warm December day.

"Here is fine, mom," I yelped suddenly, as we stopped at a red light on the 20th block of Chestnut Street.

My mother pulled behind a car parked in a row of meters. She flicked on her hazard lights. We were blocking a fire hydrant.

"Thanks alot for brunch, Mrs. Dubois," Remy said, finally breaking his silence.

"You're welcome, Remy. It was very nice to meet you," my mother answered.

"Now Claudia, you call soon and let me know how things are?" she asked rhetorically, as she turned toward me in the front seat.

"I will mom. Thank you for everything—it was great to see you," I told her with the beads of wet tears growing in the corners of my eyes. I did not want her to see me cry.

"Here let me give you a hug," she said, as she leaned over in her seat.

She held me and whispered very softly into my ear, "I never thought your life would end up like this, Claudia. I had always wanted something more for you."

Her words were like a hot metal branding iron, which seared into my skin.

That was the last time I spoke to my mother. I called her this Christmas but was at a loss for words and hung up the phone before she even knew it was me.

Looking back at that day, I find it funny that my most vivid memory I have is of my mother bitching about the fallen ginkgo berries squishing under our feet as we walked. Although I admit the berries emit a more than unpleasant smell, I have grown accustomed to them.

To me, they represent a change in season.

I pick up a tattered copy of *The Unbearable Lightness of Being* and flip through its pages. With the dull tip of my pencil, I scribble a tiny "25¢" mark in the upper right hand corner of the front cover.

I steal a look at Audrey and ask her to finish what she is doing so that we can close the shop. In a whirlwind, I show Audrey how to lock the safe and both the front and back doors. I rush through the lesson on how to arm the alarm, feeling only slightly guilty in knowing that Audrey will more than likely set it off the next time she opens the shop.

Audrey thanks me for helping her and invites me to a party in Northern Liberties. I explain that I have some errands to run before leaving town and decline the offer, telling Audrey to go on without me. Audrey leaves and I am left alone among the books.

Third Street

Old East coast cities breathe history through every pore. Underneath the bright patterns of graffiti and the stench of metropolis garbage, grin brick faces littered with intricate stained glass windows, vinca-lined flower boxes, and lattice wrought iron railings. Such understated detail is charming because such understated detail is something to hold onto from a past that's long forgotten.

Characterized by specific architecture, occupants, and trade, each finitely carved boundary of an inner city neighborhood creates an unmistakable personality. I love many distinct sections of Philadelphia; I have often fantasized of living in Queen's Village, Headhouse Square, Antique Row, Rittenhouse Square, Northern Liberties, and even the Badlands.

My favorite area of town is Olde City.

The neighborhood lies within a few cramped blocks surrounding the end of Market East. Sprinkled with historic landmarks, Olde City has emerged from the continuing renovation of abandoned warehouses and restaurant wholesalers. Its once industrially raped streets have grown infested with starving artists, dedicated musicians, and the tragically hip.

Olde City is now an exciting and budding art district, filled with the craftsmanship of both unknown local talent and widely appraised nationally and internationally acclaimed virtuoso. Galleries, quaint restaurants, bohemian coffee houses, and antique shops have sprouted up in many of the low-rent lofts. Daytrippers are constant and the night life is rich.

In the evening hours of the First Friday of each month, the shop vendors and fifty of the gallery owners in Olde City open their doors to Philadelphia for a gallery crawl. Exhibits at mainstays, such as Veem, Zone One, Vox Populi, and Phantom serve wine and cheese catered to art aficionados and those wishing to see and be seen. Extravagant bouquets of fresh flowers purchased just hours before color romance into the air. The sounds of bongos, saxophones, and fiddles drift from stoops and through the fading light of day.

Because I worked in Olde City, I had a great deal of time to wander through the crooked walkways and alleys tucked away between the river and Sixth Street. Hidden just off Market amidst the shadows of a pawn shop and a deserted office space, sat a CD shop called Third Street Jazz and Rock. Third Street overflowed with Jazz and Blues treasures that could be found nowhere else in the city.

I often lingered outside the entranceway of the store. On my lunch breaks and in between shifts, I would stop to peruse the bills posted on the store front, which advertised local music shows, theater events, and movie engagements. Then, I would pop inside to see what was new.

On one such occasion late in the dog days of August, I was standing in front of Third Street. Puffing furiously on a Camel Light, I watched as two lanes of traffic whizzed by on the tight, one lane street. The day's air was still but the tires of the cars and buses forced hot gusts of wind up into my face as they passed me by.

I finished my cigarette and flicked the butt into a sewer grate. It narrowly missed the base of a city parking meter, which was just off to my left. I paid special attention to the parking meter because someone had left a small dinner roll on top of it. I found this odd because I wasn't sure why anyone would leave a dinner roll atop a parking meter. I watched the roll curiously as it teetered under the rush of the cars. Its crust looked hard and stale.

I turned back around toward the store and pushed the heavy handle of Third Street's door down until its latch released. I thrust the door open inwardly and leaned against it. I scanned the bright room. The white fluorescent lights, which hung above my head, forced hazy halos and hurt my eyes. The air felt cool and I wriggled in my gray dress as I settled into my skin.

I recognized the wailing of Bessie Smith in the background. Her songs alternated between some other sensually scratchy, blues tunes.

There were two guys working behind the front counter. They were both rhythmically tapping pens or pencils against any surface through which sound could resonate. They were dressed in carefully selected thrift shop/I. Goldberg attire.

My eyes focused immediately on one clerk in particular. I watched him as he drifted toward the back of the cramped store room. He stopped periodically to straighten the albums and CD's lining the wide aisles. I had noticed him on other visits that I'd made to Third Street. I often invented excuses to talk to him. This was not difficult to do—he was a walking Jazz archive with discriminating taste. By asking him innocent questions, he had turned me on to the likes of Coltrane, Lady Day, and Miles Davis.

I walked past a dirty looking boy with mangy hair, which was skunked pink. He wore oversized jeans with a thick, silver chain hanging from his back pocket. I planted myself next to him in the vocalist section and started fumbling through the familiar names and titles. I stumbled across the words "Nina Simone" scrawled in indelible black marker across one of the white dividers.

I began to thumb through the clear plastic cases of CD's. I lifted a select few up toward my face and searched the songs lists for a particular Simone tune. I'd heard the song years before in the movie *La Femme Nikita* but didn't know its name. I figured I just might get lucky and find it.

I had been busily enthralled in my quest for more than a few minutes when I sensed a sudden surge of energy surrounding me. I felt a pair of eyes on my back, which made me grow uncomfortable. I shifted slightly to my left in time to see his figure directly approaching me. He stopped just inches from my side and seemed to focus his attention on my hands. I could feel the warmth of his body.

Excited, I turned to stare into his face. I smiled. I recognized the faint shadow of a goatee surrounding his mouth. I couldn't tell if he was just beginning to let it grow in or if he had recently trimmed it back. A small, gold hoop earring hung from his ear and drew my attention to his natty, sexy dreads. They were neatly rolled into tight mattes and tied back in a loose ponytail, which hung heavily against his neck. There were a few light streaks of brown kissing the top strands of his hair.

He wore a clingy white T-shirt and wrinkled khaki pants. I could barely distinguish the dark ink of a tattoo peeking from underneath his shirt. I wasn't able to see exactly what it was. His brand new sneakers were a white pair of Nikes or Reeboks or some other very expensive basketball type shoe that meant nothing to me except that they were his. A sparkling gold rope chain dangled over one of his wrists.

I was consumed in all that is male; I was drinking it in through my pores.

I heard his deep voice echo beside me. It sounded like maple syrup.

He purred, "Simone is hot, white hot."

"I don't know about this one though," he said, as he took the CD I was holding in my grasp.

I blinked stupidly. Dumbfounded, I was amazed that I had nothing to respond.

"I think you gotta go for something that tests her emotional level a little more than this," he explained as he shook the CD up and down in his hands. He brushed his palm over my knuckles and pulled out *Pastel Blues*.

"Try this one," he said. "It's fat," he added, even though I hadn't tried to elicit his opinion.

I looked at him as nonchalantly as possible. Pointing to the CD, I replied, "Yes, I've heard of this one before."

"I'm actually looking for one of her tunes they used in *La Femme Nikita*," I told him.

"Which one?" he asked bluntly.

"It's in the scene when she's gazing out of the window in her new apartment," I started to explain.

"Isn't that the French version of *Point of No Return*?" he interrupted me.

"You've got it reversed," I said, correcting him. "*Point of No Return* is the American version."

He took my remark well and asked, "How's it go?"

I began to hum a few bars aloud from my tone deaf ear: "Birds up in the sky, you know how I feel. Sun up in the sky, you know how I feel. It's a new dawn, it's a new day . . ."

He smirked at my pathetic Simone rendition.

"I know the song," he continued. "You won't find it on *Pastel Blues*," he said, as he began to flip through the other Simone CDs. As he reached the end of her section, he shook his head to confirm it wasn't there.

"You know, I think your best bet may be in the movie soundtrack section," he suggested, pointing to the row behind us.

He scuttled off to the other aisle and submerged his head in a row filled with soundtracks. He pulled an orange colored CD case up from the stacks. The reflection of the sun on the plastic bounced from the wall to the ceiling and back again. I watched him mouth the list of songs on the compilation to himself as he traced the words with his index finger. I slowly began to walk toward him.

"Here it is!" he exclaimed with a white smile.

He extended his arm in my direction and handed me the CD. I stared blankly at the fuzzy picture of Bridget Fonda, which was emblazoned on the cover.

"Track number six," he told me, pointing to the song.

"Uh, uh, umm. Thank you," I stammered, forcing the words from my tongue.

I searched for a response to keep him engaged in conversation but could not capture my normally quick witted genius. He turned from me, and be-bopped away to the beat of an unrecognizable tune that was reeling in the background. My eyes were glued to him. I noticed him pause briefly to straighten up a few titles askew on the shelves. Finally, he slid between the box sets and one of the cash registers behind the busy counter, and offered to help the next customer.

I forced myself to look away from him, and tried to dedicate my attention again to the soundtracks. Unable to concentrate, I glanced up at him once more and started toward the downward leading staircase. I was tempted to turn back to see if he had noticed my movements, but did not. I gripped the hand rail tightly and listened to my chunky black heels clomp noisily past the framed antique prints announcing tour dates for Fletcher Henderson, Ella Fitzgerald, and Dizzy Gillespie.

The windowless basement was dimly lit. It appeared far more congested than the first floor. I wandered past another register, which sat on a small isolated island. I nodded hello to the short, balding cashier who wore a pair of tiny gold-rimmed glasses. He reminded me of Ben Franklin.

"Indie Rock?" I questioned him.

"On your left," he instructed me monosyllabically. With the jerk of his head, he pointed to a corner filled sparsely with inventory.

Instead of voicing a formal thank you, I smiled at him and then followed his directions. Many of the white Indie Rock dividers announced the names of bands whose CDs weren't in stock. Many of them were unfamiliar to me. I started to look for Don Carlos' new release.

"Hey girl," interrupted a high pitched, sing-songy voice from behind me.

"Oliver? Is that you?" I buzzed cheerfully in response.

I worked with Oliver at Oz and Endz. He had been with Gus even longer than I. He claimed that his position at the book shop was the only steady day job he could hold on to in addition to his weekly drag stint at Bob & Barbara's, a jazz house on South Street.

"I thought you were supposed to be in the shop today, cher," Oliver said. He spun me by the shoulders and leaned to kiss me on the cheek.

"Just on lunch," I answered, inhaling deeply.

I clutched his thin elbow with my hand and added, "I'm headed back in a few minutes. What are you doin' in here?"

"Couldn't you find something more interesting to do on your day off?" I joked.

Oliver pried my grasp from his arm and wrapped his fingers through mine. We stood holding hands like small school children. When he squeezed his grip, I could feel his tarnished silver and turquoise stoned rings dig into my flesh. I blushed innocently and glanced down at his scuffed, maroon wing tips.

"I was on my way over to Jabez on Market to get my nails done and I thought I'd stop in to see how *he* looked today," Oliver giggled.

He grinned and displayed a brilliant smile for me, which was broken only by the front tooth he'd lost months ago in some vicious pillow fight. His nose scrunched up a little and he pushed his thick black, coke bottle glasses up even closer to his blue eyes.

"Oliver!" I scolded slightly.

My now wide eyes searched the basement excitedly to see if *he* had followed me down the steps. I didn't want him to inadvertently overhear Oliver taunting me.

"Come on Claudia, did you see him yet?" Oliver whispered. I shook my head yes.

"Wellllllllllll?" Oliver slurred, as he tugged at my dress sleeve playfully. "Did you talk to him?" he pushed further.

"A little bit," I responded coyly.

"And?" Oliver pressed again.

"*And* what?" I teased, turning my head and flinging my curly, red hair from my shoulders.

"I'll get it out of you sooner or later," he threatened.

Oliver paused and cracked his neck, rolling his head from side to side. He abruptly changed the subject by asking, "Do you have time to help me pick out a new shade?"

Confused, I stared at him inquisitively.

"My nails!" he exclaimed, answering his own question. Oliver lifted his arm and fanned his fingers out for my benefit. The flame-red colored enamel that covered them was chipping and in obvious need of a touch up.

I snuffled in response.

"Let me see those," I said, pulling his left hand toward me.

"Oh, dear, how could you let these get such a mess?" I asked, melodramatically, trying to imitate his normally campy tone.

"You *need* new tips, dahling! First, we'll buff them. Then, the polish. Then, I have an absolutely fabulous new spotlight pink I think you'll love," I continued, rushing my words together.

I could sense Oliver was growing fidgety. He jerked his hand away from me awkwardly. Breathily, he clucked, "Claudia, you are sooo insensitive. I mean really. You just don't take me seriously."

I was taken aback. Realizing that I'd offended him, I rolled my palm lightly in circles on his back in an apologetic gesture.

"Oliver, sweetie," I whined, trying to comfort him. "I'm only joking. Come on, I'll walk you over to the shop."

He pouted for a moment and then beamed his toothless grin in my direction. He extended the crook of his arm for my taking. He lifted his chin proudly and inflated his chest in an almost militaristic gesture. I accepted his offer and placed my hand on his bare skin as if I were a gloved New Orleans debutante coming out during Mardi Gras.

"Shall we?" Oliver proposed. We drifted back upstairs together, chatting nonsensically.

Once Oliver and I reached the top of the stairs, I nervously jerked my hand from his arm. My eyes darted around the room. I recognized the outline of the dreadlocked ponytail I was hoping to see.

He was still behind the front counter, leaning forward languidly to speak to another customer. He connected his words with wide, sweeping gestures. Watching him, I became entranced. I coquettishly swung my limp and droopy arm, twirling the CD's I had been holding against my hip from side to side.

Instinctively, Oliver sensed my change in mood almost immediately. I was sure he was enjoying the tension of my emotions with me, as I myself experienced them. I felt my body become rigid. Oliver turned toward me to see my expression. I wore nothing more than a disquieted smile.

"You wanna look for anything else?" Oliver asked, trying to bide us more time. I shook my head no in response.

"Come on then," Oliver said, as he pulled me forward by my black leather satchel.

I continued to fiddle with the CD's and playfully fondled the plastic case of *Pastel Blues*. I stared ahead at the line of customers winding haphazardly in front of the counter. Oliver and I walked forward and listened intently to the clacking sounds of the cash registers' keys as they grow louder. I bent my head to rummage through my purse for something. I wanted to appear busy.

"Claudia, baby, I need to get some air," Oliver said, as he interrupted my search for nothing.

"How 'bout I wait for you outside?" he asked.

My head shot up with the speed of a cat startled by an unexpected sound. I stretched my eyes open wide, as if to tell Oliver "no." I wanted him to stay with me so that I did not have to struggle through an awkward conversation alone.

Oliver knowingly ignored my unspoken plea and started for the door. He turned back to wink in my direction and wiggled his fingers in a flirtatious wave. I felt my cheeks flush pink and made a brief and feeble lunge after Oliver. I missed latching onto his smooth arm by only an instant.

In leaning forward, I bent too closely to the edge of the counter. My cotton dress snagged with a pull on one of the umpteen staples that pinned posters to the wooden facade. My interest in Oliver quickly subsided. He slipped out the front door as my sigh reverberated in my own ears. My attention was drawn to the tiny hole that I had torn through the fabric. I couldn't sew and I instantly began fretting that I'd ruined one of my favorite dresses.

"Hey take it easy there, kiddo," came the smoky voice from behind the register. "Ya'll right?" he asked.

Embarrassed by my own awkwardness, I became self-conscious of my body. I clenched the muscles in my legs tightly and stood solid ground. Intentionally, I inflated my chest. Although he did not show it, I knew that this gesture made it impossible for him to ignore my breasts. I was blushing more than I had been earlier during my brush with Oliver.

He bent at his waist over the counter and focused his eyes on my dress. With a sensuously warm and welcoming grin, he held out his hand for the CD's I had collected. I wasn't sure what he was reaching for and glanced down, not realizing I was holding anything at all.

"What's this one?" he asked, thumbing through my treasures.

"The new Paula Cole," I replied, moving closer toward him. I crossed my forearms and rested my elbows heavily against the top of the counter. I dug my nails slightly into my skin and let my head sink into my chest. I was careful not to break my stare.

"I think I've heard a track or two off that one on WXPN," he said. "The rhythm was pretty cool but it jus' sounded like one a those male bashing feminist albums to me," he continued, trying to make conversation.

"Male bashing?" I questioned. "Do I look like the kind of girl who'd be into one of those male bashing feminist albums?" I joked.

He paused for a moment, seemingly to collect his thoughts.

"You could be trouble," he answered. He flashed his eyes toward the keychain that I twisted and rolled through the fingertips of my right hand. I shot him an inquisitive look.

"It may be the way you're holding those keys," he explained. He lifted his right arm and rested it on his left wrist. He raised his index finger and touched the tip of his nail to his lower lip.

He hummed softly and then he added, "On second thought, maybe it's the way you jerked from this counter when I tried to move toward you."

He tilted his head back to stare at the ceiling as if it were the work of Michaelangelo. His ponytail swayed with his subtle movements.

He inhaled deeply and met my stare once again. "No. You know what? It's your eyes," he decided.

My heart sank into my stomach. I felt like a fourth-grade school girl who had just been caught gawking at the boy who lifted up her dark plaid, fourth-grade uniform to see what he could see. I reached for my calves as if to pull up an imaginary pair of argyle knee socks that the little boy had pushed down around my ankles. With no escape, I began to giggle.

"So you decided to go with this one instead of the soundtrack?" he asked, waving Simone's *Pastel Blues* in the air in front of him. He removed the CD from its plastic casing with the turn key.

"Yup," I answered him. "Something new and different," I laughed, tossing my red hair back from my shoulders.

"You gotta take your chances when you get 'em," he said with a wink.

"Or your chances pass you by," I said, finishing his sentence for him.

His body stiffened, as he stood up straight and inhaled deeply. With business like air, he announced, "That'll be $30.11."

"$30.11," I repeated his words. I handed him my VISA card and said, "Full refund if I'm not satisfied, right?" I joked.

"You don't trust my judgment?" he shot back, accepting my credit card. He scrunched his eyes up and crooked his head sideways.

"A girl's gotta be careful," I replied, coyly.

He steadied the credit slip on the counter top in front of me. I signed my name nervously, embarrassed that my hand was shaking. I hoped he didn't notice. Gingerly, I accepted my CD's from him. They were neatly wrapped in a brown shopping bag.

"Thank you. Thank you very much," I whispered.

"Big day for Jazz and Rock," I said, jerking my neck backward to the long line of anxious customers. He shook his head and snickered at me.

I turned and made a feeble attempt to smile at the short, black woman who was standing behind me. She was holding a Sydney Bechet box set. The old woman shifted her feet, clearly annoyed. She made it painfully aware that she was disturbed by the length of time it was taking me to make my purchase.

"Hey, we're performing at the Painted Bride this weekend if you'd be into it," he proposed, before he took the other woman's purchases.

"Gimme a call if you want. I'll put you on the guest list," he added. He leaned forward and picked up one of the store's business cards from the disheveled stack next to the register. He reached toward me and tried to slip the card into my bag.

"Thanks," I muttered, as I motioned to push his hand away.

I was careful not to touch him. "I know where to find you if I need anything else," I said.

He shrugged his shoulders. I watched him open his mouth again, as if to speak. He stopped himself though and accepted my rejection as if it were part of a game. I turned around and began to walk away. Instinctively, I felt his eyes on my body. I did not turn back when I reached the door. With the flick of my wrist, I twisted the cold, smooth handle of the knob and stepped outside.

Oliver was sitting on the front stoop of the pawn shop. His shoulders were swaying slightly as he danced to an imaginary beat. He heard Third Street's door creak shut. His dancing came faster and he jumped up at the sight of me. He snapped both of his hands, clapped once, and twirled around in a 360. Then, he shot his index fingers forward in my direction.

"You luuuuuv him. You luuuuv him," Oliver taunted in his own little rhythmic ditty.

He repeated himself over and over. I ignored him and tossed my new CD's into the depths of my near bursting black leather bag. I fumbled frantically around inside of it for my Camel Lights and my Circle K lighter, which I had acquired during a long ago road trip to New Orleans.

Enveloped in the sickeningly, stifling Philadelphia air and burning bright sun rays, which penetrated the city's smog, I lit my cigarette. I inhaled a long, smoky drag and began to release a puffy white trail of clouds into the still air behind me and over my head. I stepped toward the parking meter where the stale dinner roll remained untouched. The meter was out of time.

I smiled to myself. I began to bob my head to the cacophony of Oliver's chant and we both began to laugh uncontrollably as we danced together in the street. I stumbled in one of the sidewalk's cracks and knocked the roll off the parking meter. Attracted by my sudden movements, two hungry pigeons swooped to the curb to devour through the crust.

This made Oliver and me laugh even harder.

I was already fifteen minutes late for work but I didn't care. Arm and arm, Oliver and I skipped toward Jabez on Market Street, so he could get his nails done. I did not look back through the windows of

Third Street Jazz and Rock. But I guessed that my friend was inside, watching me dance like a love sick fool.

(*"You're slipping away from us," admonished the laos. "You're playing games with him as if you thought there could be more. You promised us that it would always just be us," they reminded her angrily.*

"I don't think that wanting more should necessarily carry inherently negative overtones," she said.

"You should be careful what you ask for. You just may get it," they answered brusquely.

"Let me have this. Please, let me have this," came her invoking chant.

The laos chattered amongst themselves. "We shall lose her to an open mind, should we not be careful.")

Again, Coffee

C rushes. I love having crushes.

You get that giddy feeling in your belly as if a butterfly is flapping its wings deep inside of your stomach. You wake up in the morning with a smile on your face because you've been having great, erotic dreams. You take every step of each new day with a boingy spring, hoping to catch a glimpse of him walking into work or catching the bus home at night. You concoct wild fantasies all day long in your head as to how you will meet, fall in love, and live happily ever after. You phrase, rephrase, and even jot down the conversations you rehearse yourself having with him in your thoughts.

Yes, I love having crushes. They make me feel so young and free.

Crushes are oxymorons. Crushes are oxymorons because they're almost always a Catch 22. Waiting for reciprocation keeps you hanging on. The waiting becomes equally as frustrating as it does exhilarating. Your heart can ache for someone for months, even years, until you experience the climax of the relationship. They call this *closure*.

You may never meet and so your crush just fades away. You may meet him and find out that he's a jerk, so you're left with nothing more than a shattered crush. Or you may meet him and hit it off, then your crush actually develops into something more. Until the day of closure, however, you have no choice other than to sit and wait, rewinding your sightings of him over and over in your head.

Meeting *him* at Third Street was enough to keep the wheels of my mind spinning for weeks. I made excuses to roam Second and Third

Street between Arch and Market as often as possible, hoping to bump into him. Gotta look cool; gotta look casual; gotta look like I was just passing by on my way to or from work.

There was a coffee house nestled low on the corner of Church Street, the tiny alleyway a few hundred yards from the CD shop. It was called The Last Drop. Because Oz and Endz was only two doors away, I often found myself settled at The Drop, hiding in its dark corners. I would sit alone after work for hours on end, pondering the state of affairs in my life and everything that touched it.

I liked the place because it was easy to get lost in the cushions of its couches and huge armchairs. Since the "Best of Philly" rankings hadn't discovered it yet, The Drop was guaranteed status as an acceptable spot to frequent if you were one of those dark, brooding artist types. With $1.50 you could stretch a cup of joe over hours of stimulating conversation, countless cigarettes, and the innumerable pages of a journal or book.

Above every table of The Last Drop hung a frosted, floral-patterned glass lamp, which dangled from a long cord in the ceiling. The lamps filtered a weak light onto the tables beneath them. Each table was littered with mismatched mugs and saucers and an Elliot's Amazing Juice bottle filled with a bouquet of fresh flowers.

Ashtrays in the shape of Texas and other random ceramic shapes were shuffled constantly from one side of the room to the other. Shelves of books and games like backgammon, chess, and Scrabble covered the back wall. Local artists' work was regularly displayed and rotated through all available space including the basement, which was also open to the public.

My friend Nathan opened The Drop long before the 1990's made coffee houses in America hip. Nathan had his fingers on Philly's pulse. I often joked with him that he invented the word "opportunity." At the least, I am sure he never let one pass him by. The Drop set the stage for the coffee house explosion in Center City but Nathan always managed to keep it a step above the rest.

Nathan let The Last Drop run on what he called "auto-pilot." He hired a bunch of artsy-fartsy PCA kids to do everything. He never asked them any questions and never got hung up on the way things worked. Once in a great while, Nathan would breeze in to make some calls on the portable phone and devour a slice of cheese cake but that was about it.

Although The Drop was one of Philly's better kept secrets, I knew that if you lived or worked in Olde City you were bound to stumble in for coffee sooner or later.

I figured it was only a matter of time before I ran into *him*.

Although it was already October, Philly was still writhing in the humidity and funk of Indian Summer. I sat alone at The Last Drop on a particularly sunny Thursday afternoon. My table was sandwiched between the tall, open windows of the coffee house and an odd shaped wall, which hid the plumbing. The windows covered the entire store front.

Usually, I chose not to sit by the windows because I found them far too distracting. However, on that day, I forced myself to recall the feeling of an icy, cold January wind on my face. The thought made me decide to take advantage of the last few remaining breaths of warm summer air. I sat alone before the window. From my table, I discovered that I could extend my reach outside to scrape my fingernails along the bricks of the coffee shop. They were chipped and weathered.

On the whole, Church Street was not heavily trafficked. It was only in the distance that I could distinguish the sounds of horns shrieking, sirens wailing, and buses spewing exhaust into the already toxic smelling air. The people that passed by were few and far between; they usually paused only to lock or unlock their bikes or to tie a shoelace. I eyed them each curiously and smiled at them on a select basis.

I remember that the espresso machine was broken that day. Because you couldn't get a latte or a cappuccino, nearly everyone was sipping the blend of the day, including myself. It was New Orleans chicory.

I was reading Camus' *A Happy Death* and trying to block out the faint crooning of Bing Crosby, which was rumbling in the background. I looked up from my book long enough to light another cigarette. Reaching for my Circle K lighter, I knocked my mug and splattered droplets of black coffee onto the stark, white reports from Oz and Endz that I should have been muddling through. I swore under my breath and smeared the dribble that had fallen from the edge of my cup. The reports were stained a drab yellowish-brown color.

The Last Drop's front door occupied one corner of the shop. It was difficult to open because it stuck to the frame. The regulars knew to bang the wood about a foot-and-a-half up from the doorknob. It was like a secret knock or password. As I puffed on my cigarette, I spied an older man standing outside on the stoop. He was clad in a tattered red sweatshirt. He struggled with the door, tugging and pulling at it. This sent his body into odd shaped convulsions. He avoided my eyes, knowing that he had captured an audience in me.

I looked past the man and into an empty bank parking lot, which faced The Last Drop on the other corner of Church Street. The brick lot had only five to seven spaces and was partially fenced in along three sides. A skinny black guy stood at the edge of the lot near the pedestrian entrance. He hung out there regularly. He always carried two plastic milk crates and a bulging brown shopping bag with him.

From the window of The Drop, I watched him curiously. He bent to position the crates on the ground so that they flanked him diagonally on each side. From the paper bag, he pulled two scraggly looking puppets, which hung from strings fastened to popsicle sticks.

I strained my neck for a better view. The female doll was unattractive. Her hair was made from a yellow mop. The shape of bright red lips were sewn across her face. She was stuffed full and burst through the stitching in spots along her raggedy dress. The male doll was a chocolate brown color. He wore a striped T-shirt, which reminded me of the one Ernie used to wear on Sesame Street. His pants were ripped and slatternly patched.

The man primped and fluffed at the puppets. From a square suit case he yanked a transistor radio. He opened the suitcase wide and placed it next to one of the crates to collect charitable donations. The man steadied the radio precariously on the uneven top of the suitcase and appeared to tune in a station. All the while, the puppets clanked heads and tangled their strings as they dangled from his right hand.

The man straightened his back and stood tall with his arms extended level to his shoulders. He began to move his arms fervently and the puppets began to dance. The man's lips moved with his motions. I could not hear his words over the cacophony of strange city sounds that filtered in through the open windows.

I shifted restlessly in my chair and rose to get my one free refill. I walked forward to the counter and passed two guys who were playing chess at a table beneath a busy sketch of an empty baby's carriage. One of the guys had a shiny, bald head. He was turned away from the board with his back to the chess pieces. He called out his moves without looking at the table. His chessmate moved his pieces.

When I reached the chess table, the bald kid stood and stretched widely, knocking me off balance with one of his arms. He apologized profusely and insisted that he hadn't seen me.

I shook him away and assured him that I was more than fine. I glanced down at his chessmate, immediately recognizing the dreads. It was *him*. He did not look up at me but the force of my realization of who he was hit me like a bolt of lightning.

I was surprised that I had not seen him when I came in earlier. I decided he must have either been hiding in the basement or had wandered in through the downstairs door without my noticing. I tried to swallow the choking lump of anticipation that was sitting in my throat; I felt an overwhelming sense of relief in knowing where he was.

I plopped my empty mug on the counter and motioned to capture Cedric's attention. He was trapped listening to a guy named Terence who was babbling on about some biblical passage or another.

Cedric had worked at the coffee house for almost three years. He started part time just after he decided that his career at Philadelphia Fish & Co. was going nowhere. He was a local cartoonist who got up early every day to draw cartoons and listen to Howard Stern. He was pretty good but he smoked too much pot, which precluded his success. My conversations with him were usually pretty brief but always very direct. We talked about things like the love of sloth, the death of the novel, and the birth of cool.

Cedric jumped to help me. He snatched my mug from the counter and cradled it in his palm. I realized that his eagerness was not so much to respond to me quickly but to escape Terence's ramblings. I gulped, knowing that I would fall prey to Terence next.

"Helllllo," boomed his thick, Fat Albert-like voice.

I stared back blankly at Terence's big, flabby figure. He wore a dirty purple T-shirt and dark blue Lee jeans. A green L.L. Bean backpack dangled from his shoulders. All of the backpack's zippers were open. From the zippers, hung crumpled, folded papers and torn notebooks, which looked as if they would shortly fall into forgotten piles behind Terence's thundering size thirteen feet.

I did not feel like talking to Terence. I ignored his greeting.

"Is something wrong, Claudia? You look sad," Terence said.

"No, Terence," I replied tersely. "Everything is fine. I'm just trying to finish up some work," I said. I hoped to excuse myself quickly so I could get back to my table.

"Are you still at the book store?" Terence pried in an attempt to capture my interest.

"Yes, I'm still at the book store," I told him, as I turned my body at the waist to watch the chess match from the corner of my eye.

"Do you know if this week is a buying Sunday, Claudia?" Terence continued, as he positioned himself more carefully along the corner of the counter.

"I have a bunch of paperbacks that I wanted to drop off to see if Gus would be interested in them," he explained.

Book buy back was twice a week at Oz and Endz—seven o'clock to eight on Tuesday evenings and one to three every other Sunday afternoon. For Gus, book buy back was sacred time because it was mutually beneficial for both him and our customers. Gus loved book buy back because it offered him the opportunity to discover hidden treasures. Meanwhile, our customers were thrilled at receiving fifty cents a piece for their trashy paperback novels, which were spotted with stale potato chip grease and reeked of stale cigarettes.

Although most of what Gus acquired during the few hours was junk, he was anxious to see what people were reading and what they were looking to read next. Book buy back fit the bill because it guaranteed a steady trickle of customers, thereby providing Gus with a venue through which he could talk to the readers one on one.

The heavy influx of books created a mammoth work load for me and Oliver but I didn't mind. I enjoyed it because it enabled me to listen and learn from Gus as he chattered on about publishers, first-editions, and the lives and influences of a broad spectrum of writers. Although Gus could afford to be more than selective during these engagements, he often accepted more than what we could obviously resell. I suspect that he did this for nostalgia's sake as much as anything else.

For an instant, I thought of lying to Terence and telling him that Sunday was not a buy back. I didn't have the heart though. Terence was harmless enough—he was just a lonely soul, whose sadness was enough to make him seductively grotesque.

"Yes, Terence. Gus will be in on Sunday," I answered. "Just so you know, he's not taking any sci-fi or harlequins."

"But I've got a bunch of Dean Koontz," Terence pleaded. "I thought that was a big seller for you guys," he added.

"It's not up to me," I replied. "I guess it's worth a shot. Gus may be interested in seeing them," I said, as I lifted my piping hot mug of chicory flavored coffee from Cedric's hands.

I ran my left hand down the side of my green polyester dress, brushing off some lint. I watched as my bright red nail polish fanned in waves along the material. I turned my head down and to the side for a better view of the chess match. From the corner of my eye, I could see *him* shove one of his knight pieces forward, across the board. My interest in Terence was quickly waning, like a waxy moon.

"O.K., then," said Terence in a dopey, slow voice. "I'll stop by on Sunday," he continued.

I had already begun to walk away from Terence with my coffee in tow.

I sauntered passed the chess match on the way back to my table and met *his* stare. Our eyes were deadlocked, as if we were in a battle to see who would flinch first. I forgot to breathe. I became self-conscious for a moment, wondering if anyone else in the coffee shop were watching us. I forgot to breathe, again.

I wondered if we could break the Guinness Book of World's Records statistic for the longest stare ever. I felt almost disappointed when he surrendered with a smile. He nodded his head and rubbed his eyes with his large hands. He blinked widely as if waking from a deep sleep. I knew he recognized me. A surge of warm energy tingled and teased the hair on my arms and I felt tiny goose bumps begin to puff up on my thighs.

I stopped at my table and clunked my mug against its hollow wooden top. I sat down. His back was facing toward me. He rocked back and forth unsteadily on the two hind legs of his chair. With each roll, his dreads skimmed the top of my bag, which was laying on top of a mess of paperwork.

He was chomping on a processed-looking pastry that was packaged as if it had come from a convenience store. He crumpled the pastry's plastic wrapper with his fist in an annoying rhythm.

Cautiously, I interrupted the chess match, "What are you eating?"

He turned his head toward me. He smiled, hinting that he welcomed my question. It was his opponent's move.

"Pumpkin pie," he answered.

"Tastykake?" I asked, demanding more specifics.

"Tastykake," he confirmed.

"I didn't know Tastykake made pumpkin pie," I told him. "It's sort of an odd flavored pie to market commercially."

"Yeah, I guess so," he replied. "I think it's a seasonal thing. I can only find 'em between September and December," he added.

"Once in a while," he continued, "I'll find one on the shelves as late as February. But then you gotta start to wonder how long the thing's been around."

"Yeah, February seems like a stretch," I mused. "January would even be pushing it," I surmised.

I grabbed for my Camels but inadvertently pushed them off the table. They fell to the floor beneath his feet. He dropped his chair back to its four legs and bent to pick up my cigarettes.

"Takin' a break," he said to his chessmate who appeared to be deep in thought. His chessmate jerked his head up from the chess board and shot him an annoyed look.

He pushed himself up and turned to walk toward me. He rested a hand on the back of my chair and crouched down next to me. I pretended to be engrossed in my work. He flipped the top of the box of Camels open and pushed one of the cigarettes out with his thumb. I crooked my head slightly in his direction.

"And I thought Tastykake's were bad," he said sarcastically, as he motioned with his eyes for me to accept the cigarette.

I lifted it to my lips and handed him my Circle K lighter. He lit my cigarette. I inhaled and leaned back to look at him. "Thanks," I said.

He nodded in acknowledgment. "What are you working on?" he asked, nudging my pen.

"Just some accounting stuff from the book store," I replied.

"I've seen you at Oz and Endz before," he said.

"I've seen you at Third Street before," I rebutted.

He raised his eyebrows and laughed lightly. He drummed the cigarettes against the nylon of his black jacket. He slid the corner of the box between the white stripes on his sleeves. This made a high-pitched zipping sound.

"How was your performance at The Bride?" I asked earnestly.

"It was fat," he exclaimed. "Why didn't you show?" he remarked.

"I wasn't sure what type of performance it was," I answered.

"Street dance," he explained. "Don't worry that you missed us. You can stop by Group Movement any time and catch us."

"The studio on Fourth Street?" I clarified.

"You got it," he said.

"Remy Thomas Pure Motion," he buzzed. He pulled his hand from my chair and dropped the cigarettes on my table. He made a locking hip-hop move with his hands. It was so quick that he stopped moving before I could focus on the gun shape formed by his index finger and thumb.

"Lemme guess," I said. "You must be Remy Thomas," I stated rather matter of factly.

"In the flesh," he replied, sticking out his chest in a proud posture. I rolled my eyes at him.

Our conversation was interrupted as one of the waitresses dropped an empty coffee cup to the floor with a crash. Glass shattered in countless directions. I watched the waitress mouth the word "fuck" with her lips. She stood for a moment with her hands on her hips, twirling her pierced tongue through her open mouth.

The waitress slipped away behind the counter. Nathan quickly appeared with a broom and dust pan. The waitress returned and offered to take them from him. He pushed her away, pointing to the kitchen. He began to sweep up the floor furiously. He winked up at me as he sifted the broken glass into the dust pan. I was surprised to find him working.

The furor subsided and the chessmate that Remy had abandoned called from the other table. He looked irritated.

"Hey Remy, what's up bro? It's your move," the bald kid announced. He waved at the board with exaggerated hand gestures.

"I'm distracting you," I said apologetically. "Group Movement, huh?" I teased, as I turned my attention back to Remy.

"A pleasant distraction," Remy flirted. "Group Movement," he confirmed as if he were extending an invitation.

He lithely stood and slithered back to his chess match. Before he sat down again, he turned back to me. He said, "You didn't tell me your name."

"You didn't ask," I told him.

"I'm asking now," Remy shot back.

I hesitated in an attempt to be coy. I replied, "It's Claudia."

"Claudia," he repeated in a whisper. He spoke the word just loud enough for me to hear. He sat and began to eye the board carefully.

I began to fumble with the papers, books, and pens that were strewn across my table. Although I was nervous, I started to shove my belongings deep into my bag. I tried to appear as nonchalant as possible and paused to glance outside the open windows. I sensed that it was growing late because the afternoon was slowly drifting away into dusk.

I recited the word "Remy" over and over again in my head. I could feel a smirk manifest itself on my face. I flipped my hair back from my eyes in an elaborate gesture and eventually managed to scrape up the last of my things. I slung my bag over my shoulder and lifted my half-empty coffee mug. I drained a last sip of the now cold brew.

I walked to the front counter and slid my mug across the smooth surface. It stopped near a pile of other dirty dishes, which were waiting to be washed. Nathan was perched comfortably on a wobbly, wooden stool that was positioned next to the toaster. He was chatting on his portable telephone. He flagged me to wait for him to finish.

I tapped on my left wrist as if poking at an imaginary watch. I had nowhere else to go but I wanted it to look as if I were in a hurry. Nathan nodded his head and lifted his index finger motioning for another second. He jumped up and began to shuffle through an enormous pile of books, notepads, and newspapers. From somewhere in the midst of the mess, he pulled out an orange and black colored flyer. His eyes scanned it quickly, as if checking for errors. Nathan offered me the flyer.

"Halloween," Nathan explained in a whisper, ignoring the babbling voice on the other end of the line.

I accepted the flyer. It was an invitation to Nathan's annual Halloween extravaganza. I tossed my bag onto the counter and adjusted my stance so that Remy would have a clear view of me. I unzipped my bag and pulled out my calendar. I placed the invitation in the book as a page marker. I hoped that Remy was watching.

"Thanks, Nathan," I said, lifting my bag again.

"Hold on," he commanded the anonymous voice on the phone. "Got your costume yet?" he asked, switching his attention to me.

"I've still go two weeks," I answered mischievously.

"Topping last year's slinky is gonna be tough," Nathan said.

"Don't worry," I promised. "I gotta run. I'll see you soon."

My hand was resting lightly against the cash register. Nathan squeezed it gently and continued talking to the voice on the phone.

Church

My college days at Bryn Mawr were passed with privileged freedom. My parents believed in the American Dream and imposed this fallacy on me. I always assumed there would be someone else to pay my bills so that I could just play. I figured that once I finished my grueling liberal arts degree, I could move to New Orleans where everything would be O.K.

I didn't make it to New Orleans after graduation. I realize now that I didn't make it because there was no one else to live my life but me. My dream of moving to New Orleans just wilted into my soul and became my paragon.

Alligator, crawfish, and oyster po-boys. Marie Laveau. Peep show lined Bourbon Street. Hurricane's at Pat Obrien's. The Garden District. Jackson Square. Listening to WWOZ at the levee. The Moon Walk. Pralines and cream. Dr. John. Mosquitoes biting my legs at a camp site in Fountainbleu State Park. Plastic Mardi Gras beads. Street cars running on St. Charles Avenue. Early morning chicory coffee and beignets. The sign for JAX Brewery. The bust of Professor Longhair at Tipitina's. Doubloons. Jambalaya. The second floor porch of Ann Rice's house.

("If I had this," cried angel number one.
"If I had that," cried angel number two.
"If I were there," cried angel number three.
"If I had more money in the bank," cried angel number four.
"If I could retire, I would just play golf. That's all. Just play golf,"
cried angel number five.

"But you don't even know how to golf," she reminded herself.)

One of the first conversations I ever had with Remy was about how much he hated the East Coast. He said he wanted to be somewhere else. I remember getting very defensive because I had never known anything else but the East Coast. Neither had he really. It was in our blood.

In the same conversation, I told Remy that Halloween was my favorite holiday. He laughed and said Halloween was as close as the East Coast would ever get to Mardi Gras. I told him I didn't care. It was my favorite holiday because it *reminded* me of Mardi Gras.

Then he asked me what I thought of when I watched the Mummers' Parade on New Year's Day.

"Mardi Gras," I answered.

I decided to be a hanging plant for Nathan's Halloween extravaganza.

It was a very basic costume. I bought a tall plastic trash can and cut it down so it fit around my waist. I hung the trash can from my shoulders with a pair of rope suspenders. Then, I scattered Spanish moss and Pathos leaves around myself and stuck a hanger in my hair. Walla—a hanging plant!

For good measure, I painted my nails with black polish.

Nathan lived in an old, renovated church on the corner of Forty-Fifth and Pine. He kept a small apartment on the main floor where the sacristy had once been and rented out the space downstairs. The church's architecture was classic West Philly. It had the kind of woodwork, stained glass windows, vaulted ceilings, and one-of-a-kind doorways that they just don't make anymore. Its atmosphere was at once ethereal and institutional—and perfect for Halloween.

At the time, I was living alone on Ninth and Catherine. I took the trolley from town into West Philly for the party. I got off at the stop on Fortieth and Baltimore and wandered through the cold in my costume. I had to move slowly because I kept losing my leaves. I cut through the University area. There was a great deal of mayhem with all of the college kids running around their fraternity rows.

I could tell when I was nearing the church. People were filtering in from all directions. I was almost knocked over by a guy who was riding a rickety, rusty Huffy bicycle. The guy was dressed as a four foot tall, bright orange carrot made out of paper-machie. He pedaled passed me furiously, missing me only by inches. He brushed against me and handed off a burning roach. I tried to thank him but he was moving too quickly.

"It goes with your costume," he yelled to me with laughter.

In an instant, the carrot was a few hundred yards ahead of me. I watched him stop on the front lawn of the church near a sign, which was perched on the street corner. The sign was bright white and anchored on each side by a metal post. With a u-lock, the carrot struggled to secure his bike around one of the posts. I walked toward him. Slowly, the sign's black, block letters came in to focus for me. In crooked lines, they spelled out cheesy phrases like "Come and Dance the Demon's Dance," "Boo!" and "Happy Halloween!"

By the time I reached the sign, the carrot had already disappeared inside. I was greeted instead by the Denorex man and a beguiling mermaid, both of whom were quite scantily clad for the weather. Together, the Denorex man and the mermaid were arranging the letters into nonsensical jumbles. I helped them form the word "succubus." Unfortunately, we were missing a letter "c."

I ran my hand along the smooth, oak railing of the church's front porch and waddled up the steps in my garbage can. I heard giggling behind me. I was high now. The dark night felt surreal and circled me in paranoia. I turned around to see if the laughter was directed at me. My eyes were met by a thin, pale girl who was wearing an ivory silk slip. She carried a thick book about dream analysis.

"Oh, I *love* your costume," she said, tugging lightly at one of my wilting leaves. "How did you think of it?" she asked.

My lips forgot to answer her and pursed to survey her instead. "What are you?" I prodded.

"A Freudian Slip," she replied with a twirl and a curtsy.

With that, she flitted past me and to the front door. She paused to talk to a lesbian couple, each of whom was dressed like Rambo. The three of them walked into the party together. I followed behind, leaving a fluffy trail of Spanish moss at my feet.

A young boy covered in colorful fall leaves kept dropping to his knees to pick up my moss. He tried to stuff the remnants of my costume around me again but I jerked away. He repeated himself over and over, "You dropped this. You dropped this. You dropped this." He sounded like a broken record that I wanted to smash against my thigh.

Immediately inside the door, stood an elevated lectern. Tacked to the lectern was a single piece of notebook paper on which was scrawled in crayon, "Donations, $10.00." Behind the lectern was a funereal-looking Elvira who was thumbing through a stack of crumpled bills. She towered above me, stiff as a board.

She smiled at me in her black lipstick and purred, "Ten dollars please."

I raised my eyebrows at her and struggled to pull money from the green corduroy jumper, which was buried beneath my plant. I handed her my donation. She directed me to a set of stairs on either side of us and told me that I would find drinks to my right.

She accepted my bill and dropped back slightly. She regained her composure quickly. I squinted to see her eyes because I didn't think she was blinking. A guy dressed as a priest appeared from a red curtain behind her. He was holding a pack of Neco wafers and dropped one into Elvira's mouth. He began to run his tongue along her neck as his hands rolled against her tight black dress. Her smile grew more sinister with his lingering touch.

I thanked Elvira and took the stairway to my left. A white cat teetered menacingly on the landing above me. It was Nathan's cat named Pastor. When I reached the top of the stairs, I bent clumsily to pet his fur. Frightened by my awkwardness, Pastor scampered away and left me grasping at empty air.

I followed the sound of the heavy bass, clomping my heels against the hollow hard wood floor. Thick tapestries hung down, hiding the party as heavily as if they were iron clad doors. I pushed through the rippling waves of the fabric and crawled through to the next room. A couple dressed as a pair of salt and pepper shakers tumbled in after me through the hole I had left in the curtain.

It took a moment for my eyes to adjust to the light and fervid activity. Candelabras were strategically positioned along each wall. The flames of single, non-drip candles danced in lines along the communion rail, food tables, and bar. Distorted shadows from the poor lighting moved against the corners and blank spaces of the church. Nathan had removed the pews to create a wide open area from the center of the room to the walls.

Although the crowd didn't seem at full force yet, a determined excitement was growing. A few giddy girls roller skated about in unsteady figure eights. As I stepped forward and free of the tapestries, a petite, blonde Alice in Wonderland in a short powder blue dress and white headband whirred past me in a blur. I nearly toppled over from the force of her speed.

I was sure the rollerskaters would wear out their welcome before the bobbing for apples or jack o'lantern contests got well underway.

I turned full circle to get my bearings. A tattered looking scarecrow dangled from the balcony above me. Two hockey players had wrenched their way between the pumpkins, which were perched on the ledge. They poked at the scarecrow with their hockey sticks as if it were a piñata. The scarecrow swayed violently, dropping strands of hay to the floor below.

The tangled cords from which the puppet hung jerked as one of the hockey players knocked a pumpkin off the balcony. The pumpkin's flame blew out in an instant as it smashed to the floor, coating the hard tile surface with a stringy, orange mush. It missed me only by inches. The balcony erupted in laughter as Big Bird roller skated over the mess and tripped. He snapped his plastic beak with his fall.

As Big Bird struggled to roll back onto his feet again and repair his beak, I escaped to the bar.

"Claudia, why didn't you call me?" came Oliver's voice from the behind the bar.

"I could have given you a ride," he explained. Oliver was juggling keg cups between one hand and the other. His outfit was filled with complicated paisley patterns—from his socks to his pants to his shirt. It was all very cluttered and very loud.

"Thanks, Oliver," I replied. "I don't mind the subway though. I wanted to save you the trip to South Philly," I added.

"That's a lot of paisley," I commented. "Part of the costume?" I asked.

"Don't you know what I am?" he demanded.

I shook my head. Oliver quickly shouted, "My car!"

I shook my head. Oliver's car was an unreliable 1978 Volvo that he drove only "on special occasions." The car was so rusty and unsightly that Oliver recently painted it with pink, purple, and blue paisleys. The project took nearly a month. The car had since become infamous on the city's streets. I secretly hoped that someone would offer to buy it from him soon; I hated the thing.

Oliver pulled a black keg cup from a short stack for me and asked, "Light?"

"No, how about a Lager?" I responded hopefully.

"Not a problem," he answered.

"I'll give you a ride home, Claudia," said Oliver, as he handed me my beer. "I figure since it's Day Light Savings Time you can just stay with me at the loft tonight."

"That'd be great," I agreed. "I'll be able to roll out of bed in time for my shift at the shop tomorrow," I added.

"Oliver! Oliver!" screeched a high-pitched voice from behind me. A small, bubbly girl dressed as a belly dancer jumped toward Oliver in a fluid motion. Although she looked familiar, I pulled away from Oliver with my drink in tow.

I moved toward the center of the room. In a comfortable circle, Nathan had strategically arranged two fluffy couches and three rickety rocking chairs. The seating sat over a deep blue oriental rug and surrounded a long coffee table, which was lined with food. I was getting the munchies and dove quickly in a bee-line toward the only available rocker.

I tried to wriggle my way into the rocking chair but my garbage can proved too wide. Instead, I opted to squeeze myself into a tiny space on one of the couches. In moving, I tripped over a tall white bucket anchored by the weight of heavy sand.

A square sign sprouted from the sand on a thin metal post. The sign read, "BUTTS."

"Yo! Watch it," warned a guy sitting at the edge of the couch.

The guy was dressed as the Una-Bomber. He was tapping a blunt against the bucket. The smell of pot crept from his lips. The smoke wafted up from the cigar shell as he handed it off to a friend who was one of the few people in the church not in costume. He looked miserable. He grunted as I wedged my way between him and the food.

The spread was pretty impressive—chips, dips, pretzels, creme puffs, twinkies, chocolate malt balls—the whole nine yards. I stretched toward the table, leaning to reach the salsa. An elbow shot me in the upper arm, forcing me to drop my tortilla chip into the bowl.

"Oooooo, salsa," sang a deep voice from my left.

I turned to see a tall, Latino man dressed in an oversized plaid suit. A Minolta camera hung from his neck. The camera kept catching on a laminated "press" badge, which was pinned to his jacket pocket. His glasses hung low on his face and a cigarette dangled from his lips. His crooked hat was pushed back on his head. Stuck under its red band was a gnawed yellow number two pencil.

I eyed the press man curiously as he danced a strange rhythm. He scribbled furiously on the pages of a white pad and smiled at me as he continued on with a silly tune about the salsa. When he'd finished writing, he ripped out one of the pages and handed it to me.

"Oooooo, salsa!" he said again, as his eyes trailed over my body.

I blushed. He tipped his hat and wandered away into the crowd. I stared at the words on the paper he'd left me. It was a love poem about me and salsa. He captured my attention with his description of the murky red color of the dip but lost me when he tried to make weak rhymes with words like jalapeno and my libido.

I crumpled the paper into a ball and shot it into one of the butt buckets. I moved back to the couch but the Una-bomber's friend shot me an evil look. I plopped down instead on an antique wheel chair, which wobbled on the uneven floor. I rolled the wheels back and forth in a rocking motion and nestled in to watch the crowd move to the rhythm of the DJ's House.

The DJ played on a stage, which was covered by a plush, red carpet. It filled the space where the church's altar had once stood. He artfully dodged a giant swing that undulated from a hole in the ceiling where I guessed a crucifix used to hang. Big Bird was standing on the swing, swaying higher and higher to the steady beat of the music.

A small crowd had gathered below Big Bird, each waiting for his or her turn on the swing. There were orange pylon cones marking off the area. The cones were intended to maintain a certain safe zone. I didn't think they were working very well though. In the few minutes that I watched, three different people were nearly impaled by Big Bird's beak.

"Pretty cool, huh?" remarked a familiar voice from my side.

I felt soft, warm breath on the nape of my neck. I quivered with the sensation of a moist kiss, which was placed on my forehead just beneath my plant hangar.

Nathan whispered, "Hello, Claudia. I'm glad you made it."

"Nathan," I sighed, welcoming the sight of a friendly face. I leaned toward him and pressed my lips lightly against his cheek.

"I wouldn't miss this one for the world. You've out done yourself," I told him. "I love the decorations."

"Cedric helped," Nathan answered.

"Cedric from the coffee shop?" I questioned quizzically.

"Yeah," Nathan answered. "He's renting some space from me downstairs," he added.

"I didn't see any 'Pathetic Potato' comic strips."

"They're around," Nathan told me. "Cedric *was* my personal costume designer this evening."

"Step back," I commanded, expecting a better view of Nathan's outfit. I twirled my index finger in the air, indicating that I wanted him to do a 360°.

I felt a grin creep onto my face.

"Robin Hood," I exclaimed. "Clever."

Nathan wore a quirky, little elf hat, which sat high atop his head. A faded orange pull-over covered his thin chest and hung loosely over his black jeans. It was laced in a criss-crossed pattern. Monogrammed across the left pocket of his shirt were the initials "RH." He even wore green boot-shoes that curled markedly at the toes.

"What's this?" Nathan asked, tugging at my sweater.

"It's cold outside," I explained.

"Go stash it my room. It's back behind the stage," Nathan offered, twisting his neck toward the sacristy.

"I think some people are hangin' out back there but you can put it in my closet. Nobody'll fuck with it there," he said.

"Are you sure you don't mind?" I asked politely.

"Come on, Claude," Nathan chided. He bumped my shoulder unexpectedly. He started to apologize but was interrupted by the grunts of an elderly balding gentleman.

"Dad," Nathan bellowed. "I didn't know you were here already."

Nathan's father muttered something that was inaudible to me. He stumbled in circles around us, filming our movements with a battered-looking video camera. I watched him curiously. He was dressed as a doctor in wrinkled scrubs and a white lab coat. Wrapped around his head was a thick elastic headband with a round light in its center.

"Claude, have you met my father?" Nathan introduced.

"No, I haven't had the pleasure. Mr. Kaplan," I said, extending my hand for his dad to shake.

"*Doctor* Kaplan," he said, correcting me. I giggled thinking that he was making a joke.

"Actually, Claudia," Nathan interrupted, "it *is* Dr. Kaplan. My pop's a professor at Penn."

Slightly embarrassed, I apologized to Dr. Kaplan. He seemed unfazed. Rather than accepting my hand shake, Dr. Kaplan grabbed the end of the stethoscope that hung from around his neck. He began to mouth words into it, as if it were a microphone. He stared at me with a growing smirk that seemed sleazy to me.

The buttons of Dr. Kaplan's lab coat were crooked. It was covered with red splotches of paint that looked like fake blood. The name tag above his pen pocket read "Dr. Kevorkian."

Dr. Kaplan dropped his stethoscope back to his chest and fluttered a flirtatious wave at me. Nathan bumped his father at his hip and tapped me on the shoulder.

"Claudia, why don't you put your sweater in the back," he suggested.

I nodded in agreement. Taking my cue, I drifted off leaving Nathan alone with his father.

I started toward Nathan's bedroom. I finagled my way passed a cow, a bear, and a piece of salt water taffy, only to reach an impasse at the swing. Big Bird was pushing the squealing Alice in Wonderland back and forth into the air. Her short skirt and white gartered thighs had captured a rather large audience. I tried to dodge the action by following the line of orange pylon cones. Alice's foot, however, found contact with my arm and pushed me back into the communion railing. My fingers brushed through the rippling flame of one of the candles that was positioned there.

I jerked my hand away quickly and scuttled passed the DJ. I smiled as apologetically as possible to him and hurried off the stage. I forced open the door to Nathan's room and nearly fell inside.

The room was surprisingly quiet. The space was oblong and felt loft-like.

A few acoustic guitars strummed softly against the back wall, while a tone deaf midget belted out an almost unrecognizable version of an old Cheap Trick tune. A young couple groped furiously on Nathan's fluffy, down comforter. In addition, there were a number of small groups of party-goers randomly scattered about. They seemed to be keeping unobtrusively to themselves. I guessed that they were probably all smoking pot and having deeply intellectual conversations.

I scanned the room desperately for the closet door. I found it just off to my right and dove toward its recess. I leapt up a step with an exaggerated stretch. I struggled with the doorknob, thinking that it was stuck. I forced it open, not realizing that it was locked. I must have popped it just the right way. I hoped I hadn't broken it.

"Claudia," came the noise of a startled, deep voice.

I stumbled upon him merely by happenstance.

> *(The laos handed her a dictionary and told her to look up the word happenstance.*
>
> **hap pen stance** *(hap'en-stans') n.: placing yourself in the right place at the right time, so that it will happen to you*
> *It was Remy. It was Remy, as if it had always been Remy.)*

"We keep running into each other," I said, stating the obvious.

"Must be fate," Remy responded.

"Must be," I mumbled. I inhaled deeply.

"Hello, Tomas," I said, greeting a beautiful, blonde surfer boy who looked as if he had been carved straight from California marble.

Tomas fidgeted uncomfortably and shifted to cover a square mirror with the width of his body. He began to gnaw on a handful of ice cubes, which he pulled from a white plastic bucket perched next to him. Tomas tried to straighten his legs but the closet space was cramped and cluttered with piles of clothes and stacks of crumpled papers and magazines.

"Hey, Claude. Waa'sup?" Tomas said.

"Watch your shirt," I told him.

"Huh?" he grunted, as he jerked his hand from his side. He was holding a lit cigarette that was looming precariously close to the fabric of his costume. A thin girl, sitting slightly off to Remy's side emitted a high pitched, squealish giggle. The sound pierced my ears.

"What *are* you?" I asked Tomas.

"Come on. Can't you guess?" jeered Tomas, as if I should know.

I closely examined Tomas' brightly patterned pez hat from under which his greasy curls tumbled. A pair of gold-rimmed glasses with rainbow colored lenses hung crookedly on his nose. Draped over his rumpled purple T-shirt and pants, he wore a heavy, retro-looking curtain. The curtain clashed grossly with the rest of Tomas' outfit and forced an unnerving effect.

"Ya' got me, Tomas. I give up," I said.

"I'm a bad trip!" he explained. Another nettling chortle came from the small girl.

Remy jumped up, "Claudia, have you met Avery?"

I hesitated for a moment. It was the same girl that had interrupted my conversation with Oliver earlier.

"No," I answered. "I haven't met Avery yet."

"Hi," squeaked Avery with the candy-apple sweetness of a farm owner's daughter. "You know Ollie, don't you?"

"Yes, I know Oliver," I replied in a formal tone. I was not sure if I liked her.

Avery smiled with down-turned eyes, blushed rosily, and hugged herself with her arms in a childish rocking motion. The sheer robes of her belly dancer costume whispered around her supple, brown-sugar colored skin. A thick gold chain was clasped around her bare midriff just beneath her scanty bra-top. It glistened in the dim light of the closet.

Around Avery's ankles were wrapped bracelets made of tiny, silver bells. They jangled with her movements. She clicked a pair of finger cymbals playfully around Tomas' head. He stared up at her wantonly.

"Why don'cha hang out for awhile, Claude?" Remy proposed. He jumped up, approaching me slowly.

Remy gingerly took my arm and guided me across the gray carpet to where he had been sitting. He pushed away a small pile of Nathan's clothes to clear some space for me. A disgruntled meow came from beneath the mess and Pastor came scampering out into the open.

"Damned cat," Remy muttered under his breath.

"You sniff, don'cha girl?" asked Tomas.

I nodded without word. Tomas shifted to his side, revealing the mirror that he'd hidden from me when I'd come in. Streaked there were tiny granules of white powder. With a plastic credit card, Tomas began to carve the powder into a small mound. Then, he cut the coke into thick parallel lines, each about two inches long.

Tomas handed me a tightly rolled dollar bill and invited me to lean over the mirror.

"You're up," he said.

I took the dollar bill from Tomas and twirled it between my fingers. I tapped the tip of the paper to the mirror and bent down. Covering one nostril with the back of my index finger, I inhaled in a slow steady breath. At the end of the line, I closed my eyes and lifted my head back and swallowed. I could feel the cold, chemical laden powder drip down the back of my throat. I blinked widely and handed the bill to Remy.

We sat together passing the blow, smoking countless cigarettes, and sipping cheap beer until the white mound nearly disappeared. I lost count of the lines I'd done. For me, the tight space soon began to reverberate every knock, twang, and click made inside or outside of the closet's walls.

My senses were wired to the brink and the air between the four of us was electrified with tension. I began to feel nauseous and dipped my hands into the ice bucket. I sniffed at the ice so that tiny droplets of water ran through my nasal passages. I knew my nose was going to start to bleed soon.

Tomas stood up and began to pace around us in the shape of an uneven square. He methodically created dark track marks in Nathan's carpet. Avery watched him mindlessly. I could tell that everyone was growing restless, so I packed a bowl to help take the edge off.

I handed it off to Avery but she shook her head no. Her eyes were as wide as saucers and I could see that her shoulders were trembling. She slithered over to the step in the doorway of the closet and rose to pull Tomas toward her by his shirt collar. She jumped onto his back, clutching his neck like a choker. The crooks of Tomas' arms cradled her legs and he bounced with her on his hips while he made a whirring sound like an airplane.

"Let's go out and dance, Tomas," Avery whined.

Tomas hopped the step and sandwiched Avery against the door. He fell back on his heels, and wiggled his waist in a gyrating motion.

"Owww!" she cried, "you're squishing me." Tomas laughed heartily.

"What d'ya say, Thomas?" Tomas asked, as he thumped the thick black soles of his shoes in a steady rhythm on the floor. "You ready to go?" he challenged.

I felt the pressure of Remy's stare on my body. He hesitated slightly, which made me uncomfortable. I shifted from my Indian style position, splaying my legs underneath me to my right.

"Tomas, I'm gonna hang out in here with Claudia a little longer," Remy said. "I wanna finish up the blow anyway," he added.

"You got it, bro," Tomas answered. "Don't be too long though. You gotta shake it off sometime. It's got to be pretty crazy out there by now," he said.

Avery pushed the door open and an unwelcome stream of light escaped into the closet. Pastor tried to scurry outside. I caught him by his hind legs and pulled him toward my chest. I kneaded his head softly. Pastor fought me for a moment, nipping at me lightly. Eventually, he succumbed to my touch and settled into my lap for a nap.

Avery slid from Tomas' back and trailed her hand along his arm. Her fingers finally stopped to clasp his tightly. She glanced toward Remy and me as we lay lazily and dazed on the floor.

"Goodbye, Claudia," Avery said to me.

"Bye, Remy," she purred softly, fluttering her eyelashes.

I watched Remy as he commanded with a wink, "Wait for me on the swing, Avery."

Remy glided his hand along the back of her calf. I felt a pang of jealousy as Avery disappeared with Tomas into the light. Remy jumped up to lock the door behind them. He turned back to me and knelt to scoop an agitated Pastor into his arms.

Remy fell into a crumpled heap on the doorstep. He created a purposeful distance between us. We sat alone without a word, until Pastor's purr grew so loud that I burst out in laughter.

The corners of Remy's mouth upturned slightly into a smile. He pushed Pastor from his lap. The white cat wrapped himself around Remy's legs, gently nudging him with the top of his head and neck. Remy seemed amused at first but became quickly annoyed when Pastor attempted to comb his dreads with his claws and teeth.

"Owwww!" Remy yelped. "Get the fuck outta here," he shouted, tossing Pastor to the floor onto the cushion of a Mexican blanket.

Pastor embarked on a reconnaissance mission throughout the closet. He was immediately drawn to the Budweiser mirror. Before he could begin to sniff at the coke, I pulled it away with lightning speed.

I remarked, "I don't think Nathan would appreciate it if his cat OD'd on coke."

Remy nodded and took the mirror from my hands. He rested it on his thighs. He carved two small lines from the remnants of the white powder and motioned for me to lean forward into his lap.

I crawled toward him on my hands and knees. Slowly, I began to inhale my last rail. With a shudder, I felt Remy's hand on the back of my neck. The strength of his massage forced me to lose my balance. I pulled back from the mirror and was directly met with his stare.

"Alone at last, Claudia," he said.

Embarrassed, I swept the back of my hand across the ends of my nostrils. I tried to shrink into the recess of the closet. Remy moved closer to me. With each inch I leaned back, he burrowed two in my direction. I could feel his sweet breath on my flushed pink skin.

His lips quivered and lingered delicately across mine. He brushed against the thin creases and contours of my frosted lipstick. I tried to kiss him but he pulled away. I let his tongue dart into my mouth for an instant.

I shimmied and screamed unexpectedly as a violent chilling sensation dripped from my neck and down my back. I jumped up and thrust a hand under my dress. I pulled out a glistening crystal of ice. I tossed it playfully against Remy's chest.

"You think you'll ever get another chance like that, Remy?" I threatened.

"I ain't worried about it," he answered confidently.

Feeling awkward, I hesitated before speaking again. To break the tension, I said, "Come on, let's go. I bet Avery's waiting for you on that swing."

Remy popped the ice cube I'd thrown at him into his mouth. I caught another glimpse of his tongue and couldn't believe how aroused I'd become. He ran his index finger across my lips. It was wet from the ice.

We ran the rest of the coke across our teeth and gums. Remy stashed the mirror on top of one of the shelves in the closet. I smoothed my dress and adjusted my costume. Remy swung the door open to the guitar strains and shining light of Nathan's bedroom. We tumbled outside.

Remy tugged at my tangled Pathos leaves. I swept my hand behind me in a swatting motion. He grabbed it, squeezing tightly. I could tell that the party had picked up because everything was much louder. Remy pummeled through the door of Nathan's room and into the noise. He dropped my hand and bounded across the stage to where Avery was swaying on the swing to the beat of the music.

I stopped in the doorway and watched them for a moment. Remy caught her, grasped the ropes, and pulled himself up on the swing too. He stood behind her and she thrust her head backward to gaze up at him. They laughed together and screeched through the air faster and faster, attracting much attention from the crowd.

I shook my head and was whisked away with a jerk of my arm.

Oliver was pushing me toward the dance floor.

"She's just a friend," Oliver promised, as if reading the question in my mind.

He blew a kiss in my direction.

"Come on, sweetie, dance with me," he pleaded. "Dance with me till the moon changes to the sun," he said.

We wriggled our way onto the already overpopulated dance floor. We gradually acquired more and more space from a samurai man, a flapper, and the Bride of Frankenstein. Oliver and I danced for what seemed like an eternity but it was really just until I had blisters from my heels.

I mindlessly thumped and thwarted to the rhythm. Oliver eventually drowned himself, fading away into the waves of the crowd. I lost him to the night but never cared.

Animal Crackers

I'm a Romantic. I long for feelings like nostalgia. I read poets like Byron. I laugh at novels written by Bukowski and Toole. I am tickled by the cold, wet noses of kittens. I sink into the smell of Christmas trees and I shrink at the thought of the touch of the boy next door.

And, I drink.

I drink a lot. I don't know if I'm a romantic because I drink or if I drink because I'm a romantic. I just like to feel numb; it helps me to think like a tormented artist. Substance abuse separates one from the physical and frees the mind to wander.

Much of my time in Philadelphia has been spent hiding in the dark recesses of the nooks, corners, and crannies of the city's neighborhood bars.

I have many favorites. Doobies. The Haven. Chief's. Walsh's. Frank's. Fergie's. Murphy's. Turf & Tavern. McGlinchey's. Anthony's Olde City Pub. W & J's. The Rusty Nail. The Khyber Pass.

("I'd like a Rob Roy, extra dry, straight up, with a twist of lemon, please," SHE said.

"Perfect?" asked the BARTENDER.

"Yeah, sure. Whatever that means. Just make sure it's scotch," SHE commanded and threw the last of HER crumpled bills on the bar.)

The Khyber Pass sits on the Northwest corner of Third and Market, not far from the CD shop, the bookstore, and the coffee house. The Khyber is a dark, intimidating neighborhood bar that serves as home to the freaks, artists, writers, musicians, degenerates, bikers, and nameless hearts of Philadelphia. It's the place to see and be seen if you're art house chic.

I love the place. They serve animal crackers at the bar and leave full packs of Camel Lights out in empty glasses. The cigarettes are free for the taking. You can't beat anything that's free for the taking.

In early November, Remy choreographed a musical called "Tailor Made" that ran at The Painted Bride. It was a multimedia jazz opera that documented racism and how it affected the life of today's typical African-American male. I suppose, like all good and equally frustrating art, it offered its audience no answer and no solution. It only recounted the problem.

I went to "Tailor Made" opening night but missed the second showing because Don Carlos was playing at the Khyber. I promised Ethan a tour of Philly before the band went on, so I told Remy to meet me outside the bar around eleven after he'd finished up at The Bride.

I waited for Remy perched on the dirty orange "City Paper" box next to the traffic light on Market Street. I sipped a tall hazelnut latte and read a review of the band on page twenty-two. The City Paper said that Don Carlos achieved the "unattainable thrill between uptight music school precision and amateurish abandon." I thought the review was funny because it sounded so serious. They were just talking about Ethan, the guy who used to sit behind me in ninth grade homeroom and throw spit balls in my hair.

I fidgeted with my Indian-print, multi-colored gloves and tightened them around my fingers. From the street corner, I could hear the distant echoes and rumblings of the opening band, Transam, who had already taken the stage. I tapped my heels to the muffled beat and peered through the tall, glass windows of the coffee house. Nathan's salt-and-pepper curls bounced against the backdrop of a newly painted mural on the wall.

I snuck out of the bookstore a few hours early in time to meet Ethan and the rest of the band at two o'clock when they got into town. Since we only had a few hours before the show, we grabbed some coffee at The Drop, checked out some used record stores, and then unloaded the van.

The van was powder blue and had Kentucky plates, which made me smile. I helped the guys carry some of their lighter things into the bar. Mostly though, I followed Darren, the band's drummer, around like a lost puppy dog with its tail sagging between its legs.

Darren and I shared an on-going, torrid affair. It was strictly physical. We only saw each other once every few months and never bothered to keep in touch with one another in between. Normally, Darren and I didn't discuss our commitments but I told him about Remy. I figured it might help avoid any awkward situations later. I wanted to minimize opportunities for confrontation by averting temptation. To me, it seemed like a safe and most tiresome strategy.

Darren didn't say much when I told him. He just mumbled "that's cool" and dragged a buzz saw from the van to the stage. The saw was embedded into an old school desk. Don Carlos used it during one of their songs to split a cymbal in half. It made an uncomfortable sound to say the least.

Remy or no Remy, Darren and I still managed to brush close to each other throughout the day. Here or there, we'd share one of his Marlboro Red's or split a Snapple while the other guys in the band bought their own. When I pointed out a rainbow in the evening sky, Darren said he'd grab me the pot of gold at the end of it if I wanted it. All I could think of were his fingers lightly tracing my forearm as I drew on the sidewalk with a piece of pink chalk I found on the Khyber's stoop.

Before long, Darren started to tease me about Remy, which helped me feel a little more at ease.

It was quarter after eleven. I was still waiting on the "City Paper" box, finishing my latte. There was no sign of Remy yet, so I lit a cigarette to kill some time. The door by the Khyber's stage was open; I caught a glimpse of Ethan setting up. He'd taken off his bright-blue, down jacket and was running around in his Jackie Chan T-shirt, which already looked rumpled with sweat. I saw Darren talking to one of the MTV guys that he'd pointed out to me earlier. They were trying to cut some deal to do some instrumental stuff for one of the network's new shows.

There was a short line outside the bar, waiting for admission. Cedric was working the door. He often picked up shifts at the Khyber to supplement the pittance he made at the coffee shop. I watched him pocket a couple of bills from the cover charge he'd been collecting.

Once the line dwindled down, he left his post and walked toward me. He grabbed my shoulders with a light, quick massage.

"Hey girl, I didn't see you at the party. Did you show?" he asked.

"I was there," I replied. "I was hangin' out with Remy. Where were you?"

"You probably didn't recognize me in my potato head costume," he answered.

"Good news, Claude," Cedric said.

"I'm pickin' up some extra shifts here at the bar. The other bouncer quit. He movee out to Cal to pursue his music," he told me. Cedric stepped back toward the bar and propped the corner door of the Khyber open wide.

"No way," I said, sounding disappointed. "He didn't even stop in the shop to tell me."

"He's been pretty quiet about it. I think he's trying to stay focused," Cedric said.

"He'll be around. This place sucks you in and won't let you go," Cedric predicted.

"I got bad news too," he mumbled.

"Shit, what's up?" I asked.

"I almost bit it today, Claude," Cedric said. "Missed my morning shift at the coffee shop."

"Ouch. Was Nathan pissed?" I asked.

"Not after I told him what happened," Cedric explained. "You're never gonna believe this one."

"I was walkin' to work down Locust Street, minding my own business, when the cops pulled up to me. They jumped out of the van, threw me down on the ground, cuffed me, and dragged me down to the Roundhouse."

"Shut up," I yelped in disbelief. "What did you do?"

"Nothing—that's the bitch. They claimed that I was a dead ringer for some nigger that knocked off the 7-11 on 22nd Street last night," Cedric explained.

"It took them the whole morning to fill out the paperwork and all the other red tape. Meanwhile, I miss half-day's pay and my boss thinks I overslept. It could only happen to me, Claude. Nobody else," he said.

"What could only happen to you, Cedric?" interrupted a husky voice from behind us.

"Hey Avery," Cedric replied.

"Don't worry about it, baby," Cedric told her. "You don' even wanna know."

Avery approached Cedric and planted a soft kiss on his vulnerable cheek. The kiss made me feel out of place. Avery smiled a look of recognition in my direction and began bantering back and forth with Cedric, excluding me from their conversation. She invited him to the upcoming "Taking Tiger Mountain" lip synch show at Group Movement. She pulled a stack of gold colored fliers from her bag, handed one to Cedric and slipped another into my hand.

"We've been trying to get into Group Movement *forever*," Avery declared.

"That's the Big Mess production that Oliver scheduled through Remy," I said.

"*You* know Remy Thomas?" Avery demanded.

"Yes, he introduced us at Nathan's Halloween party," I reminded her.

"Oh, I remember you," Avery admitted. "How do *you* know Remy?"

"He's my boyfriend," I confessed.

Avery immediately pulled an attitude with me and I knew that I didn't want to talk to her anymore. I asked her a few questions about Big Mess and the show. She appeared disinterested in me and concentrated instead on Cedric. I watched her fondle the back of his neck with her fingertips.

An obnoxious, loud voice from inside the bar shouted, "Avery!"

Avery quickly switched her attention from Cedric and me to wave to her friend.

"God, it looks crowded in there. I'm only staying for *one* beer," she lied.

"It was good to see you again," I mumbled after her as she drifted inside the bar without another word. Cedric winked at me and followed Avery toward the door to check some more ID's.

I rubbed my chin against my chest, laughing to myself. When I lifted my head up again, I saw Remy walking on Third Street. He was dressed in black from head to toe and wore a red bandanna, which pulled his dreads back from his eyes. His bright, white sneakers were hard to miss—even in the dark. Remy reached me, grabbed the mass of tangled hair drooping down my neck, and pulled my head back and upward to meet his kiss.

"Hello," he said. I kissed him back.

"You're early. They're not on yet," I told him. "I didn't expect you until after the first set," I added.

"It's good to see you too," Remy joked. "What are you doin' out here anyway? I thought you'd be inside hanging out with Ethan."

"They had band things to do," I answered. "Besides, I didn't want to go in there without you," I laughed, exaggerating my syllables with a long draw.

I leaned into Remy and kissed him again, hard on the mouth. He rolled his eyes and cupped his hands over his heart. He fell back on his heels, losing his balance slightly. He caught himself and clasped my knees in his palms.

Remy ruffled his hands through the loose fabric of my long skirt. After a long search, he found my calves and rubbed them, warming them with his strength. He began to tease my thighs with his touch but I pushed him away with an almost violent thrust.

Remy looked confused. I nodded to the small gang of trendy girls waiting in the doorway of the Khyber. They were watching us intently. Remy had minor celebrity status in town.

"Come on," Remy started, tugging my sleeve. "Let's go in. I'm dyin' to see these guys."

I jumped down from the "City Paper" box and took Remy's hand. My legs were cramped and my right foot had fallen asleep. I hadn't realized how long I'd been sitting there. I wiggled my leg until the creepy pins and needles feeling started, became intolerable, and then finally stopped as I started to take a few steps.

Cedric waved us to the front of the winding line. He and Remy exchanged their usual "hey nigger," "what's up bro?" greetings. They tousled and punched each other like little boys playing in a schoolyard. Cedric mocked a bow and tipped an imaginary hat in my direction. He stepped back and made a wide, sweeping motion with his arm for me to follow him.

Inside, the bar was packed. I recognized most of the regulars but was surprised with the draw of people I'd never seen before. It was an impressive following for Don Carlos.

Remy dove immediately toward the bar. I attempted to follow him but got lost in the crowd. I struggled desperately to keep an eye on Remy. I watched him mouth the words "Rolling Rock" to the bartender. He held up two fingers, signaling the number of mugs we needed.

A woman we knew named Lilly approached him. She was a bad drunk, who favored wearing tight, ribbed halter tops in all types of weather. Tonight, she carried a pair of bright red, stiletto heels slung over her shoulder. Her feet were filthy. I watched Remy mouth something to her and then nod in my direction.

Lilly flipped around abruptly. She screamed out my name with an ear-piercing squeal, "Claudia!"

Lilly thrust her arms straight-up, high in the air. She lunged toward me and captured me in a mammoth-sized bear hug that nearly knocked me over. My eyes grew wide as I felt the air within the cavity of my chest being pushed out of me. Lilly stepped back and flashed me a huge smile. A number of her teeth were black and rotted. There were also large gaps between them that needed to be filled.

"Hi, Lilly," I uttered softly.

I had turned my body during our hug. I was now comfortably positioned against the bar. I grabbed a fistful of animal crackers from one of the glass bowls resting there and began munching away. Remy handed me a foamy, ice cold mug to wash down the cookies.

I ran my fingertips lightly down Remy's back as I listened to Lilly talk about her new job at the Chestnut Cabaret. She was the bathroom attendant who handed out paper towels for tips. She dutifully guarded the "free" hairspray, perfume, and other primping necessities that were arranged on the counter top. She said that the best part of the job was that she got to sit high on a wooden three-legged stool reading books all night.

"So you like it?" Remy asked her.

"I love it!" exclaimed Lilly.

"Good for you," I said.

"Good for me," Lilly agreed. "Let's hear it for the girls!" she shouted, attracting attention from around the bar.

I looked at Remy. He smiled, seemingly amused. Lilly saw him and took his smile as a sign of encouragement.

She shouted again, this time more loudly, "Let's hear it for the girls!"

Lilly was wasted. I chugged a quarter of my beer.

A low buzzing sound started up from the stage in the side room opposite from the bar. I craned my neck to see what was happening.

I couldn't get a clear view because so many people were sandwiched together in the smoky, stifling-hot air.

I leaned closer to Remy. "It sounds like they're coming on. Do you want to move in there?" I said, motioning to the side room.

Remy nodded in agreement. He began to push ahead through the mass of people. He carved a small pathway for me to follow through the entangled crowd. With the exception of a spinning disco ball that twinkled high in the air, the room was blindingly dark. We gained space by sneaking along the right wall of the room. We stopped next to a stack of metal chairs that were hidden in the darkness.

I stood next to Remy but couldn't see the stage because I was too short. I teetered on my tippy-toes, trying to see the band. Remy snickered at me and freed a chair from the pile. He patted it for me, instructing me to stand on it. He pushed the chair slightly to the side, so it wouldn't obstruct anyone else's view. I jumped up and rested my hand on Remy's shoulder to steady myself.

I recognized Ethan's shadow front and center. He was sliding his finger nails along the metal strings of his guitar. He swung the guitar strap from side-to-side around his neck.

Ethan wandered around the stage with awkward, animated movements. He bumped into various pieces of the band's equipment, which were scattered around on the floor. He knocked over the microphone, hit the bassist with his shoulder, and ricocheted back and forth off the two Marshall speakers. After a short pause, Ethan began to jump straight up and down into the air. He hit his head a number of times on the layer of foam egg crates that lined the low ceiling.

While Ethan appeared to attract the most attention from the crowd, my eyes turned to watch Darren. He was tucked away against the back wall, pounding on the drums with a determined furor. He wore a dazed look and was already dripping with sweat. Darren wasn't wearing his thick black glasses; I noticed them on the sill of one of the Khyber's boarded up windows. His shaggy hair flopped over his eyes.

Don Carlos created a numbingly loud noise entirely with instruments—there were no vocals. They drove through the set recklessly, mesmerizing the crowd with cacophony. Remy and I stared straight ahead, almost brain dead. I clutched his shoulder often to steady my balance on the chair.

Although it was difficult to determine the beginning or end of any of the band's songs, their final number drew a roar from the audience. Darren jumped up from his drums and ran through the crowd with a blank stare across his face. He lunged toward the bar and the bartender handed him a dripping wet bottle of Yuengling.

Rather than return to the stage, Darren exited the bar through the side door. He disappeared into the crisp cold night air, as the three remaining members of Don Carlos droned on incessantly without percussion.

The guy standing next to me started to scream like a banshee when Mike, the second guitar, lifted the buzz saw to the center of the stage. Ethan stepped to the back and grabbed the sides of the wood tightly with both of his hands. He placed it underneath the microphone. Mike grabbed one of the gold, Zildjian cymbals and plugged the saw into the wall.

Eric lowered his bass so it sounded like a violin. Ethan flicked the red "on" switch of the buzz saw and began to carve steadily through the metal. The fluorescent "Selina's House of Beauty" sign that dangled from the ceiling behind them flickered from the power surges. Mike brushed flaking chips of metal off his blue Hawaiian shirt while a large sound filtered through the crowd.

After dividing the cymbal into four uneven quarters, Ethan shoved the buzz saw away. Mike jumped quickly back to his guitar. Ethan snatched the wobbling microphone from the edge of the stage.

Screaming into it, he sang, "Rock"

> *(SLUR, PAUSE)* we
> *(DEEP BREATH, PAUSE)* haven't
> *(PAUSE)* got
> *(PAUSE)* a
> *(LONG PAUSE)* chance."

Then, Don Carlos' music stopped.

The crowd started to break apart. People began to shuffle aimlessly about between the bar and the exit doors. The lack of noise was deafening.

The guys in the band filtered past Remy and me to get drinks. With the exception of Darren, I introduced them each to Remy. They moved back and forth between the stage and the bar, sifting through their belongings. They haphazardly began packing their instruments and loading the van again. They were leaving for New York City that night.

A few petite, grunge chicks followed Ethan around as he worked. They all wore tiny, baby doll barrettes in assorted, cheap colors pinned in their hair. Their T-shirts revealed their mid-riffs and pierced belly buttons. One of the girls, who was dressed in silver stockings and a shiny black slip, appeared to capture Ethan's attention for an instant. He tired of her quickly and wandered off in search of ice water.

Remy kissed me lightly on the cheek and left to grab another pitcher for last call. I sat down on an empty chair.

Darren was back inside now and sitting on the stage. His hair was slicked back from his face with sweat. He flirted shamelessly with a cute blonde girl who giggled a lot. Every few seconds, however, Darren glanced up in my direction. He squinted and pulled at the corners of his eyes as if he couldn't see. I guessed that he'd lost his glasses.

After a few minutes, Darren dropped his conversation with the blonde girl. I watched as he tousled her hair and jumped down from the stage. The girl's tight pink T-shirt jiggled eagerly with her laugh. She leaned toward Darren and kissed him full on the mouth.

Darren slowly began to walk toward me. He reached me and pulled both of my hands from my sides. Then, he lifted my arms up and traced my body with his eyes.

"Where's your friend?" Darren asked.

"*Remy* went to get some more beers for last call, Darren," I answered. "I'm sure he'll be right back."

"Yeah, I'm sure he will," Darren laughed. "He's a fool to have left you alone this long."

I scanned the room nervously for Remy. Darren clutched my hands in his and leered, "Claude, I *need* a few minutes alone with you."

I gently pulled away from his grasp and eyed him with curiosity. Darren knew my will power was that of a reformed con man.

"I'll be a perfect gentleman, I swear," he lied. "You asked for no strings and I'm a man of my word," he told me.

"Christ, Darren. You know I can't handle this," I said, with a deep breath.

"Just for a little bit," he begged.

I shook my head, hanging it in defeat. I took a moment before I spoke again.

"Remy can't see us walk out together," I gave in. "Let's grab some stuff and take it out to the van," I said.

"Trying to look inconspicuous?" Darren questioned.

"Shut the fuck up," I shot back. I picked up a guitar case and crossed the stage to the side door. Darren followed closely on my heels, carrying some heavy bags. I did not look back for Remy.

(There is fear within me. Fear of solitude. Fear of companionship. Fear of rejection. Fear of acceptance. Fear of disenchantment. Fear of passion. Fear of all that is feminine. Fear of all that is masculine. Fear of loving. And, the fear of being loved.

"I would be the one, if I could be the one," she told herself.)

I stepped out into the fresh, open air. The usual stagnant and claustrophobic feel of the city streets did not touch me. Instead, I was consumed with a warped sense of exhilaration as I inhaled deeply and looked up into the smoggy, night sky. I could not see the stars.

Darren took the guitar case from my grasp and threw it into the back of the van. I fell against the leather interior of one of the open doors and watched people push free from the smoky haze of the Khyber. The street became cluttered with laughing, screaming drunks who scattered off in infinite directions.

A well-dressed bum started to haggle me for change. Darren wrapped his hands around my waist. I closed my eyes tightly and winced, tickled by his touch.

"Git! Git away!" Darren barked at the street urchin.

"Darren," I whined, scolding him with my eyes.

Darren ignored me and pushed past the bum. Ethan was mulling about in the belly of the van and shouted a lewd comment toward Darren. This elicited chuckles from some of the passersby and infuriated Darren. He grunted a response to Ethan and pulled me across Third Street by my right hand.

I remember thinking to myself that I should turn away while I still had the chance but I did not stop myself. I followed Darren's lead toward the dark parking lot on the corner of Church Street.

(You.

You cannot hear me thinking. I am not civilized. I am merely an animal. I will try to convince you that my subservience is a result of my own boredom.

Then you will laugh and know that I was afraid all along.)

Darren and I crossed through the shadows of the parking lot. We nestled against the brick wall of the building furthest from the Khyber. I thought I heard someone repeating my name over and over again in the distance.

Darren started to kiss me. He ran his tongue along my neck while his hands explored the small of my back and wandered through my hair. His breath was warm against my flesh. I think Darren thought I was quivering because I was aroused. I wasn't though. I was quivering because I was nervous and jumpy and knew that being alone with him was wrong.

"Claudia?" I heard Remy's voice calling for me. He was met with silence.

"Claude? Hey, Claudia!" Remy shouted from Third Street. I could tell by his voice that he was turning around to yell in different directions.

Darren stopped kissing me and laid his head on my shoulder. He giggled mischievously in my left ear. I stared into his eyes as if to challenge him. His laughter stopped. The look that he returned to me shook me to the core. I knew not to trust him and pulled away from his hold.

Our eyes remained deadlocked together in a deep trance. I screamed to answer Remy, "I'm over here, Remy."

Darren and I stood perfectly still, waiting to be discovered. Neither of us stepped into the glow of the street lights. Darren remained pressed to the wall and I swayed uncomfortably just inches from him.

Remy turned the corner, trailing after my voice. He saw me standing with Darren and repeated himself quietly. We exchanged uncertain glances.

"Claudia," he whispered. He shifted his stance awkwardly.

"Hey," Remy addressed me directly. His voice was soft.

"I been lookin' for you everywhere," he shrugged with a grin. "I gave Lilly that whole pitcher. I got worried somethin' happened to you," he told me, ignoring Darren.

Remy seemed so nonchalant that I believed him to be innocently unsuspecting.

"Everything's fine, baby," I said.

"I was just helping the guys with the last of their stuff. Darren asked me to show him where the book store was," I lied, nodding down Church Street.

"I thought you would have stopped there earlier today," Remy prodded, making me feel uneasy.

"Hey man, what's up?" Remy said, greeting Darren coolly.

"Hey," Darren responded in an edgy tone.

"What's your name, bro?" Darren asked seething tension.

"Remy. My name's Remy," he answered. He stepped behind me and pulled me into his arms against his broad chest.

"So, what's up? I hear you guys are headed to New York next," Remy said, posing the question directly to Darren.

"Yeah, we're playing at the Mars Bar," Darren responded, looking disinterested. "Claude told me you guys stopped in The City on your last tour," he added.

"My company did a piece with Dance Africa at the Brooklyn Academy of Music," Remy explained, shaking his head yes.

"My company," Darren repeated, mimicking Remy.

"How does somebody like *you* make it to the Brooklyn Academy of Music?" Darren challenged.

I studied Remy carefully and watched as the muscles in his face grew taught.

"Like me?" he said defensively.

"Yeah, like you," Darren taunted, shaking his head at Remy.

"Sounds like the nigga's made the big time," he added, looking at me.

"You gotta kiss a lotta white asses to make it that far, doncha?" Darren slurred viciously. He arched his shoulders back and straightened his posture to exaggerate the few inches he held over Remy.

"What's your fucking problem, man?" Remy snapped.

"I come out here to talk to my girlfriend, find you alone with her, and you're the one that ends up startin' with me. What the fuck?" he screamed, raising his voice angrily.

"I'm out here with *your* girlfriend because *you* couldn't give her what she needed," Darren blurted out.

"She knows what's up," Darren said, glaring into my eyes. "Claudia knows where to come when she needs the good stuff," he screamed as he moved closer to where Remy stood behind me.

I pushed Remy backward with my arms crooked in an awkward position. I meekly exclaimed that Darren had just one too many vodka martinis and didn't understand what he was saying. I begged them both to stop fighting and asked Remy to take me home.

Remy shoved me out of the way. I fell hard against the cold, brick wall at the edge of the parking lot. I rubbed my temples from the impact and blinked blankly at Remy and Darren.

I bowed my head in surrender—the events were beyond my control.

I do not feel my body. Not this shell that shields my thought from vicious circles.

No. I am not here.

I am sitting on the River Walk in New Orleans waving at tiny ant-like figurines who are passing by me on a drifting barge. I stare at the river. It is growing dark. I sit on a rock. My friend named Cameron sits next to me. We have just finished playing backgammon together in Kaldi's, a coffee shop on Decatur Street two blocks from Jackson Square.

I am lighting a bowl that is perched between my teeth. It is a warm night and we laugh at the possibility of loving one person to the end of time. We also gaze at the rising, full moon. Cameron wonders if the government has begun experimenting there with prototype human settlements.

Cameron and I nibble on stale beignets and sip chicory coffee from Kaldi's. We talk about going to Benny's to see some Blues. This is one of the happiest moments in my life.

I pick up a pebble from the ground and thrust it deep into my pocket. It is my gris-gris that will keep me safe in the dark.

"You are special," promise the laos. "Remember that you are special."

I couldn't see who threw the first punch.

I think they both reached for each other in the same instant.

Darren doubled over from the force of Remy's fist. He cupped his already broken nose with both hands and cursed wildly. He spit at Remy's feet and swung back blindly. Remy lost his balance and became more enraged. He pushed Darren into the brick wall of the bank. Darren grunted, losing his breath.

I brushed my hand at the droplets of blood that soaked my pretty floral skirt. I began to cry. I turned back at the bystanders who had begun to congregate in the street and heard someone yell for Ethan.

Ethan jumped from the back of the van and sprinted toward the fight. I watched his flailing arms tear at Remy and Darren. He struggled to pull them apart, calling for help from the crowd. Mike broke forward and rushed toward Darren. He pushed me further out of the way. I fell to my knees.

Ethan screamed at me to snap out of it. The tone of his voice made me cry even harder. I wobbled back to my feet. He kept asking me why I hadn't tried to do anything sooner. He said "fuck" a lot too. I remained silent though, paralyzed with confusion and fantasizing about thoughts of the Mississippi.

Once separated, Mike held Darren in a giant bear hug. Ethan pinned Remy against the fence. I was left standing alone with blood on my pretty floral skirt.

Somewhere, in the distance, I heard the echoing wail of police and ambulance sirens drawing nearer.

Cameron and I hitched a ride Uptown with a young couple who told us that they would like to go to Benny's too. Cameron said O.K. and gave them directions.

We parked the car about a block from the bar and walked the rest of the way. I waited on the front porch while Cameron went inside to get us some beers. The music was loud but I didn't mind. I slumped into a ball on the pavement and listened to the noise. I listened to the noise in New Orleans knowing that listening to noise in New Orleans was better than listening to noise anywhere else.

All she ever wanted to do was to feel magnolia. But Philadelphia swallowed her up and wouldn't let her go.

Oh, Those Aimless, Meandering Muses Again

*S*ee, I told you there were laos in the trees. no, those were just those *little boys who stole her journal and laughed at her thoughts when she was six years old.* "I TOLD YOU IT WASN'T A DIARY," *she screamed at them, as they ripped out her pages and ran away faster than she could catch them.*

My heart flutters again. I can't keep my thoughts on anything but his face.

When he kisses me, my body quivers and my heart shakes. Oh yes, and my knees grow weak.

I can't fall asleep at night because I'm thinking of him. He even permeates my dreams.

I create scenarios in my head of what it will be like after we've grown old together and we're just sitting on a porch swing. I with my knitting; he with his glasses perched low on his nose and a newspaper in his hands.

"YOU DON'T EVEN KNOW HOW TO KNIT!" *taunted the little boys whose voices were so high pitched they sounded like laos.*

I watch him dance and I become aroused. It tingles between my legs. I smile a lot.

When I wake up in the morning, he is the first face I picture. I wait by the phone until he calls.

I find myself doing things I would never normally do, just hoping to please him.

"HOPING TO PLEASE HIM," *the little boys laughed.* "BUT YOU SUCK IN BED," *the laos flapped with their wings.* (that was what you were always afraid of, wasn't it?)

It has been a long time since I've been in love.

"Was I the first girl you picked up there?" she asked.

"Yes, the first girl," he answered.

"And the last," she said as she kissed him with her tongue.

I've caught myself dancing again. And singing—incessantly. Blowing bubbles. Ignoring obligations. Not caring. Just wondering when I shall see him next.

(I can do this. I can do this. I can do this. I can make a commitment.)

"Bies, ami"

"Non mi toklas."

"WE DIDN'T WANT TO ANYWAY," *screamed the mean boys again.*

He uses cheesy lines on me. Like my eyes are like the mar blue. I groan, "these cheesy lines."

He answers, "I hope they are working."

I kiss him. I don't mind the lines. It's the first time in a long time that I don't mind the lines.

God—his body. His arms; those abs. I shall suffocate if he makes love to me. I'll probably be his slave for a little while too. He takes my breath away, when he's not even there.

"YOU ALWAYS ENJOYED STANDING ON SAND, STARING AHEAD OF THE SURF, AND BREATHING IN. CLOSING YOUR EYES. LISTENING TO THE POPPING BUBBLES OF THE WATER AS THEIR WORLD IS DESTROYED BY RELENTLESS WAVES," *said 'wait, who said that? that wasn't the mean little boys or the laos in the trees'. these voices.*

and these voices. "Please don't break my heart," she pleaded. He wasn't there when she asked the question.

She was going to love him anyway. She didn't care if he loved her back.

"I wrote about you last night."

"Really," he said with a smirk. "Can I read it?"

"No. Not yet. You won't court me anymore."

"I will court you to the day I die."

His eyes undress me shamelessly.

In one of the few moments we are not touching, I stand on the phone. He sits by the couch. He watches my legs move.

"You have beautiful legs."

She shakes her head, blushing wildly. "God do you have beautiful legs," he repeated himself.

"HE SHOULD ALWAYS TELL YOU HOW BEAUTIFUL YOU ARE," *echoed the laos.*

"HE WON'T ALWAYS TELL YOU HOW BEAUTIFUL YOU ARE!" *warned the mean little boys.*

kISS me theRE. uessssssssss . . . . riGHT THERE. that was supposed to be a "Y". got it. god do you got it. WHO!!! (that's what the black girls on the bus say when they get really into a conversation.) right there baby, AND DON'T PICK YOUR HEAD UP TILL YOUR DONE.

Swimming

*(W*ished into the wind. All of my beautiful friends; they've all gone away.)*

Some of my favorite college memories are of Hunter S. Thompson-esque road trips and wild excursions that my mom and dad never knew I had. Although my traveling escapades now seem all but forgotten, I still keep in touch with some of my trust-fund blessed pals from the good ol' days. On occasion, these pals make mystical and magical return trips to Philadelphia from far-off, exotic lands.

Phoebe, my closest confidante from college, long ago fell hook, line, and sinker for the promises made to her by writers like Kerouac, Farina, and Kantzakasis. From the time she grew wings, she fought desperately to fly West with the same spirit and anticipation of the Pioneers.

Although distance and the unstoppable flipping pages of the calendar forced us apart, my heart always skipped a beat when Phoebe called with word she'd be visiting soon. She excited my imagination and sheltered me with her hippie ideals. She always reminded me that greener grass would always stay greener unless you followed your heart.

I *loved* listening to Phoebe ramble on about times she spent speeding through Arizona deserts in convertibles headed for Vegas, selling margaritas on Tour, cleaning hostels in exchange for room and board in Amsterdam, and moving whimsically for a year to Tahoe or a month's breath to the grunge capital of Seattle. A cherished part of me I gave to her for each road on which she embarked and I pray she knows that I've been with her everywhere she has gone.

Phoebe's world always seemed a step or two ahead of mine.

In late November, Phoebe phoned unexpectedly to tell me that she and her new boyfriend, Manuel, were flying into town for a week in between leases in Big Sky and San Francisco. She invited Remy and me to spend a night with them at her parent's empty summer house on the Jersey shore. I eagerly accepted her offer as a welcome respite from the dull and dismal grayness of the Philadelphia winter.

Phoebe's call came around the time Remy and I decided that we were "officially" dating. We created constitutionals centered around dance studios, book signings, CD release parties, and coffee flavors. I remember sipping a pot of "Balzac Brew" with him at the coffee house, not long after I'd hung up the phone with Phoebe.

After Remy and I had finished joking about the idiocy of naming a coffee after a literary figure, I told him of the invitation. I could tell from his grin that he reveled in the opportunity to escape the city more than I. I looked behind his eyes with wonder and tickled my fingers along the wiry hairs of his goatee with endearment.

I arranged for Phoebe and Manuel to pick us up at Oz and Endz after closing on Friday night. I finished changing and was lolling around at the front desk when I heard the distinctive toot of a car horn calling from the parking lot. I knew it was Phoebe.

I could hear thuds and creaks coming from the upstairs where Remy was sifting through the disarrayed titles of the cooking section. I hoped the new shelving Gus had just built was sturdy enough to sustain the weight of his heavy hand. I called up to Remy, announcing that it was time for us to go.

I fumbled through the hidden compartments of my bulging backpack for my lipstick and listened intently to the rhythmic thumping of Remy's footsteps moving across the second floor landing. He gripped the rickety stair railings on each side of him for support and took the steps two at a time. I watched his feet appear first in the hallway and then his loose jeans belted over the plaid boxers which were sticking out under his T-shirt. His smile met my own.

I locked the front door behind one of my favorite regular customers, a truck driver from Trenton. He shuffled out to the porch with a brown paper bag full of books for his little girl. This week, he bought her *Jemima Puddleduck*.

I routinely spun the dial of the safe, flicked off Harrison Ridley, Jr.'s "Positive Approach to the Power of Music", and perused the stack of books carefully selected as gifts for Phoebe. Remy grabbed my bag, slung it over his shoulder, and bent to peck a kiss on my cheek.

He pressed me against the countertop. I struggled in a meager attempt to fend off his leering advances. I was saved by the sound of the horn piercing my ears a second time and I gently nudged Remy out the back door. I grabbed the day's garbage, plugged the secret code into the alarm, and dashed in full sprint after him.

"Hey, girl," Phoebe yelped from across Church Street. She was beaming brightly from the driver's seat of a sporty red jeep.

She flung her thin door open wide and nearly tackled me in her excitement. After we caught our breath from laughing so hard, I introduced her to Remy. She greeted him with a demure curtsy.

"*And*," Phoebe began, "I'd like you to both meet Manuel."

She pronounced the word melodramatically with an exaggerated air. She rolled her tongue thickly over the initial letter "R" of his name, thus dragging out her first syllable as a breathy call to attention. The "oool" got lost in the back of her throat.

"Hello, Claudia," Manuel drooled in a deep, Latino accent. He paused for a moment, then nodded to address Remy by speaking only his name.

"It's a pleasure to meet you both," he added as the seductive promise of humid, sultry rain forests dripped from his tongue.

Manuel's pudgy form climbed slowly from the passenger side of the jeep and popped the front seat up so that Remy and I could crawl into the back with our bags. I glanced up at the patriotic "Steal Your Face" sticker plastered to the upper right hand of the jeep's front windshield and wriggled into the tiny space behind Manuel. Phoebe pulled her seat forward so that Remy had more leg room. Her knees were nearly touching the dash.

"Claude, Manuel smuggled a few treats back home for tonight's festivities," Phoebe said. She tossed a clear baggie bursting full of dirty, white mushrooms with brown lungs into my lap.

"Sweet," muttered Remy. I could tell he like her already.

I leaned back awkwardly into the cramped backseat and listened as Phoebe flicked the key in the ignition. The jeep began to speed through the cityscape and into the heavy traffic of I-95. I could distinguish the strings of lights twinkling along Delaware Avenue. Their reflections on the river looked crisp and clear.

I looked up at Manuel as Remy politely asked him where he was from.

"Columbia," Manuel responded, rubbing his hands along his sideburns.

"But my folks are in Miami now," he continued. "My dad was a dignitary in South America. He got kidnapped twice while he was traveling so we moved up to the States."

"Anywhere near South Beach?" I asked.

"Nah, Hibiscus Island," Manuel answered. "I used to help my dad out at his club on Ocean Drive but then I fell into sales."

"How'd you end up in Big Sky?" Remy asked.

"Was doin' the tourist thing," Manuel said.

"Then I met this one and decided to try life as a ski bum," Manuel added. He tweaked Phoebe's chin between his fingers. She giggled girlishly.

"Did you try it yet?" I interrupted, questioning Phoebe.

"Try what?" Remy asked, looking at me with a confused expression.

"Skiing," I said. "Phoebe's the only person I know who moves to the mountains but hates the snow."

"I just don't wanna fuck up my legs, Claude," Phoebe whined, trying to explain herself.

"Phoebe dances too," I explained, directing my remark to Remy.

"Cool," he mumbled. "Are you doin' any work out West?" he asked.

"I've tried but there's not much there," Phoebe answered. "I talked to Rob about working with him in New York but Manuel and I really wanted to try this San Fran thing first," she added.

"Rob Jenkins?" Remy questioned, raising his voice over his last syllable.

"Yeah," she said.

"All right," Remy commented, lifting his eyebrows at me. I could tell he was impressed.

"I met Rob through the Annenberg when I was at Penn," Phoebe told him.

"Yeah, they touted him pretty heavily for 'Next Move'," Remy said.

"Speaking of touted," interrupted Manuel. "Where's this New Jersey Dragon that you keep telling me about?" he asked.

I snickered under my breath as Phoebe corrected him, "New Jersey *Devil.*"

A smile slowly crept onto my face. I leaned back into the seat of the jeep and listened to Phoebe's voice as she started to weave the tale of the New Jersey Devil. I curled up into a childish ball under Remy's protective arm and fell into the limbo existing halfway between consciousness and sleep. Remy brushed his lips through my hair. Relaxed in the fleeting reflection of security, I slept as we wound ourselves through endless backroads, dodged deer, and moved closer to our destination.

I stirred not again until the New Jersey Devil scattered himself between the trees.

I woke feeling the jeep slowing to a stop. Phoebe said that we needed stuff from the store. She said that we should get some beer, cigarettes, and some snacks like Twizzlers or Doritos. Phoebe turned the jeep into a bustling intersection just off 55 and we picked up a case of Molson from the liquor store on the corner. Then, we pulled into the WaWa parking lot and each of us darted toward the bright fluorescent lights that screamed convenience.

Once inside, the four of us split up in different directions. I headed toward the ice cream cartons that were stacked against the back wall in frozen cases and Remy left me to find the pretzels. They were a staple of his diet. After agonizing over which flavor of Ben and Jerry's to buy, I picked up a pint of Cherry Garcia and grabbed a bottle of water from another refrigerator case. I turned to look for Remy. Instead, I discovered Manuel and Phoebe tucked away at the end of the snack food aisle.

Manuel nonchalantly stuffed two bags of potato chips under his oversized coat while Phoebe stood behind him, carefully examining the nutritional value chart on the back of an Oreo cookie package. I watched Manuel step backward and grab Phoebe by her slim waist. He skillfully traced his tongue over her right ear. Phoebe closed her eyes, tossed her head back, and shook her hair loosely over her shoulders.

As if sensing my presence, Manuel switched his eyes toward me and winked. He made me feel dirty, so I looked away. I left the two of them standing there and dropped my purchases on the counter next to the register. I paid the Indian clerk as he tried to make me laugh by telling me bad jokes in his choppy foreign accent. Without waiting for Remy, I walked back to the jeep alone, puffing on a Camel Light.

I leaned against the front tire of the jeep and gulped down large, wet mouthfuls of bottled water. A flash of lightning filled the sky line and I felt an unexpected drizzle begin to trickle down upon me. I lifted my face up to meet the droplets. It felt cold and welcomingly cleansing. I stuck out my tongue to taste the rain, knowing I hadn't done anything so impetuous in years.

By the time everyone had reassembled outside, I was already reclining in the backseat. The skies released in a torrent. Phoebe, Manuel, and Remy clamored to escape the rain. Once inside the jeep, Remy flipped his dreads upside down to brush the water off. He shot me a strange look.

"Didn't wanna get stuck in the rain," I answered smugly.

We began the drive over the last few miles to Phoebe's house. Although it was dark, I could still distinguish that the front lawns of the passing houses were more frequently littered with sand rather than grass. We gradually ascended the bridges connecting the islands, stopping to pay two thirty-five cent tolls along the way. As we drew closer to the shore, the all-encompassing smell of sea air wafted into the jeep through the cracks of its soft top. I want to die with that scent teasing my nostrils.

A long time ended abruptly as the jeep made its final right turn up the slim slope of Phoebe's curving driveway. Her house was nestled back against the bay, hidden from the road by a tangled mass of pine trees and brush. Our headlights shone a dim glow onto its mammoth, gray-wooden shadow. The windows of the house were boarded up, creating the eerie look of a giant blank face.

Remy nudged me sharply with his elbow, "Nice digs, Phoebs."

"Thanks, big guy," Phoebe chirped, as she jerked the emergency brake up.

She tousled Manuel's buzz cut playfully and grabbed another set of keys from the center consul. She jumped outside into the storming New Jersey air and dashed for cover under the side porch. Phoebe fumbled through her keys frantically, struggling with the lock. She pushed the door open and flicked on the outside light. Her outline waved us forward.

Manuel, Remy, and I tumbled out into the rain. Manuel cursed the weather under his breath and started to unload our bags. Without looking, he threw a heavy looking backpack into my arms. I stumbled backward with the impact. Remy took the bag from me and stepped closer the jeep, edging Manuel out of his way. He doled the rest of the cargo between Manuel and himself.

"Damn it, Phoebe," Manuel barked under his breath. He furrowed his brow and muttered, "that girl can't fucking help for shit."

I blinked at him, dumbfounded by his short temper. Remy rubbed his hand over the back of my neck. With meticulous care, he guided me by my arm up the slippery, water beaded steps toward the house. His exaggerated chivalric gesture made me smirk with the thought of Manuel following behind us.

We burst through the doorway and into the laundry room, discarding our possessions in our wake. Phoebe gave everyone a quick tour and led Manuel and Remy upstairs to help her put away the food. After I finished in the downstairs bathroom, I tossed my bags into the guest bedroom and walked up the fluffy, carpet-padded steps to join the others in the kitchen. The boys were busy stocking the Molson into the refrigerator. Manuel, however, quickly lost interest in the occupation and wandered off in search of the television.

I opened a set of sliding glass doors to allow a crisp, winter air to creep through the stuffy rooms. I helped Phoebe remove the white furniture covers from the two main rooms. We piled them into a crumpled heap behind a tacky, art-deco sculpture that her mother purchased in Milan.

Manuel was sprawled fully across one of the three couches. Phoebe yelled at him to take off his muddy hiking boots. He grumbled like an old man, kicked off his boots, and moved to the electronic massage chair. He whined until Phoebe found the chair's remote control for him. She gave him a quick lesson on the different types of massages with which he could experiment. Phoebe then disappeared from the room in a huff.

Remy emerged from the kitchen with a round of Molson and plopped down on another couch. He tore off his shoes before putting his feet on the coffee table. I cuddled up next to him, brushing my lips lightly across his. He smiled and pulled me into a loose hug. He started to flip through the t.v. channels and stopped on ESPN's "Sports Center". Keith Obermann was busy making dimwitted jokes.

Mercifully, I was saved by Phoebe's call to me, "Claude, could you please give me a hand?"

I followed her voice into the kitchen.

Phoebe placed a white tea kettle on the stove top and lit the burner.

"I thought that we could seep these mushies into some tea," Phoebe said. "Can you grab a couple of mugs for us?"

I pulled four mugs from the cupboard and rinsed them each in the sink. Phoebe sifted through a jar of different teas and asked me which flavor I would like. I chose Earl Grey as did she. She selected chamomile for both Manuel and Remy.

It didn't take long for the water to boil. The teapot whistled meekly prompting Phoebe to quickly remove it from the stove. She filled each cup with steaming hot water and told Manuel that it was ready. Without interrupting his conversation with Remy, Manuel walked into the kitchen and grabbed two mugs filled with tea. He continued bantering with Remy about football statistics and returned to the t.v. without a word to us.

I snatched up a striped, pastel pink mug and arranged myself in the kitchen cove at the large country-style table. I took a long gulp of tea and let the warm steam blanket the skin on my face. I closed my eyes and waited for the drug to take effect. Its awful taste was masked by the flavor of Earl Grey.

(*"Civilization imprisons the raw freedom of the spirit," she told the laos.*

"Bury your feelings beneath a coat of beautiful armor, so that no one knows that you are vulnerable," advised the laos.

She promised that she would try to do this and realized that her true self would eventually become incommunicable to all, including herself.)

My body began to quiver as Phoebe's words became jumbled and harder to decipher. I felt a churning in my stomach that sent shivers along my spine and clutched the arms of my chair so tightly that my knuckles beg an to turn white. I kept my eyes closed because, when I opened them, I was overpowered by a deafening buzz reverberating in my ear drums.

I was tripping.

"Claudia, honey, you all right?" Phoebe asked.

I tried to shake it off and swallowed the lump growing in my throat. Phoebe's words slowly came into focus again.

"I miss spending time with you, Claude," she said.

"I wish you were traveling with me. We'd have so much fun together," she added.

I blinked, following her confession. "I know, Phoebs. I think about it too."

"But I'm comfortable here," I admitted. "Traveling doesn't seem to be a big deal to me. Maybe some day, just not now," I continued.

"God, I wish I could be comfortable somewhere," Phoebe said. "I can't seem to sit still anywhere for more than five minutes," she sighed, sounding exasperated.

"Phoebs, you've got Manuel now. You guys seem to get along *great*," I told her.

"Yeah," she laughed. "The only problem is that he's even less stable than I am."

"Don't get me wrong, part of me really believes that he's *the one*," Phoebe mused. "But then I realize that I can't settle down yet because I don't feel like I'm in the right place," she said.

"Are you happy?" I asked.

"Sometimes," she answered. "Sometimes I'm happy. Other times I just feel like there's something that I'm missing because I'm not where I should be."

"What about you, Claude?" Phoebe turned the question to me. "This thing with Remy looks pretty serious."

I giggled shrilly; it sounded as if I were trying to be coy.

"Did you tell your parents?" she asked.

"Tell them what?" I responded, playing dumb.

"What do you mean 'tell them what'?" Phoebe yelped. "Tell them that he's black. For Christ's sake, your dad must have flipped!"

"I don't know what my dad thinks," I said curtly. "I haven't talked to him in a while," I explained.

"My mom knows there's a Remy. She doesn't know there's a color thing though," I told Phoebe.

"I don't feel like it's an issue between us," I added.

"Yeah, right," Phoebe jabbed.

"Yeah right, Phoebs," I countered. "I adore Remy. What my parents think doesn't matter," I said.

I stared mindlessly into the abyss of my mug. I had drained it dry. I wrapped my hands around the mug and squeezed tightly. Suddenly startled, I winced as the ceramic popped and sliced through the flesh of my palm. A long, thin cut appeared across my skin. It did not open up right away.

I waited for a second and watched as a bright red trickle started to slowly slide its way down my forearm. Phoebe was busy rummaging through the cupboards with her back turned toward me. I remained quiet and she oblivious to the fact I'd even hurt myself.

I stood up and wobbled to the kitchen sink. The blood flow was heavier now. I grabbed a towel and watched it soak into the cloth.

"Claudia!" Phoebe cursed, as she noticed me. "What did you do?" she cried.

"It's these cheap mugs, Phoebs," I droned.

"I can't leave you alone for a minute, girl," Phoebe said, as she walked toward me at the sink.

With her strong, muscular hands, she clamped the towel down even harder on my flesh. My cut wouldn't stop bleeding though, not for a long time. When it finally stopped, it just sort of caked itself into clumps around the slit.

I found out later that if I moved my hand in certain ways I could make it start to bleed all over again.

After the excitement surrounding the trauma subsided, Remy stepped into the kitchen. He tapped the last few drops of liquid from the bottom of his mug into his mouth. He shouted to Manuel about some college basketball recruit and saw me standing over the sink with a magnificently, red stained towel covering my hand.

"Claudia, what the hell happened?" Remy yelped. "Why didn't you call me"? he scolded, rushing in my direction.

Without giving me a chance to answer, Remy commanded, "Come here; let me look at it. I want to see if you need stitches."

He pulled my hand toward him, dropping the towel to the floor. I jerked away and flopped back into my chair at the table.

"Remy, please," I insisted. "Phoebe and I have everything under control. I'm fine," I reassured him as I wrapped a bandage over my palm.

"She's right Remy," Phoebe interrupted.

"If you want to make yourself useful come over here and rub my neck for a minute," she instructed Remy. "I'm so tense," she explained, reaching to pull up her hair.

Remy bent to pick up the discarded towel. Phoebe took it from him and threw it to the counter. She lifted Remy's hands from his sides and lead them to her shoulders.

With a wringing motion, Remy thrust Phoebe's neck forward and down. He began to knead in steady circles over her back; his hands could massage tension from a tightrope. Phoebe's eyes were sealed shut and a smile perched itself upon her lips. Her head bobbed about in relaxed ecstasy.

I quietly slid my chair back and stood up. I moved toward Remy. I brushed my fingers lightly through Phoebe's hair, pausing for a moment to caress the back of Remy's hand. I traced his forearm with my touch and broke away from him when I reached his elbow.

I took two steps backward and rested my weak grasp on the handle of the kitchen's sliding glass door. I tugged half-heartedly. The edges of the glass swished as they moved over the cold, metal tracking fixed to the floor.

My barefeet pitter-pattered down the gray, paint-chipped steps of the deck. They fluttered over the chilling, glistening surface of the black tarred road and made tiny splashes along the way from the force of my impact in the post-rain environment.

I descended to the bay. My pace quickened to a run as I reached the boards of the dock. I breathed in the comforting and reassuring feeling that the clunking of my heels made with each strike against the wood. When I reached the edge of the water, I stopped and listened to the break waves lap and churn under the watchful gaze of the bright moon. Its rays seemed strong enough to light the skies of a slightly cloudy day.

I bent down with the pop of my ankle and dipped my toe into the frigid water. I shivered and folded my legs underneath me, Indian style. I stared across the expanse of the bay and watched a few scattered boats drift against the night sky. My eyes followed the outline of tall marsh weed pressed beneath the island's bridge, which was barely discernible in the darkness. I sat for what felt like an eternity.

("What do you see?" asked the laos.

"I see a curious pattern of purples and blues melting into a strangely misty skyscape that never saw a sunset," she answered. "I see that which has no meaning for me—a montage of wavy lines, swaying colors, and flashing lights. That is all I see," she concluded.

"Colors are different in each world," the laos pushed her. "As are the vultures."

"As are the pleasant thoughts of blends of jasmine and fresh oranges. As is the curve of the lilac. As is the nostalgic scent of sandalwood," she combated, clinging to her own optimism.

"Cry a prayer of serenity, for these are the days that must happen to you," instructed the laos. "You arrive at the city to which you were destined," they foreshadowed.)

I cocked my head to one side and listened intently. As I anticipated, I heard the sliding glass door of Phoebe's house open in the distance. Its sound pierced the crisp silence of the thin air. I didn't turn around. I traced the path of Remy's approaching footsteps in my head.

I was surprised that he didn't rush up at me from behind. Instead, however, he began to rustle about in the boat slip on my left.

I sensed movement in the water. Out of the corner of my eye, I glimpsed Remy's shadow crouching low in the hull of Phoebe's parents' boat. Remy bent toward the dock and pushed himself along the splintered wood with his sinewy muscles. He guided the boat in my direction, stopping to stand tall before me. Without a word, he beaconed me forward with his outstretched arms.

Expressionlessly, I stepped off the dock and closed my eyes as I entered the image.

I positioned myself in the front of the boat. Remy coaxed the engine to a sputter and then to a start. He took the helm with an air of command and we began to move across the bay. A steady breeze filtered through my hair, penetrated my nostrils, and sunk into my pores. It was almost cleansing.

I stared straight ahead, following our course. I became astutely aware of Remy's presence. We rode for a long time—neither speaking nor looking at each other. I was barely breathing. We slipped away from the houses, passed under a causeway bridge, and began to trace the shore's edge. I felt distant and free.

Remy stopped the engine at the lighthouse inlet. The silence forced my re-awakening. Remy lowered the anchor into the sand. I turned to face him. A tear slid from the corner of my eye and glistened as it slithered down my cheek. Trembling, I watched as Remy's finger lightly traced the trail of my tear. The same finger then danced in a circular outline over the unyielding features of my face.

My lips parted slightly to taste his skin. I extended my pink tongue and molded it to his fingertip. Remy cupped my chin loosely in his palm and pulled my face toward him. He brushed his lips against my own. His kiss felt like sweet, sugary honey seeping out of the corners of my mouth.

Remy's hands glided slowly along my skin, exploring my body for the first time. His touch lingered over my bandaged hand for only an instant. He then ventured under the folds of my shirt, loosening my bra and caressing my breasts delicately.

Remy released the buttons on my shirt and rolled it from my shoulders. He tossed it onto a water ski, which was lying in the stern. He knelt down and molded his tongue to my flesh, alternating between soft sucking and licking motions. I fell against him unsteadily as a wave struck the boat. I heard a moan escape my lips. I dug deeply into his shoulders with my finger nails and struggled not to lose my balance.

Remy's hands chased his tongue. He fumbled over the pleats of my skirt and pushed the fabric up to reveal the crest of my inner thigh. I shivered and collapsed to the deck of the boat. I pulled Remy toward me, tearing at his shirt until his chest covered me. His nappy dreads cascaded in tangled sections against my cheeks and rested on my shoulders.

I parted my legs and guided his mouth downward. His lips hummed methodically against me for longer than I thought I could bear. He relinquished his hold with my gasp and pressed himself into me. I welcomed him, as our bodies melted into each other.

Desire overcame me as I dug my nails deeper into Remy's back and tightened around him. Rings of ecstasy seized my body, releasing me only so that I could scream for air.

Again, I felt a tear escape me. Remy rolled away. I winced and stretched slightly.

Standing on my own, I dove rigidly into the icy black water, let its spell envelope me, and swam for shore.

The Devil's Pocket

When we met, Remy was living at Twentieth and Fairmount about a block from the Eastern State Penitentiary. Pure Motion did a few shows out of town in D. C., New York, and Chicago and Remy forgot to pay his rent. His landlord ousted him within a matter of days. The situation seemed rather bizarre to me because I always thought you had much longer than that before you could be evicted. I didn't ask Remy any questions though; I took him at his word.

Wilfried Wetekam, the director of Group Movement, let Remy crash in one of the rooms at the studio for a couple of weeks. It was convenient but uncomfortable. There was no shower, no phone, and no kitchen. On top of that performances, rehearsals, and parties ran late nearly every night, making it impossible for Remy to get to sleep before 3:00 AM.

Remy started to crash with me more often than not. I didn't mind; it was better than sleeping alone. My place was small though and always reeked of garlic because it was directly above Gus's, one of the best Italian restaurants in South Philly. I'd put on a couple of pounds since I moved in.

My lease ran month-to-month, so Remy suggested we look for something bigger. He tried to hook me on the idea of moving to New York or out West for awhile but I wasn't ready to leave Philly yet. I was pleasantly settled in my every day routine. Remy kept asking me why I felt the need to limit myself. I didn't think my scope limited, just merely manageable. Besides, I looked at the photographs from my last trip to New Orleans all the time.

Convinced with the idea of staying in Philly, I flipped through the Classified section of the "City Paper" every Thursday. Initially, I concentrated on ads listed in Olde City and Rittenhouse Square but Remy reminded me over and over again that we were on a budget. We had to stick to places like West Philly and Northern Liberties.

I tried pounding the pavement with no luck. I checked out a bunch of places with those yellow and red "APTS" signs posted in the doorway but I was consistently told that someone had just beaten me to it. I even contacted a few Center City realtors. They were always very cordial but none of them would talk to me when they heard that I was looking for something for $400 a month. They'd just hand me a business card and tell me to check back later. I started to get very discouraged.

By dumb luck, one of Remy's friends named Ezra Williams knew somebody that was trying to sublet a place uptown in the Devil's Pocket. I figured it couldn't be too bad. I'd met Ezra a couple of times at Oliver's loft on Third Street and he seemed O.K.

Oliver lived on the third floor, while Ezra's dance troupe, the "Two Streeters", occupied the second. The two of them liked to dress up in drag together and haunt the city. Ezra's alter-ego was called "The Countess" and was quite infamous in Philly's Performance Art circles.

I didn't know much about the Devil's Pocket. It was on the edge of Gray's Ferry just below the bridge into West Philly. It made the local news alot because it was the bevy of racial tension in the city. The only other time I'd heard mention of it beyond that was when some local band that made it big named their first CD after it.

I ran over to see the apartment on a rainy, dreary day just to make sure the place wasn't completely cock roach-infested and mice-ridden. It had two bedrooms and was located at the top of a tight, curving staircase. The walls were paper thin and in dire need of a fresh coat of paint. The bathtub was striped in uneven patterns from contact with some sort of toxic substance. But it was nearly fully furnished and well lit by tall, uneven windows on three of its four sides.

I grinned at the sight of my new home, realizing I really didn't have much of a choice in the matter. Remy made the deal with Ezra on good faith—no lease, no security deposit, just good faith.

We moved in on a brilliantly crisp, sunny Thursday during the first week of December. Remy had to work at Third Street during the day but promised that he and Ezra would be home before night fall to help with the bigger stuff. I figured we were going to have to leave alot behind because the stairs were so small.

I borrowed Gus's truck late in the morning and had most of my apartment packed and across town before my favorite soap opera came on at two. I lugged huge box after huge box. My progress was steady until my fourth trip when I dropped my keys to the ground onto the cold pavement of our new front stoop.

The keys made a comfortably solid, clanking sound, giving me a sense of where they'd fallen. I put down the heavy box I was holding and grabbed for my keys. The key chain had come unloose. It was a thick metal square screwed together at one corner by a rust colored marble. The key chain was a gift from my father, who bought it for me during a business trip to Denmark. The rust colored marble ball had rolled away.

"Fuck," I spewed angrily.

I fell to my knees and began to rummage over the pavement with my cracked, dry hands. I squinted and continued poking around until I attracted the attention of an old man I recognized but couldn't place. I tried to hide inconspicuously behind my dark DKNY sunglasses. As a distraction, I tousled my curly red locks, which were piled high above my head.

"What are you looking for, Miss?" the old man slurred politely. He was drunk.

"I dropped part of my keychain," I answered without looking up. I've never been very good at being abrupt.

"I see. My name is John," he said, introducing himself. "Could I help you look for it?" he asked. I continued my search in silence.

"I ain't askin' you for any money, dear," John insisted. "I jes like to help you look for your keychain, if you don' mind," he continued.

The bones in his legs cracked as he bent down beside me. He made an odd gurgling noise. I was struck immediately by a pungent stench, which crept from him. It was a mixture of smoke, sweat, alcohol and urine. It reminded me of Penn Station.

John's thick olive green coat flew open. An empty bottle wrapped in a brown paper bag tumbled to the sidewalk. The glass did not shatter. I looked at him sadly. Embarrassed, he smiled back at me toothlessly.

John wore a faded oversized work flannel, dirty tattered blue jeans, and clunky black shoes with gaping holes in the soles. His brown winter hat was pulled down low over his forehead. Tiny pills were sprinkled like snow flakes over its cotton fabric. He adjusted the hat with his rickety hands that were clothed by a pair of fingerless gloves.

I turned to him, suddenly realizing where I'd seen him before. I clenched my teeth and tried to wish him away. He was going to try to hustle me.

At night, the old man worked the corner of Fourth and South outside the Copabanana Cabana. The Copa served the best Margaritas and Spanish fries in Philly, so I'd been there often.

I was surprised to see John this far uptown. He was usually camped among the South Street window shoppers, waiting for pretty girls. When one would pass by, he would point up at the sky and howl loudly at the moon. The girls would giggle and then John would hit them up for whatever they had. Sometimes, he would heckle over the corner with a blind woman. She was also a full time waif, who rocked back and forth on a milk crate playing a recorder for change.

"So what does your keychain look like, Miss?" John asked. He swept his old hands over the pavement, sifting through the dirt on either side of the stoop.

"It's just a tiny marble, about yea big," I said, motioning with my hands. "It's almost this color," I added.

I pointed to a piece of rock, which stuck out from one of the cracks in the cement.

"By the way, my name is Claudia," I said. "I appreciate your help but I really can't give you anything in return," I clarified.

"I tol' you, Miss Claudia. I don't expect nothin'," John reassured me. "I'd jes like a few minutes a your company," he schmoozed.

Unconvinced, I smirked at him.

"Look John, you've brought me luck. Here it is," I declared as I lifted the round marble from the pavement.

Avoiding his eyes, I held the marble up between my index finger and thumb for him to see. I steadied myself with the top of the box and pulled myself to my feet. John moved to help me up but wobbled under the weight of his age. He kicked the bottle he'd dropped earlier into the street and rose to where I stood. I held a foot over him at least; his posture was crooked and weak.

"Miss Claudia, do ya' think you could help me out a little?" John started quickly. "Jes a lil' change so's I can get a cuppa coffee to warm me up," he explained.

I shook my head, "No."

Without flinching, I stared unforgivingly into the face of poverty. I keyed the lock to the apartment and pushed myself inside. I slid the box through the archway with my foot and slammed the door on John.

It is the true test of the humanist to delve into the existential and still come out a believer.

I fell back against the cold door, holding my head between my hands. A winter draft wisped inside from behind me, slipping through the gaping spaces of the front wall of the house. I slumped over to lift the box from the floor, cradling it in my arms. I ascended the cramped stairwell as if attending a funeral march. I tripped over my own two feet and crashed into the banister. I managed not to drop the box.

I reached the second floor landing and let myself into the apartment. My steps echoed as I passed over the hard wood of the near empty room. I unrolled a throw rug and positioned Remy's folding chair in its center. I sunk into the red and white striped fabric of the chair. I flicked on Remy's stereo and tuned in a heavy house beat from WKDU.

I flipped through the crisp pages of some books stacked in a dusty milk crate. The bass brought me slowly to my feet and I began to tap my toes. I closed my eyes. The music made me smile and nod my head as its monotonous refrain took over my thoughts. Soon, I was jumping and clapping throughout the empty space of the apartment.

Dancing harder, I laughed aloud. I lit a Camel Light, which I pulled from behind my ear. I swished my skirt around and around, making silly patterns with it. I lifted it higher and higher, until my thighs were exposed in a mirror hanging at the end of the hallway.

The scarf in my hair loosened and slid to the floor. I caught the thin fabric in both hands and toyed with it to see what sorts of erotic shadows I could make in the mirror. I found myself out of breath. A damp sweat began to flow from my pores.

Happiness is living lost in a moment before the moment reminds you where you are.

I stopped moving when I realized that the smoke from my cigarette had filled the room. Remy would be upset with me for smoking in the house.

I flung the front window of our bedroom open. The air was still and the winter sun unusually warm. I stepped out onto the tar covered roof. The roof was my favorite characteristic of the apartment. It served as a make-shift porch.

I lined a row of brown paper shopping bags underneath the window. I sat down gingerly to finish my cigarette and leaned my head back on the sill. I flicked the butt into the street below. I managed to fall into a light sleep in the midst of the day's last dwindling, lingering sunrays.

I heard the door open. I was jolted awake by a loud bang. I recognized voices. Remy asked Ezra if he wanted a beer. Although my eyes were still squinty with sleep, I managed to peek inside. Through the bedroom window, I could distinguish the top of Remy's head. He was sitting on the couch.

I decided not to let them know I was home.

"Where's Claude?" Ezra asked.

"I don't know where she is," Remy responded.

"Maybe she went back to her old place to pick up some more of her stuff," Remy continued.

"Was she pissed that you weren't around to help today?" Ezra asked.

"I don't know," Remy answered. "What was I supposed to do? Gotta work if we wanna keep livin' the high life," he said.

One of them burped. They started to giggle like little boys. I guessed that they were nearing the end of their beers. I heard a glass bottle slam on the table. A bottle cap dropped to the floor and rolled out of the reach of our slow, fat cat named Mojo. I followed the trail of Mojo's paws as she slid across the hardwood floor after the tiny piece of metal.

"Well, bro," Ezra started. "I gotta run. We're headin' to Dirty Frank's later—I need a little nap if I'm gonna make it."

"Hey Ezra, thanks for helping out," Remy said. "I know Claude appreciates it too. Once we're settled in, I'll get her to make up a big pot of her veggie chili as repayment," Remy offered, promising my services.

"Cool," Ezra said. "Why don't you meet us out later for some beers?" he invited, slamming the door behind him.

I peered over the edge of the roof, as Ezra quickly emerged in the street. His black, bald head glistened as he turned to walk toward Spruce Street. He jerked back around in the direction of the apartment for an instant and I thought he saw me hiding. I realized though that he was looking at John, who had been badgering him from amidst a blooming holly bush.

Remy was alone, rummaging in the kitchen. I pulled myself up to sit on the bedroom window sill and watched as he ransacked the refrigerator. He arranged some vegetables, cheese, and crackers inside a make-shift tray, which he fashioned from the empty lid of a copy paper box. He knew it was my favorite meal in the world.

Remy paused for a moment, wondering if he'd forgotten anything. Mojo scurried about under his feet, crying to be fed. Remy kicked her lightly. I almost jumped up to stop him but I didn't.

Instead, I waited for him to turn around and see me. He balanced the box lid in one hand, with two glasses and a bottle of chardonnay in the other. His head was down. He was humming to the radio, which was still wailing faintly to his right. He jumped slightly when he looked up and noticed me smiling at him. My eyes turned downward flirtatiously. I crossed the tips of my feet the way Holly Hobbie used to on a pair of bed sheets I had when I was a little girl.

"Hi," my eyes shone brightly in his direction. "Welcome home."

"Thanks," Remy said. "I slaved over dinner for us," he joked, lifting up the box lid.

"To the verandah then, my dear," I gestured, spinning my legs back around onto the roof.

I jumped down from the window sill, landing on the rough black slate below. I walked to the edge, kicking a crooked drain pipe in my wake. I teetered a little and turned toward Remy. He was arranging our feast on an old Mexican blanket that he'd carried over his shoulder. You had to sit on something or you'd end up with black smudges of dirt all over your backside.

By now, it was all over the palms of my hands. I was fairly sure it was lingering on my cheeks too.

Remy patted on the blanket for me to sit with him. I collapsed and laid my head on his shoulder.

"Just in time for the sunset," he said.

You really couldn't see the sun very well. It was almost completely settled behind the University's hospital. The flashing red and blue lights of the hospital's helicopter pad had already begun to spin in the dusk in preparation for the night ahead. However, you could still distinguish pastel hues of pinks and purples painting the Western sky.

"Not many people seem to be able to appreciate the meaning of a sunset," I thought out loud.

"Or even the meaning of a sky, for that matter," Remy answered me.

He pulled some pennies from his pocket. He lofted them into the air, aiming his fire at a pair of discarded, white chucks hanging over the telephone wires above us. He only hit the sneakers once. The other pennies fell to the ground. We couldn't hear them hit the cement because of the street sounds.

"So what do you think, Claude?" Remy said. "This place is all right for us now. It's cheap, so we should be able to save up enough cash to take off in a couple months," he added.

"Take off, Mr. Thomas?" I purred as I crawled into his lap, slipping my legs around his waist. I was left staring directly in his face.

"Just where is this mystical, magical land we'll be running off to?" I questioned. I popped a cheese covered cracker into my mouth.

"Come on, Claude," Remy chided. "Philly's great but it'll always be here for us. I been here my whole life," he said.

"Remy, wait," I tried to interject. He cut me off, wanting desperately to continue.

"No, Claude. I've finally found you," he said.

"I want to walk nameless alleys with you on hot, humid nights in towns like Charleston and Savannah. I wanna take in stray cats from abandoned lots while we're lost somewhere deep in the Dakotas. I wanna live in a tiny, adobe shack in a New Mexico desert with you. Just you," he rambled, running his hand along my neck.

"I know Remy," I answered him. "But there's something within me that feels safe here."

"Safe doesn't mean happy," he snapped, sipping his wine.

"No, but it gives me control," I said. "I find something new here everyday, even if it's just a quote from Yeats on my Elliot's Amazing Apple Juice cap."

"But imagine the *something* new you could find *somewhere* new," Remy tried.

"This is home to me now, Remy," I explained. "I don't need to go anywhere else to find *home*. This apartment, you, Mojo, the bookstore, these are the things I need," I said, fingering the alfalfa sprouts.

"I don't think you know what's out there," Remy interrupted, bitingly.

"What about New Orleans?" he asked rhetorically. "Your face fucking lights up when you tell me stories about that place. It's in your soul," he said.

"And my face fucking lights up when you bring me cheddar cheese and stoned wheat thins on the first Thursday in December, Remy," I grunted, angry that he'd sworn at me.

"New Orleans is just another place," I said, denying myself. "Maybe I'll make it there someday," I whispered wistfully.

"Why is it always someday, Claude?" Remy demanded. "Why not now?" he pushed again. His knee knocked over his glass of wine.

"Because I believe the things that are meant to happen to me will find me here," I answered. "My spirit may be restless but it does not feel the need to wander."

"I see," Remy barked. "Taking your restless soul to the Ritz on Saturday night for an art house flick is more than enough to settle your emptiness," Remy taunted.

"What emptiness?" I jumped at him, pulling myself off his lap. I moved to another corner of the blanket.

"I don't think I'm restless because I'm empty. I'm restless because I'm too full," I mused.

"Oh, Claude," Remy sighed. "We don't have any responsibilities now. No high powered careers, no kids, it's just us. We won't have this chance again until we're old and gray and arthritic," Remy said, sounding discouraged.

"And then," I smiled. "Then, Mr. Thomas, I will move away with you—all the way to New Orleans."

"We'll sit on our white wooden porch swing in front of our house on Tchoupitoulas Street on the first Thursday in December. We'll just sit there, gnawing on chicory sticks, and tossing pennies at the banana tree in our side yard," I laughed.

Growing tired, Remy conceded, "Promise?"

I knew though that his soul was not only restless, it was wandering. Remy would always feel an interminable emptiness until he hitched rides alone on the country's turnpikes, worked odd jobs in ski towns, and explored the big cities he'd always read about. These were things that only experience could cure.

I only knew that Remy's emptiness was something for which I never wanted to be responsible. Listlessness is not a character trait I've ever found attractive. My heart foretold me that this difference would eventually become a chasm between us which was too deep to cross.

"C'mere," Remy whispered, pulling me back into him. He kissed my lips softly.

"What d'ya say we flare up a little hooch and head out for a celebratory house warming?" he asked.

I smiled, winking at him. I tackled him in a bear hug.

"Bring it on," I cheered.

We kissed heatedly for a few minutes. Pushing Remy off of me, I said, "Before we go, I wanna head down to the cop shop to pick up milk and some smokes."

Remy rolled his eyes at my mention of cigarettes. He was trying to get me to quit.

We smoked a bowl and started to clean up the mess we'd made on the roof. As I crawled back through the window into the nearly pitch black bedroom, Remy ran his hands over my legs. I moved to the kitchen to put away the food. Remy rooted around in our boxes for candles and lit them strategically around the apartment. Remy loved lighting candles.

When I was through, I pulled a heavy flannel from a pile of coats and left Remy dancing in the empty bedroom. He'd turned WKDU up to deafening decibels. I screamed goodbye to him but he couldn't hear me. I slung my mountain bike over my shoulder and dragged it heavily down the stairs.

I struggled with the bike in the doorway and clumsily tripped outside. It was significantly cooler out than when I'd spoken to John earlier. I scanned the sidewalk for him but guessed he'd probably left the Devil's Pocket by this time for his corner on South Street.

I hopped on my bike and headed in the direction of the big curve on Locust before the Spruce Street bridge. I rode quickly because I was cold. Standing on the pedals, I balanced myself over the umpteen potholes in the road. You needed a mountain bike in Center City; it was almost as bad as trail riding.

Five minutes later, I screeched to a halt in front of the red and white cop shop. The locals called it the "cop shop" because it was owned by two retired policemen. There are alot of corner stores in Philadelphia that are owned by old cops. They usually attract the most corrupt activity in the city.

I lifted my bike onto the dull metal bicycle rack. Expertly, I locked the frame and the front tire with my u-lock. Mine was the only bike there. I opened the front door and stepped inside. I immediately sensed a tension that wanted me to leave. My stomach became queasy.

A guy with a curly brown mustache and mismatched sandy blonde hair stood behind the over-crowded front counter. He wore faded jeans and a comfortable looking red T-shirt that screamed "Yo!" in black print. Underneath, was written the word, "Philadelphia." The T-shirt made me chuckle.

A plastic shelf filled with cigarettes packs loomed above his head. The shelf made it difficult to read the man's eyes. He leaned over a small basket overflowing with stale looking brownies, muffins, and cookies. He began to flick at the flame of a lighter. The lighter was white with the Harley Davidson emblem printed on each side. He spoke loudly in a raised voice to another man who was swaying on the opposite side of the counter.

The second man bumped awkwardly into the single serve bags of chips and pretzels lined neatly beneath the cash register. He lifted one of the bags to his lips and popped the wrapper so that chip crumbs tumbled into his mouth. The man was black and his clothes were dirty.

Both men turned toward the door, as the bell above me clanked in deadpan monotone. They stopped speaking and stared at me, shifting nervously in their shoes.

Over the silence, I heard the buzzing of the eerily bluish, fluorescent lights. My stomach wretched at the stench of the death dogs that had been browning for hours on the black grates of an encased turning wheel. I hated that smell. It always lingered in my hair and on my clothes when I went back outside.

I grabbed a shopping basket from a stack towering against the counter and smiled politely at the men.

The guy in the funny T-shirt greeted me, "Hey, how you doin'?"

He had a thick, Philly accent. I nodded my head and moved slowly past a magazine rack to the coolers in the back of the store. I scanned the shelves for a half gallon of 1% percent low-fat milk. I wanted to buy skim but Remy wouldn't drink it.

Steadying myself against the edge of the cooler's door, I yanked a blue and white carton of milk from the shelf and positioned it in my basket. The glass fogged quickly from contact with the warm air of the store. I stopped to eavesdropped on the men's conversation.

"Yo, man. All's I need is sixty-five cent," begged the black man pathetically.

"I don't care," answered the man in the funny T-shirt.

"There ain't no handouts in my store. Get the fuck outta here," he yelled. His voice was growing more excited.

"Come on man, I need it fo' the bus fare home," explained the bum.

"Look, I ast you to leave," reminded the man behind the counter.

"But Mista, is cold outside," said the black man.

"Out," demanded the store clerk. I watched him point authoritatively to the door.

Without another word, the bum turned away from the counter. He kicked furiously at the snack shelves, knocking a number of bags to the floor. He stomped on the bags, crushing the food across the tile. He left the store, banging the door against the magazine rack. The bell jangled above his head. The noise sounded surreal to me.

I looked into the street to see where the man had run. He was long out of my sight. The store clerk emerged from behind the counter with a broom and dustpan to sweep up the mess. He was cursing audibly, which made me feel awkward. I wanted nothing more than to be home dancing with Remy.

I balanced my over-flowing basket precariously on my knee, surveying its contents. I fumbled through the pockets of my oversized flannel and pulled out crumpled dollar bill after crumpled dollar bill. I tried to calculate the total in my head. When I shopped, I liked to pretend Bob Barker was the host as I played "The Price is Right" in front of a live, studio audience. Bob was always warning me not to guess over the actual price of the items.

I decided I didn't have enough money on me to pay for everything I'd picked up. I stopped suspiciously and hid a box of Pop-Tarts, two frozen chicken burritos, and a bag of cough drops in an empty space in the wrong aisle. My mother would have been disappointed in me.

I was about to make my way toward the cash register when I heard the door bell ring again.

"What the fuck?" screamed the cashier. "Didn't I fucking tell you to get lost?"

The black man had entered the store again. This time, he was wielding a long, splintered piece of wood high above his head. He cackled and made freakish, gurgling noises. He waited for a moment, almost suspended in time. Then, he began to grunt barbarically and smashed the wood hard into the candy display. He squished the stale looking brownies, muffins, and cookies under the weight of his force, scattering lighters into the air.

"Jesus Christ," yelled the cashier, clearly shaken.

He threw the broom to the floor and rushed behind the counter. He moved quickly beneath the register, struggling for cover. He tried to shield his head with his arms, as the black man continued to thrash about the store. When he pulled himself up, he was gripping a nine millimeter firmly between his hands. His aim was unwavering.

"That's it, mother fucker," he warned, pointing the gun at the vagrant.

The black man did not flinch. He raised the wood up again and knocked out one of the fluorescent light panels in the ceiling. I was surprised at his reach. He lunged forward over the register and started to bring his weapon down in the direction of the cashier. He was stopped short by the gunfire, which struck him in the center of his chest.

I'd only ever heard a gunshot from a distance before.

I guess it just sounds louder when you're five feet away. It's really just a hollow pop that echoes and leaves a lingering smell of gun powder wafting in the air. I suppose I would have seen some sort of a flash of light coming from the pistol if I'd been staring down its barrel but I wasn't, so I didn't any flash of light.

Frozen with shock, the man stood poker straight, staring at the hole in his chest. He released the piece of wood from his grasp. He looked up again at the cashier before he fell to the ground. I wanted to see the expression on his face as he went down. It was important to me. I wanted to remember the precision of the moment as if it were an indelible mark on my life.

("I believed lies," she cursed at the laos. "Somewhere, there was poison, which I ingested."

"Never you mind," they said. "Come here. We have a rocking chair for you," they added, patting on white, puffy clouds.

"I don't even think like an artist anymore," she sighed, shaking her head.

"Did you ever?" asked the laos, heartlessly.

"Yes. Once upon a time, there was this love that was greater than love," she snapped, with emotion.

"But you were careless. You stopped to love the people no one understands and you didn't have enough room," they surmised.)

In my prison cell, I bide my time. Then I was reminded. Reminded, as the cashier called 911 frantically, swearing under his breath.

I wasn't supposed to be there. No, I was lying on the grass outside Benny's, at 4:00AM during Mardi Gras. People had their faces painted and masks hiding their eyes. A random blues band played behind the metal cage in the dark one room bar. I laid there under a magnolia tree with my eyes closed, tripping my face off. Smiling.

I didn't see the spattered blood puddling around the snack size Frito-Lay bags. I didn't trip over the yellow police flags and I didn't grow dizzy from the red and blue flashing lights, which forced kaleidoscopic pictures in the night sky. I didn't see Channel 6 or Channel 10 because ice cream has no bones.

"Me?"

"Sure, I'm fine."

Questions, everyone asking me questions.

"No, I don't need to talk to anybody."

"I want to go home. That's my statement. I just want to go home."

Ask the guy behind the counter with the sandy brown hair what happened. I have to call Remy; he'll know what to do. I just want to go home. That's all, nothing else. I'm tired. I'm always tired.

There is blood on the sole of my right shoe. I loved these shoes. My mother bought them for me the last time I visited her.

Now, I am sure tomorrow will hold more of the same.

Dream Sequence

They say that you begin to have strange dreams when you're pregnant. I had this dream two months after Remy and I moved in together:

Lee's Hoagie House made great Italian hoagies but they just didn't sell the right potato chips. My mother, who was driving me around the Main Line in the early evening, was very particular about her junk food. She insisted munching on nothing other than Gibbles.

She kept exclaiming in different inflections, "What's a hoagie without the right chips?"

My mother didn't seem to care that we were already an hour and a half late to meet my aunt; she was intent on making a quick run to the Acme for the "necessities". We made a left turn off City Line Avenue into the parking lot of the Acme and mom began her tiresome search for an adequate space to dock.

Parking with mom was always interesting.

You had to find the perfect spot before pulling in; her SAAB convertible was never allowed to rest beside a "knicker" let alone a "bomber". Maybe that was what caught my attention. She was in such a hurry that she completely neglected the dilapidated, rusty, Chevy Nova standing still in the space to our right like a dull green dinosaur.

I spotted it right away; it reminded me of a tank.

My mother flicked off the engine and turned to me, smiling brightly. She lifted my hand from my side and placed a small piece of paper in my palm. It was a shopping list. I was a little surprised when I read it. I thought it would say Gibbles or the name of some other substitute brand of chips. Instead though, scrawled across the page, was the name of a book called Confederacy of Dunces.

That was the only thing on the list.

I opened up the car door and listened to the comforting thud of it closing behind me as my thick-soled heels delicately struck the surface of the black tar pavement. I walked determinedly to the Acme. I reached the glass encased entrance of the store and stepped onto the grooved mat, which signaled the electric doors to glide open for me.

I crossed through the doorway.

My eyes were met by a flurry of activity. Registers were clacking. Baggers were bagging. And, a health nut was purchasing cigarettes at the Customer Service Counter.

Instinctively, I ran to grab the last red, plastic basket with metal handles to carry around with me inside. I was disappointed as some fat lady chomping on peanuts beat me to it. The fat lady kept dropping her peanut shells onto the floor. They crunched under my weight as I followed her begrudgingly.

I wrung my hands together firmly, pretending to hold my own basket. I passed through one final electric door and stopped steadfast in the floral department. There were carnations, cyclamen, and other scattered pots of greenery.

Small puddles had accumulated in the more heavily trafficked areas of the store. This was because it had been raining outside earlier. I almost slipped on one of them but caught my footing before I embarrassed myself. I rested my hand on a center display stand. There, I spied a tall tree, which was sprinkled with dates. The tiny fruits were dangling precariously over the wet floor.

I walked around the pools of water, slowly approaching the tree. I admired the elasticity of its branches and realized that I had never touched a date before. As a matter of fact, I had no idea what a date was. I glanced around with shifty eyes, scanning the area for any noble Acme employees who may prove bitter enough to bust a good-intentioned Acme shopper.

Once I was sure that the coast was clear, I stretched on my toes and managed to grab one of the oblong fruits. I pulled it from its perch with a tug. It fought me for a spell but eventually gave way with a snap. I squeezed it, until a quarter inch piece squished into my hand. Then, I popped it secretly into my mouth.

A spot of juice trickled down my chin. I wiped it away hurriedly, hoping no one had seen my indulgence. I swallowed the date, trying to place its flavor. It reminded me of a prune.

I wished that I had stolen a grape instead.

Not being one to let everyday obstacles stop me from moving on bravely down the road of life, I continued down the produce aisle with pride in every stride. I moved past the bananas, oranges, ecru, and even the sun-dried tomatoes that I usually had to search for in vain for a solid twenty minutes on my normal Sunday shopping spree.

At the end of Aisle #1, appeared the sparkling splendor of the Acme salad bar. Cubes of cheese, cucumbers, tomatoes, onions, and fluffy sprouts were strategically positioned there. With the exception of the gelatinous looking pudding, my wanton eyes grew wide at the possibility of carrying such delicacies home on top of a cool bed of lettuce.

My attention was quickly drawn from the magnificent sight. Diagonally and to my right, was a display of glass deli cases which I prayed contained the item on my shopping list. I studied the tiny piece of crumpled paper, embedding the name of the book in my brain. I reached the deli counter and plucked a number from the jagged edges of the red and black ticket dispenser.

I patiently waited in line for my turn.

The people around me were all black. They looked at me as if I did not belong. I remember swaying slightly and adjusting my feet often because their carriages were dangerously close to my toes. The cries of their children were piercing my ears.

I was growing nervous and turned to glance over my shoulder.

The outline of a couch became recognizable. It was conveniently positioned in a daisy—strewn meadow. Upon closer observation, I noticed that it was green. It seemed like a clever and purposeful attempt by Acme management to distract weary customers from rushing through the store.

I ran to the couch, sinking back deeply into its soft pillows. From the end table next to me, I grabbed a yellow-brown banana peel. I lit the banana peel with a butane, metal lighter that I had dug from deep within my pocket. I began to puff away quietly.

A girl with long, straight blonde hair flopped down lazily next to me. She began to pull at the front of her hair. She told me that someone had just put it into a French braid for her. She complained that it was too tight and made her look too severe. She had a smile behind her eyes.

Without a word, I knew that the girl with a smile behind her eyes liked to read Richard Brautigan books late at night when she was all alone. I figured that sometimes she even smoked cigarettes and drank coffee. Of course, though, I knew that she always sat alone.

I smiled back at her.

It was then that I noticed that there was a never-ending staircase leading upward from behind the deli counter. On the staircase, sat many figures who stared down at the meats and cheeses. Some stared too at the sky. Yet still others stared at each other.

My beautiful couch companion and I were approached by a man who descended from the staircase. He began to speak to us with wild, exaggerated gestures. He held a quarter pound of Healthy Choice chicken breast in one hand and an umbrella in the other, even though it had stopped raining hours ago.

For some reason, this man began poking his umbrella in our direction. I clicked glasses with my fiddler vase, as he motioned for my couch companion to stand up. She did. She pulled off her sweater. Underneath, she wore a loose fitting, floral print dress, which hid her curvy figure. I continued to stare at her and reached up to pull out her braid.

Another man suddenly jumped into the scene. My friend and I both became annoyed, while the man with the umbrella started to poke at the new character in our defense.

Before I realized it, my beautiful, now-unbraided friend and I were kneeling with our faces pressed against the deli counter's glass. Our mouths were watering over the tapioca pudding.

When the two men began their inevitable assault on each other, my friend and I rose from our knees. We walked away from the counter and back to our couch. We sat down again and each grabbed another banana peel. Together, we lit them and began to throw oranges at the sky.

We sat like this for what seemed like hours, until the woman who was operating the deli slicer called my number. She began to slice out the pages of the book on my shopping list for me. I accepted her presentation, noticed the $2.48 price tag, and hummed an indistinguishable little ditty. Then, I started to walk into the chicken section.

I turned back briefly to wave good-bye to the girl with a smile behind her eyes, but she was already gone. A trail of tapioca pudding marked the route of her departure.

I covered my nose and mouth, as I darted past the red meat chunk and particle section. Knowing that my mother was still waiting outside, I decided to take a short cut through the pet food aisle. My arm was growing tired because my book was growing heavier and heavier with each step.

When I reached the pandemonium of the check out lines, I felt my throat begin to close. It became harder and harder to breathe. That nagging thought in the back of my mind that Americans spend one eighth of their lives waiting in line, kept creeping into my head. (I have somewhere else to be. Something more important is happening in that other place and I am missing it. Hurry, I need to hurry.)

I scanned the row of cashiers to see, which line would be my best bet. I decided that the one marked "CASH ONLY, TWELVE ITEMS OR LESS" was the one for me. I positioned myself behind the four other people already waiting there. With lowered eyes, I nonchalantly scanned the magazine rack. I found "Cosmopolitan" and "Good Housekeeping" disinteresting but was intrigued by "The Star's" headline that Hank Williams, Sr. was still alive. They said that he faked his death in 1953. I wondered why he would feel the need to fake his own death.

I flopped my book onto the rotating, black rubber mat. I used the plastic divider covered in Marlboro advertisements to separate my order from that of the fat, red-haired woman before me. She was the same woman who I'd seen gnawing on the peanuts in the produce aisle earlier.

At long last, the cashier handed the woman her receipt and turned to help me.

"Any coupons?" asked the cashier politely.

"No. No, thank you," I replied.

Bleep. The cashier ran the bar code of my deli bag over the computer.

"Your total is $3.15, please," she announced confidently.

"$3.15," I repeated after her, clearly shocked. "But the lady at the deli said it was only $2.48," I said.

"Tax," she snapped in response.

"Tax?" I mumbled.

I began to fumble around inside the pockets of my jeans for change. There was nothing there but lint and pennies. I tangled my fingers through my oversized purse but was almost swallowed by its endless mouth. More pennies. Time was ticking. Maybe in my shoe? No, nothing there either. I was beginning to grow embarrassed.

"Ma'am?" the cashier inquired impatiently.

(Ma'am?!$%#*0^@&)

"I must have left my wallet in the car," I lied.

"Could you hold this for me please? I'll be right back," I implored.

"I'm sorry," the cashier answered snippantly.

"Acme policy does not allow us to hold deli meats for any extended period of time. Those Ecoli scares have proven a bit to close for comfort for our company," she explained.

"But it won't be an extended period of time," I whined.

She promptly interrupted me and threw the deli bag into the blue trash can beneath her register.

"Have a nice day," she smiled.

"Fuck off," I thought to myself.

I pounded across the white block-tiled floor of the store, which was speckled with gold paint. The electric doors could not open fast enough for my dejected soul.

Slam. A gust of cool, fresh air crashed into my face and seeped into the pores of my skin. I saw my mother's SAAB convertible parked in the distance. I felt like I was lost in one of those Alice in Wonderland dreams where the hallway keeps growing longer and longer. I was trying to run faster and faster but the car kept moving further and further away.

With a final burst of energy, I reached the passenger door of the car. I opened it with a snap of the handle, sat down, and looked into my mother's eyes.

She had an inquisitive look on her face. Her question was like a knife in my back: "Where's the book?"

I tried to explain my experience to her. She stared at me in disbelief. She quickly forgave me and handed me four crisp, new dollar bills from her Chanel bag. She instructed me to hurry back inside again. She wrote out another shopping list and pressed it firmly into my hand.

Mindlessly, I obeyed her and walked toward the Acme a second time. As I lost my thoughts in the rhythm of my clicking heels, I dropped all of the dollar bills that my mother gave me. I lost them to the wind. I didn't notice because I was too anxious to return to the green couch where I could smoke banana peels while waiting for my deli order.

The dream repeats. Over and over again. And I wake up in a cold sweat, too afraid to fall back asleep.

I've never been one to remember my dreams. Except for the one I used to have when we lived in Williamsport, Pennsylvania when I was ten years old. In that one, I dressed up as Superman and saved the world from an untimely, painful destruction of Biblical proportions. The weird part of that dream was that the world wasn't inhabited by humans; it was inhabited by apes.

The Superman dream recurred for me for a long time. The one about the Acme cropped up for me about eight times between February and May. Hell, I could even taste the dates when I woke up in the morning.

I'm late. I only missed one pill.

(You always told yourself you would be proactive and *not* reactive. You never thought this would happen to you. And now, you (YES YOU!) are scared. You are afraid to tell him. You cannot tell your parents. You don't want to tell your friends. You want to forget about this and hope it will all be gone in the morning after you wake up and have your chamomile tea.

But your stomach feels queasy, you want to stay in bed, and you just keep crying. Christ, if you could just stop crying, you could figure out what to do.)

Say, "Cheese!"

My mom and dad always thought that I was so smart and so special I'd end up in medical school or law school at the end of my childhood.

When it was painfully apparent that I wasn't headed in either direction, my dad put a dowry on my head in the hopes that I'd *marry* a doctor or a lawyer. He figured that way he wouldn't have to pay my bills anymore and the grandkids, at the least, would be a good excuse for both of us to ignore my idiosyncrasies.

I disappointed my parents because I was selfish. I lived life to satisfy myself.

I sought comfort in the uniform, brutality of an East Coast city. I planted my feet firmly in the urbane and discovered an existence bound by an intangible love for the written word. I became the store manager at Oz and Endz.

I've held countless odd jobs in the past for which I'd roll out of bed twenty minutes late. Grumbling and sick to my stomach, I recall dragging myself to tedious, clock-watching hours spent waitressing, stuffing envelopes, or answering phones.

Work at the bookstore was not like this for me. Oz and Endz hung like a painting standing in the halls of the Louvre, suspended in time and space.

Gus, the storeowner, masterminded the eccentric labyrinth that was Oz and Endz. He held a doctorate in Physics from Penn, owned a farm in South Jersey, vacationed for two months out of the year in a tiny cabin in Newfoundland, and was obsessed with woodcarving.

Gus paved our over-crowded aisles with stacks of classic literature, science fiction, poetry, how-to-manuals, non-fiction, and children's books. He acquired antiques and artwork from estate and garage sales and crammed them into every inch of available space. He grew organic fruits and vegetables on his farm and arranged things like green peppers, eggplants, and containers of maple syrup in wooden baskets to entice customers.

Gus sold scratched LP's for a nickel and maintained an obscure collection of CD's and tapes, which no one ever touched. We carried candles, incense, and glass bottles. A mixture of scents like vanilla, magnolia, and peaches wafted through the cramped air like a subtle aphrodisiac.

Although we failed inspection regularly and only five percent of our merchandise actually moved, Gus taught me that true love for one's craft could sustain the soul. Once you discover your calling, you do not let it go.

I cleaned and protected the store's treasures with the loyalty and stupidity of a pet dog. I ran a purple-feathered duster over Civil War medals, jews harps, and a merry-go-round horse from Coney Island. I shelved books with no rhyme or reason and I used to cry alone after hours curled up tightly in the gold, velour armchair hidden in the sun porch.

I cried because I knew I was happier in that chair than I would ever be again.

It was spring. God, it was spring again. The ice melted and the cold rain and snow gave way to crocus, daffodils, and tulips plummeting to their death. The magnolia tree bloomed a cheery pink and then frowned at the bright weight of the sun. The air at night was crisp yet cool and smelled new, piercing my nostrils with unspecified memories of youth.

I rubbed my belly. It was pregnant and bursting like spring.

I still rode my bike to work. I hadn't told Remy about the baby yet. I figured he'd make me stop riding my bike if he knew. I loved riding my bike, especially in the spring. I loved Remy but I couldn't bring myself to tell him about the baby.

It was Saturday. I screeched through the bank's gravel parking lot onto the smooth pavement of Church Street. The rocks crackled and popped under my tires. I was fifteen minutes late for my shift but knew Gus wouldn't notice.

Gus' dusty, blue Suburban truck was angled high on the sidewalk between the store and Christ's Church. It was blocking the end of North American Street, our delivery alley. I snuck around the front of the truck. Shielded by its enormity, I steadied myself on one of the porch posts. I jumped off my bike and struggled with my rusty u-lock.

Once free of my bike, I wrapped my hands around the corner post and peered down the alley looking for Gus. The metal doors leading to the basement of Oz and Endz were thrust open and lying on the cement like wounded butterfly wings.

Gus was standing there in the dark hole, hunched over swelling cardboard boxes. I could only see his upper torso. He was intently sorting through our new stock with a discriminating eye. He categorized the arrivals on the steps, making separate piles for first editions, fiction, non-fiction, and "porch books".

"Hello, Gus," I said, calling his attention to me.

"Hello, Claudia," he responded with the haphazard disinterest of a mad professor.

Gus was pushing the season; he wore scraggly jean shorts that were too tight and a mismatched, tattered flannel. A pair of white tube socks was pulled up to his knees. The socks were heinously decorated with a primary color red pinstripe. His blue and yellow running shoes squeaked as he skidded along the honeycombed pattern edging that covered each step. The sound made me cringe.

Gus flipped through the pages of a hard back and slammed the cover shut. He pushed his wire-rimmed glasses closer to his washed out blue eyes and scrunched his nose up in my direction.

"Mmmm," he said, glancing up at me. "You smell great."

I shifted uncomfortably under his shameless candor. "Thanks," I whispered.

"Sorry I'm late, Gus," I apologized.

"Late?" he echoed, twisting his watch over his wrist. "I hadn't noticed it was so late. Damn it, I missed an estate sale up in Cranbury," he lamented.

"Jersey? What time were you supposed to be there?" I asked, carving my thumbnail into the bare wood of the porch post. The facade badly needed a fresh coat of paint.

"Four o'clock," Gus answered.

"I don't think you're gonna make it, Gus," I told him, stating the obvious.

"No, it certainly doesn't look like it," he agreed. "Claudia, would you be a dear and line some of these books on the shelves out front?" he asked, pointing to two of his piles.

"Sure, no problem," I said, moving toward him.

I lifted one stack in its entirety and shuffled back to the porch to arrange the books on the already overcrowded and dilapidated shelves. Gus had generously discarded three National Geographics, a high school Calculus textbook, and an outdated SAT study guide.

I smoothed my hand over a crumpled sign posted above the shelving. Scrawled red in my handwriting were the words, "PORCH BOOKS, TEN CENTS A BAG." Porch books were give aways that sat in the rain until they grew mildew and made their way into the trash. In the city, it's difficult to lose what you don't want.

I flung open the screen door and clomped noisily down the long hallway in my clogs. Instinctively, I knew that Oliver was already upset with me for being late. I paused anyway to peruse the "New Arrivals" section for anything of interest. I smiled at the thought of Oliver grumbling; he was so endearing when angry.

"Oliver!" I exclaimed brightly, turning the corner into the first edition's room.

"How are ya', sweetie?" I squealed, with a wink. I clucked my tongue against my cheek.

I climbed behind the wooden island in the center of the floor and tossed my bulging backpack under the bottom shelf of the counter.

The counter top was covered with a thick, brown paper that was stapled over the unfinished wood. Its texture felt like gravel. I pushed myself onto it and spun my legs back to the floor with a showgirl flutter kick. I moved back to the doorway and straightened the frame of the "Curse to the Book Stealer".

"Claudia, you're late," scolded Oliver. He was pushing back his cuticles and did not bother to look up in my direction.

"Traffic," I feebly excused myself.

"Traffic?" he shot back. "On your bike?"

"Oh, forget it," he muttered, clearly frazzled. "Here," he said, as he thrust the bright purple jacket of *Little Birds* by Anais Nin into my hands.

"I found this earlier when I was pricing the paperbacks," Oliver explained.

"Thanks, Oliver," I replied with downturned eyes. "Anais Nin?"

"Yeah, girl," he said, drawing out his syllables rhythmically.

He shifted his neck evenly from side to side and explained "You finally gettin' your groove on, you better make sure it's worth your while."

"Trust me, Oliver," I warned him. "It's worth my while," I added with a smirk.

Oliver chuckled under his breath. His pale white hands darted over the area surrounding the register as he straightened pens, scraps of paper and phone books. I moved back to the counter and rested my elbows on the counter. Earl Grey, our store's gray cat, sauntered past my face. The fur of his tail tickled my chin.

I leaned forward and followed the grain of Oliver's olive green, yellow, and brown plaid trousers with my eyes. They hung loosely from his hips and skimmed the bottom of a white, V-neck T-shirt. The T-shirt was short sleeved and looked ratty and threadbare. Oliver grabbed his hat from a freestanding lampshade, which was perched low on a pole lurching over the plastic garbage can.

He gripped the hat by its indentations and placed it high on his head. The oversized, striped band reminded me of one my grandfather used to wear at his tailor shop. Oliver tilted the hat low on his forehead and ran his fingers along the stripe. He tapped the front for an instant.

Oliver shoved a loaned paperback in his back pocket and retrieved a Marlboro Red from behind his left ear. Brushing a hand over my shoulder, he turned toward the door.

Stopping suddenly, Oliver said, "Oh, I almost forgot. Spring Fling's tonight."

He pulled the paperback book from his pocket again and lifted two yellow and black fliers from between the wrinkled pages. He fanned the fliers out, extending them in my direction. I read the invitation.

"Spring Fling?" I asked.

"Big Mess!" Oliver cried, insulted by my ignorance.

"I thought 'Blue Dog Cognescenti' at Group Movement was their last show," I said, remembering the flier that Avery gave me the night Don Carlos played the Khyber.

"No," Oliver responded, with a "tsk" falling from his tongue.

"'Blue Dog' was just a scaled down version of Big Mess. This time, PAPA's agreed to sponsor us—we're going all out with a cabaret show at the Trocadero," he said.

"PAPA?" I inquired.

"Philadelphia Association for Performance Art," Oliver explained, in a tone that clearly indicated he felt I should recognize the acronym. His brow was furrowed too.

"Rumor is," Oliver gossiped, "if Spring Fling goes over well, we're gonna schedule a second show at Christmas. So, your attendance is *very* important."

"Remy is expected too. But I'm sure The Countess has already commissioned him," Oliver added.

"Ezra's performing?" I asked.

"Yes, they finally persuaded him," Oliver spewed, shaking his head. "He was in a tizzy because they'd asked Miss Bea Haven to MC instead of him," he added.

"Really, how'd they convince him to do it?" I questioned.

"They promised Ezra two runs down the catwalk, auctioning off dresses," Oliver said. His words were coming so quickly; they'd begun to run together.

"As soon as The Countess heard he'd get to do a strip tease, there was no keeping him away," he swooned. I snickered as Oliver rolled his eyes.

Without giving me a chance to speak, he continued rambling. Oliver's arms were lifted at his elbows. He was flailing them about, making exaggerated gestures.

"Stuart's doing Butterfly Fairweather," Oliver told me. "I also heard there's gonna be a flea circus, *and* Lava Lou's gonna eat fire," he added. Oliver emphatically whispered his words, as if revealing top secret information to me.

"Are you bringing Gabe?" I asked, listening to the rhythmic rise and fall of my tone. Oliver blushed.

"Claudia, I invited him," Oliver told me, spreading his fingertips along the base of his neck. "He's been so obsessed lately with this trip to Paris that I don't think it even registered."

"Trouble in paradise?" I joked.

"I just wish I were going away with him," Oliver whined in a high pitched squeal. He tapped the back of my hand lightly and bounced up and down on his heels.

"Anyway," he started hurriedly, "I have to go. I have nothing to wear tonight."

"So you'll be there?" he asked rhetorically. Oliver pecked a kiss onto the smooth, white skin of my cheek and walked toward the doorway.

"Look for us in the balcony," I called after Oliver, who was already lost deep in the hallway. I listened to the deadpan clomping of his thick-soled wing tips until the noise of his footsteps disappeared outside.

I sat down on the rickety, wooden stool, which teetered behind the cash register. The light of dusk filtered through the yellow-stained lace curtains that framed the store's front windows. I felt safe.

I stared blankly throughout the room, allowing my eyes to languish over the expensive books lined in glass cases. I noticed a new red cover next to the pirated American edition of Henry Miller's *Tropic of Cancer*. I squinted to read the title—*ABC's of Learning*. It looked in mint condition.

I pushed the "sale" button on the register and snatched a set of keys from the open drawer. I started toward the case to examine the book more closely but tripped over a stack of unyielding cardboard boxes. I dropped the keys among the tattered paperbacks.

"Fuck," I fumed.

I cursed Oliver under my breath. He knew we weren't accepting paperbacks now because we were so overstocked. I hoped that he'd at least taken them on donation and not paid out or offered a trade in. Sometimes, Oliver was a sucker.

I crouched at the waist and knelt down to rummage for the keys in one of the boxes. I heard them fall further to the bottom. One of my fingernails snapped under the weight of the books, which made me even more upset. I yanked my hand from the box, pulling with it a rather respectable-looking copy of Oscar Wilde's plays.

My curiosity peaked, I lifted a pencil from the Barney mug on the desk and positioned myself on a short stepping stool. It was the perfect height for sorting through the books. I started to price them inside on the upper right hand corner of the first page. I adhered to a rather methodical system, marking most of the cheesy novels and sci-fi at twenty-five cents. I decided that anything even remotely interesting warranted fifty cents.

I lost track of time but figured that it took me over an hour to finish the boxes. By then, I'd found the keys. I was starving, so I dug some grapes and a granola bar out of my backpack. Once back on the stool, I swirled a swig of Evian through my mouth.

I cringed at the sound of the screen door creaking from the hallway and became anxious with the sound of approaching footsteps. I hadn't seen a customer since I'd started my shift. The footsteps broke into two distinct rhythms, eventually revealing the awkward profile of one of our regulars, Mr. Jennings. He was voraciously examining the non-fiction new arrivals and chatted half-heartedly to a lanky boy who looked no more than fourteen.

"Bernier," Mr. Jennings said to his companion, "why don't you go ask Claudia to show you where the records are?"

The boy did not answer Mr. Jennings directly but turned to walk in my direction. Embarrassed, he stole a glance at me and shoved his hands deep into his pockets. He managed a shy smile, brimming with stark white teeth. His complexion was dark, almost blue-black like a character in a Richard Wright novel. I motioned toward the back room where we kept our LPs. The boy followed my lead and disappeared without a word.

Mr. Jennings continued to scrounge the shelves of the hallway. He lifted his glasses from his nose periodically, pulling them back and forth from his eyes like a magnifying glass. Within moments, his arms were filled with more books than he could hold.

I watched him wipe the dust from his palm onto his sweat-stained, white T-shirt. The T-shirt made me smile; it depicted a map highlighting the best fishing spots in New Jersey.

"Hello, Claudia. How are you?" came Mr. Jennings's bellowing, loopy voice as he walked toward me. His words were slow and marked by the leisurely tone of the well educated.

"Great, Mr. Jennings. Thanks for asking," I replied.

"Would you mind holding these for me until next week, Claudia?" Mr. Jennings asked, as he plopped his purchases in front of me.

I lifted a book about World War II fighter plane disbursement from the top of the pile and straightened the spines of the other covers against my forearm. I hesitated before answering him.

I shook the fighter plane book in my fist and said, "Gus doesn't like us to hold more than five books per customer in the cage, Mr. Jennings."

"Oh, I see," he mumbled in disappointment.

Mr. Jennings shoved one of his hands into the back pocket of his pale brown, polyester slacks. He retrieved his wallet and began to fumble in the billfold for money. He came up empty handed and asked if he could purchase the books on his credit card.

I shook my head no. Our credit card machine wasn't working.

"Well," I gave weakly, "let me check in the cage to see how much you have in there now."

I scuttled for the keys and moved from behind the counter to unlock the closet, which was hidden in the space just before the recordings room. My eyes darted into the stacks where I spied Mr. Jennings's friend peeping out in my direction. I winked at him flirtatiously. The boy bolted behind the shelves.

I unlocked the rusty gate of the cage. I hated searching through it—it was a dark, dank pit infamous for swallowing the refuse of characteristically poor credit-risk patrons. Whatever was discarded in its bowels, usually rested there for eternity.

I didn't go into the cage for just anyone. But I pitied Mr. Jennings. He was a packrat. He bought books for their mildewed pages, their faded print, their fabled pretense, and to read them next. His wife threatened to leave him because she'd become second best to his obsession.

Mrs. Jennings had said, "No more books in the house." So, Mr. Jennings started hiding them in his car.

I'd watched him driving on Market Street. I figured he'd have to sit on the roof in about two more weeks.

"All right, Mr. Jennings," I said, "I'll let these go until next Saturday."

"But you have to remember to pick them up or I'm putting them back," I threatened.

"I will, Claudia," he promised idly.

I crammed his stash down the throat of the animal in the cage and twisted the key into the dime store lock again. Mr. Jennings was busy emitting guttural, phlegm-filled noises into an already soiled handkerchief.

"Who's you're friend?" I asked, twisting my head toward the record room.

"Bernier!" Mr. Jennings exclaimed as if he'd forgotten. "Yes Claudia, that's Bernier," he stated the name again matter-of-factly.

"Bernier?" he called. "Where have you wandered? Come out and meet my beautiful Claudia," he demanded, projecting his boisterous voice throughout the store. My cheeks flushed red.

I watched as Bernier moved steadily toward us. With cat-like grace, he maneuvered around and over the cardboard boxes strewn about the floor. I stepped aside, offering him space. In doing so, I bumped into a wobbly, file cabinet and knocked over a plastic container filled with black and white photographs on sale for twenty-five cents each.

The pictures fell about the room in a snow-swept flurry. I dropped to my knees, scurrying after them. Earl Grey appeared from out of nowhere to sniff aristocratically at the debris.

"Bernier, this is Claudia," began Mr. Jennings, introducing me.

Bernier crouched down to the floor to help me gather the photos. I matched his smile with my own and held out a gracious hand, which Bernier accepted and shook gingerly. He nodded his head in acknowledgment of me. It seemed a sincere and respectful gesture.

"Bernier is visiting us from Cite` Soleil in Haiti. He'll be staying with my wife and me for a few weeks," Mr. Jennings explained.

"How interesting," I remarked.

"I'm presenting a lecture to our D. C. chapter tomorrow afternoon. We're driving, so we wanted to stop by to pick up some books for the trip," he continued, following Bernier's movements carefully.

"That sounds exciting, Mr. Jennings. "Will you have time to see any of the sites?" I inquired. He snatched two thin books from the boxes on the floor and handed them to me. I shuffled them over and under each other again and again.

"Cherry blossoms and all," he joked. I had never heard him make a joke before.

"I think you'd like the lecture, Claudia," he told me. I blocked his words and concentrated on totaling the prices penciled in his books. I punched my sub-total into the register, which calculated the tax due.

"What's that?" I said, absent-mindedly. I caught myself and tried to refine my question, "I mean, what's the lecture on?"

"I'm still trying to push the Haitian controlled immigration issue along, using Guantanomo as a transfer base," Mr. Jennings answered. "As you can expect, the hard-liners haven't received the idea very well," he added.

"That's a shame," I said, shaking my head. "I would like to hear the lecture sometime," I agreed with him.

"Great, I'm opening a discussion on it at the Free Library at the end of the month. You'll come?" Mr. Jennings posed. Bernier was tapping the jacket of an LP against his leg. The white tissue paper covering the record crinkled to the beat of his movements.

"What d'ya find, Bernier?" I asked, holding out my hand. He lowered his eyelids and passed the record to me.

"Sweet. George Clinton," I said, reading the title.

"Take it. It's yours," I instructed, returning it to him.

"Claudia, you don't have to do that," Mr. Jennings fumbled. I ruffled through a pile of old grocery bags, pulled out a white one from Acme and held it open for him to drop his books in. I smiled generously.

"You two have a safe trip tonight," I smiled again to Bern. He waved modestly in my direction.

"Thanks, Claudia. I'll see you next week," Mr. Jennings answered. He twisted the plastic bag from my hold. Clutching the books against his chest, he plodded down the hollow boards of the hallway. Bernier followed quickly after him.

I rubbed my palm over the back of my neck and sighed. The store was empty again. I glanced at the clock. Its white face told me that it was only 7:05 PM. I groaned and mulled anxiously about. I grabbed a box of the paperbacks and wandered into the other room to cram them on the overcrowded shelves.

I dropped the box in front of the Harlequin section with a thump. I hung my head, kicking one of the two other boxes, which were already there. My footsteps creaked on the loose hardwood floorboards. I searched for the paint-splattered stool that could usually be found near the cash register.

I spied the pink stool trapped in a corner cubbyhole, lost amidst our outdated Cartography section. I dashed after it, tangling myself in the heavy, maroon tapestry that hid the basement staircase. I sneezed delicately, tickled by the dust the tapestry spewed into the air.

"G'bless you," came a soft voice from the basement.

Startled, I jumped from the sound and knocked the stool on its side.

"Gus, is that you?" I called down the steps.

I listened carefully to the rustling I heard beneath me. I lifted the corner of the tapestry and peered into the cool, dark space. A damp, musty odor wafted up, slamming me in the face.

The basement was entirely Gus's domain. It was once open to the general public but the city health inspectors had since condemned it. Now, the basement was a cluttered maze filled with towers of books, magazines, and paintings. Most of the tiles on the floor were broken or chipped away. The dirt from the ground beneath was visible in certain spots, while the wooden support beams of the store's foundation were framed by the intricate designs of cobwebs.

"Hi Claudia, it's me. I'm sorry, I didn't mean to scare you," Gus apologized.

"Have you been here all this time?" I asked.

"I lost track of time—I just finished unloading that last truckload," he said.

"Is there anyone up there?" he shouted.

"No, Gus," I replied, dragging out my syllables. "It's been pretty slow. Must be because it's Saturday night and all," I added, waiting for him to suggest that I close up early.

"Mmmm, that's not very good," he mused. His words trailed off at the end of his sentence and I heard something metal clank to the floor. Gus remained silent.

"You O. K., Gus?" I yelled to him.

"Sure, I just dropped my glasses," he muttered. "Go on and lock up, Claudia. I don't think we're in for a big rush in the next hour," Gus instructed.

"Yes!" I exclaimed in a muffled whisper. I closed my fists and threw my elbows backward in a thrusting motion. Closing early was another thing I loved about working Saturday nights.

"Claudia," Gus called again. "Are you in a hurry?" he asked.

Without waiting for my response, he continued, "I've got my photo album from our last trip to Newfoundland. I thought you'd like to see them."

I hesitated for a minute and knelt to scoop Earl Gray into my arms. I figured I had a few hours to kill before "Spring Fling" started.

"Sure, Gus," I agreed. "Come up when you're ready. I'll start cleaning up," I said.

I righted the stool and filtered back through the bookshelves to the register, turning off lights as I walked. I locked the front door and flipped the "OPEN" sign closed. I moved the cash drawer of the register into the safe and snatched a translucent blue lighter from the one-dollar bill slot before locking it.

I dug a tightly rolled plastic bag from the depths of my backpack. I expertly packed the residue covered shell bowl of a femo pipe. Oliver kept the pipe tucked away in the metal box used to file book requests. I brushed some of the shake from sides of the shell and inhaled a quick puff.

I looked up in time to see Gus stumble up the second basement staircase, positioned across from the cage. His hair was ruffled over his patchy bald spots and his glasses sat crooked on his nose. He waddled to the counter, his feet inverted from his normal pigeon-toed stance. He was dwarfed by a stack of books, which he steadied with his chin.

"What a day," he moaned under his breath, balancing the books on an empty chair. He stopped to wipe his brow with a handkerchief that he pulled from the back pocket of his shorts.

"That smells good," Gus said, referring to the pot. I passed the bowl off to him. He refused the lighter, using his own Zippo lighter.

Gus exhaled a puffy cloud of white smoke. He lifted his eyebrows and nodded his head in approval, "Tastes good, too."

He tossed a thick red photo album onto the counter top. It skidded to the edge, threatening to drop to the floor. I stretched to catch it from falling.

Apprehensively, I opened the cover of the album. Gus used his photography as the basis for his woodcarvings. He'd been trying to convince me to pose for him for months but I was hesitant. I had agreed to look at the Newfoundland shoot and then make my decision.

Gus and I flipped through the pictures together, discussing position and shadow. We smoked way too much pot and giggled over glaciers, tugboats, and flannel-clad fishermen. There was an endearing frame of his son climbing a rock on the deserted beach—free of clothes, inhibition, and age. I laughed at his wife, running from the frigid edge of the sea, with her breasts flopping and hair blowing in the wind. I squirmed, staring at a shot of Gus holding himself in a pool of water surrounded by mussels and sand.

I sat looking at the pictures for a long time because, in the back of my mind, was the realization that looking at the pictures would sometime stop. I ran my hand over the clear plastic of the last page. Gus snatched the photo album closed and balanced it between his body and the counter.

"Claudia, I can offer you a hundred bucks for an hour long session tonight," Gus offered quickly.

Dumbfounded, I blinked widely before answering him.

"I'll do it, Gus. Remy and I could use the money," I mumbled, not hearing my own words. I nodded my head, swallowing hard the growing lump in my throat. I was as nervous as the time I'd gotten my first tattoo.

Gus smiled maniacally at me. He looked a little shocked but did not hesitate. He grabbed the flesh of my upper arm and squeezed it tightly, as if he were trying to comfort me.

("I AM NOT WEAK. I DO NOT NEED COMFORT," she screamed.

"But you're shivering," laughed the laos.

"I am?" she asked with the innocence of a five year old little girl. "Those men in the construction boots are staring at my body. I feel separate."

"That is how you are supposed to feel. Your subservience is manifested in your own femininity. You are still a virgin, aren't you?" the laos demanded.

"Oh, yes," she answered without hesitation. "They told me sex was dirty."

"And cock?" they quizzed again.

"And cock was king," she scribbled in a number two pencil.

"Good. Now write it all down in that notebook. Then, you can call it art," they promised.)

Gus darted from the first edition's room with lightning-quick speed. He disappeared again into the basement. I could hear him rooting around downstairs for his camera and lights. I figured he was probably looking for some props too.

I slipped away into the bathroom with my backpack and began casually undressing. I primped, fluffed, and prodded furiously. I smeared bright red lipstick across my lips and blotted them together into a powder blue tissue.

When I finished, I stood barefoot and naked on the toilet seat. I tried to strike an alluring, seductive pose in the tiny mirror. The queasy feeling in my stomach spread downward slowly into a warm, tingling sensation between my legs and thighs. I was alive.

I slipped my faded, oversized denim shirt over my shoulders as a cover up. I pulled the door open with a creak and listened to the pitter-patter of the tips of my feet guide me again to the front room. Gus was bent over, setting up his equipment. He glanced up at me with a wink.

"So what do ya' want me to do, Gus?" I asked, my tone quivering telltale.

"Just try to move about naturally," Gus advised. "*Feel* your body," he said with innate artistic sense.

"O.K.," I muttered, slurring my tongue at the end of my words. I raised my eyebrows curiously. I had no idea what he was talking about.

I walked over to the staircase in the front hallway. I slumped down on one of the lower steps. Gus followed after me like a lost puppy dog. He commented that the banister would be a great backdrop. I jerked my shirt off my shoulders and tossed it on the padded carpet of the landing up above.

Gus asked me to straddle the banister and lean back, arching my torso in a severe gesture. I followed his direction and placed my left arm high and crooked above my head. I turned my face away from Gus. He began to snap the shutter release of his camera from the floor below.

I brushed against the wood of the banister. I grew wet and became more comfortable with my nudity. I didn't try to seduce the lens as I thought a real model would. Instead, I struck typical poses, adjusting my posture and cramped muscles. Gus ate it up. His eyes grew wider with every second. His breath came so hard that he seemed to smell the secretions of my body.

The stairs offered only limited mobility. Gus suggested that we move to the sun porch for better lighting. I picked up my denim shirt again and crossed the store through the children's section. I turned down the blinds and flopped lazily onto my favorite chair.

Gus lagged behind me but quickly appeared holding the wheel of a ten-speed bicycle. He handed me the wheel, lowering his eyes as I undressed again. I pulled myself up from the chair and steadied my stance against the bike tire. I lay down on the grungy, yellow carpet and stretched. I ran my fingers through the coarse, tangled loops of shag that covered the floor.

I lost track of Gus as he mulled about the room, adjusting lights. I writhed and gyrated, moving my hands between my legs. It suddenly felt good to be unaware.

Watching me, Gus jumped hurriedly for his camera. I closed my eyes and smiled wildly.

("I don't like letting go of control because I am afraid of not being beautiful," she confessed.

"We taught you that inhibition breeds distance, which results in class, which makes you better than they are," assured the laos.

"But when I don airs, I feel fake."

"Never admit to donning airs," advised the laos.

Enlightened, she whispered to herself, "I shall acquiesce to freedom. Then, I will be pure."

I pushed my left leg between two spokes of the bicycle wheel. I wiggled strategically so as not to lift my head or right foot from the floor. I pulled the wheel up next to my crotch and brushed my hair forward so red curls cascaded and covered my face. With an unbreakable grip, I squeezed the dusty black rubber of the tire as hard as I could.

And the film kept slipping through the chamber of the camera.

After awhile, my motions became more fluid and I was better able to ignore my awkward poses. Gus and I ran around to other corners of Oz and Endz.

I hunched up in a ball on one of the oversized bookshelves, threw myself over the top of an old school desk, and extended my torso taught over the brown paper of the front counter. Occasionally, Gus would make a joke or ask me to adjust my stance slightly. Silence though seemed more comfortably oppressive for both of us.

By 10:30 PM, I'd long missed Lava Lou eating fire because I was late for "Spring Fling".

A few weeks later, I found myself alone on a splintered bench in Independence Mall. I tickled the purple petals of a lilac bloom beneath my chin and looked back at the photographs from the shoot. They told me it was spring again. God, it was spring again.

I didn't recognize the strange poses of my body. I thought my skin looked dirty and my hair greasy. I didn't know the person in the pictures and I remember thinking I could never get myself into those positions again.

I never got to see any of the woodcarvings that Gus made using me as a model.

Part Two

Death

Free Tickets

M y favorite radio station in Philadelphia is WXPN. Lost somewhere between the definition of public and commercial radio, 'XPN stepped up its ho-hum status as The University of Pennsylvania's college radio station to become one of the top contenders for Philly's alternative listening market. I love it. Rarely does my dial move and I pledge to make a donation to them every fund drive. I still have a yellow sticky on my refrigerator from the one last summer, reminding me to mail the check.

I have a favorite show too—Johnny Meister's Blues Show on Saturday nights from 8:00 PM to 1:00 AM. I decline all sorts of Saturday night invitations, so that I can sit home with a bottle of Bully Hill Love Goat red and sink into "soulville" with John Lee Hooker and friends.

Oh yeah, that and I win free tickets from them all the time.

MALE, RADIO VOICE ON AIR. Johnny Meister here. I've got two tickets for next Friday night at The Barclay on Rittenhouse Square. The American Music Theater Festival (AMTF) presents The Jon Faddis Sextet's 'Lulu, A Be Bop Opera'. They're goin' to the ninth caller.

MALE, RADIO VOICE OFF AIR ON PHONE [*click-click*]. Hi. You're caller number three.

CUTE, RED-HEADED, FEMALE CALLER. Shit.

[*Redial.*]

MALE, RADIO VOICE STILL OFF AIR ON PHONE [*click-click*]. Number seven.

[*Redial.*]

MALE, PHONE VOICE [*click-click*]. Hellooooooooo, you're caller number nine.

CUTE, RED-HEADED, FEMALE CALLER. Sweet.

(One seeks to sow seeds. The other waits to bear children and build a home. This is the difference between the sexes as they break fast. She sews buttons on eggs.)

It was Friday night. My home still felt new. Even though it had been weeks since Remy and I moved in together, there were times that I wasn't sure I really lived there.

It was almost 7:20 PM. I was sitting in front of a half opened window at the dressing table Remy had salvaged for me from someone's garbage on the sidewalk of Spruce Street. He'd done a great job fixing it up. After he'd sanded it down, he painted it a matte antique red and replaced the knobs on all of the drawers with shiny brass handles.

My legs were propped up and spread slightly, so that the pads of my feet rested on the edge of the table top amidst strewn make-up brushes and perfume bottles. Remy sat behind me, bare chested. He watched as I expertly applied my pink lipstick. We had to leave in twenty minutes to make it to the Barclay on time.

"You look beautiful, Claude," he said.

"This will be good for us tonight, I promise. Everything with Pure Motion's been so crazy this season that I think we just need some time alone," Remy spoke anxiously as he ran his fingers over his dreads. He stood up to find a shirt. I smiled at him blankly, hoping I could choose a feeling and stick with it.

It had started for me already. That churning in my stomach and in the back of my throat when I know something is wrong. When I don't want him to kiss me anymore. When I cringe at the thought of him touching me. When I want to be alone. When I want to argue with him about everything under the sun. If he says black, I gotta say white.

I hadn't told him yet. I didn't know how or where to start. With every passing day, I realized how badly I didn't *want* to tell him and wondered how long I could keep it a secret. I kept attempting wild, whirlwind escape plots in my head. The whole thing just reminded me of the one time I tried to run away from home when I was a little kid and only made it to the Ferris wheel at the Oakland Firemen's Festival.

I stood up, smoothed my short dress, and leaned over to straighten the back seams of my fish-net stockings. I pushed Mojo off my patent leather bag and began to shove things in the over-cramped pockets. I took a last scrutinous glance over my body in the mirror and announced that I was ready to leave. I heard Remy click off the stereo and we met at the door.

Remy hailed a cab for us as we turned onto Spruce Street. In minutes, we were dropped in Rittenhouse Square. Remy told the cabby to leave us in front of The Ethical Society because the traffic was hiking up our fare. We walked the last few hundred yards to the fancy hotel. The face of the Barclay loomed before us, reaching high into the sky. It edged the Southeast corner of the park like the end pieces of a puzzle.

We pushed through the shiny gold, revolving doors and skated over the plush maroon carpet. It felt soft and welcoming enough for my high, heavy heels to sink an inch down. The twinkling glass chandeliers swaying from the ceiling helped me to imagine I was a regal princess visiting from an exotic land. I pretended to be dripping with rubied tiaras and diamond tethers from my neck to my ankles, capturing the gracious approval of all those around us.

I smiled to myself at the thought of my daydream. We moved down a long corridor to one of the smaller ballrooms. I reached a large card table propped in a dark corner. A stodgy woman no younger than forty-two greeted us reluctantly with fliers, information about AMTF, and two tickets for *Ms.* Dubois.

Remy gingerly accepted the tickets from the woman. We entered a rectangular shaped room with fabulously tall, high ceilings. Rows of padded folding chairs five deep formed a wide center aisle. Remy immediately darted toward one of the back rows on the left but I managed to coax him closer to the stage. We settled somewhere in the middle of the crowd. I would have preferred to have been even further up front.

Neither Remy nor I spoke a word to each other. He began to tap his fingers against his knees in an annoying rhythm and surveyed the room nervously. I was painfully careful not to turn in his direction. Instead, I glanced intensely at the show's program.

Designed as a work in progress, the performance was a new adaptation of the first act of Alban Berg's original opera called "Lulu". Based on the work of Frank Wedekind, the act contained four "songs", three of which we would watch that night—"The Teaser", "Snakes", and "The Dropad".

Lulu told the tale of a mythological nymph who prowled 52nd Street be-bop clubs like Birdland in New York City after World War II. Tweaked with anachronism stolen from Wedekind, the woman teased and seduced men shamelessly until she herself died at the hands of Jack the Ripper.

I liked Faddis' liner notes. They reminded me of something out of an Oscar Wilde essay: *"We are deeply interested in the relationship between improvisation and 'serious music'. Improvisation was a part of classical music until the 18th century, at which point serious music became very tight, as it remains up to the present. When improvisation stopped, it was the end of the era of great musical genius. We are committed to keeping our work loose so that the performance changes according to the mood of the soloist. In this way, the piece becomes a statement by the artists at the time".*

The lights in the ballroom began to dim and the words on the gray page of the program became muddled in front of my eyes. An enigmatic sound echoed throughout the air, startling me from behind.

I turned my head to see a black man walking slowly forward down the center aisle. He was carrying a long, slender and slightly curved instrument. Remy told me later it was a didjeridoo; it just reminded me of the crazy thing they blared in the Riccollae cough drop commercials on t.v. Regardless, it grabbed my attention and refused to let it go.

Remy loved it. When I caught glimpse of him from the corner of my eye, he was grinning wildly and rolling his body to the man's sole solemn notes. Remy was whispering words like "mesmerizing" and "all right" under his breath to me and no one in particular. I placed my left hand on his knee and scratched through his jeans with strong, elongated strokes.

Remy grabbed my hand. He twisted it over his arm and cradled my wrist inside the fold of his stomach. He lifted my fingertips up, spreading them out like a fan. He brushed my cameo ring against his lips and gently traced his tongue over the knuckle of my middle finger.

Remy held me like this for a long time. We both became engrossed in the stage, until the end of "Snakes". Then, a tall, bald-headed man approached the center microphone and introduced to a hushed audience the seventy-nine year old dean of jazz bass, Milt Hinton. One or two of those whooping background yells came out from the crowd. The noise made the performance sound like an old scratchy, live blues recording.

Hinton ambled forward to the right of the bald-headed man and positioned himself between his acoustic bass and the microphone. He greeted us in an aged, raspy voice. He softly told a funny childhood story about his uncle's dry-cleaning business on the Southside of Chicago and how they used to use grain alcohol run from Al Capone to raise money at their house-rent parties. He cackled heartily at his anecdote and began to play.

Remy shrilled out a sexy, cat call in Mr. Hinton's direction. Besides the heavy bass, it was the only other noise in the room.

Hinton's solo drove through "The Dropad" as the characters of Lulu and Femme traded the jazz vocal. Percussion was then added and Hinton slipped into "Bow Bass/Voice", which echoed and counterpointed the singers. The improv of the four musicians was like conversation and provided a fantastic finale for the opera.

The audience rose to its feet, as the entire cast took the stage holding hands and making wide sweeping bows. Hinton received special recognition, after which it took a few minutes for the applause to subside. The chandeliers were gradually turned up brighter and brighter. The room drifted into a rumbling pitch filled with noises of shifting, rising, and gathering belongings.

Remy turned to me, "That was amazing, Claudia."

I grinned smugly and blinked. It was a good show but I wanted a cigarette.

"Thank you so much for scamming the tickets," Remy continued. "I'm gonna juke up there and try to talk to Hinton. Would you mind hangin' out for a little longer?" he asked.

I hesitated but saw how excited he was. "Yeah, sure. Go 'head up. I'm gonna have a smoke. Meet me outside?" I offered.

"You sure you don't want to come?" Remy said sincerely. "He's a fucking legend. Jammed with Calloway, Holiday, Basie, *and* Ellington," he rambled.

"No, I'm sure," I answered in the most maternal voice I could muster. "Go. It'll be easier for you to get to him without me tagging along," I explained, making excuses he believed.

Remy jumped from his chair and pecked a boyish kiss on my cheek. We separated and I watched him bound to the area in front of the corner of the stage where Hinton stood. The old man was talking very animatedly with a small group of interesting onlookers.

I smiled to myself, feeling somehow in control of the moment. I stood alone, staring ahead at Remy. I realized how much happier he seemed without me holding him back. Without me by his side, he only had to worry about himself, not whether or not I needed an ice cold glass of water in the middle of the night.

Remy engaged Hinton in a one-on-one conversation. I could tell Hinton liked him immediately. I knew some hip jazz lingo that I couldn't relate to was flowing between them. Content in this fact, I turned and walked through the doorway, up three steps, and again to the long maroon carpeted corridor.

("This is temporary. This is frail. This will be here tomorrow but you won't," warned the laos.)

The lobby was very quiet and felt cold and fleeting like all hotel lobbies. The man behind the front desk smiled at me as I passed him. I clicked my heels as loudly as I could because he knew I couldn't afford any of his rooms.

I reached the revolving doors and swirled through them with a gargantuan push. The clear night air of Rittenhouse Square greeted me; I could feel its splinters crackle on my skin. Everything around me seemed clean, crisp, and aware. From my bag, I pulled out my cigarettes and lit a Camel. I caught my fluorescent pink thumbnail on fire and swore. I hated the smell of burning chemicals.

A black man was walking toward me down 18th Street from the direction of The Graduate Hospital. The guy was holding a rolled up newspaper in his left hand. The top of the paper was on fire. He held it high and thrust forward like a torch.

He stared at the flame mindlessly, as if in a deep trance. Ashes were falling around his step. Sporadically, he brushed his shirt sleeve with his free hand. He stopped next to me, as I knew he would. At first, he didn't say anything to me. We just stood there, he with his burning torch and I with my lit cigarette. I kept thinking that these are the things that happen to me when no one else is looking.

"Good evening," he opened.

"Hello," I replied.

"What are you waitin' for, miss?" he asked politely.

"Not a thing, sir," I responded sternly with equal respect.

"That's interesting," I commented, remarking on his flaming baton. "Perhaps you could audition for Miss Pennsylvania with such an amazing talent," I taunted.

"What?" he asked in confusion. I told him to forget about it—it was an old joke that I'd played on a friend a long time ago.

"You sniff, sweetie?" the man asked. "I gots a sweet deal goin' down up in West Philly. Someone's fine as you should enjoy a treat so sweet," he offered.

"Thanks," I answered.

"I do 'sniff'," I said, repeating his slang. "But I've got some things going on tonight."

I paused to inhale from my cigarette. "Umm, what's up with the newspaper? Is it the 'Daily News' or 'The Inquirer'?" I asked referring to his growing conflagration.

"Neither, sweet thang," he replied. "This is what us niggas had to do before there was 'lectricity. I'm your street light, baby. All dressed up showin' you the way home," he proposed with a leering advance.

"Oh, I thought it was Mardi Gras," I joked under my breath, moving away from him slightly.

"Huh?" his rhetoric spilled again in confusion.

"You're right, you know," I said. "In New Orleans—particularly during Mardi Gras—the parade routes were lit with—oh, forget it," I said, cutting myself off.

As I expelled my breath, Remy burst through the revolving doors. He glanced hurriedly in all directions, scanning for me with his dark eyes. His dreads snapped in the wind, as he caught sight of me.

"Hey, Claude," Remy said. "Sorry I took so long, he was just so incredible to talk to," Remy explained.

He eyed my new found friend curiously. In a protective voice, Remy addressed the man, "Hey bro, whatcha need?"

The flame of the man's newspaper crept dangerously close to his fingertips. He tossed it to the ground and crunched the light into ashes with the sole of his shoe.

"Nothin' man, jus' lookin' out for the lady. Damn, she is too fine, ain't she?" he said as his eyes crept along my body.

"Beautiful," he muttered.

I shifted uncomfortably. Remy glared at the man and snatched my cigarette from my pursed lips. He pretended to inhale a long drag. Then, he flicked the butt into a sewer grate in the road in a very James Dean-esque manner.

"Thanks, buddy. You better get movin'. We ain't got nothin' for you here," Remy warned, hurrying the street urchin along.

"I gotcha, man. I'm on my way. You two have a good night, ya' hear?" he answered.

"Ma'am," the man said, nodding to me. I smiled at him without emotion; I hated being called ma'am.

He started to walk away but turned back to Remy. He begged, "Hey bro, can you help me out a little? I jus' need some change to grab a cup of coffee."

Remy responded sternly, "No."

The guy shrugged. Apologizing profusely, he wandered off toward Walnut.

"Claude, why didn't you come back inside and get me? You shouldn't be hangin' out alone on the street," Remy scolded me.

"I know Remy," I said, feeling smothered. "Don't worry about it. Do you want to head over to Diva and grab some coffee?" I asked, quickly changing the subject.

"Diva?" Remy repeated. "The place next to Doobies?" he clarified, upturning his nose.

"Yeah. Oliver said he was gonna stop there and then try to catch a ride to W&J's to shoot some pool," I pressed hopefully.

"Damn girl, W & J's is a hike—all the way in Northern Liberties. You really up for that?" Remy asked, trying to weasel out of my proposal.

"Come on, I'm in the mood for coffee. I just feel like something different. Pleassse," I said. I slurred my last consonant, knowing Remy wouldn't be able to resist me.

Remy acquiesced. We walked quickly, cutting through the park in the direction of 22nd Street. Once on Walnut, I spotted the sign for Doobies. Beneath it, I recognized Nathan's figure teetering on the front stoop of the bar. He was running his hands through the top of his hair and talking to three shadows that I couldn't distinguish.

Remy and I reached the corner. I skirted off to his left, hiding behind his hulking frame. I clutched the back of his denim shirt tightly like a little girl.

"What's up?" Remy said, greeting Nathan.

Nathan was flanked by Cedric, Avery, and a third person who was not familiar to me. I nodded at Cedric and Avery, recognizing them immediately.

I grinned sheepishly at Nathan as he directed a "hello" at me. Remy jumped into conversation with the small group and Avery wrapped herself around his pure movement. Nathan introduced us both to Ossie, explaining that he had started "The Shack"—an artists' colony in the Badlands. I learned later that "The Shack" served as headquarters to an up-start ad agency that Ossie founded with Cedric. They called it "Cyclone". To cut down on operating expenses, Ossie, Cedric, and Avery recently moved into The Shack as roommates.

I thought about politely excusing myself to grab a boilermaker at Diva. I stayed instead to chat.

"Got the Svvvedish clogs on, huh?" Nathan said to me in his melodious voice. I watched him eye my body cautiously with stolen glances. His hands were thrust deep in his pockets.

"Danish," I corrected him with a smile. "So what's up? You guys headed over for some pool?" I asked, lifting my hands in a worldly manner.

"Yeah, you guys into it?" Nathan challenged. Although his tone clearly addressed Remy, he continued to stare at me.

"It's up to Claude," Remy said, pinning the responsibility on me.

"You bet, Nathan," I countered. "I'm up for it."

"Cool," Nathan replied. "I gotta drop Ossie off at Silk City first. His friend's band is playing there tonight."

"Yeah, it's gonna be hot," Ossie explained.

I nodded in acknowledgment. Ossie moved behind me. He grabbed my shoulders, resting his hands there for an instant. I turned my head upward and back to look into his face. Avery tugged at his sleeve and whispered in his ear that she would go to Silk City with him. She and I had not yet spoken a word to each other. I was glad she was leaving with Ossie.

We piled into Nathan's gray BMW, which was illegally parked on the sidewalk in front of Doobies. Avery sat in Ossie's lap in the passenger seat, while Remy, Cedric, and I crammed in the back. I was squished in the middle and kept jerking my head from side to side to see whose dreads were longer—Remy's or Cedric's.

We pulled up under the fluorescent lights of the Silk City Diner. Avery and Ossie leapt from the car onto the street. Avery arched her back, stretching out her muscles that were tightened from the strain of the ride. She stuck out her chest and twisted her arms behind her. A horn beeped in her direction from the pack of traffic speeding down Spring Garden Street. Ossie rested his hands on the roof of the BMW and leaned inside again toward Nathan.

"There's a private opening at Paradigm tomorrow night. Can you make it?" Ossie asked.

"Where's Paradigm?" Nathan blurted.

"You know—the place on Chestnut Street that we just finished the advertising for," Ossie said.

"Did *you* name it Paradigm?" I interrupted. "I don't think that's what you meant."

"Do you know what 'paradigm' means?" Ossie attacked me.

"Yesss," I slurred, with an agitated face. "I think *paragon* would have been far more appropriate," I commented. Ossie obviously did not understand me and glared at me through the BMW's tinted window.

Cedric threw the back door open, splintering the reflection of Silk City's lights in the window. He jumped between Ossie and the car, pushing him back slightly. He climbed into the passenger seat.

"Later, bro," he mumbled, tugging at the down, orange vest he was wearing. The ivory stone on his leather necklace twisted with his movement.

"When you gettin' back?" Ossie asked.

"Takin' the red eye on Thursday. I'll call you to tell ya' when to pick me up," Cedric answered.

(*"Her creativity is bred from reflection,"* resounded some deep, indistinguishable male voice. She could not hear the man, for she was merely mortal.

The laos tried to protect her from the sinister, male voice. They told her that those possessed by mortality were consumed by the consequences of limited potential.

"Such sad souls," said the laos, "are confined by their own jejune attempts to avert phenomena such as conclusions and thus, live in sheer terror of the death of the physical being. The dormancy of the imagination for these individuals is inevitable".

"But I am not possessed by mortality," she tried to excuse herself. "I only find solace in its reminders."

"Where is Gertrude?" she asked.

"She is out there with Carl Sagan, organizing some sort of forbidden universe," answered the laos.

"If there isn't anything after this?" came her voice again.

"Do not worry your small mind with such large thoughts," ordered the laos. You do not have enough time.")

Nathan sped away nearly before Cedric had closed his door. He flicked in a Chemical Brothers CD and Remy tried to talk over the thick electronic beat.

"Where you goin', Cedric?" Remy yelled over the music.

"New Orleans," Cedric replied.

"Shit, Claudia," Nathan said, quickly turning down the volume. "I didn't get to tell you, we're driving down tomorrow night. Borrowed ourselves a sky blue Chevy Impala," he told me. My ears perked up. I could feel my eyes growing wider.

"Avery's ex, Tomas, is moving to New Orleans. I told him that since I've never been, I'd give him a hand," Nathan added.

"You goin', Cedric?" Remy asked.

"Yeah, I'm trying to drum up some business for Cyclone," he answered.

"Where ya' staying?" Remy continued. His right knee jutted toward me and he pulled himself up from the cushiony leather seat. He positioned his elbows on his upper thighs, so that he was closer to Nathan and Cedric. I edged further away from him, almost clutching the rubbery handle of my door.

"Tomas has a friend in the Quarter. Some chick—she's a stripper, so it should be pretty nuts," Nathan explained.

"A stripper," I hmmpfd, as if I were so pious. "You should call Cameron. He lives Uptown. He'll hook you up," I promised.

"Is that your friend down there?" Remy pried, with a hint of jealousy in his tone. I nodded and nothing more. My expression remained a disinterested blank.

I turned to the Northern Liberties' nightscape. The deserted streets grew tighter and more narrow. They ignored the city grid and jutted off diagonally to the East. Dead-end alleyways snaked haphazardly to and from abandoned intersections. Blowing newspapers and

rolling trash littered the curbs and doorsteps of the abandoned
breweries, warehouses, and apartment buildings. Everything was
dark, rust colored, and empty.

W & J's sat on an oblong corner, which forced a fork in Poplar
Street's already crooked angles. "Sabotage" by the Beastie Boys was
blaring on the stereo. Nathan circled the block and began winding
his way in reverse down a one-way street. He drove staring out the
back window. He clung to the headrest of the passenger seat for
support, while his elbow brushed lightly against my knee.

Nathan found a parking space underneath a stop sign and
crammed the beamer in. He tapped the back bumper of a long sedan
just behind us. As we stepped out into the street, Nathan pressed on
his car alarm. It turned on with a bleep-boink and I bee-lined for the
bar. Cedric and Remy struck up a conversation about a hip-hop band
out of New York City for which "Cyclone" was running videos.

I stopped before the red brick building and stood on my toes to
look past the glare of the fluorescent beer signs on the barred windows.
I couldn't see inside and fell off the stoop. I picked myself up just as
Nathan reached me. He asked me if I was O.K. and stretched forward
to ring the door bell. A small placard hung there, which read:

W & J Bar
447
& Restaurant

A pair of beady eyes peeked out at us through a sliding wooden
peep hole. After a brief moment, the peep hole slammed shut and the
door's locks began to rumble. A stocky, heavy set man with pale white
skin and matching faded hair answered. The balding man's cheeks
were rosy. His pot belly was hidden under his threadbare white T-
shirt. The man greeted us in broken English and stepped back from
the doorway so that we could enter the bar. We each thanked him
individually as we shuffled past.

Shaped like a capital letter "L", W & J's was partitioned into two
rooms. The uneven carpet of the front room was red and speckled
with flecks of black. It melted into a soft velvety red wallpaper, which
covered both the walls and the sides of the bar. A faded Ukrainian
flag hung above the liquor shelves. The flag was complemented by
maps of the Ukraine and black and white photographs of very happy

people eating pierogies and halupki. The pictures made me hungry and then made me laugh.

We scattered off in different directions. Nathan ran to the bar, while Remy and Cedric wandered to the right into the pool room. I stood alone in the center of the red carpet, watching Remy. He continued his conversation with Cedric, twisting his hands over the back of a chair tucked tightly against the back wall. Remy pushed the chair onto its hind legs with his foot and rolled it back and forth while balancing his weight on it. He smiled and waved to Oliver, who was attempting silly tricks with a pool stick. The tip of the pool stick was covered with blue chalk.

I approached Nathan, who was already sipping a scotch on the rocks. Nathan pushed three bottles of porter in my direction. He was busy making small talk with the gray haired gentleman. The bartender, a stern-faced woman with a dirty apron, stood next to the old man laughing at Nathan's offhanded remarks. She spoke broken English and was wringing a sopping wet towel in her hands.

I pulled two beers up from the bar and thanked Nathan. I smiled at the woman bashfully, and walked into the pool room.

Oliver quickly spotted me. He rushed to my side.

"Claudia! You made it," he yelped, stretching the muscles of his jaw so that the words all sounded too long.

Oliver yanked the beers from my hands and tossed them off to Remy and Cedric. He shot me a "you should know better" look and glared down at my stomach. He rubbed his hand over my dress. I pushed him away.

"Remy's here," I whispered heavily with clenched teeth.

"You still didn't tell—" Oliver started.

"No," I interrupted abruptly, nudging Oliver with my elbow. I shot Remy a fake smile.

Oliver rolled his eyes and kissed my cheek. He ran his fingers over my upper arm, leading me toward his crowd of friends. His boyfriend, Gabe, missed his shot and retreated into a dark corner to chain smoke unfiltered Lucky Strikes. Gabe wore his hair in a white Caesar cut and had his nose pierced. His forearms were riddled with symbolic, religious tattoos.

Noticing me, he screeched in a high pitched voice, "Hi, sweetie!"

"I'm gonna miss you," I whined, squinting my eyes and grabbing Gabe in a tight bear hug.

"I know," he pouted, releasing me to inhale again.

Tonight was Gabe's last night in Philly. The trip to Paris was actually going to happen. Oliver clung to him, until clinging to him hurt.

I couldn't hold Gabe's attention for very long. He turned to the pool table and began joking with a girl who was wearing combat boots and a polyester dress patterned with lime green and orange flowers. The dress hung to her ankles.

Remy stepped toward me. He kissed me on the back of the neck.

"Wanna play, Claude?" he asked, outstretching a pool stick.

I shook my head no and pointed to the corner of the table. "Somebody's got quarters down."

"Those are Cedric's," Remy explained.

"Why don't you let him play with Nathan?" I suggested.

"If you say so," Remy said, handing the stick off to Cedric. Cedric stacked the balls and broke them with a loud smack.

I breathed deeply and nitched my hand underneath Remy's belt. I pulled him toward me for a kiss. I swallowed the growing lump, which had grown in the back of my throat. I led Remy to a deserted table in the empty front room.

"You need a beer, Claude?" Remy asked, naively.

"No thanks," I answered. "Remy, we need to talk," I started.

Remy's eyes shot up immediately. He pulled his beer bottle away from his lips. "Christ, Claude. What's the matter?" he said. "Anything started with those words can't be good," he foreshadowed.

"Remy, I'm not very good at this kind of stuff," I told him.

"What are you talking about?" he asked defensively.

"I'm leaving," I told him as a tear escaped from the corner of my eye. Remy remained silent.

"I can't do this anymore. I can't be an 'us' anymore," I continued. "Something inside of me just isn't satisfied."

"So you can't *love* me?" he barked.

"I love you. I love you so much, Remy. But I think it's holding us both back. Relationships are supposed to be about growing—we're stifling each other," I explained.

"Relationships are supposed to be about compromise," Remy tried.

"Compromise doesn't mean giving up your dreams," I pronounced. Remy lowered his head.

"You need more than I can give you right now, Remy," I told him gently.

"What are you gonna do? Sleep at the bookstore?" he dug bitingly.

"No. I talked to Oliver. I'm gonna crash at the loft for a couple of weeks until I get back on my feet. Gabe's leaving for Paris tomorrow, so it'll be good for both of us," I answered.

"I can't believe this is happening," Remy muttered under his breath.

"I'm sorry, Remy. I wish I could change the way I feel but I can't," I whispered, clearing out my throat. I kissed him for the last time. I ran my fingers over his dreads, touched his cheek, and embedded his face in my memory.

I apologized again and watched the trail of smoke tumble slowly from the tip of the cigarette I'd lit. The trail tangled itself into the air, making cloudy white swirls and circles, which hid my face and stung the tear that slipped from my eye. I knew my hair would reek of stale smoke the next day.

Remy didn't say much else. He asked if I'd be OK and if he could call me at Oliver's in a few days to check in. He said if I needed anything, anything at all, to call him. I told him I would and that I'd stop by within the week to pick up my things from the apartment.

That was it. Remy gulped down the last of his beer and walked out the door. I lost him to the dark night of Poplar Street.

I breathed in deeply and moved into the chair he left vacant. I stood up, stopping myself before I started to get nostalgic and reminiscent. I walked back into the pool room and challenged Nathan to a game.

I was sad. I had wanted to live with Remy in a powder pink house on Rue Dumaine with a wrought iron porch made of veve hearts that invoked the Maitresse Erzulie. But it would never happen because I left him.

I left him because I was afraid. Because the Claudia he loved wasn't me.

I collected rain water in a glass jar for a month after that night. I served the rain water up to the Virgin because I didn't want to feel the guilt any longer.

Drag

So then, I moved in with Oliver.

The loft sat just across the street from the CD shop. It felt awkward at first. I was always afraid I was going to run into Remy but I never did. I settled in easily living with Oliver. We were on the third floor, above both an art gallery and Headlong, Ezra's dance studio. People filtered in and out all the time, so I wasn't alone much to feel lonely. Mostly though, I just sat in one of our tall, front window sills and stared outside at Olde City.

Oliver was great. He helped me through my morning sickness and my cravings. He took me to my cajillions of doctor's appointments, helped me pick my midwife, Maude, and comforted me through my bouts of depression and general mass hysteria.

I was sitting with my face directly in front of a fan I bought earlier in the day. I was surprised that I was surprised that it was so hot and sticky in Philadelphia on June 26th. I ran my fingertips over the base of my neck. I loved the feel of sweat covering my skin. I knew my face was flushed pink. I closed my eyes and pictured myself standing in the French Quarter looking up at porches lined with over-flowing flower boxes.

It didn't feel hot anymore; it felt sultry.

I was waiting for Oliver to finish in the bathroom. We were both very excited. Big Mess was performing Samuel Becket's *Nothing* at the Eastern State Penitentiary. It was opening night. Oliver and I were hosting the cast party at the loft. We'd been decorating and making minor renovations for the event all day.

Oliver was pulling out all the stops and dressing up in drag for the play. He borrowed one of my tightest black skirts for which I had no use—I couldn't cram myself into it any longer. I sat patiently, hoping he didn't look better in the skirt than I did.

"Ta da!" he finally announced, emerging from the bathroom.

Oliver thrust his arms high into the air. He threw his head back with a wide grin. He had filled in his missing front tooth, while his smoothly shaven legs were poised and glistening in the dim light. I flipped around quickly. With a laugh, I applauded enthusiastically. I would have jumped up but I had cramps and didn't want to aggravate them.

Oliver looked fabulous. The hair he usually wore slicked back with some sort of crunchy gel was hanging loose in tight spiral curls around his face. In it, I could faintly detect the plum, wash-in dye he'd used two days ago. His makeup was flawless; the bright red lipstick served as perfect contrast to his pale white skin. His fake eyelashes were long and thick and blended well with his mint green eye shadow. Glitter kissed his chin and cheeks.

His body was wrapped in my skirt and a sheer black body suit. When he bent over, the straps of his garter and the tips of his fish net stockings peeked out at me. He wore floral printed platform heels and clutched a rhinestone evening bag he'd bought from the Antique Market on Sixth and South. A velvet ribbon choker held his neck and his silver rings drew attention to his black nail polish.

"Do you like this shade, Claudia?" Oliver asked, as he puckered his lips toward me in a kiss. "I wasn't quite sure if I should have gone with nouveau pink instead."

"Uh-uh," I purred. "Oliver, those lips look good enough to kiss."

"That's just what I wanted to hear, sweetie," Oliver said, releasing a deep sigh. He fluffed and patted at his hair in the cloudy mirror, which hung by the door.

"I do feel so much better," he admitted melodramatically. "It's getting to the point that I need to be in drag at least once a week or I just don't feel whole."

I winked at him and stood up. Grabbing my straw oversized bag, I asked, "Ready?"

"You bet," Oliver answered.

Gasping, he said, "My keys, wherever did I put them?"

I rolled my eyes and tossed the keys I'd retrieved from the hardwood floor up into his hands.

"Oh Claude, be a dear and drive *please*. My nails are wet and I don't want to muss them all up," Oliver said, touching the side of my cheek lightly. He grinned an insincere smile and dropped the keys back into my palm.

I took them gingerly and thought to myself how much I despised driving his car. It was still covered in pink, purple, and blue paisleys. Only now, the rust had begun to bleed through the paint. It had been sitting on Third Street untouched for months. I'd finally convinced Oliver to sell it. In yellow Dial soap, he scrawled the words "FOR SALE, 125,000 MILES" on the inside of the front windshield.

Nonetheless, we shuffled down the freight elevator, out onto the steamy streets, and into the Volvo.

The Volvo started on or about the fourth try and we jetted off uptown. We stopped at the Reading Terminal Market to pick up a bouquet of daisies, late-blooming tulips, and pink roses with some filler for our friend Stuart. Then, we headed up to the Fairmont section of the city, behind the Art Museum. We found a space on 22nd Street. It took me a few tries to parallel park the Volvo.

I glanced at the red digital clock velcroed to the dashboard, noticing that we were already late. I urged Oliver to hurry along but he couldn't run in his platforms. He just got flustered from the pressure. Looking for the entrance to the Penitentiary, I wandered ahead and combed the monstrous building on its Northwest side to no avail.

By the time Oliver caught up to me, I'd stopped a girl for directions. She was carrying home grocery bags from Fresh Fields and asked if we were going to see *Nothing*. I told her that we were and she said she had wanted to get tickets to the show but couldn't because it was sold out. This made me feel proud of Stuart.

Oliver began making sympathetic sounds with his tongue and started to invite the girl along with us. I nudged him in the stomach with my elbow. The girl told us to turn back onto Fairmont Avenue. She said that about half-way down the front of the building, we'd find the entrance.

Oliver and I turned to walk back around the cold stone wall of the building. I was struck by the enormity of the empty prison. My eyes lit up at the sight of the scattered stems of white-headed wild daisies that lined the tiny patches of dry brown grass. The contrast of the two made me smile.

Philip the Ticket Man greeted Oliver and me on the sidewalk. He was passing out programs for *Nothing*. Everyone in Philadelphia knew Philip. He had free tickets to everything from movie screenings to The Philadelphia Orchestra and he doled them out as if he were Santa Claus.

Philip amused me.

The "City Paper" ran a sensationalistic story about him once. They accused him of less than ethical business practices and claimed that he used the ticket scam to seduce pretty, young girls. The paper received nasty editorial letters for months afterward in Philip's defense. What was funny, was that they eventually named him their "Man of the Year". I thought it was cool that I knew someone who could create such a furor in society. Sure he'd come on to me before but, in life, you learn never to look a gift horse in the mouth.

Philip captured me in a bear hug and I struggled to wriggle free from his hold. He told me we had to buy tickets at the gift shop. Philip directed Oliver and me through the front door, which was flanked by city and state flags. He said that we should then follow the short hallway on our right.

Oliver and I thanked Philip, invited him to the cast party at the loft, and then rushed passed him. I wanted to stop to look at the pictures of Al Capone and Willie Sutton. which lined the Penitentiary's walls but Oliver kept nudging me in the back with his bony knuckles. He didn't like Philip.

A woman dressed all in black with small, gold-rimmed glasses met us from behind the counter of the gift shop. She made us both sign a disclaimer releasing the Pennsylvania Prison Society from any liability incurred while we were on the premises due to any unsafe conditions of the prison. Then, she sized us both up for hard hats.

Oliver bitched that the hard hat would flatten his hair and refused to put it on. He twirled it over his fingertips instead. The woman dressed all in black with small, gold rimmed glasses took our money, shooting Oliver an annoyed look. Oliver asked her to hold the flowers until the end of the play. She accepted and pointed us toward the center courtyard for *Nothing*.

The courtyard was partitioned off from the shallow rows of the audience by a tall wall of steel prison bars. The play had already started.

Avery was standing alone in the urban forest of the prison courtyard, reciting a monologue. Two male actors glared at her from a dimly lit watch tower up above and a number of straggly-looking alley cats circled about her feet. One cross-country ski slid along the ground, pulled by the invisible strings of a puppeteer. Avery began to scale the bars of the courtyard's entrance with her hands and feet. She stopped at the top because she could climb no further.

Oliver and I stood watching hesitantly in the back of the crowd. There were no more seats. Luckily, Stuart popped out at us from behind a curtain to the right of Avery. He held his index finger to his lips in a "Shhh!" motion and clasped his hands together and over his heart at the sight of Oliver. Oliver lowered his head and curtsied with a smile. Stuart rolled his eyes and pulled out two folding chairs for us from behind his curtain.

I whispered, "Hello."

Oliver and I made a slight commotion in settling down. I could tell he was getting pissy because Avery was finishing her scene and we'd missed the bulk of her performance. I listened to her and lost myself in the rapture of Becket's words. He was as base as an alcoholic could get. I guess I liked him because he wasn't about dialogue; he was about nothing. Avery stopped speaking just as I was beginning to get comfortable.

Stuart emerged from behind his curtain again, this time addressing the audience. He briefly introduced Becket and told us that he would serve as a sort of tour guide for us that evening. Stuart explained the layout of the Penitentiary and how it would be used within the piece. Having just completed Act I, the other four Acts would take place in different areas of the prison.

We walked after Stuart's lead through the *Nothing* of crumbling stone and the crushed glass of smashed sky lights. We tripped over unruly weeds and the tangle of sweet smelling honeysuckle. I kept stopping to tighten the strap of my hard hat and Oliver conveniently misplaced his altogether. I hoped that we wouldn't get charged for it.

Act II was in one of the dilapidated cell blocks. It was interactive in that each actor was seated alone in a separate cell reciting the same material. The audience roamed from cell to cell. Act III took place in an open dining hall and Act IV in a different cell block. Three male actors lay in an uncomfortable looking bed; they represented the fragmented parts of one person discussing angst and the self.

The part I liked the best was Act V. Stuart took us to a third and final cell block. He stopped at the first cell, grabbed the first girl in the audience, and pushed her into it. One by one, he assigned us each to our own. Oliver and I were the last in line.

Stuart held our hands as we walked down the long corridor. Oliver tried to go with me into my cell but Stuart wouldn't let him. They disappeared from my sight as Stuart slammed the bars of my cell shut. I just remember the look of sheer terror on Oliver's face. It made me laugh. I heard him begging Stuart to let him sit with me.

The sense of solitude was unnerving. I was alone with one chair, a television set positioned on a wobbly stand, and a pile of rubble in the center of the room. The screen of the television was filled with static but I felt compelled to sit and stare at it just the same. My eyes followed the cord along the bottom of the wall and I hoped that I wouldn't see any rats. The t.v. came on and the static was gone.

A series of shadows moved across the screen too fast to be visible. Because they were indistinguishable for me, I concentrated on the words. Soon, I was whisked away by the monologue.

"What I sought was the rapture of vertigo . . . the relapse . . . to nothingness," came a deep male voice from the video.

(A sense of time passing with the sound of Becket humming in the background.

"Girl, it's Thursday. Why haven't I received my offering yet?" *demanded the laos from her tree.*

"Yes, I've brought you this bottle of jasmine perfume," she answered, *dropping to her knees among the banana leaves.*

"I should make you my horse," laughed the laos.

"Now Maitresse, please tell me. What are these boys for? What am I *going to do with them?" the girl screamed as if she had Turrets Syndrome.*

"It is not the boys. It is you. Go to Harry's Occult Shop, Incorporated *on Twelfth and South. Ask for Lamarr. He'll help you," advised the laos.)*

"All this about staying where you are, dying, living, being born, unable to go forward or back, not knowing where you came from, or where you are, or where you're going, or that it's possible to be," the male voice concluded abruptly before I was able to get truly acclimated to my cell.

Then, the television went blank. Static filled the barren, black space. Stuart released me from behind the bars. Oliver rushed to my side. He was suddenly wearing his hard hat and looked as if he'd been crying. I put my arm around him.

Nobody really clapped because Stuart immediately led us back to the main entrance of the prison. He dropped us all back off at the ticket counter/gift shop. We shelved our hard hats behind the woman dressed all in black with small, gold-rimmed glasses. Oliver asked her for his flowers back. People started to leave. Oliver and I moved back to the center courtyard. We mulled about in front of the maroon curtain.

I could tell that Oliver was nervous because he was fidgeting. His movements kept crinkling the green paper, which was wrapped around the flowers. I told him to stand still so that he wouldn't crush them. He yanked a single, pink rose from the bunch and rolled its stem violently between his fingertips.

Stuart tumbled out from behind the curtain. He rushed toward Oliver in a big, bear hug. A wide grin covered his face.

"Thank you, guys, for coming," he slurred. "What did you think?" he said, pulling back anxiously from the hug.

"I loved it!" cried Oliver enthusiastically. "I *am* so proud of you," he screeched, bouncing on his heels. Oliver gently pressed the bouquet into the cradle of Stuart's arms. He hid the pink rose behind his back.

"The 'City Paper' did *not* do it justice. Where's Avery?" Oliver gushed in the same breath.

"I have to see her," Oliver continued. "She looked *so* beautiful!" he exclaimed.

"Oliver!" came a high-pitched squeal from the right side of the courtyard. The maroon curtain swished open and Avery came bounding out in full sprint after Oliver.

Oliver thrust the pink rose he'd been holding out in front of his chest. Avery caught herself before she grabbed him in a hug. It was good that she did; she would have squished the flower.

"Oliver," she groaned in a different tone, accepting the rose graciously.

I shrunk back at the sight of Avery shifting barefoot amongst the dust of the Penitentiary floor. It was nice to see Oliver with people he loved. To be surrounded by those who admire you, grant you comfort, and accept you, this is all any one of us has ever really wanted. To be surrounded by those who love me, this is all I have ever really wanted.

"Hi, Claudia," Avery whispered breathlessly. Her composure was filled flawlessly with femininity.

"Hi, Avery. You guys were fabulous. I loved the ski," I tried.

"You *did*?" she buzzed with a crinkled up nose. "I was worried people wouldn't get it," she whined.

I didn't get it but I didn't say so.

"Oh, you are just *so* misunderstood," Oliver proclaimed with a lisp and a bent wrist.

Avery tousled Oliver's gelled curls with her red fingernails. Oliver jerked back furiously to avoid her leering gesture. "Averyyyyy," he yelped. "You'll ruin my hair."

"Come on, you two," scolded Stuart. "Let's get outta of here," he commanded.

Oliver rushed to my side and slid his arm through the crook made by my elbow. "Back to the Volvo, my darling?" he swept widely.

It took a moment for his words to register to me. I had caught the eye of one of the other actors. Oliver followed my line of vision. He waved his hand in front of my face, pulling me out of my daze.

"Jordan, huh?" Oliver mused with a knowing nod.

"What?" I said, shaking my head back into the conversation.

"Are you ready?" he teased. I pinched him lightly in the stomach and jangled the keys in my palm.

"Owww," Oliver screeched. "Stuart, have you invited Jordan to come along?" he said, leaning around my back.

I pinched Oliver even harder. Stuart winked and told us that Jordan was riding down with some of the other actors.

We started outside into the filmy moistness of the stifling city air. I had to push Oliver along because he kept stopping to arrange carpools. He upped the number of passengers in the Volvo to almost seven. He didn't even seem to mind when Philip asked to jump in with us.

I lost my driving privileges to Stuart and had to cram up front with Avery. That pissed me off. The car was hot and smelled like sweat. The music was too loud and Oliver's laugh was piercing my ears. On top of that, Stuart hit every single pothole in the city from Spring Garden to Third Street. The ride was miserable, and made my stomach nauseous.

I just hoped we got back to the loft before I got sick.

We screeched into a parking space between The Khyber and the pawn shop. I flung the door open and shoved Avery out ahead of me. I jumped after her, tripping over an uncollected pile of fermenting garbage. I could smell puddles of urine in the side alley. My stomach started doing somersaults and I ran inside and up the crooked steps. I didn't care who saw me.

I dashed into the studio and nodded hello to the five or six people already standing in the kitchen. I could hear Oliver's voice trailing behind me and wished he would just keep quiet to avoid a scene. I slammed the bathroom door shut, dropped to my knees, and felt an enormous release.

I rested my head against the white tile of the bathroom wall. It was cool and soothing. I closed my eyes but jerked back violently as I remembered a bathroom cleaner commercial on t.v. where they magnified the mildew critters on your tile to twelve million times their actual size. The image gave me a chill.

I climbed back to my feet and stared into the mirror. I pulled the skin underneath my eyes down to see how bloodshot they were. I scratched my fingers across my cheeks slowly, leaving thin lines marking where I dragged my nails. I splashed some cool water onto my face and drank some through the cup I made with my hands.

I grabbed my toothbrush, slathered it with some toothpaste, and tried to erase the wicked taste left in my mouth. I spit into the sink and gulped some more water. When I finished, I breathed in deeply and looked down at my rounded stomach. I lifted up my baby doll dress. The tattoo next to my belly button was starting to look distorted. I could see spaces in between the black outline where the colored ink needed to be filled in again.

I laid my palm on the shelf of my skin and said to the baby, "God, what's the matter with *you* tonight?"

I hesitated for a moment, half expecting an answer.

I stepped back out into the loft to join the party. I walked slowly toward the open kitchen area through a growing buzz mixed with voices and music. "The Countess" was perched on the corner of the library table, pouring sloppy glasses of Merlot from an obese green jug. Jordan was standing next to him, trying to pull away the wine.

"Hi Ezra," I managed from my dry throat.

"Claudia, sweetie. How are you feelin'?" The Countess said, rubbing my back in tiny circles.

Sheepishly, I avoided Jordan's eyes. I answered with embarrassment, "I'm O.K."

"Whatssa matter, one too many Yoohoos?" Jordan joked ignorantly.

"You know," I started. "I've never had a Yoohoo in my entire life," I affirmed with a smug nod of my head.

"You've never had a Yoohoo?" Jordan repeated, raising his eyebrows in disbelief.

"Never had a Yoohoo," I confirmed, pursing my lips into a blank expression. "Have you ever eaten SPAM?" I asked.

"Sure, my stepmother used to make it all the time. Best thing about SPAM is the roll top cans," he concluded. "You ever eaten SPAM?"

"No SPAM," I answered, clucking my tongue against the roof of my mouth. "Never eaten SPAM either," I added for clarification.

The Countess was stretched back on the library table, leaning on his elbow. His legs were crossed and angled high at his knees. The spike heel on his right foot teetered along the top edges of used LP covers filling the boxes underneath him. He stared at Jordan and me, fascinated with our conversation. Periodically, he would lift the wine jug up to his lips and sneak a sip.

"Wow, a chick who's never had a Yoohoo or eaten SPAM. Are you a virgin, too?" Jordan snapped.

"Sure, if you believe in the Immaculate Conception," I droned dryly.

Jordan missed my remark and I realized that he had no idea I was pregnant. This made me feel more confident in flirting with him. It's always a game when you have one up on somebody. When you don't, you pretend you're lying in a field of green grass.

"So you're Oliver's new roommate, huh?" Jordan chirped, skating over my comment.

Jordan reached into the front pocket of his short-sleeved, polyester shirt and lifted out a joint. He rolled the paper between his fingertips and lit it. He handed it off to me. Just as I was about to put it to my lips, Avery appeared at my side and yanked it from my hands. She inhaled deeply.

A smile crept across Avery's face as she scolded me, "Claudia, you shouldn't."

"But Ezra, you really should," she twisted the conversation, thrusting the joint at The Countess. He accepted it graciously.

"Claude, would you give me a hand please with some of these other bottles of libido?" Avery asked. "The one's on the table over there are already gone," she pointed, referring to the table next to the DJ.

Avery pulled me away from Jordan and yanked two bottles of wine from the refrigerator—one red and one white. I stole another glance at Jordan and followed Avery to the other side of the library table. Looking for a corkscrew, I started to rummage through the mess of beer bottles and playbills scattered across the kitchen counter.

I jumped up at the resonating sound of a cork popping from behind me. I flipped around and saw Avery bent over at her waist, leaning toward the floor. She was bracing the bottle of red wine between her feet. As she lifted herself up, she folded the arms of the corkscrew together and handed me the open bottle. I chuckled and shook my head.

"What?" Avery screeched with a silly laugh. "It's easier this way. I can't get a good grip when it's on the counter," she explained.

Avery steadied the bottle of white wine on the floor in the same manner. She twisted and turned her wrist again until the second cork gave way. A single muffled cheer came from the direction of the front windows. Avery giggled and her sandy blonde tresses bobbed with her movements.

Avery poured herself a drink in a metallic pink goblet and took a long gulp. She wiped her lips with the back of her hand. The muscles of her upper arm were pulled taut and her sleeveless shirt called attention to a tattoo of a fish flopping under a leafy tree. She wore a pair of brown denim shorts and maroon Doc Marten boots that she'd spray painted silver.

I took the other bottle from her grasp and started toward the DJ. I accidentally knocked a stack of playbills from the counter, scattering them around Avery's feet. I put the wine down and crouched gingerly to pick up the playbills. I tried to support my back with my hands. Avery dropped to the floor, grabbed my elbow, and brought me back to my feet.

"Claudia, I've got it," she scolded. "I may not know much about being pregnant but you look really uncomfortable," she yelped.

"Stuart!" Avery cried loudly in a theatrical tone.

Stuart appeared at Avery's side on call, as if he'd been waiting for her voice.

"Stuart, please help us with this wine," she begged. "Claudia needs to sit down. Do you think you could make her some tea?" Avery blurted.

"Ooo, I'll help," chirped The Countess anxiously, scrambling from his spot on the library table. Oliver told me that Ezra had a crush on Stuart, so I knew he was looking for excuses to get close to him.

"What kinda tea you want, baby?" asked The Countess.

"Earl Gray would be great. I think there's some in the cupboard above the sink," I answered pointing with my left hand.

"Here, I'll get it," Stuart offered, resting his chin on Ezra's shoulder. They looked cute together.

"Thank you, boys," Avery said, as she led me from the kitchen.

We left Stuart and Ezra alone to chat cheerily about different types of tea. Avery clutched my elbow tightly and directed us through the crowded party toward an empty loveseat, which was positioned under the elevator shaft. Philip stood against the television set, flicking the "on/off" switch of a vacuum cleaner that Cedric had painted for display on First Friday.

Avery shot Philip an annoyed look and shooed him away. She pulled the vacuum cleaner to the center of the oriental rug as if calling it to center stage. Then, she plopped down next to me in the cushy loveseat.

"So have you seen Remy?" she asked me, point blank.

"No," I responded curtly.

"I heard he's thinking of going to Chicago," Avery told me.

"Chicago?" I echoed in a condescending tone. "What about Pure Motion?" I asked.

"Ezra said he's gonna keep it going," Avery explained. "I think Remy's trying to get a residency at one of the schools out there."

"Oh, yeah," I mumbled, shaking my head yes. "The one at Columbia College," I remembered.

"Doesn't that upset you?" Avery dug, lighting a cigarette. The cigarette made my mouth water but I knew she wouldn't let me have one.

"Remy should do what makes him happy," I said.

"You made him happy, Claudia," Avery reminded me.

"But I didn't make him complete," I reminded myself.

"Aren't you afraid of being alone?" she asked.

"Everybody's afraid of being alone," I answered. "But I think settling frightens me even more," I confessed.

"Is that fair to the baby?" Avery pushed.

"I don't think it's fair to any of us," I said. "At first I thought that because this wasn't planned that meant it was wrong. But I don't think that's true anymore," I explained emotionally. I could feel my cheeks reddening.

"There are a lot of people that need things to happen this way," I surmised.

"Oliver," Avery cited.

"Oliver," I repeated, scanning the room for him. He was pouring drinks in the kitchen. He was laughing and making wild, flailing hand motions. I smiled as I watched him expertly apply his umpteenth layer of red lipstick. I caught his eye and wriggled my fingers at him in a wave.

"He's really excited about the baby," Avery said.

"I wasn't sure how he was going to react when Gabe left for Paris," she admitted. "They spent a lot of time together over the last few months. I think Oliver thought that they were totally committed," Avery remarked.

"I know," I agreed. "I don't think I would have had the strength to leave Remy, if it weren't for Oliver."

"He's so funny," I laughed. "He keeps stealing parenting books from the shop. He's got a different name picked out every five minutes," I said, watching enviously as Avery snuffed out her cigarette.

As if his ears were burning, Oliver quickly appeared crouched next to me, sipping a Cosmopolitan. He reached his hand toward my enlarged middle and tickled it lightly.

"What are *you* two whispering about?" Oliver interrupted in an out-of-breath hush. He swirled the paper umbrella in his drink and then crooked his elbow so that his right hand was poised demurely in the air. His wrist hung limp and he rolled his thumb mindlessly over the rings on the inside of his hand.

"Oh, it doesn't really matter anyway," he said, nearly forgetting himself. "Now what do you think about the name Kennedy if it's a boy?" he asked.

"Too Democratic. What's the matter? Have you given up on Oliver?" I joked in monotone.

"Just exploring other options," he responded smugly, shifting on his ankles. "If it's a girl, it's got to be Olivia!" he exclaimed, exaggerating his words.

"Olivia," I mumbled, liking the way the syllables dripped from my tongue.

"Why not Avis?" Avery jumped in sounding perky and trite.

"Avis?" Oliver scoffed, furrowing his brow.

"Isn't that the name of a rental car company?" he asked. Avery stuck her tongue out at Oliver and scrunched her nose up in a playful way.

"Now girls, I can't stay and chat," Oliver informed us, changing the subject entirely.

"There are *far* too many cute boys in here," he added, lifting his tone at the end of his sentence.

"Stuart just wanted me to come over and ask if you wanted anything in your tea, Claude," Oliver said, directing his comment at me. "I told him you took it black but he insisted I double check," he finished.

"You're right, O. Not a thing in my brew," I confirmed.

"You know what, sweetie, I'll tell Stuart," I offered. "I'm exhausted. I think I'm gonna go lie down for a little awhile," I said almost apologetically.

"Lie down?" Oliver cried. "Christ Claude, where do you think you're gonna lie down? It's so loud in here," Oliver spoke quickly before Avery cut him off.

"Oliver," Avery chided. "She's tired. Why don't you just sit and keep me company for awhile. I'm dying to hear what you thought of the play."

"Thanks, Avery," I said gratefully. "I will be fine," I insisted, directing my words to Oliver.

I ran my index finger across Oliver's chin and covered his lips in a silencing gesture. Oliver smiled and crinkled his eyes. When I lifted my hand away, I noticed some of his lipstick had rubbed off on the pad of my fingertip. I licked it off with a rolling, cupping motion of my tongue. I was surprised; it tasted like raspberries.

I purposefully walked toward the kitchen. I accepted and thanked Stuart for my tea. I wandered off down the makeshift hallway to the corner of the loft where my bed was hidden by a wall of curtains. I swished my teabag through the piping hot water. I loved watching the brown swirls of the tea slowly overtake the clear water. I could watch tea seep for hours; I always found it very soothing and therapeutic.

With its corner, I pulled back the heavy fabric of a deep blue tapestry partitioning off my room and disappeared behind its covering. Moments of privacy in the loft were few and far between but I knew Oliver would try to keep things quiet for me.

I placed my full mug on the upside-down wooden barrel, which served as my nightstand. I tore off my dress and unzipped the front of my one-man tent as it wobbled unsteadily on my futon bed. I crawled wearily onto cool blue sheets and closed my eyes with a sigh. I listened intently to the smooth strains of Sidney Bechet seeping through the background and thought of the word "home".

Drifting off to sleep, I caught quips, phrases, and the broken words of random conversations from the party. I made a bet with myself that I would remember on which side of my body I fell asleep but I knew I'd forget in the morning. My last thoughts were fuzzy and I fell asleep thinking of the statue of Sidney Bechet in Congo Square.

I awoke with sleep ridden eyes and peeked outside my tent to glance at the red, digital numbers of my clock radio resting on the upside-down wooden barrel. It was 4:26 AM. The loft was pitch black and silent. My mouth was dry and I reached for my mug. I stopped myself, thinking how much I hated the taste of cold tea.

I wiggled my toes and moved my feet. Mojo got pissed off because she'd been sleeping comfortably behind my knees for hours. I laid perfectly still, hoping to fall back asleep but my stomach was grumbling. My senses came into focus and I listened carefully for the sound of any remaining voices from the party. I thought I heard the faint whispering of the stereo.

Pickles. I was craving Jewish deli-style pickles. I rolled out of bed and tugged on an old T-shirt I'd stolen from Remy. I got tangled in the blue tapestry but pulled myself free. I stumbled into the kitchen.

I surveyed the countertops and slanting tables. Strewn everywhere were discarded beer bottles, half-full wine glasses, pillows, and ashtrays overflowing with cigarettes. I knew smoke was in the air but couldn't smell it because my nostrils were so accustomed to its toxic odor.

There was a faint light emanating from the stovetop. It was a white candle, which had been left burning. I walked to it and blew out the flame. I began to sift through bags of stale chips, empty pizza boxes, and the playbills I'd dropped earlier. I came across an open bag of Sweet-Tart's Chicks, Ducks, and Bunnies. They were left over from Easter. I forgot about the pickles, grabbed a handful of candy from the green bag, and turned toward the front windows of the loft. A soft glow from the street lights of Third Street filtered into the room.

Startled, I jumped up, noticing a figure slumped over one of the couches edging the oriental rug. It was Oliver. I smiled at how peaceful he looked in the distance. I walked to the loveseat and picked up a pastel-colored Mexican blanket and placed it over his chest. I nearly kicked over a glass of unfinished Merlot resting on the hard wood floor next to him.

I picked up the glass and saw that Oliver had been scribbling in his journal. It was haphazardly thrown pages down on the back of the couch. I picked it up too and started to walk back to the kitchen.

John Lee Hooker was wailing on the stereo. I will never forget that noise. It made me feel like something was wrong. It was an intuitive, sixth sense that I didn't know I possessed.

I turned back to Oliver and looked down at him. His mascara had run in black, squiggly lines down his face. They were the trails of tears. His lipstick was smeared from his lips carelessly over his left cheek and also covered the pillow beneath his head.

He looked pale. He looked white. His forehead was cold and I shook him. I shook him lightly at first, whispering that he should get up and go to bed because he'd have a sore neck in the morning if he slept like that.

But Oliver didn't move. So, I shook him harder. And he still didn't move. I kept shaking him and John Lee droned on melodically in the background. A black pen rolled onto the floor from Oliver's lifeless hand. I began to cry.

I found an empty bottle of Demerol underneath the couch and lifted it up to the light of the windows. A thin layer of powder slid against the inside of the plastic. I hated the opaque brown color of prescription bottles. It was so drab.

I sat alone with Oliver for a long time. I waited for the sun to come up. I didn't really want to say goodbye. I didn't really know how.

So I listened to the city wake up from the night and thought about reading his journal. I decided against it though and placed the book on the cluttered shelf in the corner of the loft with dozens of other lost thoughts.

"I'll read it someday," I promised aloud. "Right now reality has become far too numb to touch."

When it was nearly full light, I stood up and dialed 911. I put on a pot of hazelnut coffee and lit a cigarette. I turned on the television and listened to a bleached-blonde newswoman ramble on about a fire in Parkside that had been raging out of control for two days. She said they suspected arson.

It was a new day in a beautiful city. I sipped my coffee quietly and thought about getting dressed to cover Oliver's shift at the bookstore. I thought about calling Oliver's mom in Charleston, West Virginia but I stopped myself, knowing the cops would take care of it. They'd call her and break the news to her gently.

Me?

She found me dancing naked and alone in Congo Square under the soft light of a crescent moon. I spun in tight circles around the statue of Sidney Bechet and saluted it to the four faces. Storyville laid in ruins to my right and a woman approached me from the direction of St. Louis Cemetery #1.

It was Marie Laveau. She wore a turban around her head and stood nearly seven feet tall. She handed me a piece of pink chalk and told me to mark X's on the statue with it.

I snapped the chalk in two and demanded directions to Holt Cemetery. She was insulted. She asked why I would want to go to Holt when St. Louis was so close.

"Buddy Bolden," I replied snippantly.

She scarfed at me and told me to go to the Voodoo Museum on Dumaine. She said to ask for Veronica Powers and have her give me her "Singing Bones" tour. I thanked Marie Laveau and ran across North Rampart and down Conti.

She screamed after me to put some clothes on but I ignored her. I slipped through the shadows of the street as the sun began to creep up in the Eastern sky. I started to sprint through the Quarter because I knew it was already day light in Philadelphia.

Researching Rolywholyover

I decided to stay on at the loft after Oliver's death. I didn't find the place as eerie as one would expect. I found that it made me feel safe, as if Oliver were watching over me.

Oliver's mom called me all the way from her trailer park in West Virginia to make the funeral arrangements. She insisted on taking care of everything from Charleston. When I suggested having a memorial service in Philly for all of Oliver's friends, she refused. She said his friends should have known. Her accusations made me feel small and weak and desperately ineffectual.

I should have known.

I didn't go to West Virginia for the burial. I just let it slip past me in a blur. I sent Oliver's things to his mother as she demanded but I kept his journal. I kept his journal tucked away on the bookshelf in the corner of the loft because I was going to read it later. I'll need a month of Sunday's for all the things I'm going to do later.

Avery thought it apropos to hold a simple dinner party at the loft so that we could all say goodbye. I obliged and helped arrange, prepare, indulge in, and clean up after an unemotionally bland evening. The usual crowd showed up, with the exception of Gabe who phoned from Paris to tell us that he couldn't get a flight back to the States to sit and do nothing with us over dinner.

At the end of the night, I crawled crying and alone into my tent. I realized that even though I should have known I didn't. I didn't know because there was the drag and the superficial laughter and the "I'm Too Selfish to Take the Time". But for me, there was never any real Oliver.

So I usurped shift after shift after shift at the bookstore. Gus hated dealing with new hires and I needed the money. I was left where I started: sitting alone at the big front desk of Oz and Endz, pricing paperbacks in pencil on the upper right hand corner of the first page.

It was my birthday. I treated myself to a late lunch from Lettuce Eat, the deli on the corner of Second and Market. I figured turning twenty-three wasn't a milestone but deserved to be recognized at the least with a good messy sandwich.

I didn't tell anyone about my birthday. I thought that was cool. It was that "she was filled with so much angst that no one knew it was her birthday" kind of thing. I didn't expect any gifts, I just hoped my mother would call. But she didn't call because she didn't know where to find me. I got a card at the bookstore signed by her and her two cats two weeks after the fact. It was cute; my mom had drawn two sets of paw prints above the names Amos and Leo.

I bit slowly into my tuna melt. The meat squished and squeezed out of the sides of the bread. I was licking my fingers, when I heard the jingling of the tiny bell on the front door. It was Cedric.

I hadn't seen him for months—not since his trip to New Orleans in May. He'd been busy trying to jolt sales for Cyclone and had been traveling for most of the summer months. Cedric only showed up at the bookstore when he needed extra cash. Gus had more odd jobs to be filled than full moons had freaks.

"Yo, Claude!" Cedric bellowed from the hallway. "You in there?"

I finished the last crumbs of my sandwich and wiped the corners of my mouth. I lifted a light stack of tattered and doomed porch books and followed the sound of Cedric's voice.

"Hey, Cedric. What's up?" I answered him.

Cedric rushed toward me grabbing the books from my arms.

"Damn, girl. Watchoo doin'?" he scolded me, glaring at my stomach.

"I've gotta work," I snapped. He shook his head. Two of his scraggly dreads were wrapped in colorful strands of thread.

"Where'd you get those?" I asked, referring to the wraps.

"In the Quarter," he replied. "I've got Gus' truck out in the alley. He sent me over to Mullica Hill to pick up books from some auction. He told me you'd know where to unload 'em," Cedric said, jerking his head toward the door. I rolled my eyes back.

"Let's see how many are out there," I sighed.

I struggled with the handle of the screen door and pushed myself outside into the hot, thick air. It was difficult to breathe because of the humidity. I shuffled across the creaking boards of the porch and leaned over the railing into American Street. The hatch of the Suburban was still down. Cedric plopped the books he was holding onto one of the two rickety white benches and rushed to the truck.

He opened the hatch and revealed a full load of cardboard boxes filled with books. I couldn't even count them all.

"Shit, Cedric," I mumbled, clearly overwhelmed. "I don't know what to do with 'em. Throw 'em in the basement wherever you can find room," I instructed.

I fumbled through my pockets for the keys to the grated door, which was embedded in the sidewalk of the alley. I tossed the keys into Cedric's hands and left him to his task. I turned back to the store. I stopped briefly to arrange some books discarded on the crooked shelves, which were leaning limply in the hot sun.

"Excuse me, Miss," came the feeble voice of a small, white-haired woman inflicted with osteoporosis. "Are you running the special on porch books today?" she asked me.

"Yes, Ma'am," I answered her. "One bag of porch books for one dollar on Monday's," I clarified.

The bag at her feet was almost full. She stared up at me, squinting into the sunlight.

"Miss, do you have any extra bags inside?" came her breathless voice.

"I'm sorry," I said. "We're running short on bags. As a matter of fact, we can always use donations," I told her.

The old woman ignored me and cursed under her breath. She began to lower more books into her brown paper bag, carefully positioning them as if they were puzzle pieces. I tried to pass by her but she dropped her arm down in front of me like a traffic cop. She voraciously skimmed the titles I was cradling against my forearm. Greedily, the woman snatched an insurance license testing book and a faded telephone directory of the Main Line from my hands.

When she stooped to the ground to lift her bag onto one of the porch benches, I dashed through the creaking screen door into the cool quiet of the bookstore. I leaned my forehead against the back of the heavy wooden door as I pushed it shut and felt something brush past my shoulder and widely around me.

It was the smooth yellowish-white palm of Cedric's deep black hand. He'd beaten me inside by using the basement steps. In between his index finger and thumb was a tiny perfume vial no more than an inch and a half long. I looked at it curiously, accepting it cautiously. I smiled as I twirled around to see his face. He lunged a step to his left and cocked his head toward me. I kissed him on the cheek.

"Can't take the credit," Cedric confessed. "Remy asked me to get it for you when I was in New Orleans," he explained.

I twisted the vial's tiny black cap and released the stinging, sense-awakening scent of jasmine underneath my nostrils. "We broke up, Cedric," I told him.

"I know—that night at W & J's," he responded.

"I caught Remy in between tours a couple weeks ago at Group Movement. He gave me cash for the perfume but told me to keep it anyway. I thought you should have it," Cedric said with a sentimental twinge in his tone.

"Thanks. It means a lot to me," I whispered, shaking the vial. I over turned its open face onto my index finger and brushed the oil lightly over the pulse points on my neck and the inside of my wrists. I even crouched over to dab some on the back of my knees. Cedric laughed at the amount of energy I took to complete such a simple motion.

"Come on. Give me a hand out front," I commanded, starting back to the register.

"Damn girl, shouldn't you be at home in bed or somethin'?" Cedric asked, following me from two steps behind.

I laughed off his remark and wobbled back to my stool. I snatched the white paper left over from my sandwich and crumpled it into a tight ball. I shot it into the garbage can and then crooked my arms at the elbow, thrusting them into the air in a victory stance.

"There's been alot goin' on around here," I said, teetering on three legs of the stool.

"You heard about Oliver?" I added in a hush. Cedric shook his head up and down and lifted a heavy cardboard box from the floor to the counter.

"I don't really mind the extra hours. Sometimes the loft just gets too quiet," I confessed with a pause. "I guess it won't be for long though," I joked, rubbing my belly.

"Christ Claudia, when's the last time you saw him?" Cedric jumped in suddenly. I threw him a quizzical look, as if I didn't know who he was talking about.

"He knows, Claudia," he forewarned me like a death knell.

"Are you gonna help me or not?" I responded abruptly.

I flung my tangled red mane of hair over my shoulders and violently started stabbing the keys of the adding machine with the well-worn, eraser of a pencil. My eyes were filling up with stinging wet tears and I fought to hold them back so Cedric wouldn't see me cry. I was feeling even more emotional than usual; I was like a time bomb waiting to explode.

"All right," Cedric backed off quickly. "I know when not to push *my* luck," he bellowed, rustling through the box.

"Just stack these boxes over by the Harlequins," I instructed.

Cedric nodded and went about his work. I tried to make myself look busy by grabbing the "Hold Request" box from the left of the register. Since Oz and Endz had no formal inventory or card catalogue system, it was nearly impossible to track what was on the shelves at any given moment. We took requests anyway. Once in awhile, I'd actually call people if the stuff they said they were looking for came in. I figured I had time to make a few calls.

I leaned back on my rickety stool, pushing it precariously onto only two of its four wooden legs. I lifted the telephone receiver to my ear just as I heard the weak tinkling of the tiny bell above the front door of the store.

In a loud voice, Cedric announced, "Shit, if it isn't Remy Thomas."

I closed my eyes. My heart jumped and my stomach sank to my knees. I held my breath and listened for Remy.

"Yo. How you feel, bro?" Remy slurred in a deep, raspy breath. I could hear them slapping their palms together in greeting.

Remy's voice brought a flood of emotions cascading over me. I wanted to run away and hide. I sat perfectly still though, frozen in cowardliness as yellow as the color of a box of pralines from Kate Latter's on Decatur Street.

"How's that VW treatin' you, man?" Cedric asked.

"It's pretty sweet," Remy responded.

"What kind is it again?" Cedric pressed.

"It's one a those VW Things," Remy explained. "You know, like a jeep," he added.

I thought I recognized the whimpering of a dog over Remy's words. I furrowed my brow and leaned forward slightly to see through the doorway into the hall. I saw a stubby little tail wagging wildly about a foot from the floor.

Remy had always wanted a dog. When we lived together, he used to try to drag me to the SPCA all the time. Once, he even brought a stray home with him. I flipped out though and made him get rid of it because Mojo got so freaked out. I think that was why Remy hated Mojo so much. I figured this dog was probably one of the first purchases he made when we broke up.

"What's wrong, Dozer?" Remy said rhetorically. He bent at his knees and crouched to tousle the top of the dog's head.

"Hey, you seen Claudia in here?" he asked Cedric.

I saw from his shadow that he had straightened to his feet again, seemingly waiting for a response. I couldn't hear Cedric's response but I assumed he pointed Remy in my direction.

Remy turned the corner into the front room and the hideous runt of a bulldog came panting and slobbering after him. I smiled at the sight of both of them.

Remy dropped the dog's leash and commanded, "Get her Dozer. Go get her, boy!"

Dozer wiggled himself behind the counter and started to sniff and shake himself happily around my legs. He was so ugly that he became irresistible. His stained yellow teeth protruded from his lower lip in an underbite and added to his charisma. I was in love.

"Happy Birthday," Remy said, staring into my eyes. In my direction, he extended a stark white envelope, tied in a festive red ribbon. I hesitated before accepting it.

"Go on. Take it," he instructed me.

I looked at him blankly. I was exhausted and overwhelmingly afraid. I took the envelope from him and fumbled with it. I turned it over and over again in my hands. I started to open it but Remy stopped me.

"No, Claude. Please, read it later when I'm gone," he said.

I struggled to break my spell of speechlessness and forced out the most nonchalant statement I could muster: "Dozer, huh?"

"As in 'Bull'," Remy joked. I laughed.

"Hey Claude," he continued. "I know it's short notice and all but do you think you could get out of here for a couple of hours?" he invited politely.

"I know," I responded. "There are a lot of things we need to talk about."

"Nah, I don't wanna bring you down on your birthday," Remy said. "I have a surprise for you. If you taught me anything, it was never to forget birthdays or Valentine's Day," he reminded me.

"Surprise?" I repeated with upturned eyebrows and piqued interest. "You know I'm not good at refusing surprises," I told him.

"No need to refuse then, right?" he asked rhetorically.

I smirked and thought to myself for a moment. "Cedric!" I shouted into the hallway.

Cedric was still in the other room struggling with the boxes. He poked his head into the doorway with a grumbling, "Whaaaat?"

"Listen, big guy," I started. "I gotta cut outta here for a little while. I'm only on till five. Do you think you could cover the store till then?" I pleaded, flashing a look at Remy.

Cedric followed my line of vision and asked if Gus was due in. I assured him not and tossed the keys to the register to him before he could refuse me. I gathered my few things and stepped out from behind the counter. Remy placed his hand low on my back and guided me toward the door. Dozer followed after us, panting like a fat man climbing a flight of stairs.

"Thanks, Cedric," Remy spoke sincerely. "I appreciate it."

I ignored the comment and shuffled past Cedric.

Remy and I stepped outside. I squinted my eyes, blinded by the brilliance of the hazy sunlight. We began to walk slowly and pointedly in the direction of Third Street. As we turned the corner, I knew instantly which of the parallel parked cars was Remy's.

"You haven't seen my new ride yet," Remy told me excitedly.

The car was difficult to describe. It was Volkswagen's version of a jeep. Its boxy, bright turquoise frame sat low to the ground. A poorly mended, black cloth roof covered it. A series of thick-ridged lines were etched along the side of each door. The lines wrapped around to the thing's front grill and gave way to space for two perfectly round headlights. The headlights peeked out like curious eyes with flashing hazards attracting special attention.

"Sharp," I remarked. A smile crept onto Remy's face.

"Thanks Claude," he replied.

"I'm planning on taking it out West, so I've been tweaking it to make sure everything's O.K." Remy said.

I looked at him curiously and thought of all the conversations we'd had in the past about saving up enough money to buy a car to run away into the sunset together. I wondered what was on his mind but kept my mouth shut. I pretended to look happy out of my own social responsibility.

"Let's head up to Rittenhouse Square so we can talk for awhile. It's not far from your surprise," Remy proposed cryptically. "I have some stuff I need to talk to you about," he confided.

He turned his key in the lock of the thing's passenger side door and pulled it open for me. I shifted uncomfortably in my platform sandals and plopped myself down in the scorchingly hot seat. Dozer jumped in after me and scurried into the back. His tongue was hanging from his mouth and dripping drool.

I leaned over to unlock Remy's door for him but he was too fast. He'd already swung it open before I had the chance.

"Nervous?" Remy asked with raised eyebrows.

"Only about your driving," I half joked.

I quickly learned that Remy was a terrible driver. He pummeled through more auburn stop lights than I could count, honked wildly at any and all cab drivers in our way, and nearly flattened a uniform-clad Girl Scout who was trying to cross Walnut Street. He sat with his seat back so low that he looked as if he were lying down. The Wu-Tang Clan was blaring at decibels so loud that I thought the stereo speakers were sure to blow out.

Parking was equally as exhilarating. After recklessly circling the same three-block radius for fifteen minutes, we crammed into a tiny space on Locust Street. It only took Remy three tries to wedge his way in.

"I'm a little rusty," he tried to excuse himself.

"No problem," I replied, clutching my stomach as discreetly as possible.

Supporting my back with my palms, I wriggled out of the thing. I stretched shamelessly in front of Pizzeria Uno's. Dozer dragged Remy to my side of the thing by his leash. Remy draped his arm loosely around my shoulders and began to guide me toward the park. Beads of sweat began to form on my forehead from the heat. Embarrassed, I wiped them with the back of my hand.

The streets were nearly deserted because of the soaring temperatures and oppressive humidity of the August heat wave. The few visible people were either hurrying off to another air-conditioned destination or standing still, tucked away in a premium pocket of shade.

Remy and I walked down the Southeast entrance of Rittenhouse Square, toward the center fountain. Most of the benches were taken and chess matches, which looked as though they'd been raging for years, strategically littered the park. We found a space not far from the spot Remy usually liked to play. Some of the chess players nodded at him in acknowledgment.

Remy and I sat in silence at first, each guarding separate ends of the bench. Remy tied Dozer to one of the splintered wooden legs beneath us. Dozer sniffed and barked frantically at other dogs passing by.

Remy finally moved closer to me and picked my hand up from my lap. He began to trace long, sloping lines between my fingers.

"I've known for awhile, Claudia," he said. "I didn't know what to do. I couldn't understand why you left, let alone why you never told me about the baby."

"I'm sorry. I *wanted* to tell you," I tried.

"At first, I was scared. It seemed like we both wanted very different things out of life. It didn't kick in for me until the time I won the tickets. I felt that things between us just weren't right," I continued, as Remy released my hand.

"I can't understand why you'd wanna do this alone," Remy said in confusion as he gestured toward my stomach. He was careful not to touch me.

"I don't expect you to understand. I'm not even sure I do," I confessed.

"It's me," I told him. "There was a time that our relationship made me feel very full and very alive. I almost thought I knew who I was and what I wanted. But after we moved in together, I started to feel like I'd stopped growing. I became obsessed only with the phenomenon of an us," I explained, growing near hysteria.

"It was like the rest of the world didn't matter. Then, I realized that I felt lost like I didn't have a place. We were holding each other back, Remy," I surmised.

"I know," he agreed, "I loved you so much that I didn't want to leave you behind."

Remy paused for moment, before continuing. I smiled at him with soft, wet tears growing in the outside corners of my eyes.

"I'm leaving, Claudia," he said point blank. I blinked widely in disbelief. His words did not immediately register for me.

"I gotta get outta Philly, Claude. I bought the thing so I can head West," Remy explained.

"Where are you going?" I asked.

"I got the Residency in Chicago," he answered, avoiding my eyes. "It doesn't start until after Labor Day, so I'm gonna travel first for a few weeks. I'm planning on driving North out to San Francisco and then back," he said.

"Wow," I exclaimed. "Did you quit Third Street already?"

"I gave my two weeks yesterday," he said. "Listen, Claude. I'll keep you posted everywhere I go. If you need anything, I'll be there for you. If you ask me to stay or come home or go somewhere else, I'll do it," Remy promised.

Dozer had begun to sniff and jump onto a cocker spaniel that was none too pleased with his intrusive efforts. Remy tugged hard on his leash. Dozer pulled back for a split second but continued to try to hump the cocker spaniel. Remy yelled his name sternly. I leaned my head back, rolling it across my shoulders.

Jerking back up, I said in a dry monotone, "I'm happy for you."

Remy shook his head and released a short puff of a breath through his nostrils.

"I was thinking about staying around until the baby was born," he offered, twirling Dozer's leash between his fingers.

"No," I commanded almost simultaneously. "No, you should go now. You told me once that you have to take your chances when you get them or your chances pass you by," I reminded him.

"Just promise that you'll keep in touch with me and I'll be fine," I added.

Remy looked at me innocently and whispered, "I love you."

He leaned toward me to kiss me on the forehead but Dozer suddenly yanked his arm so hard that Remy nearly fell to the ground.

I giggled. Under my breath, I vowed to myself, "I won't lose you. I know I won't."

Once Remy regained his composure, he changed the subject. "Well, I didn't ask you here today to freak you out," Remy spoke loudly, slapping both of his hands on his thighs.

He stood up, stretched his taught muscles, and inhaled deeply. "It's your birthday and I wanted to do something special for you," he continued.

My ears perked up and I thrust my head up toward him waiting anxiously to hear the surprise.

"Do you remember the John Cage exhibit we saw at the Art Museum in the Spring?" he asked.

"Rolywholyover?" I clarified, scrunching up my nose.

"Yeah," Remy sniffled. "Turns out this place called the Rosenbach Museum & Library loaned a bunch of the James Joyce stuff to the exhibit," Remy informed me.

"Cage got the name Rolywholyover from Joyce's *Finnegan's Wake,*" I told him.

"That's right," Remy remarked. "Since the show created major hype around Joyce, the Rosenbach started running a piece on Cage's influences," he said, as he wrapped Dozer's leash tighter around his hand.

"I heard somewhere that they had Joyce's original, handwritten manuscript of *Ulysses,*" I said.

"Right again. I thought it'd be cool if we checked it out," Remy concluded.

What a fabulous birthday present, I thought to myself. Remy knew me better than I knew myself.

"I love you," I whispered.

"I know," he answered smugly. Remy lifted my hand and pulled me up from the bench. He kissed me on the top of my head, letting his lips linger there for a moment.

("You thought your apathy was so strong you could never change it," cried the laos.

"I didn't invite him into my life," she told them.

"No, but you left the door to the kitchen wide open," they said.

"That wasn't me, that was Robert Johnson," I corrected the laos, snippantly. "Besides, he forced himself into my life."

"He won't be leaving any time soon," warned the laos.

"It's O.K. It will end. It always ends for me. I'll just wipe him away," she answered.

"He'll come back," they said.

"Yes, I suppose he has already started to haunt me," she muttered under her breath.)

Remy and I started to walk again through the park, exiting on the Southwestern corner. We followed a tiny alley to 20th Street. After traveling just a few short blocks, we turned left to be swallowed up by the peaceful, cool shade of Delancey.

Delancey was my favorite street in Philadelphia. It was a wonderland, deserted and gracefully suspended in time above the grime and stench of Center City. Broken regularly by numbered cross streets, it ran crookedly through town, stopping and starting wherever it so chose. Towering sycamore and maple trees carefully lined its uneven brick sidewalks. Wrought iron designs decorated the porch railings and blooming window boxes of mansions, which were protected by menacing security systems.

The Rosenbach Museum and Library was discreetly tucked away on a residential block of Delancey between 17th and 18th Streets. Remy and I almost walked past it but Dozer stopped to pee nearly directly beneath the brass historic plate, which hung to the right of the Museum's front door.

We climbed the Rosenbach's marble steps with Dozer yapping excitedly at our heels. Remy squeezed my hand tightly and rang the doorbell. I pressed my face up against the glass of the front door to see inside but a thick metal gate blocked my view. We waited a few moments. No one answered Remy's ring.

"I know they're giving tours today," Remy said. "I called earlier," he added, as he rang the bell a second time.

It took a few more tries. Eventually, a tall, sallow-looking gentleman opened the creaky gate. He greeted us with an awkward smile.

"Hello. I am so sorry," the curator apologized in a deadpan droll.

"Please do come in," he invited, stepping back into a dark foyer.

"Cool," Remy whispered. I could tell the sight of the man relieved him. I was ecstatic that we would actually be able to take the tour.

Remy tugged Dozer's leash and dragged him back to the sidewalk. He bent to tie the dog on the green iron frame of a screen that was protecting a struggling young maple tree.

"What d'ya say, boy?" Remy questioned Dozer, as he rubbed the dog's head and neck roughly. Dozer's collar shook and jingled, as he panted stupidly in Remy's face.

"Won't be long," Remy promised, as he stood up and climbed the stoop again. He took my elbow and guided me into the museum.

"Are we too late to make the 2:45 PM tour?" Remy asked the gentleman, who held the door open for us.

"Not at all," the man responded with an air of aristocracy. "It's good you're here now—2:45 PM is our last tour for the day."

The man paused and led us past a small gift shop on our left. He deposited us into a dimly lit parlor.

"Please, make yourselves comfortable," he offered. "We'll wait a few extra minutes before we start, just in case any last minute stragglers arrive," the man suggested. He turned back to the foyer and disappeared into the mouth of the Rosenbach's gift shop.

"Thank you," I called after him, politely.

The museum was still and quiet. Remy sat down gingerly on an antique rocking chair with a tall back. The wood of the chair was cherry, while the upholstery covering the seat cushion was worn nearly threadbare. The cushion's faded red stripes alternated with equally dull lines of a once courtly blue.

"You O.K., Claude?" Remy inquired. "Why don't you sit down and rest before the tour starts?"

"I'm fine, thanks," I replied forwith.

"I'm just really excited," I explained.

I paced the room. I stopped to leaf through the open-faced pages of the museum's register, which was positioned on a low-standing library stand. I flipped through the book's wrinkled pages, eagerly skimming the names of the museum's previous visitors. The tip of my index finger rested over the name of a couple from New Orleans, Louisiana.

I picked up the black pen, which was strapped to the library stand by a heavy plastic cord. I rolled it loosely through my fingers and motioned as if to sign the book. After some careful thought, I decided against it. Instead, I walked toward Remy and dragged my hand softly across the back of his shirt collar.

"No sense in putting things off any longer," the doyen bellowed, as he returned to the parlor.

"Let's get started, shall we?" he proposed.

Remy jumped up. The rocking chair he'd been sitting in swung violently against the white wall of the parlor. Remy grabbed at it but missed. The chair ricocheted back and forth again before I caught it in my palm. I shot Remy a scolding look but the doyen appeared not to notice.

"My name is Atherton," the man told us.

"Our tour today will be rather informal. Please feel free to ask as many questions as you like. I'll try to gear the tour to your interests. Although there is no charge, donations are greatly appreciated and accepted in the gift shop," he informed us.

In a monotone voice, Atherton offered us details about the history of the museum and its founders, the Rosenbach brothers. He told us that the site was listed on the National Register of Historic Places. He explained that the brothers were world-renowned collectors, who specialized in antiques, art, *and* literary rarities. Atherton asked in which area Remy and I were most interested.

As I marveled dumfounded at the paintings hanging above the fireplace, Remy quickly replied, "the literature."

Although Remy was trying to please me, I could tell that he wanted to keep the tour as short as possible.

"Very well, then," Atherton said. "Let's move upstairs."

We followed Atherton up the mansion's winding staircase. I glanced up—there were four floors. The center of each marble step was well worn from years of previous visitors. Atherton stopped us briefly on the first landing and pointed out the names of various sculptures and paintings directly in our line of vision. The only name I recognized was a piece by Thomas Sully. I knew Atherton could sense that Remy and I were unimpressed.

Once on the tight second floor landing, Atherton explained that the room to our left was an exact replication of the Marianne Moore's New York City studio apartment. He also motioned to his right in the direction of the museum's prestigious library. Atherton stated that the bulk of the expansive literary collection of the Rosenbach brothers was housed in these two rooms.

Before turning to the left, Atherton called our attention to an enormous bookcase positioned against the center wall of the landing. He explained that the bookcase was of the American Gothic style and had once been owned by Herman Melville. He motioned toward a signed first edition copy of *Moby Dick*, a number of volumes of Emily Dickinson's poems, and an exquisite leather-bound copy of Whitman's *Leaves of Grass*. My eyes lingered in awe over the titles.

Atherton waited patiently for me to finish exploring the bookcase and then led us into the replica of Moore's studio. Atherton indicated that the original architecture of the room was most remarkable in that it nearly mirrored the physical design of Moore's New York City apartment. Remy and I leaned over a drooping red velvet rope to examine the design.

The studio was sparsely decorated and meticulously neat. Its one tiny window filtered the afternoon's waning sunlight in to shine over three perfectly aligned library shelves. My eyes were drawn from the books hidden there to an archaic typewriter resting on an otherwise bare desk. I squinted to read the words on the yellowed paper in the machine's carrier.

To the right of the doorway hung two black and white photographs. One was a shot of the fully furnished interior of Moore's New York City apartment. Just above was a picture of a crowded library table where Moore was seated at center, lounging amidst literary giants such as Tennessee Williams, W. H. Auden, and Gore Vidal.

I stared at the second photograph before Atherton suggested that we move on to the library. Remy turned quickly after Atherton and I was forced to abandon the picture. I vowed to come back to the museum again when I had more time to spend.

The Rosenbach library was dark and cool. The lower portion of the walls was covered with wood paneling and the top with a royal blue wallpaper. Impressive looking portraits were scattered throughout the room. My attention was immediately drawn to a marble bust of James Joyce positioned to the right of the entrance. The bust sat between two long vitrines.

Atherton turned on the lights so that we could peered into the casings. I gawked at John Tenniel's drawings for *Alice in Wonderland*, Lewis Carroll's copy of *Alice*, and Maurice Sendak's original sketches for *Where the Wild Things Are.* As I left my fingerprints on the glass, Remy leaned over me and rested his chin on my shoulder. He snickered at Sendak's drawings, listening to Atherton explain that Sendak credits his family as inspiration for his sketches.

Remy pulled away from me and said, "Claude, look over here."

Atherton was standing in the center of the library floor, circling three vitrines standing head to head against each other.

"This is the William Anastasi display currently running in conjunction with the Cage exhibit," Atherton began.

"You'll notice three separate documents juxtaposed," he continued. "One is written in red, one in green, and one in blue. Anastasi believed Joyce was greatly influenced by the writings of a French satirist named Alfred Jarry. The three colors are intended to represent an imagined conversation between Anastasi, Joyce, and Jarry."

"Hmmm," I purred in fascination. "Where is Anastasi from?" I asked.

"He's a New York implant from Philadelphia," replied Atherton. "I've heard he's selling the piece by the page," he offered.

"Cool," Remy yelped from the other side of a partition within the room.

"What's this over here?" he called back to Atherton.

Atherton followed after Remy's voice. He responded, "That is the reading library. It is open by appointment only to researchers and readers alike. Visitors may use any of the resources you see here."

Trailing behind again, I reached the spot where Atherton and Remy were standing. Their attention was focused on a cherry wood library table.

"By appointment only," I thought out loud to myself.

Remy posed a polite question to Atherton as to how to schedule appointment hours for the library. Atherton handed him a business card and smiled at me. Remy stuffed the card deep into the pocket of his jeans. He placed his hands on my shoulders and began to rub my muscles tenderly.

Remy whispered to me softly, "You about ready, Claude?"

Although I could have wandered around for hours longer, I answered Remy dutifully, "Sure. I've gotta get back home—I've got a million things to do."

Atherton overheard our conversation and began to flick off the light switches in the library in a flurry. We all paraded downstairs and into the foyer. Atherton led us into the cluttered gift shop, reminding us again that donations were greatly appreciated. Remy slipped a fold of bills into the locked, red box, which held donations. We thanked Atherton enthusiastically for the tour and left without purchasing any souvenirs.

Remy and I returned outside into the steamy, August heat. I started to sweat instantly. The wrinkles on my sundress began to come undone, as if pressed by the heat of an iron. Remy bent down to untie Dozer. He ruffled the dog's fur as Dozer licked and slobbered over him excitedly. I fumbled through my backpack and pulled out an eight-ounce bottle of water.

"Here, Remy," I offered, extending the bottle in his direction. "The poor thing looks so hot."

Remy untwisted the cap and held the water to the dog's mouth. Dozer drank in long, lapping gulps, as Remy held it bottom tilted up.

Remy apologized for rushing me through the museum tour and asked if I wanted to grab dinner at the restaurant of my choice. I joked with him that I wanted to go to Le Bec Fin but quickly declined with the feeble excuse that I had errands to run.

We walked to "the thing" in an oppressive silence. Minutes later, Remy dropped me on Third Street at the door of the loft. Without any tearful, messy words, Remy double parked and flicked on his hazard lights. He leapt to my side of "the thing" and helped lift my enormous shape out and into the street.

"Bye, Dozer," I said, as I mustered up a cheerful tone from deep within my gut. Remy leaned over me and placed a gentle, wistful kiss on my lips.

"Goodbye," he whispered.

"Goodbye," I repeated.

I ran hurriedly toward the loft and floundered furiously for my keys. Remy tooted his horn in a "meep, meep" sound and the thing chugged determinedly away from my door step.

A few hours later, I was busily cleaning up the house. Neatness was an obsessive-compulsive disorder with which I'd been inflicted since my pregnancy.

As I was clearing dirty dishes from the kitchen counter, I broke a glass that was half filled with grape juice. Purple splattered everywhere from the cupboards to the refrigerator.

I pushed Mojo away, hoping her paws hadn't already been cut. I swept the shattered glass chunks and splinters onto a green dust pan and dumped them into the trash. As I did this, I began to think of the white envelope that Remy had given me in the bookstore. I prayed I hadn't left it at work.

I stumbled to the couch where I had haphazardly thrown my bag. With a sigh of relief, I yanked out of the envelope. I tore the red ribbon away hurriedly and ripped the flap of the envelope open. I knelt on the blue oriental rug and began to read out loud in a distant voice.

Dear Claudia,

I find myself wondering an awful lot about life lately— women, work, places, fate, destiny. Sometimes, I think life accompanied by age and wisdom and experience, ought to become easier.

I've been down this road before, I think I should be saying to myself. I ought to know how to handle it but such is rarely the case. The more people you meet, places you go, confrontations endured, friendships come and faded all combine to help one make decisions. What I find myself with mainly is a clusterfuck of conflicting ideas and wishes and wants.

I want it all, which is never available let alone possible, and would probably give me cancer anyway.

So where does that leave me?

It leaves me in the same boat with every other fool that looks for the easy way out. My problems are not special or unique. I am undoubtedly not the first to ponder my place in the universe and find myself dumbstruck. Aghast in a maze full of wonder, wanting to absorb it all because it is there and what the hell else is there to do anyway.

So we fell in love and we gave it a shot. Nothing wrong with that. Nothing at all. We leaned over, reached for the brass ring, and missed. This time—and maybe only by a little. Life is long and, from what I've seen, it's usually pretty good. It sure as hell beats the option anyway.

I leave you, Claudia, with a heavy heart but a strong conscience. I would only regret if I had not tried. As for now, live your life well. You are a great person like few I have ever seen. I wish you the very best of everything. You deserve nothing less.

I write out this poem for you for a number of reasons. I've never been that big on poetry but I went to the library yesterday to read some to help me understand you a little more.

As soon as I opened *Leaves of Grass*, I found this poem. I'd never read it before but it spoke to me immediately. I do not claim to be all that the poem envisions or embodies but I hope it helps you to see why I need to leave Philadelphia and see what else there is in the world.

Peace & Love,
Remy

Sixteen additional pages were attached to this note. Remy had handwritten each stanza of Walt Whitman's *Song of the Open Road*. Through clouded tearful eyes, I devoured each word. To this day, I find myself often slipping mindlessly into recitations of Whitman:

> From this hour I ordain myself loos'd of limits and imaginary lines
> Going where I list, my own master total and absolute,
> Listening to others, considering well what they say,
> Pausing, searching, receiving, contemplating,
> Gently, but with undeniable will, divesting myself of the holds that
> would hold me.
>
> I inhale great draughts of space,
> The east and the west are mine, and the north and the south are mine.
>
> I am larger, better than I thought,
> I did not know I held so much goodness.

All seems beautiful to me,
I can repeat over to men and women You have done such good to me
I would do the same to you,
I will recruit for myself and you as I go,
I will scatter myself and you as I go,
I will scatter myself among men and women as I go,
I will toss a new gladness and roughness among them,
Whoever denies me it shall not trouble me,
Whoever accepts me he or she shall be blessed and shall bless me.[1]

I was surprised how faithfully Remy adhered to his promises to keep in touch with me.

I received postcards from him almost on a weekly basis. I could set my watch by his promptness. In the beginning, the letters came scattered with return addresses from places like Detroit, Bismarck, and Denver. In the last letter I got, he was holed up in Vegas for a spell trying to replenish some lost cash.

I never wrote back to him, even though he left me with post office boxes all over the country.

---

[1] Whitman, Walt, New American Library, 1958, *Leaves of Grass*, "Song of the Open Road", p. 138, Stanza 5.

My Daughter's Life in the Year 2010

My water broke around dusk on October the fourth. I can't recall exactly what time my labor started because I don't wear a watch. I was nowhere near a clock when it happened.

I was riding the Philadelphia Phlash home from a shopping trip I made to The Gallery mall on Market Street. SEPTA had been on strike for almost three days and I wanted to pick up some last minute things for the baby. Being the queen of public transportation that I was, I didn't find the Phlash as bad as everyone made it out to be.

It was an oversized, purple mini-van. The word "Phlash" was emblazoned in mustard yellow on both of its sides. The plastic cab on its top extended high enough that you could stand up straight, as if you were riding a regular bus. It cruised the historic district, stopped at colorful well-marked berths, and usually ran right on schedule.

When I first found out I was pregnant, I started going to see a doctor at the HUP clinic. When I told Oliver about it, he flipped out and insisted I use his friend Maude Jackson instead.

Maude was a blue-black, heavy-set elderly woman from North Philly who'd been practicing midwifery on her own for decades. I didn't ask Oliver how he knew her; I just accepted his offer to hook me up.

At first, I was a little apprehensive about having the baby at home. But I combed Oz & Endz for books on childbirth and checked out nearly a dozen on the same topic from The Free Library on the Parkway. I read them all in one day. Afterward, I looked up at Oliver from my Indian-style perch on the brown, gravel counter of the front desk of Oz & Endz.

I closed the cover of *Having Your Baby with a Nurse/Midwife* and asked him, "Will you help me?"

With tears in his eyes, Oliver grabbed me and squeezed me so hard that I couldn't breathe. He pulled back and exclaimed, "Yes, Claudia. Everything will be perfect—I promise you."

Once Oliver was gone, I became very afraid of it all. I'd pretended to be so strong for so long that I even fooled myself. I forgot that I had to do it alone.

I almost chickened out when I got off the Phlash. I thought about going to the emergency room but I didn't because I trusted Maude. I beeped her from a pay phone. My phone was ringing in response when I walked into the loft.

Maude's voice was very excited as she spoke. She asked me how far along my contractions were and tried to get me to relax. She told me to lie down with my feet elevated and to concentrate on my breathing as we'd practiced in class. She assured me that she and her birthing assistant, Nico, would be at the loft in less than twenty minutes.

As I hung up with Maude, I shed a few tears for fear and tried to clean myself up as calmly as possible. On my way to the bathroom, I doubled over suddenly. I clutched my stomach with both hands as if I'd just been tackled by a professional football player.

I crawled to the couch, struggling to find my breathing pattern. I thought I was going to hyperventilate. A long moan escaped my lips and I thought of Remy. I wondered where he was and wished he were with me because I did not want to be alone anymore. I was so tired of being alone.

I closed my eyes and tried to think of peaceful thoughts and wistful dreams until Maude and her assistant, Nico, arrived.

Before long, I heard a knock and a rustling at the inside door. I'd left it unlatched when I'd come in earlier.

"Claudia?" came Maude's husky voice from the hallway. She was peeking hesitantly into the loft through the cracked open doorway. "Claudia, darling? Where are you?" she called again.

"Over here Maude," I cried. "Hurry, please. It hurts. It fucking hurts like you wouldn't believe!" I finished, gasping for air.

"I know, sweetie. It'll all be over with before you know it," Maude answered, as she pushed through the door with bags and towels draped over her arm.

"Go," she mouthed the word to Nico, as she nudged Nico over in my direction.

"We called the hospital, Claudia. It's purely precautionary—just in case we need anything," Nico said, rushing to my side.

"Hi Nico," I whispered, mustering up the tiniest bit of strength I could spare.

"Maude? Maude? What's going on?" I shouted into the kitchen where I could hear her noisily clanking pots and pans.

"Don't worry, dear. I'm just going to fill the sink to make sure everything's ready for us. I wasn't expecting your call so soon. How far apart are we now anyway?" Maude asked in a soothing maternal voice.

"Around three minutes," Nico replied for the both of us.

"Nico, why don't you help the poor thing into something more comfortable. Hell, anything would be better than that shirt; it looks so tight. I've got a gown in that blue duffel," Maude offered carefully.

"Check the sheets in the bedroom too please, Nico. We should move in there," Maude advised, as she continued to move about in the kitchen.

"Did you take that crazy tent down, Claudia?" she added, addressing me directly.

I didn't answer her. Instead, I wallowed miserably, fixating on the disbelief that they were going to try to move me. Nico stood up while I flinched defensively. I felt like a beached whale that was unwillingly being pushed back into the ocean.

"O.K., Claude. You ready?" Nico asked. "I know you don't want to do this but trust me. You'll feel so much better in your own bed," she said. She took me by the arms and started to force me up.

"Wait!" I screamed deafeningly. Nico smiled and stopped to brush my hair from my sweating forehead.

"I know," she whispered. "It won't be long now," Nico continued.

I inhaled deeply, arched my back, and placed my hands behind me for support. Nico helped to steady me. My eyes popped wide open, blinded by pain. We settled in the bedroom and Maude joined us within minutes.

My labor lasted for five hours. I insisted on going natural and refused an epidural. I was O.K. for awhile but eventually the force of the ordeal made me beg Nico for something to help me through. By that time, however, it was too late. I was passed the point where they could safely administer Demerol.

When my contractions started coming one minute apart, I became so exhausted that I couldn't move anymore. Soon, I started to become delusional and began to black out in between my feeble attempts at pushing.

I screamed as I tightened all of the muscles in my body. I held my breath and flushed more droplets of sweat from all the pores in my skin. Maude told me to try to keep my eyes open but my instinct was to close them tightly. *Push. Push. Out. Out. Breath. Breath. Not here. No, I am not here. There is a black blanket over the landscape of my reality and I can only slip into other worlds.*

(We moved to Grays Ferry when Olivia was twelve. That was three years ago.

When Olivia came into my life, I was alone and afraid of much of the world surrounding me. Now that she is fifteen, I am alone and terrified of all of the world surrounding me.

I fear all that is different than I am.

However, Olivia has become both my comfortable crutch and the breadth of my existence. My purpose now is to divert my personal neuroses from fixations centered around my own misplaced position in the universe. Instead, I seek to protect her morality and mortality from the wicked, weary world.

I sit now at a table in the center of the kitchen of my row home on the 1900 block of Corlies Street. The five neighborhoods of Grays Ferry are still plagued by the same racial tension that has existed here since the Rizzo administration. Sentiment has not changed nor does it appear likely to in the foreseeable future.

The legs of my kitchen table are cold, ridged metal. The Formica table top is white and speckled with gold dots. It is covered with hurricane remnants of unfinished homework, dirty ashtrays, and plates that hold the crumbs and crusts of stale sandwiches. This table reminds me of the one where my Nana used to sit and drink Black Label beer late at night in her high-ceilinged, echoing kitchen.

As I sit here, I sip luke warm coffee and skim the morning paper. It is the second Tuesday in June.

Olivia bounds down the steps in a flurry. She pecks a dry kiss on my cheek and yells, "Bye, mom!"

As I glance up at the clock above the sink, I think to myself that she has already missed the 8:05 A. M. bus. I shake my head and pull my fuzzy, pink bathrobe shut. The fluffy plastic pads of my slippers brush with a swish over the cold tile of the floor.

She's gone. There is nearly complete silence. If I strain myself, I can hear the city's voice in the background.

I shuffle through the papers that Olivia has forgotten behind her. I pick up a piece and try to decipher the handwriting. It looks as though she tried to scribble the answers to the review questions for Doris Lessing's "The Rocking Horse Winner." I wondered what lie she would concoct for her teacher when she was called on to answer question number five.

I've been unemployed now for nearly six weeks. Once in awhile, I scan the newspaper looking for a position worthy of my adept skills and invaluable qualifications. The phone hasn't rung yet and I still have a few more months to collect. So most days, I opt to mull around the house inhaling Camel Light after Camel Light.

I haven't been myself lately. I haven't been myself in years but I'm thinking of making a change.

I need to make a change. I worry far too much about Olivia; her childhood has not been as privileged as mine and that troubles me. I am ready to leave Grays Ferry. I have been ready to leave since the day I got here. Other places beacon to me—places like New Orleans. But I know Olivia skipped school today, so it's easier for me just to sit here and fret.

I know exactly what she's doing. She's been pining away for weeks after this boy named Andre.

Andre frightens me. It's trouble that draws Olivia to him and I hope he hurts her soon, so that she can quickly get on with her life.

Andre heads the Junior Black Mafia in Grays Ferry. He hangs out at Lanier Park. Over the past few years, the park's turned. It's all black now. Although Olivia is light skinned, she's welcome there. I expect she's almost revered in a way because of her relationship with Andre.

I cannot set foot near the fence of the park because I am white. From time to time, I drift into Gabber Deans, the Irish bar on 29th and Tasker, and try to spy on Olivia from the corner. Olivia doesn't know I do this.

Today I decide to get up, get dressed, run some errands, and wander to Gabber Deans for a late morning cocktail to see her. I know she'll be in the park, watching Andre play basketball.

I yank the last of the pink, sponge curlers from my hair. I don a bright green Eagles jersey, a pair of Jordache jeans I bought at K-Mart, and my *yellowing, low-top chucks. A cigarette dangles from my lips with the poise of a truck driver. I chomp on a piece of Juicy Fruit gum as loudly as I can. I even crack it once or twice.*

I grab a couple of crumpled dollar bills I discover tucked away in another pair of my jeans and run downstairs to scrounge around for some change. I look everywhere, even underneath the pillows of the couch in our dusty living room. I come up with an additional fifty-three cents and some hefty sized lint balls.

I step out into the bright sunlight and blink the last remnants of sleep from my face. My eyes start to water slightly. I push a pair of plastic, Mickey Mouse sunglasses up over my nose and turn my head down. Eagerly awaiting my first Rolling Rock of the day, I start to walk slowly East toward the park.

Nothing has really changed much from last night. There is a bit more broken glass crunching underneath my feet from one or two of the cars that have been stolen or broken into in the dark. I move in a wide circle past the Tasker Homes, the projects that dictate much of the politics in Greys Ferry. Nearing the park, I think that I recognize a few of the figures guarding the corner in front of Gabber Deans. I lift my hand to them in a wave but stop myself. Unnoticed, I duck into the Chink store next door for another pack of smokes.

The Chinese guy behind the counter speaks politely to me in broken English. I ask him for a hard pack of Camel lights. He fumbles through the different brands of cigarettes dangling from a plastic dispenser high above his head. He is too short to reach them, so he pulls a stepping stool over to gain a few inches.

He teeters on the wobbly stool and struggles to pull down a soft pack of Camel's unfiltered. He apologizes to me for not having any in hardpack. He methodically begins to ring up four dollars on the register. I thank him but say that I can't smoke unfiltereds and turned to walk back outside.

I am too lazy to walk to the newsstand one block down. I curse to myself underneath my breath, knowing that I will be forced to bum cigarettes all day.

It is almost 10:30 A.M. as I saddle up to the bar inside Gabber Deans. Rick has just opened up. I am the first one here. At this hour of the day, the bar seems seedy to me. I realize that this is because I find myself in it so often. Anytime you find yourself sitting alone on a barstool hiding behind the dark desolation of alcohol while being pummeled with the smell of stale beer and loneliness, you can't help but feel as low as the curb you stepped over to get there.

"The usual, Claude?" Rick asks, as if reading from a torn and tattered Bukowski novel.

"Yeah, thanks Rick," I answer. I am not in the mood to chat. I pull my bar stool over as close to the doorway as possible. Rick had propped it open to let some fresh air inside to cleanse the place; it isn't working.

I stare out toward the park and scan for Olivia. I don't see her. I recognize Andre playing ball. He makes a shot and jogs lightly off the court to a dilapidated set of bleachers. He sits down next to a tall kid in a black leather jacket. They shake hands. I notice Andre drop something to the ground. He kicks a small vial over in the direction of the other kid.

Andre deals snap. Snap is the *new drug running on the streets today. I heard it gives you a rush like heroin without the needle. I stumbled across some once when I was looking for some cash in Olivia's room but I wasn't quite sure what it was. In my mind, that realization reaffirmed exactly how old I'd become.*

With abandoned eyes, I watch Andre adjust his sunglasses. Stretching the muscles in his bare chest, he leans back and juggles his basketball between his feet. He mouths a few words, which I cannot hear. I can tell that his voice is very loud.

Within a few seconds, a group of young girls comes into my view. I see Olivia emerge among them. She quickens to the bleachers and jumps up from behind Andre to wrap her arms around him. She lowers her lips to his, enveloping him in a long, pornographic kiss.

Andre's hands roll over Olivia's legs and linger on her thighs. I can't believe I let her out of the house this morning in a skirt that short. Either my hangover had been too thick to see through or she'd changed her clothes the minute she left home. I hope it is the latter.

I slug back the last sip of my first drink and order my second. I think to myself that the crowd of kids all looks very happy from a distance. I watch Olivia bow her head and inhale deeply from a vial no longer than a two inch long carrot stick. I turn my head down toward the bar and twirl the lemon around the bottom of my glass.

Rick interrupts me and slams another Rob Roy down in front of me. He decides that he wants to make small talk.

Rick is still washing glasses left over from the night before. "Still" is a word I often use to describe Rick. He has been working the same bar at Gabber Deans for over fifteen years.

"So Claude, how's your job search comin' along?" Rick asks.

"I haven't heard you say a word about applications or interviews," he adds loudly. His voice carries over the noisy swishing sound of the steaming hot water that is pumping through the sink's spicket.

"Not much luck right now, Rick. Thanks for asking," I answer.

"I'm takin' my time because I've still got the unemployment comin' in. I want to find something I'm really interested in. Ever since the book store closed, I just haven't been able to find my niche in the working world," I muse nostalgically.

"Yeah, what the hell ever happened down there anyway? One day, I'm buyin' books there for the best price in town—next day the place is all boarded up," Rick says.

"Yeah, Gus got sick," I tell him. "He couldn't handle the maintenance or the rent on his own."

"That's a shame," Rick mutters.

"Ahh," I continue in a drone. "Olde City's gone to shit anyway. It's almost as bad as around here by now."

"Whole fuckin' city's like that anymore, Claude," Rick says. "All the good people just got up and moved away. The rest of us just got trampled on and over. Now we've sunk too deep to get out," Rick theorizes with the sincerity only a bartender would know.

"Yeah, I guess that's part of it," I agree. "Sometimes, I think I stay here in town though because it's not really all that much better anywhere else. I figure, why waste the energy?" I add.

"You may be right—the grass is always greener. You gotta hold on to your dreams though, Claude. Without 'em, you don't have shit," Rick muses eloquently.

"Hey, you never told me why you didn't take over the shop, Claude. You woulda been perfect for it," Rick says.

"Yeah Rick, sometimes I think I would've been. I'm not really sure why I didn't. I just let the opportunity pass me by," I answer.

"Part of it was Olivia. Part of it was my innate fear of commitment to anything. Alot of it was the booze and the apathy that inevitably comes along with it," I say.

"Whatever it was, I let it go," I mumble, shaking my head. "Now the place is just a boarded up, abandoned building. Once in awhile, I walk past it and try to remember if it was ever really there at all," I whisper with a faraway look in my eyes.

"Have you seen Gus?" Rick asks.

"No. I hear he's pretty bad though. He's been in the hospital for over a month. I keep trying to get over to Camden to see him but getting into Jersey by public transport is such a hassle," I admit unenthusiastically, taking another sip of my scotch.

"Olivia out there?" Rick asks, motioning his head in the direction of the park.

I don't answer him. I gesture "yes" with a nod and turn to look outside again.

Andre has returned to the court while Olivia and her friends have moved to the bleachers. Olivia's best friend, Mahogany, is standing behind her. Mahogany's knees rest on Olivia's back. She starts to braid Olivia's extensions together.

I smirk remembering the thought of the first day Olivia came home with her extensions. She walked around for a week popping Tylenol because her head hurt so badly. Her eyes were stretched and pulled so far out to the sides that she looked like a dark skinned Asian girl. I thought she looked beautiful. She reminded me of Remy.

Andre makes a shot, causing some of the girls to stand up on the bleachers to yell and dance. Olivia doesn't budge except to sniff occasionally from her vial. Meanwhile, I sit inside Gabber Deans taking it all in. I swill another slug from my cloudy glass. I look up again in time to notice a beat-up, faded blue Saturn circling the circumference of the park.

I feel my stomach drop to my knees.

There are moments in life when the thought that something is wrong feels so strong that your instinct becomes more necessary than your breath. In these moments, the blanketing existence that is forced by certain sounds combined with certain smells and the aura of a certain time of day can almost smother you.

The sight of the beat-up, faded blue Saturn makes me feel the same way I did the night I discovered Oliver lying alone on our couch in the loft on Third Street so many years ago.

The Saturn jerks to a stop on the other side of the fence just behind where Olivia is sitting. I cannot see how many people are in the car. Olivia's back is toward Andre. Recognizing the Saturn, he immediately slams his basketball to the cracked black tar pavement below him.

The ball bounces high above Andre's head and crashes back to the ground. It hops up and down until it finally slows itself to a wobbly roll, stopping at the corner of the basketball court's fence.

Andre storms past Olivia toward the direction of the Saturn. I can tell he is angry from his cocky stride. In an attempt to prove his masculinity to both his girlfriend and his dedicated entourage, he struggles to maintain his composure.

I sip my scotch again and listen to the rusty creak of a car door from outside. A stocky boy of about sixteen thrusts the passenger side door of the Saturn wide open. He stumbles out of the car. He is holding a crinkled, brown paper bag in his right hand. He takes a long pull of a drink from the bottle inside the bag. I figure that it is a forty ounce of Colt 45.

The boy begins to make animated gestures with his hands and arms. His head lolls back and forth on his neck as he shouts at Andre. Andre lunges toward him but stops himself short before making contact with the fence.

The other boy does not flinch. Instead, he turns his attention toward Olivia. He flutters his fingers through the air and draws out the shape of an hour glass. Still yelling, he musters a sinister laugh from deep within and points directly at Olivia with his index finger.

I stop my thoughts for a moment and wonder to myself whether or not I should wander outside. I push my bar stool back. It jerks and screeches loudly against the cold, unyielding floor.

"Be back in a second, Rick," I mumble mindlessly. I don't wait for his response.

I plod outside and onto the pavement in front of Gabber Deans. I move toward the park, trying to keep my distance so that Olivia does not see me. It is difficult to hear their conversation because of the noise of the morning traffic.

"Yo, motha fucka," cries the kid from the Saturn. "That bag was bum. You ripped me off."

"Look, bro," Andre speaks coolly, with his head leaning back. "I tol' you, it din't come from me. Anything goin' through my hands is one hundred pe'cent pure."

"Besides man, you party and there ain't never no money back guarantee," he adds, straightening a pair of dark sunglasses across his face.

"What that mean, man?" the other kid screams in anger.

"You pro'lly spent the money on yo' fuckin' pretty white girlfriend already. Ain't that right?" he says, jerking his head back in Olivia's direction. I cringe as the hair on the back of my neck begins to prickle.

"Leave her the fuck outta this, you hear me bro?" Andre snaps viciously. "This between me an' you," he threatens, moving closer toward the fence that separates the two boys.

"Yeah, that cuz she so fine. Ain't it?" taunts the kid.

"That's why you gettin' so mad. Gots me why she'd want an ugly lookin' nigga like you," he says, pushing Andre further. The boy's eyes turn to Olivia.

He addresses her directly: "Whatchoo doin' sweet thang?"

"Why don'chew come out here and come for a ride wit me?" the boy asks. "I gots somethin' nice an' big I know you gonna love, girlfriend," the boy prods, grabbing his crotch in his right hand with an exaggerated movement.

"Get the fuck outta here, man," Andre yells, jumping in front of Olivia.

Olivia moves to the side so she can still see the boy. She screams at the top of her lungs, "Kiss my black ass, and big, fat, black titties!!!"

Olivia lifts up her shirt to expose her bare chest to the boy. I shake my head sadly.

"You be beggin' for it soon enough, sweetie," the kid answers her with a sinister laugh.

"Awww, girl. Come on," Andre demands as he lunges at Olivia. He tries to tug her shirt back down. She quickly jerks away from him.

Infuriated, Andre begins to scale the fence in the direction of the other kid. Then, Olivia starts after Andre in a feeble attempt to pull him back down to the ground. Olivia is stopped short as the kid yanks the near empty forty ounce from its paper bag sheath. He launches the bottle directly into Olivia's face.

The bottle crashes through the metal fence, spraying in glass splinters around Olivia's head. She is not able to shield herself. The fence provides no protection from the flying glass shards, which spiral toward her flawless, smooth skin.

Just as Andre clears the top of the fence's barbed coils, the kid jumps into the back of the Saturn. The car speeds away furiously, leaving behind clouds of billowing dust and gas fumes. Andre lands back on the ground with a dull thud. He is left standing alone between the Saturn's tire tracks, which lay crookedly in the dirt.

I stand on the street corner, frozen in my own footsteps. I want desperately to run to help Olivia. Instead, I turn and run. I don't know what else to do. I stiff Rick for my drinks, knowing he will add it to my tab.

I run from Gabber Deans. I run from the park. I run from Andre. And I run from Olivia—just when she needs me most.

I should be ashamed of myself.)

Thoughts so sad ought never to occur. I will take all to the grave long before.

To some, control may prove relative. To me, control remains ever-evasive. Running away is what I have always done because running away has always been easier than chasing my dreams. Selfishly, I believe my own redemption will find me while I sit still and waiting.

Then, there was this tiny baby girl and I still sat—waiting.

After five hours of labor, Maude placed my seven pound, fifteen ounce daughter into the cradle of my arms. Tears filled the corners of my eyes and I thought of Remy. I remembered again that I was alone. I was alone because I was different and Remy moved away without me because I was afraid.

I pictured the feeling of New Orleans in my soul, kissed her forehead, and declared her name.

"Olivia Prytania Thomas," I muttered to all and to no one, in the same breath.

My head fell back deeply into the pillow, exhausted and spent. So small. So small. So small.

This child will be brought up to believe that no difference of any kind is wrong.

Thanksgiving Dinner

Control.
    Relationships are all about control. Who has it—and who doesn't.

But everyone—whether they wear it on their sleeve or bury it deep within—everyone wants to believe in the romantic ideal. Everyone wants to believe in their soulmate because they don't want to be reminded that they're really alone.

Companionship is conveniently comfortable. It allows one to pretend that the complete loss of his or her existence as an individual is possible. Becoming a "we" requires the surrender of the "I" and the "you".

Phoebe called me in mid-November, crying hysterically. She and Manuel were having problems.

San Francisco treated Phoebe and Manuel well for almost a year. At the end of the summer, Manuel announced that he was ready to move back to Columbia. He flew out of SFO in the second week of September. He invited Phoebe to follow him.

Phoebe worked her ass off to save money to get out of the States. She flew out of San Francisco almost a month later and called me from Newark during her lay over. She was in Bogota later that night. I wasn't home when she called, so she left a message on my machine. I didn't even get to tell her about Olivia.

Manuel's father was a big-shot diplomat for the Colombian government. He was heavily involved with one of the more infamous drug cartels running to and from Miami. Political unrest in the country was so commonplace that the family kept a second house on Hibiscus Island for times when they were forced on the lamb.

Manuel's dad got him a cushy office job in one of Columbia's domestic affairs offices. He moved into his parent's mansion to keep up appearances and rented a flat buried deep in town for Phoebe to live in. Phoebe wasn't allowed to visit Manuel unannounced, for fear his parents would disapprove of his involvement with an American girl. She met his mom once and was introduced as nothing more than an old friend from his Wharton days.

Phoebe and Manuel seemed happy enough for the first week or two. In between meetings with his father's cronies, he would take her out shopping or to eat long lunches. And he stayed with her nearly every night.

But Phoebe decided she wanted to play house. She started to smoke more and more pot. She started sleeping an average of over twelve hours a day. She developed all sorts of strange neuroses fixating on an unhealthy obsession with Manuel. She wouldn't leave the flat without him. She wouldn't see other people without him. She wouldn't leave the phone unattended for a minute for fear that he would call and she would miss him.

Then, Manuel stopped coming around as much.

I knew what was happening the day Phoebe called and declared, in a mopey tone, that Manuel went out to dinner with some of his friends. He'd gone without her. She'd stayed home alone and called me.

After a few weeks of less and less Manuel and many, many tears, I finally convinced Phoebe that it was best for her to come home to Philadelphia. Coming home is inescapable. Leaving is a part of growing up but letting go isn't necessarily part of the process.

Phoebe's flight was due to land in Philadelphia at 6:45PM on the Tuesday before Thanksgiving. Despite Phoebe's protests, I vowed to meet her at the airport. We agreed that she would stay with Olivia and me at the loft. I was excited to see her. As much as I hated to admit it, I desperately needed help with the baby.

I bundled Olivia up in the fleece, pink parka that Avery had given me at the shower she'd thrown for me in September. The parka was humongous on the baby. You could only see her chubby, flushed cheeks peeking out from behind the fuzz of the hood. I kissed her lightly on her forehead and paused to inhale the soft smell of baby. It made my heart flutter.

Holding Olivia against my hip, I looked in the mirror at myself. I let out a deep sigh. I hadn't worn makeup in weeks. I had dark circles under my eyes and my hair was so dry that the curls looked more like frizz than ringlets. I worried that it might be growing straight. I tried to run a brush through the tangled mane but tossed it aside in disgust. I ran a thin layer of lipstick over my lips and slipped into my black leather jacket.

I stocked the stroller with Olivia's diaper bag and two bottles of milk I'd pumped the night before. I crammed Tinky Winky, her purple Teletubbie, and her favorite rattle into one of the pockets already overflowing with baby powder and "Kiss My Face" lotion.

We plodded down the freight elevator and slowly worked our way over to the Chocolate Works. The condos ran a shuttle van to and from the airport. The shuttle was for tenants only but I was determined not to schlep across town on the subway and train that day. I even wished for a minute that I still had Oliver's Volvo but I'd sold it in August to some punk with a mohawk to make rent. I'd seen it parked on Fourth and South a couple of times since then.

The driver knew we didn't live in the condos but he let us on for ten bucks anyway. I made small talk with him about Olde City and the traffic on 95. I tipped him well and he helped me and the baby out of the van in front of the "International Arrivals" terminal.

We passed the ticketing and baggage check and moved toward the escalator to our left. I tilted Olivia's stroller onto its hind wheels and stepped onto the flat grooved metal, which crumpled into a rolling staircase. I was already exhausted from carrying Olivia and all of our paraphernalia.

Once on the second level, I stopped to scan the bed of televisions above my head for Phoebe's arrival gate. Her flight was supposed to be on time. She was coming in through C-9, the last gate in the corridor.

I wandered through the maze of overpriced gift shops, understocked newspaper stands, and "Real-Philly" pretzel trucks. I struggled to dodge the beeping airline carts carrying old people and their luggage to different gates. I passed an airport bar and thought, for a moment, about stopping in for a quick Rob Roy. I stopped myself though, remembering how expensive airport drinks were.

I pushed Olivia's stroller through the security clearance at Gate C and followed the long hallway nearly to its end. We plopped down into one of the plastic chairs in the row beneath the wall of windows.

I lifted Olivia into my lap and turned to watch the incoming and outgoing airplanes. I loved to see them lift off the ground. I pulled out a bottle and began to feed Olivia. I sat and waited patiently for Phoebe.

I closed my eyes and took in a deep breath.

("Separations in life lead to different experiences," she proclaimed.

"Separation is a fact of life," the Iaos reminded her.

"There are certain relationships that one hopes to keep frozen in time in an untouchable, safe vacuum," she told them.

"Relationships such as these are few and far between," laughed the Iaos.

"Yes, but coming back to them after much time has passed and testing them against one's new self—as it is bred from separation—remains the true measure of life-long friendship," she assured herself.)

I tucked Olivia's bottle away into the diaper bag and watched as Phoebe trodded up the ramp with her two carry-ons. Olivia coughed and let out a small cry with my sudden movement. I struggled to my feet and waited to catch Phoebe's eye.

Phoebe was blinking and turning her head from side to side, scanning for me. I lifted my arm above my head and waved. A slow, steady grin overtook her face. She rushed toward me. Phoebe reached me, dropping one of her bags to the floor. She grabbed me in a bear hug, which tangled us among the straps of the other bag still hanging heavily around her neck.

"Claudia," she said.

"Phoebe," I whispered.

"And this must be—" Phoebe started with a smile.

"Olivia Prytania," I interrupted her with a proud posture.

"She's beautiful, Claude. Absolutely beautiful," Phoebe commented. "Just like her mother," she added, kissing me on the forehead.

Phoebe twirled her index finger over and around Olivia's hand. Eventually, the tiny hand opened and clasped itself around Phoebe's giant finger with the blinding strength of a child's grasp.

"So how are you, sweetie?" Phoebe asked with a sigh, shifting the conversation and her stare back to my direction.

"Glad to see you," I replied. "I told everyone you were coming into town; they're so excited."

"What d'ya say we head back to the loft, so you can get settled in?" I continued.

"I'd like that," Phoebe replied.

We trampled down the escalator to the baggage claim where we captured the rest of Phoebe's scant belongings. I looked around for a pushcart so we wouldn't have to drag everything through the airport by ourselves. I couldn't find one though. So Phoebe and I giggled furiously as we wrestled with bulging bags, suitcases, a straw sombrero, a stroller, and a baby.

We stepped outside into the crisp, November air and Phoebe flagged a Yellow Cab. The driver was Indian and did not offer to help us load the cab. Phoebe pounded on the trunk with her fist and yelled at him. He jumped out, clearly agitated. He shot Phoebe an irritated look and popped the trunk. He started to lift some of the bags from the ground but Phoebe snapped at him.

"No. Her," she nodded at me. "Go help her," she demanded, instructing him to help me into the back seat. I shook my head, laughing at her smugly.

We took I-95 and came into the city from the Delaware Avenue exit. I watched as Phoebe took in her surroundings. Her eyes were as wide as saucers. She looked excited to be home.

The cabby dropped us off in front of the loft. Phoebe paid him generously and we hurried inside from the cold. Phoebe wandered through the loft, discovering all the discarded pieces I'd acquired from beloved old friends like Oliver and Remy, trinkets I'd borrowed from the bookstore, and unwanted art I'd adopted from housing starving artists showing at First Friday.

Phoebe unpacked while I put Olivia to bed. Once we were settled, Phoebe and I sat around the library table, nibbling on cheese and crackers and celery and carrot sticks. We got drunk on Bully Hill wine and talked until the streets cleared themselves of Olde City's unruly bar patrons.

We decided the best way to announce Phoebe's return to Philly was to make Thanksgiving dinner for all of our friends. We made plans to shop all the next day for our feast. We passed out on the couches late that night, anxious to sleep so tomorrow would come.

I remember thinking to myself that nights like that are so perfect and come so few and far between that my only remaining wish was to stop time.

The next day was Wednesday. Phoebe slept until noon, while I tried to keep Olivia as quiet as possible. Around 11:30 AM, I started to make phone calls to try and recruit people for Thanksgiving Dinner.

Stuart and The Countess were ecstatic with the thought of seeing Phoebe. They insisted that they couldn't wait until tomorrow. Stuart suggested that I call The Shack because a celebration was rumored to be brewing there. I hit the jackpot when Avery answered the phone. Ossie and Cedric were trying to force her into cooking a feast at The Shack. Avery was just looking for an excuse to get out of it. She jumped at my invitation for the three of them.

By the time Phoebe rolled out of the tent, our guest list stood at five. Phoebe's eyes started to perk up as she sipped her coffee and listened to me tell her who would be coming. She seemed excited enough but asked if I would mind if she also invited her friend Nico.

Nico was one of Phoebe's friends from Penn. Nico lived in Manhattan and danced with the Rob Jenkins Dance Company. Phoebe told me that Nico was dating a "guy" from Philly, so she'd been spending a lot of time in town over the last few months. Although I was none too fond of Nico, I grinned and agreed that she would be a welcome addition to dinner. Phoebe later confessed that the "guy" was Ossie. She said Nico would probably show up on his arm whether we invited her or not.

After we'd washed up and dressed, Phoebe and I dragged Olivia outside. We took the Market/Frankford line up to the Reading Terminal and shopped. We shopped for the turkey and all of the trimmings. From the seventeen-pound bird to the cranberry sauce to the pumpkin pie with whipped cream, we bought it without much of a clue as to how to cook it all.

But we tried.

In the end, I was pleasantly surprised with how well everything turned out. The bird had been cooking for hours and looked as if it would be ready not long after we'd told people to arrive. The pies were baked and all of the sides prepared, waiting to be plopped into the oven or microwave.

Phoebe finished setting the table. She then busily began to light candles throughout the loft. I changed Olivia and slipped myself into a forest-green, crushed-velvet dress that I should never have been able to fit into so soon after being pregnant. I must admit that I was quite proud when I managed to zip it up in the back all by myself.

I came out of the bathroom to find myself thrilled at how great the place looked. An ivory-lace tablecloth covered the library table, which was lined with an enormous bouquet of autumnal flowers from Olde City Flowers. Each chair was adorned with place settings that looked nearly as exquisite as my mother's china. Phoebe and I had talked an old man at the antique mart on Sixth and South down to forty-five bucks for the whole set. I felt a little guilty about it because it was such a steal.

"I *am* impressed," I said to Phoebe, admiring our work.

"Yes. So am I," Phoebe agreed. "Cocktail?" she asked.

I shifted Olivia on my hip as I said, "As a matter of fact, I believe I will."

"Here, let me take her. You pour," Phoebe said as she lifted Olivia from me.

"She looks adorable, Claude," Phoebe added.

In the same breath, she continued in Olivia's direction, "You look adorable, Ollie." Phoebe shook Olivia's hand lightly.

I pulled one of umpteen bottles of Miss Love white wine from the refrigerator. I watched Phoebe play with Olivia and thought to myself how precious the two looked together. Phoebe had given Olivia a red velvet dress with black buttons that wrapped snugly to her neck. Shiny, black patent leather shoes with a thin strap kicked on her tiny feet. The colors of her outfit made the dark fuzz of her hair look softer than I remembered it feeling to my touch.

Mojo jumped down from the kitchen counter, startled by the sound of the front buzzer.

"I got it, hon," Phoebe shouted as she carried Olivia away to the door.

I immediately recognized the squealing, awkward voices of Stuart and The Countess.

"Hi guys," I chirped from the kitchen. I peeked around the refrigerator for a better view. It was one of the few times of late that I'd seen The Countess not in drag. I figured he was going by Ezra for the evening.

"Hi Claudia," they both echoed in synchronicity.

As Ezra began making goo-goo eyes at Olivia, I turned to open the oven and check on the bird. Stuart snuck up behind me and bumped me lightly on the hip. I shot up straight, dropping the turkey baster to the floor. Stuart giggled, standing in front of me. He was holding the boys' coats and a heavy-looking, brown paper bag.

"Hi," Stuart whispered, leaning to kiss my cheek.

"The place looks great," he said as he paused and handed me the bag. "A gift for our fabulous hostesses," he added. I accepted the bag gingerly. I could still feel the cold air coming from the package.

"Stuart, you guys didn't need to bring a thing," I scolded, peering to see what they'd brought. Inside the bag were a bottle of Stuart's favorite Portuguese wine and three jars of honey. The tops of the honey jars were covered with blue and white checkered cloth secured with white ribbon.

"I got the honey from that guy in my building who keeps bees out in Bucks County," Stuart told me.

"The one that always used to hit on Phoebe?" I asked.

"The one and the same," Stuart replied. "Where do you want our coats, Claude?" Stuart asked, holding them up for me.

"Just toss them into my tent so Mojo can't get at them," I instructed.

"What can I get you guys to drink, Stuart? Beer? Wine? Phoebe even made a great big bowl of sangria," I offered.

Before Stuart had time to answer, Ezra piped up from the front, "Ooooh, sangrrrria puh-leeze."

"Yes, sangria," Stuart chuckled, as he moved to drop off their coats in my bedroom.

"Claudia. She is sooo precious," Ezra purred, rubbing his nose against Olivia's. "May I please hold her?" he asked, reaching to take her from Phoebe.

I could tell that Olivia was in store for a full night of shifting, cuddling, kissing, and patting. I hoped she wouldn't get too fussy. "Sure, Ezra," I answered, as I spooned ladlefuls of sangria into punch glasses for them.

The doorbell rang again and Phoebe moved to answer it. I could hear heavy footsteps clomping up through the stairwell as she opened the door to the loft. Avery and Cedric trailed inside following Phoebe's lead. They brought with them a fresh bouquet of flowers and two additional bottles of wine. The loft grew noisier. It was welcome noise that filled an all too often silent loft. I smiled at the thought of feeling happy again.

Everyone seated themselves on the couches and chairs arranged in the open center of the loft. I regained possession of Olivia from Ezra and climbed onto one of the windowsills facing Third Street. Phoebe circulated among our small crowd of guests, serving trays of veggies and cheese and crackers. She also refilled glasses of sangria and wine. Everyone began to chomp and chatter cheerily.

I thought about putting the finishing touches on dinner but we were still waiting on Nico and Ossie. We couldn't start without them; they were bringing the Pictionary. I sat quietly and listened to my friends make conversation.

"So Ossie, I hear Cyclone's gonna be working with The Wu-Tang Clan," Ezra said, musically.

"Damn, boys. How'd you manage that?" asked Phoebe, in her best hip-hop voice.

"Cedric's been workin' it," Avery chided, with a grin.

"Yeah, I been up in The City a lot lately," Cedric started, nodding his head back and forth. "Wu-Tang needed some serious graphics for their next video. I gave the brothers the pitch and they're psyched," he said, stabbing his fist into the air in front of him.

"What are you doin' for them?" Ezra asked.

"Their next album's called 'Killer Bees'. In the video, my boys are runnin' around The City tryin' to escape this swarm," Cedric explained.

"You guys gonna do the bees?" Ezra jumped in.

"Yeah, we're doin' the bees," Ossie repeated. "I gotta get up to PCA on Monday to see if I can get some kids to work cheap. We've only got two graphic artists on staff now and they're costin' way more than we're bringin' in," Ossie complained.

"Yeah man, but if it fuckin' works out they're gonna let us do the cover art for the album too," mused Cedric.

"And if doesn't, you guys are fucked," laughed Avery.

"What's up?" asked Phoebe.

"Ask 'em what Wu-Tang did to their manager on their last tour," coaxed Avery, squirming in her chair.

"Lay off, Avery," Cedric warned, angrily.

"Nah, ask 'em," Avery continued, putting Cedric on the spot. Everyone in the loft stared at him with wide-open eyes. He couldn't escape without answering.

"It was a totally different fuckin' situation, man," Cedric said, gesturing uncomfortably.

"The dude fucked up some tour dates and the brothers did a little number on 'im," he said.

"Little number?" cried Avery in disbelief. "The dude was in the hospital for over a month," she screeched, scrunching up her face.

"Whatever, Avery," Cedric said. He dismissed her with the wave of his hand.

"O.K." Ezra slurred awkwardly, in an attempt to change the conversation. "Hey Avery, what time did you say Nico and Ossie were getting here?" he asked.

"The turkey smells great—I'm dying to eat," he added.

"Ezra's probably right, Claude," Phoebe agreed. "I hate to start without her but you know Nico's always late," she said. "We should finish getting things together. I'm sure those guys are gonna be here any sec," Phoebe added as she started to get up.

"No, Phoebs. You relax. Play with Olivia for a bit. I can handle things in the kitchen just fine," I answered her as I got up from the window ledge.

"You sure?" Phoebe asked.

"Positive," I said as I handed her Olivia. "I'll call you when I need help," I finished.

"Claude, I'd love to help you out but wanna play too," Avery chirped in a whiny voice. She walked across the floor on her knees stopping next to Phoebe who was still sitting on the smallest of the three couches.

"Not a problem. Anyone need anything?" I asked.

"SSSSSangria," tumbled from Stuart's tongue. He tried to make the letter "s" sound like the hissing of a snake.

"Here, let me spoon," he pleaded as he grabbed my waist from behind and pushed me into the kitchen.

"Another glass here, please," Ezra called after us, batting his eyelashes in a flurry.

Gingerly, I peered into the stove. I poked, prodded, and squirted at the bird. I checked the stuffing and shoved the biscuits in afterward to bake. I drained the gravy, mashed the potatoes, and got the veggies going all before Stuart filled one glass of sangria from the giant fruit bowl.

"Veritable Julia Childs, aren't we?" he joked.

I grunted after him, too wrapped up in my cooking to make any sort of a half-witted comeback. After Stuart finished filling Ezra's glass, he pushed himself up onto the kitchen counter top, which was closest to me. He sat perfectly still, sipping his sangria with a pensive, far-off stare. I didn't want to know what he was thinking. I could tell it was going to make me sad and I didn't want to be sad right now.

"This is the first time I've been in the loft since Oliver died," Stuart said. "It looks different, but it feels the same."

"Feels the same?" I repeated, stirring the green beans.

"Yeah, it feels like I've been away for a long time but then like I never left at all. The voices in the background. The light coming in through the front windows. The way everything is empty but overcrowded. It just all reminds me of him," Stuart mused, shaking his head. I stayed silent.

"He liked to have people here," Stuart continued. "He didn't like being alone."

"Being alone scares a lot of people," I commented, sneaking a taste of the potatoes.

"Yeah, I guess that's why they invented television," Stuart muttered.

"And the Internet," I added.

"I miss him," Stuart said.

"I know," I whispered.

The doorbell rang, interrupting us. Stuart jumped down from the counter, kissed me on the cheek, and scuttled away to give Ezra his drink.

I heard Phoebe answer the door and listened for Nico's awkward voice. I watched her enter the room gracefully. Ossie followed after her with his head bobbing and jerking about as he spoke in animated sentences. He wore a pair of black vinyl pants that were ripped in the crotch. Shaun Cassidy's mug was emblazoned on the front of his orange T-shirt. I thought that his shoulder-length, dirty blonde hair looked greasier than usual.

I watched Nico brush her hands over the soft peach fuzz atop Olivia's head and smile faintly. Ossie left Nico's side and joined the small crowd in the living room. After he called into me, he began to shake hands and mutter hellos.

"I've got the Pictionary," Nico yelled in my direction. She held up the box in one hand and toted an enormous jug of wine into the kitchen.

"Happy Thanksgiving," she said as she kissed my cheek.

"Happy Thanksgiving," I repeated after her in a deadpan tone.

Phoebe exchanged Olivia with me for the spoon and turned to stir the mashed potatoes.

"Help yourself to a cocktail, Nico," Phoebe offered. "Beer, wine, sangria. We've got it all," she explained.

"Damn, you girls went all out. Ossie!!" she cried in the direction of the crowd.

"Ossie, baby, what would you like to drink?" she screamed. Olivia started to whimper from the volume of her voice.

"Everything smells great," Nico said, not waiting for Ossie's response. "What time do we eat?"

"It looks like everything's almost ready," Phoebe said. "Would you mind trying to get everybody to the table?" she asked.

"Not at all," Nico answered and drifted toward the others.

Phoebe and I bustled about, dragging food out from the kitchen. Everyone was seated and waiting to eat within minutes. Phoebe and I took our places at opposite heads of the library table. Phoebe smiled a bright grin in my direction. My heart sank to my knees with a feeling of safety.

"I think we need a toast," Phoebe bellowed, raising her glass. Some hooting and hollering erupted from the group. Everyone followed Phoebe's lead and raised their glasses as well.

"It's wonderful to be home," Phoebe began, hovering over the cranberry sauce. "It's strange as well. I've been away for a long time. But, in my heart, each of you has remained exactly as I remembered. Each of you—even Oliver," Phoebe whispered in a soft voice.

"I am thankful because I can think of nowhere else I'd rather be just now," she said, pausing to inhale deeply.

"Happy Thanksgiving," she finished.

Phoebe pushed her glass forward to the sky and then pulled it back to her lips. We all mimicked her and sipped thirstily. A wave of "Happy Thanksgiving's" circulated about the table.

I was nervous that people would hate the food. But if anyone didn't like it, they didn't let on. I sat content, stuffing my face and cradling Olivia in my left arm. She was wide-eyed and happily gurgling. I could tell though that she was growing tired. She coughed periodically and started to emit the first small sounds of a cry.

I nearly cleared my plate. I stood up and announced that I was going to put Olivia down. Ezra jumped up and asked if I wanted help. I declined his offer and told him to enjoy the pumpkin pie.

I slipped away beneath the tapestries. Listening to my friends' voices, I changed my daughter. With a warm feeling tingling in my gut, I fed her quietly. I could hear her tiny mouth sucking hungrily as I rocked her to sleep.

Pictionary. If Stuart was in the room when we were playing Pictionary, I did everything in my power to finagle myself onto his team. We played four games. My team, with Stuart as our leader, kicked ass the whole way through.

It was nearly midnight by the time we'd finished the fourth game. Everyone started to make excuses as to why they had to get home. First, Stuart and Ezra announced they had to be going and then Nico and Ossie not soon thereafter.

Avery and Cedric stuck around a little longer. We played some corny CD's full of raunchy blues and finished off the last of the wine. We attempted to ponder deep, nonsensical thoughts about love and the notion of a soul mate. I fidgeted during this conversation, worrying that Phoebe might break down. She held her ground, however, and only brought up Manuel twice.

I stood up and ran the palm of my hand through her smooth straight hair. Phoebe arched her head back and looked up at me with a smile. She took my hand in hers and pulled it to her left shoulder where I let it rest briefly. Phoebe squeezed it tightly and brushed her lips over my knuckles.

I listened carefully as Avery rambled on about Plato's writings on love. I found it to be the perfect segue for me to interject my theory of the afterlife as it was based on quantum physics, continuing cyclical energy, and reincarnation into the mix. I spewed it out in less than five sentences and drifted into the kitchen to clean up. I started gathering scattered plates and glasses into the sink. Avery followed after me and asked if I needed help.

"Don't worry about it, Avery. Phoebs and I will get it all in the morning. I just want to get the food away, so Mojo doesn't have a field day," I told her. I didn't want to get trapped into a conversation; I only wanted to curl up in my bed.

"Good deal," Cedric exclaimed, as he carried a handful of empty wine glasses into the kitchen. "I'm exhausted and don't feel like sitting around watching the women clean up," he added.

"Cedric," Avery scolded him in an short voice.

"Claudia's right, guys," Phoebe said.

"You guys should get home. But you've gotta take some pie. I'm back out on the meat market again and can't afford any extra pounds around my waist line," Phoebe explained. She jumped up from the living room and started to wrap three slices of pumpkin pie in foil for them.

"Well, if you guys are sure," Avery said, sounding almost relieved. "I've got tons of shit to do tomorrow. Will you give Olivia a good night kiss for me?" she asked, in my direction.

"No problem," I answered.

Phoebe led everyone to the door and closed it tightly after them. I heard her flick the dead bolt and then pitter-patter off toward the stereo. I rinsed the gravy bowl methodically and lost myself in the sound of water running from the sink's spicket.

I recognized the sounds of the CD player shifting between disks. My head fell back between my shoulders. I closed my eyes and listened as Nina Simone's voice filled the quiet air of the loft.

"Do you miss him, Claude?" Phoebe said, moving back into the kitchen. I could feel her body behind me, shadowing my stance. I didn't turn around.

"Remy?" I asked. I didn't realize how stupid my question sounded until I heard it escape my lips.

"Claudia," Phoebe said, in a disappointed tone. Her breath was on the back of my neck. She moved away from me and pulled herself onto the counter top next to the sink. She sat cross-legged, sipping a glass of wine.

"I miss the idea of him," I answered.

"It's funny. I think about it sometimes but I can't remember him," I said. "I can't remember the things we used to talk about. I can't remember the way he felt to my touch."

"Sometimes, I feel like I can almost remember his smell but that's about it," I continued.

After a long pause, I concluded, "I think the only thing I miss is the idea of having someone."

"Have you heard from him?" Phoebe asked again.

"I still get letters," I answered. "I thought he would've stopped writing by now. Last I heard, he was thinking of spending the winter in Jackson Hole," I said.

"I didn't know he skied," Phoebe said.

"He doesn't. I guess he's looking to learn," I joked with a weak laugh.

"Do you think he'll come back?" Phoebe asked.

"Not for a long time," I said.

"Do you want him to come back?" she pressed further. Her words struck me as hard as if someone had thrown a basketball in my gut.

"Sometimes I can't help but wonder what things would be like if he were here. But then I realize it's not about him," I explained. "Something within *me* is unsettled and Remy can't change that."

"No one can change that but me," I said.

"That makes me sad, Claudia. I just want you to be happy," Phoebe muttered, almost under her breath.

"I love you," I told her. It was the first and last time I ever said those words to her.

We stood alone then in the silence of the kitchen, weary from so much thanksgiving.

Once you get what you want in life, you conjure up another dream. Then, you chase it. The farther away something is, the more beautiful it appears because you cannot touch it.

Something new. Something new. Someone. Where? I turn. I wonder. My vision? My eyes are closed to this world. I pray you do what you want and that you do it well. To be surrounded by well wishes. I wink. I blink. I just decide to close my eyes again.

If I could run away and hide. If I could change. If something different suddenly happened. If all of these same selfish people would stop making wicked evil demands on my time. If all this, then I could be free.

Dropping. Slipping. Disappearing. Satisfaction will come when I. When I. When I. When I wake tomorrow?

But what about "they?" "They" are still out there. "They" haven't gone away. "They" want me to do things. And yet, it is I who binds my life to triviality. It is this innate fear that I possess. This innate fear to do what I want. This innate fear of letting go.

My faith in tomorrow comes in believing that I have time. As if time were mine to be had.

To Come

*T*o *is a preposition.*[2]

I never said a word to Phoebe when she stopped dancing. She never formally declared that she was stopping; she just moved away with Manuel and didn't dance anymore. Perhaps there isn't room enough in the heart for more than one great love.

When Phoebe came back to Philly, her friends from the city's dance scene seemed to hunt her out. At first, I thought Phoebe seemed uncomfortable with even the utterance of the word "dance". But she wasn't able to hide her excitement from me for long.

On Thanksgiving Day, Nico told Phoebe that the Rob Jenkins Dance Company would be in town performing at the University of Pennsylvania's Annenberg Center on the first Wednesday in December. Nico put us down on the guest list for two and invited us both to the champagne cocktail hour afterward.

Phoebe accepted the invitation and arranged for Avery to watch Olivia before I had a chance to even think of declining.

Come is a verb.

I found myself peering into my closet in the loft at 6:45 PM on the first Wednesday in December. I was struggling to find an appropriate outfit to wear to the dance recital at the Annenberg. I always felt slightly uncomfortable around Phoebe's dance friends. They all weighed under a hundred pounds; I didn't.

---

[2]   All italicized entries this chapter excerpted from "To Come," *The Story of Lenny*, Lenny Bruce. Copyrighted by Douglas Music Corporation.

Phoebe was sacked out in front of the television, gorging on Doritos and Pepsi. She was clad in black jeans and a black silk blouse—the combined effect of which were tight enough to pass as a second skin. Her profile was thin enough to see through. I was only comforted by the fact that I knew she would wear her bulky, black leather coat over her skeleton.

The verb in transitive.

After I finally settled on a loose-fitting, red rayon dress, I pulled my hair up into a black velvet scarf and joined Phoebe and Avery in the center of the loft. Phoebe was holding Olivia, while she and Avery took turns smothering her with kisses.

It would be my first night away from Olivia since she was born.

"Avery, the bottles are in the fridge. She napped earlier, so you should be able to put her down around eight. I'll call from the performance to see—" I rambled on before Avery cut me off.

"Come on, Claude. You're insulting me. We'll be fine. Go," Avery commanded.

"She's right, Claude. We gotta get movin'," Phoebe said.

Phoebe rose crookedly to her feet, crinkled the Dorito's bag closed, and stretched widely. She dumped the bag in the kitchen and slinked into her black leather. She walked slowly toward me and wrapped her arm through the crook made by my elbow. Then, she laid her head on my shoulder in a playful way.

"All right, I know," I answered in a feeble attempt to appease both women.

"I'm ready. Let's go before I change my mind," I added.

"Don't act so excited, Claude," Phoebe spoke, sounding almost hurt. "Come on," she said as she tugged at my sleeve.

To come.

I kissed Olivia goodbye and Phoebe and I left for the performance. The air outside was crisp and cold. Olde City was buzzing with people. I could sense excitement in the air. The city's holiday-kickoff parade had started at 5:30 PM and was just beginning to wind down. Market Street was closed off from Fifth to Broad for the occasion. I shook my head thinking that Philly loved to close its streets for parties.

Phoebe and I toyed with the idea of walking the parade route but decided against doing so because of the crowd. We opted instead to grab the subway at the Second Street stop. I paused and glanced up Market before we turned down the steps.

I could feel Christmas. The lampposts were lined with twinkling lights, which hung in the shape of snowflakes. Green wreaths and red ribbons adorned the storefronts. People rushed around quickly on the sidewalks but the nameless faces seemed happier to me than they did yesterday. I closed my eyes and tried to imagine the sound of bells jingling, the taste of gingerbread, and the smell of pine. The image made me think of my mom. That made me feel warm.

When I opened my eyes again, I noticed tiny snow flurries fluttering through the already dark night.

To come.

Then, there was the smell of the subway.

A cold gust from one of the passing Eastbound trains hit me hard as Phoebe and I walked down the steps. Everything seemed metallic and dirty to me. The tunnels smelled like piss and everyone around us looked scared or angry. The subway ruined my thoughts of Christmas. I remember thinking to myself that if I could live in the pictures in my mind all the time, I would always be happy.

I swiped my SEPTA pass through the turnstile and plopped myself down onto one of the graffiti ridden benches to wait for the next train. Phoebe followed my lead and sat down next to me. I had been quiet for a long time. She turned to me and lifted up my face by my chin. She smiled and pushed a stray curl off my forehead.

I heard the train coming. We got on it without saying a word.

I've heard these two words my whole adult life.

After you cross the river into West Philly, the subway train climbs up to the city's surface and then is called a trolley. I don't mind riding the trolley as much as I mind riding the subway. On the trolley, you don't have to stare blankly at cement walls whizzing past you under flickering lights.

We crossed the river and our train was a trolley in fifteen minutes. Phoebe and I jumped off at the Fortieth and Baltimore stop and started quickly toward the Annenberg. It had stopped snowing and now felt colder outside.

We reached Penn's campus within minutes. I stole a glance at Phoebe before we started down Locust Walk. I recognized excitement in her face. I figured she was thinking of the past. When we climbed the steps of the entrance to the Annenberg, she turned to me with a wide grin, which shone her white teeth. She bounced up lightly on the soles of her shoes and rubbed her mittens together. Suddenly, I knew she was thinking of the future.

Phoebe flung the door open. Once she stepped inside onto the carpet, she stopped to look around her. She moved her head quickly from side to side, taking in the crowd. She turned back to me and tried to hurry me along. I stood back for a moment, staring at her. She looked beautiful and strong. She looked alive.

And as a kid when I thought I was sleeping.

"Nico said we had to pick up tickets at Will Call. I'm gonna run over to get them. Do you wanna come with me or do you want to wait by the steps?" Phoebe asked.

I scanned the room and noticed some people congregating around a television in a corner opposite from the ticket counter. It was previewing artists who would be performing at the Annenberg during the upcoming Next Move Spring Series.

"Phoebs, I'm gonna check that out," I replied, gesturing toward the television with a nod of my head.

"Cool," Phoebe said, as she squinted her eyes to see the t.v. screen.

We each drifted off in opposite directions. There was a small swarm of people immediately surrounding the television. I couldn't see what was on, so I turned back to watch Phoebe. She had reached the ticket window and was laughing with the girl behind the glass. I smiled too and the people in front of me moved away. I stopped dead in my tracks and stared at the screen until Phoebe came back.

To come.

"Oh my God, is that—" I could hear Phoebe's voice from behind me.

"Remy," I finished for her in a whisper.

"Wow," she exclaimed. "Is he coming back?" she asked.

"Pure Motion," I said.

"When are they performing?" Phoebe demanded.

"February," I answered.

"Did he tell you?" she asked, scrunching up her nose.

"I haven't spoken to him," I responded blankly.

"Oh Claude," Phoebe groaned. She seemed suddenly aware of me. I could tell that she thought I was sad. But I wasn't sad. I didn't feel anything inside. There was just a void.

To come.

The usher in front of the Zellerbach Theater announced that we could begin seating. I walked away from the television.

I slipped into the line of people who had begun to filter into the theater. Phoebe and I handed our tickets to another one of the ushers and I accepted a program from a girl with thin shoulders. She offered one to Phoebe also but Phoebe refused it. The girl shrugged her thin shoulders and extended the same bill to another couple behind us.

Phoebe ran her index finger across my jaw and then grabbed my right hand. I eyed her curiously. She pulled me hurriedly into the theater and led me down the center aisle. Phoebe and I moved past two elderly women and took our seats. They were great—only five rows away from the stage. I took off my coat and draped it over the back of my chair. I nestled myself into the coarse, red cushion and began to fan myself with the pages of the program.

It's been like a big drum solo.

Phoebe was clutching my hand again tightly. I wanted to pull away from her because my palm was sweating but I didn't. I looked around from the stage to the aisles to the seats and back to the stage. As I scanned the crowd, Phoebe seemed to recognize an older couple sitting across the room. She quickly dropped my hand back to my side and waved her fingers through the air in the direction of the couple.

"Oh look," Phoebe exclaimed, "it's Nico's parents."

"I'll have to go say 'Hi' during intermission," she said.

I nodded my head, acknowledging Phoebe's words. As she sat grinning, I pulled my free hand away from her and laid it in my lap. I began to flip through the pages of the playbill. It was pretty bare-bones—four pages of black and white biographies and a listing of Annenberg contributors. I ran my fingers across the program and casting. There were three pieces: "More Wine for Polyphemus," "Bite the Wax Tadpole," and "Narcoleptic Lovers."

Did you come? Good.

Phoebe burrowed back deep into her seat and stared straight ahead at the stage. She muttered, "God, it's good to be back."

I couldn't tell if Phoebe was talking to me or to herself. She was quiet for a moment and began to fiddle with the buttons on her black leather jacket. I kept my head turned down toward the program, only half-listening to her. For some reason, I wanted her to be quiet.

I did not want her to talk to me because I was afraid to hear what she was going to say.

"Claude, I talked to Rob the other day," Phoebe said to me. She sat up straight so she could see me more clearly.

I cut her off before she could continue speaking. I tried to change the subject as nonchalantly as possible but I heard my words. They sounded abrupt.

"Who's Polyphemus?" I asked.

"Huh?" Phoebe purred with a disturbed look and furrowed brow.

"Right here," I demanded, pointing to the word on the top of the program's second page. I tapped my index finger on the smooth, cool paper for emphasis.

"Oh, that," Phoebe said. "Polyphemus is a character from *The Odyssey*. He was a giant Cyclops who imprisoned Odysseus and his men in his cave by pushing a stone across its entrance," she explained. "The men escaped by deceiving him."

"How?" I asked.

"They blinded the monster with a poison they mixed in his wine," she replied.

I blinked at her. I knew what she was going to tell me but I had stopped her for now. I lifted my hand and cupped her face in my palm. Now I was sad. I missed Phoebe before she even told me she was leaving.

Did you come? Good.

"Aaggh," Phoebe moaned to break the tension. She jerked away from me and slammed her back into her chair. She slumped down low and breathed out a heavy sigh. She twisted her knuckles around the corner of her eyes to stop them from tearing.

"It says they're using Lenny Bruce in the last piece," I said.

"God, would you knock it off with the fucking program, Claude," Phoebe snapped. She tore the program from my hold and threw it into the empty seat in front of us. Surprised, I looked at her as if I were seeing her for the first time.

"I . . . I . . . I'm sorry," Phoebe stammered.

I leaned forward, searching for the program. It had slipped to the floor below and was lying face down with its pages flittering through the air. I wanted the program. I needed to hold it. It was like a security blanket that could protect me from her. I moved forward to recapture the program.

"No. Sit," Phoebe demanded. She rose and walked into the next row. She picked up the wounded pages from the rippled carpet and handed them back to me without saying another word.

We sat in silence until Rob Jenkins took the stage.

Did you come? Good.

Rob was short. He was probably only a few inches taller than I. He wore a tight orange and navy striped rugby shirt that reminded me of the costumes the characters used to wear on the t.v. series "Zoom." Underneath the shirt, his arms were riddled with tattoos. He adjusted the microphone and stood drowning in an oversized pair of jeans, which hung low over his Air Walk sneakers.

Rob thanked the Annenberg for inviting his Company to perform and graciously lauded the upcoming Next Move Series in order to garner support from the crowd. In conjunction with the Series, he mentioned Remy's name to a short rumbling of applause. I squirmed uncomfortably in my seat and could sense that Phoebe was purposefully avoiding my eyes.

Jenkins introduced the performance and invited the audience to attend a champagne reception in the Harold Prince theater after the show. The lights dimmed on cue.

I come better with you, sweetheart, than I do with anyone else in the whole damned world.

Mesmerized, I sat and watched the dancers spin delicately through their routines. They were each wrapped in mint green or ice blue leotards with matching flowing, chiffon robes, which they rolled and waved through the air. The dancers' movements were all consuming. I drank in the sound and the visual as if the combination of the two were my life's blood.

Nico performed in both of the first two pieces. She looked like a fragile china doll that would shatter if she were dropped to the floor. Nico held a long solo with Rob, during which a captivated Phoebe sat perched on the edge of her seat. I looked back and forth between the two of them as if I were watching a tennis match. I felt a pang of envy at the look that they each wore.

I really came so good.

After "Bite the Wax Tadpole," the lights came up to signal intermission. I blinked hard several times to accustom my eyes to the switch. I sat perfectly still and watched as much of the crowd rushed out to the lobby where rest rooms, cigarettes, and cold beverages anxiously awaited them.

Phoebe excused herself from me and slipped away to the opposite side of the theater to meet Nico's parents. Her face looked as if she wanted me to go with her but I did not. Instead, I stood up and enjoyed a deep stretch.

I thought for a moment about going to the lobby for a change of air but decided against it. There were too many beautiful people in the crowd. I felt safer staying where I was—alone and gawking. My eyes scanned the seats immediately surrounding me. Two rows ahead, a pixyish-looking girl stood against the back of the chair in front of her. She was directly facing me. The girl looked to be about my age and seemed virile and lithe. I, on the other hand, felt as if I were clumsy, giant, and awkward.

The girl exuded a sense of youth that seemed untouchable and foreign to me, as if youth were something that I could no longer possess within myself. The sight of her made me feel old and tired and alienated. It made me picture myself sitting on a porch swing in the Garden District of New Orleans, rocking slowly under a twilight sky.

The sight of the girl reminded me that I was not where I wanted to be. The sight of the girl reminded me that life was moving on in the place where I wanted to be. Life there was moving on without me, as I stayed here—silent and stagnant.

I really came so good.

"You O.K.?" Phoebe asked, returning to my side.

"Hmmm?" I mumbled, not hearing my sound. I started to turn my focus away from the girl and toward Phoebe.

"What's the matter?" Phoebe said.

"Oh nothing," I responded. "I was just thinking about where I was."

"Where you were?" Phoebe pushed.

"Never mind," I said. "How are the Falin's?" I asked.

"They're doing well," Phoebe answered. "They flew in from Pittsburgh last night. They asked if we were going to the post-show reception," she added. She threw the remark out rather nonchalantly. I could tell she was trying to gauge my responsiveness to attending.

"Really," I spoke in a hollow tone. I didn't want to go to the reception. I wanted to go home to see Olivia. Phoebe knew this.

"Nico's dad is soooo cute," Phoebe continued, ignoring the tension coming from me. "He's nervous about the next piece. It sounds like Nico's got a pretty racy lead in it," Phoebe explained.

"That's funny," I remarked, absent-mindedly. I was becoming more anxious and wanted the performance to start again. I was pleased when the lights began to flicker, calling the audience back to their seats for the final piece.

I really came so good.

The final piece was called "Narcoleptic Lovers." The dancers all wore black and performed to songs by Gavin Byers, Mio Morales, Mozart, Sinead O'Connor, and Urban Species. I didn't recognize most of the songs but I *was* especially intrigued by the Lenny Bruce monologue, which close the show. I even wrote myself a note to remember to track down the script later so I could use it in my own work.

It was called "To Come." During the text, Bruce bantered back and forth, enacting an imaginary conversation between a man and a woman. They talked about orgasms—having one, not having one, why the man wasn't having one, what not having one said about the relationship, what not having one said about the man, what the listener's reaction to the word meant. It was about hang-ups and how worrying about the implications of an action eliminated its very possibility.

Nico and Rob held the leads. They moved with and yet separately from the monologue. Their twisting and writhing was fast pointed and determined. I could hear their bare feet squeak against the stage floor. The squeaking made me cringe because their make-up and hair and perfection were just make-up and hair and perfection. They were touchable; they were not an image in my mind.

I watched Nico and Rob dance, listened to Lenny Bruce's voice, and began to feel aroused.

I hadn't been aroused since Remy and I had broken up in May. It made me feel dirty and excited at the same time.

Because I love you.

The lights came up again to a roaring applause. The Company took the stage with wide, sweeping bows. I smiled because I was happy and I clapped too because I thought it was a good show.

But don't come in me.

The theater began to clear out quickly. Phoebe and I filtered out of our row and into the lobby. She headed immediately to the Harold Prince Theater for the cocktail reception. I followed her begrudgingly.

We bumped into the Falin's at the door. Phoebe introduced me and began to chat with them. I felt out of place but stayed with the group.

We slipped into the dimly lit theater, in which a slowly increasing buzz of voices began to reverberate from wall to wall. I didn't recognize anyone in the room and noticed that the dancers had not yet arrived. I assumed they were undressing out of costume and busily collecting bouquets of flowers.

But don't come in me.

I spied an hors d'oevures table in the corner of stage left. I decided I was famished and excused myself from Phoebe and the Falin's. I started off in the direction of the long table where cheese, crackers, and other munchies awaited me.

I began to survey the grub and tried to choose my vice. As I seized possession of a stringy celery stick, the strong-looking hand of a man curled around my right side and stopped in front of me. The hand was holding a tall glass of champagne. It waited for me to accept its offering.

"Go on, take it," said a deep voice from behind me.

But don't come in me.

I took the glass and twirled around slowly. The face looked familiar but I couldn't place him. He realized this but did not flinch.

"Jordan," he said. "The name's Jordan," he added, as if the name would make me remember. I still had no idea who he was.

"I'm with Fringe," he told me. He drew out the word "fringe" with his voice and shook his head up and down.

"We met in the Spring after the opening of 'Nothing' at the Penitentiary," he explained, squinting his eyes in the nervous hope that he would jar my memory loose.

"Oh yeah, that's right," I remarked. I was a little embarrassed that I'd forgotten him but flattered nonetheless that he'd approached me at all. "I'm Claudia," I stated matter-of-factly.

"I know," he said, laughing softly at my need to remind him of my name.

"Hey, I'm sorry to hear about Oliver," Jordan offered, in a morose tone.

I can't come.

His words made my stomach churn. Jordan said "I'm sorry" as if "I'm sorry" could make the grass greener and put me in another place like New Orleans where I could cuddle up with Oliver on the day bed on a sleeping porch.

I gulped a large mouthful of the champagne and replied, "Yeah, you missed one hell of a party that night."

Because you don't love me, that's why you can't come.

I could tell my response made him uncomfortable but I didn't regret my comment.

"So what's goin' on?" I asked. "Drink any good Yoohoos lately?"

He snickered slightly. "Good memory," he answered.

"I've been living back and forth between Philly and New York," he said. "My girlfriend's in the Company. She's got a sweet studio in Hells Kitchen," he added.

My heart sank nearly to my knees. A girlfriend. I left Remy because I wanted to be alone but now I was jealous of everyone else that had someone. Watching other couples made me fear that I would never love someone. It made me afraid that I would never be happy.

I love you. I just can't come, that's all.

"Girlfriend, huh?" I said hoping not to appear shaken. "Did she perform tonight?" I asked, trying to sound interested.

"Yeah, she was great," he replied, with a smirk. "Her name's Kristin. She had the lead in 'Bite the Wax Tadpole'."

"So how's New York?" I questioned.

"Cool," Jordan exclaimed. "I've been auditioning for some stuff. Kristin travels a lot though, which kinda sucks because we don't get to spend much time together. Once my lease is up I think I'm gonna move for good," he explained.

"Awesome," I muttered with shallow enthusiasm.

I noticed that the dancers had begun to fill the room. I saw Nico move immediately toward her parents and Phoebe. She wore a baggy pair of Adidas sweats and a sports bra. She looked toned and in shape. I watched the other dancers and tried to guess, which of the sickeningly tiny girls was Jordan's girlfriend. I gave up in disgust.

"Well Jordan, I gotta get these back to my friends," I lied, referring to a plate of cheese and crackers that I lifted into the air.

"Yeah, Kristin just got here," Jordan said. "Claudia, it was really good to see you," he added. His tone sounded sincere.

"You too, Jordan," I lied again, as I turned to walk away.

That's my hang up. I can't come.

I heard his trailing voice exclaim he'd love to see me again sometime but I had already disappeared from the conversation. My stomach had started to hurt and all I wanted to do was go home. I approached Phoebe and the Falin's, dreading the thought of small talk.

Because you don't love me.

"Hello," I said with a long "O" as I joined the small group.

"Hi Claude," Phoebe said as she grabbed my hand and pecked a kiss on my cheek. "Who was that?" she pried, glancing back in Jordan's direction.

"Just a friend of Stuart's," I replied. "Hi Nico," I said, quickly changing the subject.

"Hi Claude. I'm so glad you came," Nico answered.

I cringed when she called me "Claude." Only people who were close to me called me "Claude." Nico knew instantly that she'd overstepped a boundary. Phoebe rubbed my back in tiny circles as if she were trying to calm me down.

"How's Olivia?" Nico asked, trying desperately to recover.

"She's great," I said. "Avery's watching her for me tonight."

"Mom, Claudia just had a baby in October," Nico turned to tell her mother.

"Ohhh, that's wonderful," Mrs. Falin crooned, smiling in my direction. "How big was she?" she asked, glancing down at my left hand for a wedding ring. She looked back into my face. I could tell she disapproved of me.

"Seven pounds, fifteen ounces," I answered, moving closer toward Phoebe.

Just what the hell is the matter with you?

I brushed a lock of Phoebe's silky hair from her ear and leaned into her. I whispered, "Phoebs, I don't feel very well. Do you wanna get out of here soon?"

"You all right?" she questioned.

"Fine," I said. "I'm just really tired."

"O.K." Phoebe said. I knew the Falin's couldn't hear our conversation but they were curious what we were talking about. Mrs. Falin looked at me as if I were taking the spotlight away from her daughter.

What does that got to do with loving you?

"I'm sorry," Phoebe addressed the Falin's loudly. "Claudia needs to get home to check on Ollie," she stated matter-of-factly. Phoebe was great at making excuses.

"Oh, that's too bad," Nico whined. "We're heading over to Walsh's later on, and I thought you guys might want to go," she continued. Even though Nico used the word "guys," I knew she was specifically speaking of Phoebe.

"I wish I could," Phoebe said. "But I've got a ton of stuff to do for tomorrow."

"All right. I'll give you a ring when I wake up," Nico gave in.

I felt threatened by Nico's answer, as if she were going to take something away from me—something I loved very much. I stole a glance in Phoebe's direction to try to read her face. She avoided my eyes. I felt her slipping away from me. My face flushed and tears began to swell up in the corners of my eyes.

"Claudia, it was great to see you again. Thanks so much for coming," Nico offered, as if she felt sorry for me. I hated pity more than any other emotion. It symbolized weakness and made me nauseous.

"Have fun with Olivia at Christmas," she added smugly.

"Thanks, Nico," I responded, half-heartedly. I knew I'd lost Phoebe to her. My pride was so wounded that I thought it would burst in front of everyone and embarrass me in their eyes forever.

"You really were terrific tonight. Good luck with the rest of the tour," I said with a nod. The well wishes took all of the strength I could muster.

We bid goodbye to the Falin's and Phoebe gave Nico a final bear hug. After bundling ourselves feverishly into warm layers, we were off again into the frigid December cold.

I just can't come, that's all.

We cut back through Penn's campus in the direction of Baltimore Avenue to catch the trolley. We hugged the shadows of the sidewalk and Phoebe started to furrow through her bag. I knew she was looking for her dug out. I was glad we were going to get high. I was upset and knew it would help me to relax.

"Here you go," Phoebe said. Her words sounded funny to me because she was holding her breath to keep the smoke she had inhaled swirling inside her lungs.

"Thanks," I replied, accepting the bat. I took off my right mitten and touched the metal. It already felt hot. I interrupted my step for a moment to light the weed again and took a quick puff as we neared the trolley stop.

"Shit," Phoebe yelled abruptly, as we both spotted the trolley rattling down its tracks. "Come on," she barked, tugging at my sleeve.

Now, if anyone in this room or the world finds these two words . . .

I thrust the dug out back into her hands and we jogged our last few steps. I jumped onto the car, and offered the driver a weak smile. It took me awhile to find my TransPass because I was already high. I could tell it was really good weed.

I grabbed hold of one of the trolley's silver metal poles to steady myself and fell into a dirty vinyl-cushioned seat. Phoebe and I sat next to each other quietly. I only caught her eye once. Her stare was glassy and bloodshot. When she caught me looking at her, she yawned and put her head down against her chest as if she didn't see me. I started to giggle because I felt awkward.

At first, Phoebe didn't move. She nudged my side once with her elbow but she soon realized I couldn't stop laughing. She started to giggle too. For a moment, I was afraid she was laughing at me instead of with me. But then I realized that I didn't care if she was. It was just good to laugh. It was just good to laugh alone on the trolley with Phoebe on the first Wednesday in December. It was just good.

Decadent, obscene, immoral, amoral, asexual . . . .

We were back in Olde City in less than half an hour. Phoebe and I flared up again before we got to the loft. I didn't even notice the walk home but knew I was glad that Ollie would be asleep when we walked through the door.

The front room of the loft was dark and didn't feel much warmer than outside. I spotted Avery asleep, curled up in a tiny ball on the longest of the couches. Her outline was visible only through the eerie blue iridescent glow of the television. As I moved toward the tube to turn it off, Phoebe jumped over the back of the couch and tackled Avery in a big bear hug. Phoebe began to tickle her hard and wild. Avery was startled awake. She looked miserable almost immediately.

"What the fuck?" Avery screamed, tossing Phoebe to the floor. She rubbed her eyes, which were blurred with the stickiness of sleep.

"Phoebe, come on," I scolded. "Let the poor thing sleep," I said, as I slowly unwrapped myself from my protective layers of winter clothing.

"Forget it," Avery moaned grumpily. "I'm up *now*," Avery said as she stood up and began to search for her shoes.

"It's so late, Avery. Why don't you just stay here tonight?" I offered. "We can get up early and all go for breakfast at Blue in Green," I added, hoping she'd say yes.

"No, that's all right. I've got to help Stuart with a script tomorrow," Avery said. She stretched a long wool hat over her head as she spoke; her coat was already on.

"Olivia was great, Claudia. She went down around eight o'clock," Avery told me.

Phoebe jumped up from the floor and moved to stand behind Avery. She rested her chin on her shoulder and whispered something into her ear. Avery ignored her but smiled slightly. I figured Phoebe had asked if she wanted to smoke.

"All right, I'm outta here," Avery announced. She started toward the door but Phoebe stopped her before she had a chance to pull away. Phoebe clutched her arms around her throat in a loose hold and continued to whisper in her ear.

"Good night, Phoebe," Avery remarked shortly, sounding exhausted. Phoebe sulked away.

"Claudia, gimme a call. We'll go for coffee," she offered. I nodded a "yes" and told her to be careful on the way home. She shut the door behind her with a hollow thud.

If the words 'to come' really make you feel uncomfortable . . . .

It was near silent in the loft. Phoebe flopped down on the couch, which Avery had just abandoned before she left. I guessed that it was still warm from her body heat. I lit some candles throughout the room and put on a Nina Simone CD that Remy had taken from Third Street for me. The strains of "Feeling Good" began to echo in the empty space of the loft. Phoebe started to snicker at the lyrics.

I pinched her lightly on the arm and plopped down next to her on a papasoon wicker chair we recently acquired from The Shack. Ossie and Cedric were remodeling Cyclone's office space and had asked us to "store" some old furniture indefinitely. I didn't really like the papasoon chair but Mojo had already claimed it as her own, so I didn't have the heart to get rid of it.

Phoebe cleared her throat and stated matter-of-factly, "I'm leaving, Claude."

I waited a moment before responding to her. I said, "I know."

My words were spoken without emotion. I accepted that Phoebe was moving on. When she came back from Columbia, I'd wanted very much for her to stay with me in Philadelphia and live the same life that I did so we could find safety in being together. But Phoebe had outgrown Philadelphia and, maybe to a certain extent, even our friendship. Leaving was right for Phoebe. What I wanted of her was irrelevant and purely selfish.

"Nico said a spot's opening up on the tour. One of the girls from the Company is headed to Korea with her boyfriend to teach English. Supposedly you can make a ton of cash there and then move back to the States in a year and live off whatever you saved," Phoebe explained. "Rob all but promised me the slot."

"All but promised?" I snapped in a viciously biting tone. I was clinging to the dim hope that maybe the whole thing would fall through. Maybe the whole thing would fall through and she would stay with me in Philadelphia.

"I know," she said in a wavering voice. "But Nico thinks she can persuade Rob to bring me on for at least a few performances. Even if I only get a little stage time, I think it'll still be worth it," Phoebe spoke with upturned eyes and a wistfully distant voice.

If you think I'm rank for saying them to you . . .

I wriggled in the papasoon chair. It creaked and teetered slightly on its wicker frame. I thrust my hands out on each side to steady myself. Phoebe laughed softly and rolled to the floor beneath my feet. She laid on her back, shoeless. She started to press the soles of her feet into the cushiony pillow, which surrounded me like a cloud of peach cotton.

"Where are you gonna stay?" I asked.

"Nico said I could crash with her till I figured out what was going on," Phoebe answered.

"She's really going out of the way for me. I don't have much cash because of the move here to Philly but I told her I'd help clean and cook her dinner all the time," Phoebe added.

"Make the cold tuna noodle casserole thing with the peanut butter and apples for her," I said, trying to be supportive.

"You like that one?" Phoebe whispered, blinking her eyes widely.

"Yeah, I like that one," I smiled with an "it's O.K." kind of look.

"I'm going to miss you, Claudia," she said, pulling herself up and into the huge chair with me. Her arms looked taut and strong as dancer's should be. "I'll try to visit soon as I can but it's gonna be tough with money and all for awhile," she promised.

"When are you planning on leaving?" I asked.

Phoebe hesitated as if she were afraid to tell me. Then, avoiding my eyes, she said, "Nico's driving back to The City tomorrow and said I could come with."

She turned to look at me again and waited to read my reaction. Tears started to grow in the corners of my eyes.

Phoebe continued to speak as if it would make me feel better, "I know it's quick Claude but I don't have much stuff. I'll leave you with enough cash for two months worth of bills. If you need more you can let me know."

"Don't worry about it," I said, as I felt her sweep a straggling red curl off my face.

"Thank you, Claudia," Phoebe whispered. "Thank you for everything," she repeated as she wiped a teardrop from my cheek. She leaned closer to me and brushed her lips lightly against mine.

I flinched nervously and pulled back from her.

If you, the beholder gets rank from listening to it . . .

Phoebe waited for my reaction but I stared back at her blankly. After a moment, she leaned into me again and I felt her tongue and index finger softly trace my upper lip. This time, I did not pull away.

I started to kiss her back but she stopped me gently yet sternly.

"No. I want to do this for you," she whispered into my ear. Her breath was warm.

"You deserve beautiful things, Claudia," she spoke in a quiet voice. "And I want to give you beautiful, beautiful things," she said as she let her tongue slip to outline my ear and then expertly allowed it to glide toward my neck where she began to suck tenderly with small kisses.

Her fingers wrapped themselves through my red curls and she pulled my scarf free so that my hair tumbled down onto my shoulders.

"Relax," she said, as she pulled back to better position herself above me.

She placed her cool palm on my chin and spread her fingers out widely. Her grasp slid to my neck and pushed my head back and down. She straddled me and, with strong hands and long strokes, massaged my chest, shoulders, and arms.

I felt safe. I felt the safety that was Phoebe and my friendship with her. Phoebe was leaving and I needed confidence. Confidence to keep with me when she was gone. Phoebe knew this and gave to me a passion like I had never experienced before and knew I would never touch again. I accepted her gift and enjoyed it selfishly.

You probably can't come.

I fell asleep late that night in my bed with Phoebe still cuddling and kissing me. I was drunk with emotion and deliriously drifted into a deep sleep sometime in the wee early hours of the new day.

When I woke up, Phoebe was gone.

She mustn't have slept a wink that night. It was much easier not to talk about it and to have just been in love with the moment for the moment. I hoped to see again her soon but knew it would be a long time before our next visit.

I rolled over, hugged a pillow that still smelled lightly of Phoebe's jasmine oil, and listened to Olivia gurgling blissfully in her crib.

Big Mess

I t was Christmas Eve.

I missed my parents. I missed the image of my beautiful family sitting around a crackling, roaring fireplace on a snow flurry dusted Christmas Eve drinking mugs of egg nog or hot chocolate laced with peppermint sticks. I missed the picture of my beautiful family on a blustery, cold Christmas morning, padding down our winding staircase in footed pajamas and rushing toward stockings stuffed with fluffy and plump surprises. I missed sitting around the Christmas tree, sipping mimosas, debating politics, and wishing the Never-Never never to end.

My parents *believed* in Christmas. My parents believed in a faith that I never understood. But belief made my parents happy. They believed and that made them happy and I didn't understand so I disappointed them.

I yearned for the tradition that my parents followed. I yearned for the solace that they found in the disciplined safety of routine. I yearned to give Olivia a snow flurry dusted Christmas Eve in front of a crackling, roaring fireplace with a mug of egg nog or hot chocolate laced with a peppermint stick. I yearned to give Olivia a blustery, cold, Christmas morning, where she and I padded over hardwood floors in footed pajamas and rushed toward stockings stuffed with fluffy and plump surprises. I yearned to give Olivia Never-Never land.

I just started back at the bookstore. With Phoebe gone, it was tough trying to juggle work and the baby but Avery helped out a lot and so did Gus's wife, Anne. It was tiring though and I'd become pretty depressed. I started smoking pot more often too. It seemed to be the only thing that made me feel better.

Gus was so ecstatic about my returning to work full-time that he offered to give me a fresh pine tree from his next-door neighbor's farm. He dropped off the tree early on Christmas Eve morning. We decorated it together in the quiet hour remaining before Olivia woke. We wrapped strands of bright, white lights from the base of the tree to tip, testing them as we went along. Then, we inter-layered the lights with strings of iridescent pearls, round plastic apples, and red ribbons, which I'd purchased the day before from the Antique Mart on South Street.

Olivia finally stirred after eight o'clock and was uncharacteristically restless. Her whimpering soon became intolerable, so I dressed her warmly and decided to run my errands while Gus finished the tree. Gus insisted he didn't mind; I left him alone in the loft where he dangled fragile candy canes precariously on limp pine branches and cheerily hummed maudlin Christmas carols.

Olivia and I returned home in time to watch my favorite soap opera. I pushed her carriage forward into the silent loft; Gus had long since disappeared. The smell of pine usurped me and forced me to stop in my tracks. I closed my eyes and laid down my bags to inhale the scent of the season that made my heart drop to my knees. I felt as if I had stepped into a scratch 'n sniff Richard Scarry children's storybook.

In order to strategically position the tree in the center of the loft, Gus and I had pushed the black and white television back against the wall of windows, which faced Third Street. The short stump of the tree stood bushy and plump in the awkward space between the couches. I smiled at the sight of our first Christmas tree and bounced Olivia lightly against my hip. I wished Remy were with us.

"Your Daddy loves you," I whispered into Olivia's soft, pink ear.

I shook her tiny fist in my hand, "I know your daddy loves you."

Olivia stared back at me with heavy, drooping eyes. We both needed a nap. I wanted to ensure that we were both well rested because I was planning on going out again later in the day to see the Wanamaker's Christmas light show. I prayed she wouldn't be cranky and put her down in her crib, amidst a sea of rattles, dolls, and block-shaped toys.

Like a responsible mom, I returned to the kitchen and hurriedly put away the milk and all the other perishables. But I left the dry food out on the floor in brown paper bags because I felt a migraine coming on. I just wanted to flare up and sprawl out on the couch.

I moved to the library table to fumble around for rolling papers. I couldn't find any but instead discovered a wrinkled note Gus had left behind for me. He had deliberately tucked it away under a glass ashtray I'd stolen from the coffee shop.

I unfolded the note slowly. I had to squint to read the words because I didn't have my contacts in. It was an invitation from Gus and Anne to join them for Christmas dinner. He even offered to drive into the city in the morning to pick us up so we wouldn't have to take public transportation. I smiled at his gesture but knew we wouldn't go. I wanted to spend the day at home, alone with Olivia. I tore up the note and threw it away.

I flicked on the Christmas tree's lights and yanked out my bong from behind one of the bookshelves. I sunk into the couch and smoked until my body felt numb. As my eyes grew heavier, I wrapped myself into a fuzzy, warm blanket and rolled onto my side, still staring at the blinking lights.

"Such a pretty tree," I sighed. "Such a pretty tree," I whispered as I fell into a lazy sleep.

I woke up later in the afternoon to the sound of Olivia crying. I glanced at the clock in the kitchen; it was well after four. The light trickling through the windows was waning as the sun was already starting to go down. I struggled to pull myself from the couch and stumbled toward the back corner of the loft. Olivia stopped crying as soon as I lifted her into my arms. I held her straight against my shoulder and moved into the kitchen so that we could both eat.

My mouth was cotton dry. I slurped two glasses of ice cold water as quickly as my throat could gulp it down but still couldn't quench my thirst. Olivia fed quietly as I ate a bowl of Grape Nuts mixed with apple sauce and raisins. I wasn't in the mood to cook anything extravagant and I didn't want to endure any strenuous clean-up efforts.

I was beginning to feel rushed with the thought that Wanamaker's last show of the day was at seven o'clock. I started to plan outfits for both Olivia and myself. I remembered that Remy and I had tried to make arrangements to see the light show together the year before. We never made it because we became lost in the shuffle of our move to the Devil's Pocket.

I tried to picture spending last Christmas with Remy but couldn't. My memory of that time alone with him was blank.

"We won't miss it this year," I promised Olivia.

I whisked the baby away to her changing table, the face of which was a sturdy, red door resting on two columns made of cinder blocks. Once Olivia was changed, I bundled her tightly into a giant round pink puff of fleece and cotton. Her arms and legs jutted straight out from her sides and looked stiff and difficult to move. Her chubby cheeks were the only part of her skin, which remained exposed. I couldn't help but chuckle at the sight of her tiny body. She looked like the Pillsbury Dough Boy.

I tugged a gray fisherman's sweater over my head and knotted a chenille scarf with fraying tassels around my neck. Then, I pulled on my sheepskin hat and tied the strings of both ear flaps together underneath my neck. The hat was furry and warm and made people stare at me when I walked down the street. Sometimes, it even made my head sweat if I ran around too quickly.

I safely tucked Olivia into her carriage and turned off our Christmas tree lights. Then, we scuttled outside into the remnants of the season's first major snowfall. The air I took in tickled the pit of my stomach with nostalgia. I loved the smell of the first snowfall. I figured it would be something I'd miss if I ever moved to New Orleans.

The flurries looked beautiful on the first day of the storm. I stayed in bed and peeked out of my tent for an extra ten minutes that morning just to watch the fragile, crystalline flakes flutter to the ground. They danced delicately through the crisp air and eventually melted into a thick blanket of white, which covered the patches of garbage lining the city's streets. The accumulation had been so heavy that some Philadelphians took to skiing down the long, front staircase of the Art Museum. I thought this image was funny.

The El was delayed, so we took the 121 bus to Fourteenth Street. We had to wait in the cold at the berth for over half-an-hour because only two lanes of traffic were running on Market. I resolved to myself that we would catch a cab home.

Wanamaker's sat on the Southeast corner of City Hall. The store had been there for as long as I could remember; my parents used to bring me to see the light show when I was a little girl. I was surprised how often I'd been thinking of my parents this Christmas.

Olivia and I used the store's main entrance on Market Street. As I opened the door, I glanced above our heads toward an enormous evergreen wreath, which was festively decorated with a red, velvet ribbon. The fabric of the ribbon rustled through the gusting wind as it swept unforgivingly along the block. I paused and listened to the hollow, bone-chilling whispers of the night air.

I escaped the cold and moved inside with Olivia.

Wanamaker's was bustling with holiday shoppers. I stood in the center of a wide, tiled aisle between racks of Women's clothes and coats and scanned the open center of the store. Although the enormity of the space made me feel small, I still felt welcome as if I would soon be comfortably swallowed up by a sea of expensive designer and brand names. I glanced upward at the brass railing, which lined the second floor balcony. The unlit metal frames of the light show's figures were pinned there amidst a loose trim of seasonal garland.

Isolated groups of people had begun to cluster on the floor between glass display cases, which were filled with perfumes and purses. The noise level was already high and growing steadily. Small children were sprawled in heaps, lying on their fluffy, down jackets. Some were sledding across the store's freshly waxed tiles on their knees, dirtying their tiny corduroy pants or denim overalls.

I scanned the floor around Olivia and me for some standing room. With each passing second, another patch of space quickly disappeared, snatched up by mommies and daddies for their little boys and girls. I was dumbstruck at the ferocity of the crowd but forced myself toward the statue of the famous Wanamaker's eagle, looming in the center of the store. I carved some room for us with my elbow and nestled in just as the voice of the master-of-ceremonies began to echo across the public address system. The buzz of Christmas carols reverberated behind him and soon overtook his sound.

The lights burst on to a giant roar of applause. A parade of characters, including Rudolph, Frosty, and the Grinch blinked on and off in rapid succession. Amidst the more recognizable of these figures, flashed the shapes of Christmas trees, snow flakes, gingerbread men, and candy canes. I smiled, listening to the squeals of delight and awe, which swelled up from the mesmerized audience.

I tried to draw Olivia's attention to the lights by pointing upward and repeating her name over and over again in a hushed voice. Although I knew she didn't recognize any of the holiday symbols, I could tell from the gentle kicks of her toes that she approved of the bright colors and quick animation. She gurgled happily. I winced at the thought that I knew her innocence to be fleeting with each passing day.

The show lasted only half an hour and ended promptly at 7:30 PM. The crowd began to disperse almost immediately after the MC thanked everyone for making another Wanamaker's presentation the best one ever. I spun in circles trying to collect Olivia's toys from the floor and gather them back into her carriage. People rushed passed me in the direction of the door while I hid, protected under the shadow of the wings of the giant Wanamaker's eagle. I bundled both Olivia and myself warmly and waited patiently for the furor to die down before we moved back outside. By that time, it was a quarter to eight.

I thought for a moment of returning straight home but had trouble catching a cab on Market Street because of the traffic. I decided to walk down Arch Street instead, in hopes of having better luck there. Arch Street reminded me of Oliver. The noisy gangster-rap stereo shops, the peep shows, adult bookstores, and make-shift incense stands reminded me of Oliver because their combination made Arch Street feel seedy, like the forbidden fruit of the Philadelphia underground. Mostly though, Arch Street reminded me of Oliver because of the Trocadero.

The Trocadero was the only burlesque hall in the country still open to audiences. The building has been bought, sold, remodeled, and repainted more times than I can remember but remains a Philadelphia landmark. Oliver loved the Trocadero because it was the perfect place to book the Big Mess Cabaret. Big Mess *was* its vision: "a big mess of people making big messy things on a big messy scale."

I loved the Big Mess Cabaret because it reminded me of Oliver.

(An aphotic shadow moved past her.

"Wait!" she cried. "Who was that?"

"Godot," replied the laos offhandedly. "Quickly. Run and catch him, before he goes," they told her in their droll tone.

She should have known who it was, she thought to herself.

"I cannot catch him," she said. "He walks too fast."

"Look!" the laos screamed. "He is standing on that patch of green grass in the deserted church yard."

"Among the tombstones," she whispered in reaffirmation.)

Big Mess' *Christmas* Cabaret had been running for the past three days; tonight was the last showing. I rocked Olivia back-and-forth in her carriage, struggling to decide if I should go inside. She was squirming, which made me nervous that she would soon break into a restless tantrum. I crouched at my knees and pulled one of her rattles from underneath her blanket. I shook the rattle lightly in front of her face. The bright colors made her eyes twinkle. Olivia flailed her arms as she tried to capture the sound of the toy. She quieted almost immediately and sunk deep into the cushion of her carriage. She reminded me of a doodlebug.

"What do you think, Ollie?" I asked the baby, half expecting an answer from her.

"Do it," whispered a man's voice from behind us.

Startled, I spun around to see who it was. I breathed a short sigh of relief as I recognized Stuart standing there toting some heavy looking bags and clothes, which dangled from wire hangers.

"Stuart, you scared the hell out of me," I jumped.

"I know. I'm sorry, I couldn't resist," Stuart explained.

"Come on," Stuart said. "Please come," he begged, referring to the show.

"I don't know, Stuart, Olivia is awfully cranky," I told him. "I don't think anyone's gonna want to listen to her crying."

"Don't worry about it. You'll be with me," he said. "We can hide back stage if you feel uncomfortable," Stuart added supportively.

I hesitated before answering him and then accepted his invitation, "Thanks, Stuart. I think I will. I don't want to go home alone just yet."

"No one should be home alone on Christmas Eve, Claudia," he said, as he nudged me with his shoulder. With a nod of his head, he motioned for me to take one of the bags he was carrying.

Stuart slung the hangers over his back and grabbed the plastic handle of Olivia's stroller. He waited for the traffic light to turn green and led us across Arch Street. I smiled to myself, feeling confident in the luxury of being able to follow someone safely. I hadn't allowed myself to follow anyone in a long time. Since Remy left, I'd become accustomed to being alone. Since Remy left, I'd become a grotesque, double-jointed, three-headed monster that no one knew how to love because no one could touch.

Stuart pushed ahead of the short line of people waiting for tickets to Big Mess. He flashed a wide pearly-white smile at the burly bouncer who was clad all in black. We shuffled inside the Troc. The bouncer looked displeased, so I tried to muster up a seemingly appreciative expression on my face for him.

"Where do you want to sit, Claude?" Stuart asked. As he said this, he fanned his hand out first in the direction of the stage and then in a sweeping gesture across the room.

"Let's sit toward the back," I suggested. "Olivia and I aren't going to stay long, so it'll be easier for us to leave without attracting much attention," I added.

"You got it, girl," Stuart agreed, as he turned to pile the clothes he was carrying onto my already over-burdened body. He did this to free his reach so he could lift Olivia from her restless sleep.

He held her high against his chest and said, "You'll at least stay until after my song though, right?"

"We'll try," I lied. "What are you performing?" I asked.

"Oh Little Star of Bethlehem," Stuart answered, proudly. "Wait till you see my costume. Ezra helped me with the design—lots of bright yellow sequins," he grinned.

"Ezra," I muttered to myself. "Did he get the MC slot this time?" I said, posing the question cautiously. The Countess had been passed over as MC for Spring Fling, so I knew the matter was a sensitive subject.

"Yes," Stuart said, raising his voice emphatically.

"He muscled Miss Bea Haven out of it *this* time. And, Claudia, thank god he did. I don't mean to sound biased but Miss Bea really doesn't have the stage presence to carry the whole thing off," he whispered, glancing around the room to be sure no one could overhear our conversation.

Philly's drag queen circuit was filled with gossip hounds who scrambled to embellish juicy tidbits amongst those in the inner circle. I instinctively knew that the Reckonwith camp was already secretly plotting a coup to overthrow the Duchess from his prestigious post within Big Mess. Comments like Stuart's would only add fuel to the fire.

I snickered slightly at Stuart's remark and rolled the wheels of Olivia's carriage along the cigarette-ridden red carpet of the Trocadero. I was starting to get fidgety but tried not to let Stuart sense my anxiety.

I replied in a small voice, "You're right, Stuart. The Countess brings so much to a performance."

Stuart and I stopped talking for a moment to concentrate on the buzzing crowd, which had begun to grow steadily inside the dimly, candle-lit theater. Everyone looked tragically hip. I felt suffocated by the hush of what it meant to be cosmopolitan and was grateful when Stuart pulled out a joint for us to smoke.

"Claude?" Stuart offered, as he lit the cigarette and extended it to me with a straight arm. He leaned closer to me to take Olivia from my hold.

"Thanks, Stuart," I whispered, accepting the joint cautiously. I cupped it in my hand to hide the glow of the fire. Now that I had Olivia, getting high in public made me nervous. I was always afraid other people would think that I was a bad mother or something.

"Humboldt kind," Stuart explained proudly, with regard to the origin and grade of the pot.

It *was* good weed. It had been a long time since I'd smoked weed that good. It made me feel separate from my body. It made my chin drop downward against my neck and forced my eyelids to droop as if they were about to close. The weed made me fixate on my state of being alone, of not fitting in, of feeling different, of always standing two steps back.

And then, I knew I was old.

I remembered that I had recently begun to notice the tiny lines of crow's feet growing in the corners of my eyes. I knew my hair felt dry and brittle to the touch from the oppression of the winter months. And I realized that something in my dress was missing too. I recognized that people were younger than I was—that everyone was not only older.

And it hit me that the spirit called youth is fleeting.

"Stuart, I need to leave," I announced suddenly, listening to the sound of my own voice. My tone was crisp and sharp.

"I shouldn't be here," I whispered.

"Claude, you O.K.?" Stuart asked with a startled expression. "You don't look so good. I'll get you some water," he offered.

"No," I declined. "No thanks, Stuart," I repeated as my eyes began to well up with tears. I thrust my head and face downward to the direction of the floor and struggled through blurred vision to gather my things.

As I finished my remark, three stilted figures stepped onto the stage. They were all clad in fluffy, white clouds of cotton and began to recite a tasteless poem about abominable snowmen. I turned toward Stuart and tugged Olivia loose from his grasp. He resisted me slightly, so I pulled harder and finally she was free.

"But Claudia, you haven't even seen my costume," Stuart tried again with fake cheer. His words fell on deaf ears.

I puffed a light kiss on the top of Olivia's head and placed her gently in her carriage again.

"Come on, Claude—you're worrying me," Stuart continued in a weakly convincing tone.

I tried to say goodbye to Stuart but the words wouldn't come out. I was already alone. There were dozens of people surrounding me but I was alone.

The instant I turned away from Stuart, a flood of tears rushed down my cheeks. I closed my eyes because they were stinging so badly from my cheap mascara. I grasped the handle bar of Olivia's carriage and pushed it toward the door. I listened to the sound of the wheels rolling across the floor of the Trocadero. The wheels squeaked with each full rotation.

The squeak developed into an intermittent rhythm coaxed along by the sound of Stuart's voice calling after me as I walked away: "Claudia. Claudia. Claudia."

The front of the baby's carriage crashed into the door with a loud metal clanking sound. Olivia began to cry. Children sense fear and instability. It is a terrifying thought to be helpless and not in control.

(Something is wrong. I know I am not as happy as I try to convince others I am.

I must leave.

I must leave.

I must leave.)

I stepped outside into the winter night. The air that slammed into my face was so cold that I could not bear to take it into my mouth or nostrils unless I first filtered it through the weave of my scarf. My tears had begun to freeze into meticulously clear diamond drops on my cheeks. My eyes were no longer crying; they were full of water from the shock of the subzero temperatures.

Olivia was whimpering softly in her carriage. I paused on the sidewalk and made a feeble attempt to quiet her. She fidgeted and waved her arms through empty air. I put a pacifier into her mouth and she began to suck on it noisily. I switched my attention from the baby to the traffic on Arch Street searching for a cab. I caught one on my first try.

I think the cabby felt sorry for me because he got out to help me with the stroller. We were about the same age. He was tall with blue eyes and long blonde hair. I remember thinking to myself that I should find him attractive but I didn't because I was numb. He tried to talk to me but I didn't answer. I gave him the address to the loft and stepped into the back seat, clutching Olivia tightly to my breast.

We sped away on a bumpy ride that felt like it was taking far too long. I lifted my eyes from Olivia's face and glanced out the cab window. The night was black. There were no stars littering the city skyline. I looked up into nothingness and tried to find the moon. At first, I couldn't see it among the labyrinth of buildings and billboards. But as we turned onto Race, I spied it hanging low on my right against the shadow of South Philly.

It was a crescent moon. It was the kind of moon that looked like the tip of your thumbnail. It kept peeking out at me from the empty spaces created by the city's cross streets and parking lots. It seemed to be lying on its back like an elongated letter "U." It was a long, peachish colored moon that looked like it was stretching out, lazily, yawning from boredom, poised to get up soon to walk away and be full again. The moon was telling me it was tired and ready to move on.

I handed the cabby a crumpled clump of cash and found myself standing alone on Third Street outside the loft. Before I keyed the lock, I rang the front buzzer just to hear its noise. I closed my eyes, inhaled another icy gasp of December air and ran upstairs as quickly as I could.

I stepped into the quiet safety of the loft and kicked off my shoes. I realized that I was shaking but knew it wasn't from the cold. I kept my coat on just the same. I lifted Olivia from her carriage and undressed her on the library table. She was gurgling happily as I placed her in her messy play pen, which was filled with toys.

"We can't forget to leave cookies and milk for Santa," I told Olivia, as I turned from her to light the tree. I was pleased with how bright it shined in the otherwise dark room.

I popped a tape of raunchy holiday blues into the stereo and listened as Olivia made loud, whirring noises in response to the stimulus surrounding her.

"I know, I know. I won't forget Rudolph's carrots," I said, as if answering her.

I moved to the kitchen and pulled a bag of bright orange carrots from the crisper drawer of the refrigerator. I cleaned and peeled the carrots in the sink and sliced them with a serrated knife so that the edges were lined with pretty shapes. I arranged the carrot sticks on one plate and a small pile of chocolate chip cookies and gingerbread men on another. I left both plates on the corner of the library table nearest the front door and positioned a tall goblet of Bully Hill Love Goat red wine between them.

I returned to the couch with my own glass of wine and watched as Olivia rustled softly in her play pen. After a few minutes, I picked up the telephone and dialed my parent's phone number with a continuous motion. I dialed the number as nonchalantly as if I called it three times a day on a regular basis. I had nothing to say but I wanted to hear the same, familiar voices that I had loved all the days of my life.

The ringing signal that followed on the line sounded hollow to me and repeated itself a number of times. At first, I thought that maybe my parents were already talking on the phone and not accepting the call waiting blips. But then, just as the ringing became monotonous enough to seem inaudible, I heard someone answer on the other end.

"Hello," cried the voice, with its tone upturned as if it were asking a question.

The word sounded more like "hal-lo," with emphasis placed on the first syllable as if the voice were calling a turkey. I recognized that the voice was my father's. I stood, frozen in time, all-consumed in the moment. I listened intently to the resonating sound of the second call of the voice, which my father emitted like clockwork. This time, his words echoed with a more hurried and bothered tone.

My father. I did not speak. I did not shed a tear. I did not move. I just waited to fall away, completely entranced in the repetition of the voice that evoked emotions in me I thought I had suffocated to death.

My father tried his greeting a few more times. I could hear my mother squawking in the background "Who is it?" over and over again but he did not answer her. He paused to allow long breaks of silence in between his words and I knew he could feel me. He knew it was me and didn't know what to say any better than I. He just wanted to sit and think of me, as I of him.

I waited until he hung up to replace the phone back on its hook.

"Goodbye," I whispered, as I pictured him standing dumbfounded with his hand still resting on the receiver. My father is the strongest person I have ever known. Memories and thoughts of him break my heart on a daily basis.

"Come on, Ollie," I chirped.

"We need to get a bath so that we're nice and clean for Santa," I said as I reached into the play pen and lifted Olivia up. I tugged from her grasp a strange plastic toy that was shaped like a wand. The wand lit up when you pushed on its sides. Olivia liked to knock herself on the head with it over and over again.

Once in the bathroom, I began to draw luke warm water into the tub. I searched for the bath seat I was given at my shower but couldn't find it anywhere. I thought it was a peculiar thing to misplace and wondered if it was really lost or if I just couldn't find it because I was high. After a few more moments of scrambling for the piece, I gave up and opted to wash the baby without it.

Olivia was in an unusually good mood for the late hour. I wrestled her from her pink flannel dress and unlaced her tiny work boots. She waved her hands, which made her look as if she were trying to clap. She made me smile. I realized that she was the only person who could make me smile anymore.

After noticing that the tub was nearly full, I rushed to turn off the faucet. Water was swishing and splashing in over three-quarters of the tub. I hadn't realized that I was moving so slowly. I finished undressing Olivia and tossed a yellow rubber duck and some other faded plastic figures into the mix. I watched the shapes bob up and down in constant, swirling motion.

Olivia didn't make a sound as I submerged her into the blurry water. Her eyes grew wide and I could tell she was excited because her breath was coming in short, concentrated puffs. She tried to reach for a floating, purple ball but couldn't catch it because it drifted from her so quickly.

I massaged the translucent orange gel of Johnson & Johnson's Baby Shampoo through Olivia's hair. The shampoo's nostalgic scent grabbed me. I twirled a bar of Ivory soap through a tattered wash cloth and inhaled deeply. I closed my eyes and concentrated on the trickling noises our movements made in the bath water.

It's not hot enough. It's supposed to be hot. Adjectives like sweltering and smoldering should be used to describe the air. When I breath in, it must be too thick to fill my lungs. When I exhale, I should feel as if I am suffocating.

No, it's not hot enough.

I squinted from the corners of my eyes and lifted my hand to turn on the hot water again. A thin stream began to flow from the faucet and steam began to billow upward. Fog crept across the mirror. I closed my eyes again, this time more tightly.

The water was much hotter now and the room felt humid. My curls were beginning to frizz, my skin felt moist, and I was away. I was there. I know I was.

Three hours of sleep was not enough for me.

Three hours hadn't given me enough time to wash the picture of Ruthie the Duck Lady and her duck peeping from his cardboard box out of my head. I'd met the two the night before in front of Pat O'Brien's in the Quarter.

I desperately wanted a shower but was forced to settle instead with sneaking into the bathroom in the lobby of the Bayou Plaza Hotel to brush my teeth. It was more than I expected. It was Mardi Gras. We'd parked our winnebago in the parking lot of the Bayou Plaza three days ago. We slept there every night since. The Bayou's staff paid no attention to us and let us come and go as we pleased.

I'd woken up earlier than my other eleven companions in the 'bago. This morning was special to me. An old high school friend of mine was stationed in Fort Polk. I'd promised him that if I were ever in Louisiana I'd look him up.

I stepped out of the darkness of the hotel lobby and into the blinding morning sunlight. My eyes met directly with the traffic running up and down Carrolton Avenue. Carrolton reminded me of City Line Avenue in Philadelphia. I crossed the parking lot toward the winnebago and spied other cars scattered about with the feet and arms of slumbering bodies jutting up and out of windows.

The Bayou Plaza was a great hotel.

On the roof of the 'bago, I recognized the outlines of two of my friends who were still sleeping. I couldn't believe they hadn't woken yet because the sunlight was so bright. I thought to myself, for a moment, that perhaps they had strangled themselves during the night with the tangle of plastic beads draped around their necks. I snickered at the sight of them. They looked as if they had just stepped from the pages of a Hunter S. Thompson novel.

I scanned the general vicinity for a pay phone. I couldn't find one. I hoped that one of the stores at the intersection of Claiborne Avenue would let me make a call. I studied my options carefully. I remembered that I hadn't taken a shower since we'd gotten into New Orleans and I knew it showed in both my dress and musky scent. I noticed a banana yellow sign hanging on rusted chain links above the doorway of a deserted looking shop. Red letters were etched across the sign. They read: "Pawn Shop."

I decided I would call my friend from the pawn shop.

I dodged the busy lines of traffic moving along Claiborne and tumbled from the humid morning air into the cool quiet of an empty room. A tiny bell tinkled as I entered. The ringing prompted a man with sandy colored hair to step out from behind a red velvet curtain. The man greeted me cheerily as he pushed a pair of wire-rimmed glasses further up the bridge of his nose.

"Hello, shire," he said with a slow New Orleans drawl.

"Hello," I replied dryly.

"I hate to trouble you," I mustered in my nasally, North Eastern accent. "May I use your phone? I've been looking for a pay phone but can't seem to find one," I explained.

"Local?" he questioned, chewing on a chicory stick.

"Fort Polk?" I questioned, unsure.

"I suppose," the man said as he pulled the chicory stick from his lips. A thin line of drool followed his hand. He thumped an off-white rotary phone onto the counter.

"Help yourself," he offered.

"Thanks," I spoke nervously. I dialed my friend's phone number, which was scrawled in my handwriting across a crumpled piece of notebook paper that I'd been keeping in my pocket since we'd left Philadelphia.

It took me three tries to reach my friend. We agreed to meet outside Tipitina's for margaritas later that day. I hung up the phone and quickly thanked the pawn shop cashier for his hospitality. The cashier began to make small talk with me. He told me that I was a beautiful woman and that he was happy I was visiting his town. His eyes leered at my chest and bare legs.

The man's stare started to make me feel awkward and painfully aware that my skirt was too short. I smiled uncomfortably and shuffled toward the store front without turning my back on him. I pressed myself against the glass of the door, pushed it open, and ran in the direction of the 'bago. I could still feel the man's eyes on my back.

My friends and I drank heavily at the Maple Leaf all afternoon. Eventually, I noticed that I was over an hour late for my meeting at Tips. I decided to go anyway even though I was sure my friend had already given up on me.

The cab dropped me off on the corner of Napoleon and Tchoupitoulas. I crossed the neutral grounds and sauntered up to an outside bar nestled on the cement walk. I asked the bartender for a margarita with salt. She nodded to me.

The bartender was scantily clad in a ribbed halter top and a pair of skin tight jean shorts. Her body was hard and attracted a great deal of attention from male patrons. She wore three strands of Mardi Gras beads draped loosely around her neck. They skimmed the tops of her breasts as she moved to make my drink. Embarrassed by watching her, I stared down at my toes.

"Knock it off, Cameron," the bartender ordered.

My eyes shot up instantly. The bartender was being harassed by a guy who looked so drunk, he appeared retarded. I smiled at the guy anyway. He was sort of cute. He smiled back at me.

"You got a cigarette?" he asked.

I had a pack of cheap menthols that I'd stolen from one of the other bars I'd been in earlier. I pulled them from my bag and offered them to him.

"Fuck. Menthols," he said, accepting one anyway. He lit the cigarette with a pack of matches he snatched from the bar and paused to take a deep drag. He blew out the match he used and dropped it to the ground. I could smell the sulfur.

"I lost my friend," he said to me suddenly.

Confused, I looked at him and shook my head. He stepped out from behind the corner of the bar and approached me.

"You better watch out for him," the bartender warned as she handed off my margarita. I guessed that she was joking but wasn't sure. The man ignored the bartender entirely.

"You from here?" he asked.

I shook my head again.

"Come on," he gestured, pulling me in the direction of the neutral grounds. We walked through the tall grass, dodging other Mardi Gras goers in our wake. We moved further up Napoleon and away from the growing crowd. We stopped next to a dying maple tree.

"What's your name?" he asked me.

"Claudia," I answered.

"I'm Cameron," he said.

"Cameron," I repeated softly. The name fell from my lips and embedded itself in my heart to be forever associated with the romance that is New Orleans.

"You dose, Claudia?" he asked.

I nodded my head again. Cameron put his hand on the back of my neck and popped a tab of acid into my mouth. I hated tripping but decided to do it anyway because I was so smitten.

"How did you lose your friend?" I asked him as I waited to peak.

"A couple of guys took him away," Cameron answered. "They said I sold them some bad acid but I didn't. I just put them in touch with a guy who sold them some bad acid," he explained.

"They couldn't find me, so they took Matthew away," Cameron added nonchalantly.

My eyes widened. I didn't like fighting and I told him so.

"Fight? Me?" Cameron laughed heartily.

"These guys would kill me. I don't know how to fight. I fight like a doodlebug. If somebody comes after me, I curl up in a ball and hide," he finished.

"I wish more people fought like that," I mused. There was an awkward silence between us.

Cameron started to tap a stick against the tree and then began to sing aloud to the rhythm he created: "I had the blues so bad one time, it put my face in a permanent frown. Now I'm feelin' so much better child—I can cake walk into town."

The acid kicked in about fifteen minutes later.

Cameron and I laid on the grass giggling and crying with each other until my stomach started to hurt. He asked me if I wanted to walk to the levee. Before I had a chance to say yes, a rusty white van with Louisiana plates rattled down Napoleon and stopped on the street next to us. A large man tossed a crumpled body out from the back of the van. The man screamed obscenities at Cameron and me as the van began to speed away.

"Oh, this is my friend," Cameron spoke calmly, as he nudged the body on the ground into consciousness.

"Hey," Matthew said in a witless tone. Recovering quickly, he proceeded to bounce up miraculously. "I found you, man," he told Cameron with endearment.

"Yeah," Cameron said smiling.

"You wanna go to the levee?" he asked, pulling me up from the grass. As he steadied my arm, he placed a string of white beads around my neck and pecked a kiss lightly on my cheek. The beads looked iridescent under the street lights. They reminded of pearls.

"Cool, bro," Matthew answered. "She comin' too?" he said, referring to me.

"Yup. This is Claudia," Cameron said, introducing me.

"All right," Matthew mumbled as if he approved of me. "Let's go," he shrieked into the sultry night air.

Matthew turned and started walking toward Tchoupitoulas. Cameron followed first and then I second. I found myself singing with them both as we embarked on the most magical, exhilarating night of my life: "I had the blues so bad one time, it put my face in a permanent frown. Now I'm feelin' so much better child, I can cake walk into town."

My knees hurt from sitting in the damp grass for so long. I stretched uncomfortably but felt as if my shoes were sloshing in a puddle.

My eyes sprang open wide. I was not in New Orleans. I was still standing in my bathroom in Philadelphia. I was standing on a sopping wet, blue rug. I started to panic because I didn't hear Olivia. I wasn't holding Olivia anymore.

I looked down into the tub. Her head was under the bubbles. I bent over and jerked her up quickly. Her body crashed through the surface of the water. I cradled her lifeless figure in my arms. She wasn't breathing. She wasn't moving. I pressed my ear against her chest. I could not hear her heart beating.

I rushed toward the phone even though I was afraid that it was too late. I was crying and shaking uncontrollably. I rested the phone between my ear and my shoulder and dialed 911. My left arm clutched Olivia's tiny body in a dark green towel. With my right hand, I squeezed the purple colored ball I had snatched from the tub. I bounced the ball against the yellow colored phone book and waited for a voice on the other end of the line to answer me.

Cameron. I miss Cameron. I miss butterflies and tulips and sandollars and sunshine and clear blue swimming pools and reading books in trees. And I miss playing tag when I was ten. And having my mom sing "You're My Best Girl" to me as I fell asleep in her arms while she brushed my hair with her palm.

Life's beauty escapes me now. It was mine once. All of the beautiful things that were mine were good. And all of the beautiful things were good in a moment that could have been bad if I'd let it be bad.

My life is suddenly over here. It has ended with all the silence with which it had begun.

After Bo-Houn, I will find myself sipping chicory coffee at Kaldi's on Decatur. After Bo-Houn, I will take a late-night ferry ride over the Mississippi. After Bo-Houn, I will visit Buddy Bolden's grave. After Bo-Houn, I will play hide and seek among the oaks at Audobon Park.

After Bo-Houn, I will know beauty again.

Part Three

Birth

The Crescent City

I t's New Year's Eve.

Today is my last day of work. I am moving far away and leaving many of the things I have loved dearly in Philadelphia behind me.

I want to leave here, yet I am home. In life, it is difficult to step on a tight rope when one knows the safety net, which has been below for as long as one can remember, is pulled away. But if you don't move when you have the chance in life, your chances pass you by.

The cops conducted a brief investigation into Olivia's death. In the end, it was ruled an accident.

I am not ashamed by the fact that I do not feel remorse over my loss, only relief.

The funeral was no frills. There was a small, non-denominational service attended only by myself, Stuart, Ezra, Gus, and residents of The Shack. Olivia was buried at West Laurel Hill Cemetery in the bone-chilling cold of a Philadelphia December. Her tombstone read:

Olivia Prytania Thomas

October 4, 1995-December 24, 1995

"From this hour I ordain myself loos'd of limits and
imaginary lines
Going where I list, my own master total and absolute".[3]

---

[3]   Whitman, Walt, "Song of the Open Road", *Leaves of Grass*, p. 138, Stanza 5, New American Library, 1958.

I placed a single, red rose on the coffin before they lowered it into the frozen ground. At that moment, I became separate from life for all those whom I had loved were gone.

I'm flying out on the red eye.

Gus said to close at five o'clock because of the holiday but I decide to stay open until nine. Only one customer has been in during the last hour. Surprisingly though, Audrey has stayed with me without complaint. I can tell that she will love the job and the job will love her.

I steal a look at Audrey and ask her to finish shelving the stack of books in her hand so we can close up. In a whirlwind, I show her how to lock the safe and both the front and back doors. I rush through the lesson on how to arm the alarm, knowing that Audrey will probably set it off when she opens up the shop in the morning anyway.

Audrey thanks me for helping her. She asks if I want to head out for a drink at a party she's going to in Northern Liberties. I decline and tell her to go on without me. I want a few minutes alone in the bookstore to take photographs with my mind's eye. Audrey tells me good bye and good luck. I shut the door behind her as she disappears into the night.

I walk to the foot of the stairs in the hallway and stand beneath the framed "Curse to the Book Thief." I smile to myself. I take my last glances of Oz & Endz, trying to rape the store of its vitality for my own posterity. I search desperately for something to take with me upon my departure. I feel that possessing a physical piece of Oz & Endz will link me inextricably to the world that exists within these walls.

I pluck a thin red journal from one of the hallway shelves. I fan its pages in front of my face and thumb through the chronological account written in an anonymous hand. There are no more than ten entries; the majority of the book is blank. The entries seem to diary the European holiday of a young male circa 1930. Although simple, the style is detailed and fluid. It is how I wish to write. I take the journal and slip it into the pocket of my baggy, denim overalls.

I think of walking through the store one last time but stop myself. It is better to leave comforted by the thought that this moment is akin to my own phoenix. I gather my things, exit through the front door, and follow Audrey's cold shadow into the new year.

Ossie, Cedric, and Avery are hosting a New Year's Eve party at The Shack, which I promised to attend before leaving town. I dropped my bags off there earlier this morning day so I wouldn't have to lug them around the city with me.

I move onto Market Street and hail a cab. I instruct the cabby to drop me at Eighth and Poplar in the Badlands. He grimaces as he registers the address.

I understand the hesitation of the cabby and am surprised that he accepts my fare. The Badlands is one of Philadelphia's empowerment zones. Ossie and Cedric purchased space there for The Shack to escape city wage taxes for Cyclone and its employees. By helping to reclaim decaying urban areas, they gained the unwavering support of both the mayor and city council. Politicking in business isn't an option; it's a way of life.

The cabby drops me off on Eighth in front of a Ryder truck depot, which is lost in the intimidating, black scape of deserted warehouses and parking lots. I am the only person walking the street. I cross toward The Shack, stepping over a sea of used condoms and broken crack vials, which line the sidewalk. A stench emanates from a fermenting pile of uncollected garbage and strikes me hard in the face. I lean against an abandoned car to steady myself from the force of the smell.

I hug the brick front of the building and move at a slow crawl toward the front door. In my hands, I clumsily juggle a clock stolen from Oz & Endz. Admission to the party is discounted by five dollars if the guest donates a timepiece, regardless of whether or not it is in working condition. Ossie plans to construct a giant, quasi-time machine from the donations. He intends to synchronize all of the components and activate them in unison at midnight.

As I lift my hand to ring the bell, Ossie throws open the front door in a wild burst of enthusiasm. I sense that he is nervous because he appears to have been waiting alone in the small foyer for the arrival of guests. His anxiousness forces me chuckle to myself. I step into The Shack beside him. The room is illuminated by the tint of a glowing red colored light bulb, which dangles high above Ossie's head. His manner is stately and urbane; he is dressed in a rumpled tuxedo and shoed in a dusty pair of brown work boots.

"Sweet. You're early, Claudia," Ossie announces sarcastically. "That means that you can help finish setting up," he jokes.

"Only if it means working the bar. I just closed up at the shop—a Rob Roy is all I'm lookin' for," I answer him.

Ossie touches his hand to my cheek. He is wearing a tattered pair of fingerless gloves. I grab him in a bear hug, which he holds for slightly longer than is proper. I pull away and study him again curiously. I lift a brass pocket watch from against his chest and peer carefully at it for a closer look at the time. It is 10:35 PM.

"Nice touch," I smile at him sincerely.

"Happy New Year," he offers. "Did'ja bring a clock? he asks.

I pry my clock from my sweaty grip and hand it to him. The clock's face is imbedded into the flat belly of a hula dancer. Two fluorescent lays are wrapped around her neck—one green and one pink. I flick her "on" switch. The foot-tall figurine begins to jiggle a tiny grass skirt around her hips. Ossie smirks as he accepts it from me.

"Don't get too excited," I say. "I don't think she tells time anymore."

"Her wiggle more than makes up for it, doesn't it Claude?" Ossie remarks leeringly. His tone makes me feel awkward and self-conscious of my gender.

"I'm sure somebody'll get it ticking before midnight," he adds, changing his voice as if he senses that he has made me nervous. "Avery!" he shouts suddenly into the life of the party. "Avery! Claudia's here."

As his last word rolls from his tongue, Avery steps into the foyer on cue.

"Claudia!" she screeches. "I'm so glad you made it. I was worried you'd bail," she explains. I wonder why she says this, when she knows that I have placed all of my worldly possessions in her kitchen. I give her a puzzled look but she does not notice.

"Hi Avery," I respond.

Avery leans forward in my direction to peck a kiss on my cheek. Ignoring Ossie, she wraps her arm through the crook of my own and demands, "Come on, Claude. Ya' gotta see the studio."

Avery pulls me into the next room. I stumble after her, kicking an empty glass with my foot. The glass rolls toward a small group of guests. They each look up at me, seemingly annoyed. I realize that I am under dressed but do not care. I eye Avery more carefully. She is wearing a crushed green velvet dress that appears both festive and sophisticated on her thin frame.

Avery stops abruptly in the center of the room. She nods her head, pointing me to the position of the bar, the liquor luge, food, and coffee. She tells me to check out the giant timepiece, which is steadily growing in the right hand corner of the space. She instructs me to get my glass early for the champagne toast and offers me some confetti. I accept a small handful. Avery tells me that I can find more in a private stash she has hidden away upstairs.

Avery drops me at the bar and drifts off to welcome some of the other guests. Before she leaves my side, she makes me promise that I will not leave the party without saying goodbye to her. I lie and tell her that I will. She leaves me I alone. I drop the confetti to the ground and turn to pour myself a tall, cold beer from a silver metal keg.

I step away from the bar and sip quietly from my cup. I stand alone and scan the room, taking in the holiday decorations. My attention is drawn immediately to the timepiece. It is secured to a wire fence on The Shack's stage. At present, it looks as though it consists of about thirty or so clocks, including one shaped like a white-faced vinyl 75 LP and another like the logo for Coca-Cola. Together, they emanate a soft iridescent glow, which illuminates the room in surreal pink and purple hues.

I recognize the shape of my hula dancer from among the collection. She gyrates alone on a granular, ivory column pushed to the far right side of the display. Her time does not match any of the other clocks. I wonder if Ossie will actually get her to work. I doubt it but hope so nonetheless.

My eyes are drawn from the timepiece toward a paint-splattered ladder, which is positioned near the center of the room. Dangling directly overhead of the top rung is a giant, papier-mâché globe. It hangs from the ceiling by a tangled thread of frayed rope. I scan North America for the location of New Orleans. An awkward Asian kid who climbs the ladder and spins the globe furiously with the palm of his hand interrupts my search.

"Look!" he demands. "I've got the whole world in the palm of my hand," he yells to his friends who are standing below him on the floor.

Bored with the idiocy of his remark, I walk opposite the stage toward the left corner of the studio. I slump deeply into one of three angled and cushy leather couches. The couch on which I choose to sit is gold. The two others are blue; one of which is patterned with white pinstripes.

I place my beer on a makeshift coffee table fashioned from a wooden door propped on legs of cinder block columns. I lift my feet onto its dusty surface and toss a near empty pack of Camel Lights next to my beer. I have been smoking incessantly since Olivia's death. It has been helping to calm my nerves and control my weight.

I light the one cigarette that I withheld from the pack and sink further into the couch. Staring at the ceiling, I spot another silly decoration hanging low—a dead Christmas tree, plucked bare of all of its needles. The branches of the tree are tied together and sculpted into the giant oval shape of a holiday ornament. Fire hazard or not, the creativity piques my interest and makes me smile.

"Severe saturnalia, huh?" bellows a familiar voice from the direction of the timepiece.

It is Philip the Ticket Man. I haven't seen him since the play at the Penitentiary this past summer. Philip approaches me while rolling the squeaky wheels of a rickety shopping cart over the floor. The shopping cart is brimming with metallic party hats, bags of confetti, horns, and other annoying New Year's party favors. On the front of the cart is a mount of a black boar's head. Fierce looking ivory white tusks jut out from each side of the stuffed animal's face.

"These guys know how to throw a party," Philip observes in his grating and raspy voice.

He parks his cart behind the pinstriped couch and snaps the elastic band of a cardboard hat around my head. The hat is white with pink plumes. It reminds me of Mardi Gras.

Irritated, I yank the hat off and respond curtly, "Hello, Philip."

"Not in the mood this evening, my sweet?" Philip taunts.

"So where you been, girl?" he continues. "I call, you don't call back. I call, you don't call back. I call, you don't call back," he says, repeating the phrase for emphasis.

I try to ignore him and turn my attention to pushing back my cuticles with the rough edge of my fingernail. Our ritual has always been simple: Philip hits on me, I shoot him down. Philip hits on me, I shoot him down. Philip offers me free tickets, I accept, and don't see Philip again for months.

Relationships are best when you take them as they are.

"Claudia, I feel such an astral connection to you. I'm not sure what it is. When I see you, it's as if this supernal agent just usurps me," Philip babbles. His purposefully exaggerated vocabulary never fails to make me laugh.

"So what do you say, babe, you wanna get wit me? We hang out here a couple hours, we go back to my place, light some candles, drink some wine. I just want to span some time together," he drones.

"Oh Philip, you know I'm still reeling from my broken heart," I answer with mild sincerity. In truth, I add, "It will be a long time before I can love again."

"I'm not asking for love; I'm asking for companionship," he tries pathetically. I glare at him with down-turned, disapproving eyes. I remain silent.

"So what's going on this week? You available Tuesday, ten o'clock for a film at the Ritz?" Philip asks, not even taking a moment to acknowledge defeat.

"I don't think I'm going to be around on Tuesday, Philip," I reply in a deadpan tone.

"All right, how 'bout SCRAP at the Arts Bank on Thursday?" he suggests.

I hesitate. Before declining again, I decide to lie, "Sure. That'd be great."

"Tickets'll be at the door. Just ask for 'em," he instructs me. "And Claudia, *call* me. I mean it—I *need* to see you," Philip whines.

"I will, Philip. I will," I lie again. "Listen, I gotta run. I promised Ossie I'd help him set up the liquor luge."

I rise from the couch before Philip can argue with me. I lift the limp party hat from my lap and snap it around his head. It settles with a "twang". Avoiding his stare, I walk through the haphazard arrangement of couches while slurping down another sip of beer.

Hitting my shin on the edge of the liquor luge, I start to make my way toward the stairs. Ossie tries to lure me into the furor of the drinking game. He offers me a fifth of tequila to pour into the mouths of participating lugers. I refuse Ossie, immediately offended by the surrounding flurry of flashing cameras and buoyant laughter. I follow the luminescence of the foyer's red light bulb. I trip my way past a steady receiving line of guests and ascend the stairwell. It is cluttered with junk ranging from dirty clothes to abandoned suitcases to speckled paint trays.

The second floor is remarkably quiet. The open loft space is logically partitioned into a bathroom, a bedroom, and an office. A small number of people are mulling about, the majority of whom are waiting to use the bathroom. They form a line between the shower curtain wall of the bathroom and the undisturbed calm of the bedroom area.

My old tent covers the top of the bed. I gifted it to Avery after I'd finished packing. I peer through its zipper, spying the dark outline of a sleeping bag, a pile of scattered books, and the unassuming glow of a clock radio.

Cyclone's office begins just beyond the bed. The privacy of the office is secured by a cropped piece of unfinished plywood. A pathos vine coils along its top, skimming a series of pencil sketches. The edges of the pencil sketches are thumb tacked to the plywood. They appear ragged, as if they have been torn from a larger pad of paper. They depict the slow degeneration of an urban property as it decays in stages—bustling market to abandoned building to vacant lot.

I follow the story of the sketches as they wrap around to the opposite side of the plywood. Beneath them lies a thin, mission-style couch. I plop down hard onto one of the couch's uncomfortable cushions. I settle in to study the sketches more carefully. I am interrupted, however, by a peculiar man dressed in a Hawaiian shirt who forces me into an inane conversation.

"Sort of depressing stuff to put on your wall, huh?" he asks loudly.

I nod to him, although secretly thinking to myself that I rather enjoy the positioning of the sketches. I do not answer him.

"I'd never bring somethin' like that into my place. I wouldn't be able to sleep," the man continues. "Doubt the neighbors would like it either—because I live in *Society Hill* and all," he explains, as if trying to impress me. I am not impressed.

"That's quite a shirt," I offer unenthusiastically. The man pushes his chest out proudly, not realizing that I intend the remark to be condescending. I smile at his naiveté.

"Where does one *find* a shirt like that?" I ask, curious how far I can lead this man into his own self-degradation.

"Key West, baby," he replies with self-assured chauvinism.

"Key West is the greatest place on earth, man," he blurts out quickly. His tone is slow and drawn out because he is stoned.

I laugh aloud. Taking a stab at his intelligence, I say, "So, you like Jimmy Buffett?"

"Hey, how'd you know that?" he asks dotingly. He appears to be genuinely astonished.

"Just a lucky guess," I respond. "So have you read *The Sun Also Rises*?" I question him.

"Yeah, I started it on the flight home. Boy, it's a tough one," he answers, offering me his unsolicited critique. "I was going to read some more of it today but I can't find the damn thing. I think I left it on the plane," he confesses.

"I use 'ta have another one of his books. Something about a bell," the guy says. I wince slightly at his ignorance. To be well read is to be worldly, which commands my respect.

"Something about a bell," I repeat to myself, registering his words.

"*For Whom the Bell Tolls*?" I propose mindlessly. "I've got a first edition copy at home," I add proudly, testing to see if he knows what a first edition run is.

"Hey, maybe I could borrow it sometime," the guy suggests, reaffirming my suspicion that his mind is vapid. "I could get your number—" he begins before I cut him off abruptly. I am flattered but unimpressed. He is indeed a hopeless romantic.

"True and pure love gives to every object in nature a power of the heart, without which it would indeed be spiritless[4]," I spew a quote from Coleridge into the empty space before me, as if he were not even present.

"Huh?" the Hawaiian shirt clad boy replies, dumbfounded by my remark.

"Oh, nothing," I reply. "Would you excuse me, please? I need to talk to one of my friends," I lie.

"Will you come back?" he asks desperately.

"Sure," I lie to him again, shaking my head yes.

I stand and walk again to the opposite side of the plywood, stepping into Cyclone's waiting room. The area consists of a wrought

---

[4]   Coleridge, Samuel Taylor, "Passion and Order", *The Meanings of Love, The World of Love Volume 1*, p. 188, George Braziller, Inc., 1964.

iron green table, three wrought iron green chairs, and a giant red fluorescent sign shaped like the letter "S". The sign is heavy-looking and stands as tall as my shoulders. It is propped up by a row of metal filing cabinets. I recognize it as stolen from the PSFS building in Center City.

I pull out one of the wrought iron chairs and settle down next to a man who is sitting alone at the table. The man appears to be in his early twenties and is dressed entirely in black. I trace the tip of my index finger around the petals of one of five Gerber daisies, which droop limply in a carafe in the center of the table.

"I'm sorry," I interrupt the man. "Can you help me?" I ask.

The man instantly turns his attention toward me. He appears to be intrigued but also cautious.

I start to speak again before he is able to answer me: "I'm trying to get rid of that guy over there. Can you pretend we know each other?" I beg.

"Where is he?" the man says with a thick Irish accent. I nod my head in the direction of the guy in the Hawaiian shirt. He is difficult to miss.

Suddenly, the man in black leather jumps up and pushes my chair back. He pulls me up, wraps his arms around me in a bear hug and plants a kiss passionately on my lips. I sink back into the chair, stunned.

"You said to make it look like we knew each other," he says.

Coming to my senses, I excuse him, "Yes. Yes, I did."

I pause and introduce myself awkwardly, "I'm Claudia."

"I'm Seamus," he answers. I grin with the expectation that I will kiss this man as the clock tolls midnight.

"On the run, huh?" Seamus asks.

"You could say that," I reply coyly, stubbing my toe against one of the table's wrought iron legs.

I am anxious to put distance between myself and the guy in the Hawaiian shirt. I suggest to Seamus that we go downstairs together. It is nearing midnight and I suspect that Ossie will soon start his timepiece.

"Sounds grand," Seamus agrees, accepting my invitation.

He glances down at his Swiss Army watch and adds, "It's almost midnight. I'll pick up some champagne for us at the bar."

Seamus steps behind me and pulls my seat out slightly from the table. I stand slowly. He rests his hand along the small of my back and guides me down the stairwell. The party has grown a great deal more crowded, making it difficult to move about. The noise of conversation and loud music fills the air. Together, Seamus and I maneuver gracefully through a sea of anonymous faces.

"Confetti?" squawks a petite girl with dark, straggly hair. With her words, she thrusts out her hand and forces a pile of confetti into my face. Her eyebrow is pierced.

I laugh aloud and tilt my head back to see Seamus' expression. He motions for me to accept the girl's offer.

"Please," I reply in her direction. The petite girl spills a heaping handful of brightly colored, plastic confetti into my open palm.

"Thank you," I say as Seamus and I continue through the crowd.

"Over there," Seamus points to the far right side of the main floor.

My pace quickens with Seamus' wide step. He nudges me in the direction of two empty rocking chairs, which are nestled snugly between the coffee bar and the wall. I plop down into one of the rockers. A fluffy, blue cushion comfortably engulfs me. Seamus crouches to his knees beneath me. He lifts my hand to his face, brushing it across his cheek.

"I'm gonna go grab the champagne, Claudia," Seamus tells me. I smile and nod my head in agreement.

"Hurry back," I whisper wistlessly. Seamus places a soft kiss on the back of my hand and walks away.

He leaves me sitting alone, rocking in the chair. I begin to count the seconds until his return. Time feels as if it is creeping along like a snail.

(*I hear a bang. "Slide, creak, slip," screeches the cold, gray metal of my tired defense mechanisms. I fear this man.*

"I and I alone possess my heart," she cried.

"No, we hold half your heart," the laos told her forcefully.

"It is cruel to give me hope that I still retain the capability to feel emotion," she answered.)

My eyes scan the room for a familiar face. I recognize no one. My ears perk up at the steady hum of voices I hear buzzing along together. The sound is foreign to me. It is as if another language fills the air—a language, which I do not speak. Invisible barriers alienate me. Although I wish to deny it, I suspect that I have created these barriers to safeguard myself from my desperate need to love and be loved.

As if by magick, the bells, whistles, and cuckoos of Ossie's timepiece begin to ring, ushering in the midnight hour. People yell, "Happy New Year!"

I watch couples kissing and others as they laugh and sip champagne together. I mouth the words of Auld Lang Sin, realizing that Seamus will not return. I stand and lift my arm above my head. I toss the confetti I'd been clutching in my sweaty palm into the scattered direction of a million lost souls. I close my eyes and turn my face toward where the sky should be. I make a secret vow to which I shall always adhere and shake confetti from my hair.

I walk through the crowd to retrieve my tangled mass of bags and back packs. I sling what I can over my shoulders and drag the rest across the floor. I make a beeline for the door, purposefully avoiding anyone I may know. I don't bother to thank or say goodbye to Ossie, Avery, or Cedric. Such is the gratitude of my heart.

I step into the piercing air of the frigid night. I inhale deeply, filling my lungs. I hail one of the cabs, which Ossie has arranged to have wait outside The Shack throughout the duration of the party. It is one of the two cars moving on Eighth Street. The other I suspect may be preparing for a drive by shooting.

"The airport, please," I tell the cabby, as he helps me arrange my bags in the trunk.

Within an uneventful forty minutes, I arrive at the Domestic Departures gate, check my bags, and find myself waiting to board a flight to New Orleans.

The feeling in the pit of my stomach when I'm flying alone to somewhere other than home is always gut wrenching. The fear of the unknown lies below me, waiting. I worry if I will be welcome because I have not yet been where I am are going. Then, I realize that I am suddenly somewhere new—somewhere different and exotic and not where I was.

So I tell you. So I take you. So I tell you. So I take you.

To the Crescent City where all of my dreams live like Willie Wonka's did in his Chocolate Factory.

There is the first sight of New Orleans. I am forced to lean over the arm of my seat because I am not sitting next to the window. It is an awkward position, which grants me only limited view. But scattered in the midst of the pitch-black sky, I spy the bright lights of the city, twinkling in a spectrum of beautiful shades.

It reminds me of the confetti I threw at midnight.

I sip the last of my Dewar's and squint down again at the lights. Their outline forms a crescent shape, which bends along the river. I fasten my seat belt and listen to the captain's soothing voice as he announces our arrival. I sink my head back into the seat and sigh. In minutes, the landing gear touches the ground and we taxi toward the gate.

I wait patiently as passengers from the rows ahead of me slowly begin to search for their bags. Forming a steady line, they make their way off the plane. I stand and stretch languidly. With my two carry-ons, I follow the somber procession and cordially wish the flight attendants goodbye. I clumsily walk through the hollow, boarding tunnel and step into the tacky, New Orleans airport.

I start to think of Cameron. I become nervous and fear that I do not remember what he looks like. It's been a long time since I've seen him last. I never even spent that much time with him to begin with. We have been more like long distance pen pals than anything else. I do not recognize him at the gate, so I start toward the baggage claim.

I walk quickly through the dark and nearly deserted airport, mindlessly following the arrows posted high above my head. There is an overweight black woman selling pretzels at a cart to my right. My eyes devour the sight of colorful prints hanging on the walls behind her, which scream things like "Mardi Gras Central," "Jambalaya Jam," and "Zataran Dirty Rice." The carpet below me is littered with trash, as if a whirlwind has gushed through the bowels of the airport.

The place has the feel of an Atlantic City casino in the early morning hours.

I reach the baggage claim and position myself at an empty area along the belt. I place the bags I am holding onto the ground near my feet. Standing alone, I find myself eavesdropping on the conversations going on around me. I recognize the rough New Orleans city accent dripping from the tongues of a couple to my right. I feel self-conscious of my Northeastern nature and wonder if I look like a tourist.

I turn my attention away from the baggage claim and scan the room for Cameron. I see no familiar face among the crowd and begin to worry that he may stand me up. Before I lose myself in paranoia, however, I spy Cameron from the corner of my eye.

He approaches me slowly as if he is afraid of startling me. His gait is light and long. His hair is much longer than I remember. It is tied back in a ponytail along the nape of his neck. He does not smile at me. Instead, he wears the stern and chiseled look of a middle-aged man. He seems nervous. It is contagious.

"Claudia," he says, stopping at my side.

"Cameron," I say, in return.

He lifts his arm to my shoulder and then grabs me in a strong bear hug. His hug tells me that everything is fine—that I can stay with him as long as I like.

Cameron releases me from the giant hug. He steps away from me and stares into my face. I stare back at him. His skin is lightly tanned. He is clad in an oversized black T-shirt, the front of which reads "Atlanta". A bed of brightly colored peaches serves as backdrop for the word. Cameron hands me a wilted daisy, which looks as if it has seen better days. I accept the flower graciously.

"Your hair," I say, with a smile. I reach to push a stray strand from his eye and tuck it behind his ear.

"Yeah, I let it grow," he explains.

"It looks great," I comment.

"Thanks," he responds with a pause. "Let's grab your bags. I thought we could swing into the bar before we head home. I could really use a cocktail before work," he says.

"That'd be great," I agree as we push closer toward the turnstile. "How was your New Year's Eve?" I ask enthusiastically.

"Girl, you must be somethin' special because you wouldn't believe what I had to give up to get here," Cameron jokes in a slow drawl that sounds like that of a Manhattan cab driver.

"Hell, now that I think about it I'm not even sure I know *how* I got here," he adds, placing emphasis on the word "how".

"I don't want to know," I laugh, holding up my hand like a traffic guard. He snickers lightly.

"Hey, there's one of 'em," I yelp, as Cameron jumps to grab my bag.

"Thanks," I say, reaching for another.

"How many more?" he asks.

"That's the last one," I answer, pointing to a bulging and clearly over packed blue and white striped bag.

"Jesus," Cameron mutters.

"Come on," I scold him. "This is my whole life. This is *everything*. You have no idea how much I left behind," I tell him. I want desperately to disown the impact of my own words.

Cameron moves closer to me and clasps his left hand around my neck and face. He responds, "Yes I do, Claudia."

"Thanks, Cameron," I whisper, almost frightened by his intensity. I know my words could just as well have gone unspoken.

Together, Cameron and I drag my bags through the abandoned airport. Walking within the terminal, we pass a pastry shop called Bag-a-Beignet and another named The Praline Purveyor, which sells loose candy and dried fruit. This terminal ends and converges with others at a central food court. The airport bar, Mrs. Sippy's, sits at the opposite end of the food court. Cameron and I stumble into the smoky room and collapse at one of the two unoccupied tables.

"Bourbon?" Cameron asks genteelly.

"Scotch," I correct him. I never liked bourbon; it was too sweet for my taste. Cameron nods and walks off toward the bar to order our drinks.

Waiting for his return, I fumble through my backpack for a tube of lipstick. The thought of drinking scotch with a man I barely know in the city that I love on the first day of the New Year excites me. I begin to feel confident and sexy. I want to flaunt my confident, sexy self to others. I search for the darkest color lipstick I can find. I settle for one called "Sangria".

I finish applying my first coat of "Sangria" as Cameron arrives back at the table with our drinks. I purse my lips together on a white tissue to blend the lipstick. I draw the tissue from my face and study the imprint of my kiss. It looks cheap and makes me smile.

"Here you are," Cameron says, placing my scotch in front of me. He pulls out a chair for himself and adds, "Got it on the rocks because I didn't know how you liked it."

"This is great, Cameron. Thank you very much," I reply.

We sit quietly for some time, sipping our drinks alone with each other. Feeling compelled to break the silence, I ask, "So you got a job?"

Cameron laughs loudly as if I have made a stupid comment, then answers, "Yes, I got a job."

"I'm the new lifeguard at the Holiday Inn on Canal Street," he announces, inflating his chest proudly.

"Putting the Math major to work, are you?" I joke, taking another swig of my scotch. The ice tumbles forward from the bottom of the glass and splashes me on the tip of my nose. Although I know I should be embarrassed, this makes me feel like a little girl. I think, for a moment, of slurping.

"It's gonna be pretty sweet digs," Cameron explains. "Just lounging by the pool all day, watching the tourists float around, checkin' out little cuties in their bikinis."

"No stress," he says as he lowers his voice and makes a straight, jabbing motion with a flat hand.

"Indoor or outdoor?" I ask.

"Indoor for now. Hopefully I'll be promoted by Spring to outdoor. Gotta get the summer tan goin'," Cameron adds.

"I'm working ten to six today so I'll set you up in your room," he tells me. "I figured you wouldn't mind because you'd want to sleep most of the day," he says, knowingly.

"You've got that right," I agree. "Will anybody else be home?" I ask.

"My dad probably," Cameron answers. "He's been hitting the bourbon pretty hard since the evil step mother left. That's it though— Sophie's staying at Vanderbilt over break and Maddox is in Dallas visiting relatives," he explains.

"Wow, is your dad O.K.?" I pry.

"I don't think he misses *her* really. I think he's just pissed off because she gutted the place. Took it all—the furniture, the plants, the pictures, the curtains," he says. "Don't expect much because there's nothing left," he warns me.

"Dad's pretty harmless but watch yourself. He'll try to hit on you since you're so hot," Cameron cautions. "I bet he'll make you his shrimp etouffe."

I shoot Cameron an inquisitive look. He finishes his bourbon after the tail of his sentence. I drain the last drops of alcohol from my glass.

"You ready to get going?" Cameron asks, jerking his head in the direction of the door. He is trying to change the subject and I let him.

"You got it," I concede. "I'm exhausted," I tell him, rising to collect my bags.

We walk from the airport and step outside into the early morning. My eyes focus on the tumbling rays of an orange and yellow sunrise as it bleeds into the blackness of the night sky. I am enveloped immediately by the warm film of the Louisiana air. When the body is lost to day after day of frigid cold and wind, the sudden submersion into magnificent sunlight makes the spirit feel so free that it becomes spiritless.

My breath is pushed from my lungs with a force so powerful I feel new again.

Cameron had parked his father's blue Suburban truck over the yellow painted warning, which screams "LOADING AND UNLOADING ONLY". I am amazed that the car has not yet been towed. We walk to the back and Cameron lifts the hatch so we can load my luggage. I smile at the sight of the white "Sportsman's Paradise" license plate and crouch on my knees to view it more closely. I wipe a smudge of dirt from the plate's lower right corner.

I pull my hand back to see if there is now dirt on my fingertips. I do this sort of like the "pinch me" test—to see if I am really here.

I am really here.

"Girl, what're you doin'?" Cameron asks, waiting for me to step back from the truck so he can close the hatch.

"Nothing," I answer, clearly embarrassed. Startled by the realization that someone is watching me, I rise to my feet.

Cameron guides me along the passenger side of the Suburban. He opens the door for me, waits until I have positioned myself in the huge front seat and shuts the door with a loud slam. I lean to unlock the driver's side for him but he beats me to it. I curse myself for not having moved faster.

Cameron starts the engine, revving it lightly. He flicks on WWOZ, an old school jazz station. Passing a police car marked N.O.P.D., we head toward Route 10, which eventually rolls into Claiborne Avenue. As we move through the more densely populated areas of the city, I begin to feel as if I am watching an old blues documentary on public television.

Everything seems old and quaint and French and tattered and slow and congested. It is humid and sultry, even at this time of year. Even the trees hang lower in the oppressive heat. The bushes and the crab grass grow wildly in front of the houses and buildings. Paint chips everywhere. It is all untamed, like I stepped back in time to a place that didn't need to hurry because there was nowhere to hurry to.

There are the shotgun houses in pink and pale yellow and pastel blue. There are the cemeteries filled with above ground tombs. There are the wrought iron porches and the white lattice woodwork, carved into the shapes of veves. There are the archways covered with ivy and the little black girls jumping rope on the sidewalk. The little girls' brothers and boyfriends tap dance on street corners with bottle caps stuck to the tips of their shoes. And there are the old men crouched and leaning on stoops, eating po-boys, drinking from paper bags, and playing harmonicas.

In moments, I think to myself, I can change into a summer dress and wear it all year long if so I choose.

We turn down St. Charles, passing stately mansion after stately mansion. We follow the streetcar line through a sea of residential houses. Sensing we are drawing closer to Soniat Avenue, I begin to focus more closely on my surroundings. It is nearly full light. I spy a slate gray cat as it disappears into a bed of tall weeds and watch as Cameron's house comes into view.

We turn down the gravel driveway, forcing rocks to pop upward beneath the weight of our tires. Cameron parks the Suburban. I jump out, slamming the heavy door behind me.

The hair on my arms begins to tingle and I feel warm inside. The house looks as I imagine Emily Dickinson's would.

The edges and windows of the bright pink two story are trimmed stark white. The trim wraps around the middle of the house, separating two porch-lined floors. A worn-looking hammock hangs on the first, while an inviting porch swing sways lightly in the breeze. A haphazard arrangement of white wicker furniture is scattered on the second.

From the outside, the house appears deserted. The front door is thrust wide open and the porch light has been left on. Hanging above the doorway is a dry, brown pine garland, which droops as low as if it has been there since last Christmas. Eyeing it more carefully, I decide that it may have been there even longer than that.

Rather than walking up the front steps, I leap from the driveway and over the side of the porch. I steady myself with one of the white columns. Careful not to misstep over any missing floorboards, I walk toward the unsteady looking porch swing. On its seat lies an open-faced textbook. I reach for the book but instead trip over a half-gallon milk jug. I knock the jug on its side. A murky substance oozes from it and seeps along the porch. I step gingerly away from the thick liquid.

Disturbed, I turn back to Cameron. He has begun to pile my bags over the side of the porch over which I had jumped.

"I'm sorry," I say, nearly having forgotten all about them.

"No problem," Cameron responds. "I wanna get them out now because I'm taking the Suburban to work," he explains.

After a deliberate pause, he adds, "I want you to have everything you need, Claudia."

"I do, Cameron," I say. "I do."

I hoist as much as I can carry over my shoulders and enter the house through front door.

The house is empty—stripped bare. Cameron is right. With the exception of Mr. Thomas' library, some rolled-up Oriental rugs, and a small grouping of rusty porch furniture, his stepmother had taken it all.

"Wow, you were right," I tell him. "There's not much left."

I balance myself on my right heel and use my other foot to pull a strand of Mardi Gras beads from a plastic bag. The bag is overflowing with fabulously bright colored necklaces, doubloons, stale candy, and plastic cups. I kick the beads into the air, catching them with my hand. I begin to braid them therapeutically through my fingers.

"I tol' you," Cameron replies. He tries to guide me hurriedly up a flight of stairs positioned to my left.

I follow his lead through the main entrance parlor and into the library. I trace my hand along the royal blue wallpaper of the room, stopping before the stairwell to admire a bookshelf lined with hardbacks of varying shapes and sizes. Perched there, lay John Kennedy Toole's *A Confederacy of Dunces*.

I place my palm gingerly across the spine of the book. I smile a smile that reeks of the wisdom gained from my past and the promise held by my future.

"Please get out of the house, Ignatius, and enter the world around you," I say, quoting Toole directly. I wait for Cameron's response.

"The bible of the vice capital of the world," he notes with a smirk and a shake of his head. He stops on the first step and leans over to scoop up the book from the shelf. "Makes for good bedside reading; I'll bring it upstairs."

"You read my mind," I tell him, as we continue to walk the steps.

I recognize the distant volume of a television set. The sound grows nearer as we approach the second floor. I jump slightly at the top stairs. The sight of Cameron's father, who is passed out cold in an abhorrent looking blue velour recliner, startles me. A half-empty fifth of Jack Daniel's is overturned and dripping onto the floor next to him. The glass he'd apparently been using before he lost consciousness is precariously positioned in his hands, which rest upon his chest. The glass rises and falls each time he takes a breath.

Cameron pauses to put down one of my bags and lifts the glass from his father's chest. He places it on a three-legged table not far from reach. Mr. Smith stirs lightly, forcing his already unkempt gray hair to flop over his eyes. I scan the room, which looks as if it has been swept through by a hurricane. Books, papers, dirty dishes, beads, doubloons and cups cover every inch of available floor space.

"What is he watching?" I ask Cameron, fascinated by the television.

"Christ, he plays that damned tape over and over," Cameron mumbles almost inaudibly.

"Don't ask him any questions about it or you'll get stuck watching it for hours," he advises.

"It's Sophie's coming out from last Mardi Gras. My dad says it was the proudest day of his entire life," Cameron says, adding the explanation strictly for my benefit.

"Cameron," I slur, focusing on the home video. "Look at him," I plead.

In the video, a well-groomed Mr. Smith is speaking directly to the camera. He is impeccably dressed in a black tuxedo. He repeatedly makes sarcastic side comments to another man who is elaborately costumed for the holiday ritual.

"He looks amazing," I proclaim, as if speaking of a dead man.

"Yeah," Cameron agrees, nostalgically. "It was a great day. She looked like a princess. Even her friends from Vanderbilt were impressed," he adds.

"Come on," Cameron commands.

We leave his father and move toward a pair of French doors, which lead to my room. One of the doors is slightly ajar. Cameron pushes it open.

"I was gonna put you in Sophie's room upstairs because it had the private bath," Cameron tells me. "But I'm too selfish; I want it for myself," he confesses.

"By default, you get my old room. It has the porch though, so you've got some definite perks," he tries convincingly.

The room is sparsely decorated, which suits me fine. The wall facing the street is filled with tall windows and a glass door, which leads to my verandah. The wallpaper has been peeled from the walls, as if someone had once anticipated either recovering them or painting over them. There are spotty patches of the old pattern interspersed within the drab brown of the undressed wall.

Furniture pieces are minimal. There is a queen size bed to my right, a small bedside table with a bottom drawer that droops open like a tongue protruding from a giant mouth, and another dresser pushed steadfastly against the opposite wall. The dresser looks nearly five feet long. Its top is scattered with bric-a-brac—candles, empty cigarette packs, books, tapes, beer bottles, and coins. All of these items are reflected in the antique mirror, which is bordered in a flower pattern and hangs above the dresser.

I grin widely, drop my bags to the floor, and collapse on the bed. "Home sweet home," I say.

"It's all yours cher," Cameron promises.

"I'm outta here—gotta snooze," he explains. "There's a fifth of bourbon and some glasses in the bottom drawer of that," he offers, motioning toward the bedside dresser. "I'm sure there's some scotch on the bar downstairs," he advises.

"Thanks, Cameron. What time will you be back?" I ask.

"Probably not till after six," he answers, as he steps over a mound of clothes to drop a set of keys on the dresser. He moves effortlessly back toward the doors.

"Claudia," Cameron says.

"Yes?" I respond, upturning my voice.

"I'm glad you're here," he says with a sincere, straight face.

"Thanks, I'll see you when I get home," I tell him. I shut the doors tightly behind him and push the brass metal lock up into the ceiling.

I fall again into the bed. Before my head hits the pillow, I drift into one of the deepest sleeps I have ever known.

Hours later, I wake still feeling lazy and exhausted, like I could easily sleep through the night. I can tell it is already late afternoon by the way the sunlight trickles in through the white lace curtains, which whisper in the breeze. Even though it's January, it is unusually hot. Tropical humidity traps sweat on my skin.

I roll from the bed slowly and stretch lightly. I rummage amidst the mess for matches or a lighter to light some of the already well-burnt candles in the room. I love burning candles in the daylight; it seems so frivolous and sexy.

I walk then to the windows, pull the blinds, and thrust them as wide open as I can manage. I glance out at the Spanish moss, which dangles and sways from the branches of the cypress tree in the front yard. As I turn back to the sea of crumpled starched white sheets, I lift the dusty clock radio next to the bed. I struggle with it for a bit but manage to find a weak signal. I recognize the yelping of an old Robert Johnson tune, even though the warped record crackles repeatedly with static.

I flip absentmindedly through the pages of *A Confederacy of Dunces* but quickly tire of the occupation. I decide instead to simply sit alone in this room. I shift my gaze from the clock radio to the mirror straight ahead and to the curtains I see when I glance to my right.

Alone in this room. I have never been alone in this room. So I will stay quietly now and feel the blanket of warmth that covers my skin.

I pull the damp sheet up to my neck. I no longer see my body.

As I close my eyes, I feel only the lingering smell of jasmine, honeysuckle, and rose that filters through the musty salt air. My mind begins to race.

Any time anything bad has ever happened in my life, I have forced myself to immediately slip from reality into a peaceful fantasia conjured up by thoughts of New Orleans.

Perhaps it is not the physical boundary and mysterious beauty of the Crescent City that has led me here. More than likely, I believe that I have been driven by a self-created ideal. An ideal that the grass is always greener here. Maybe it's not really an ideal. Maybe it's more like a hope—that it really does exist every minute of every day as it does in my mind.

I have only ever wanted to be happy in my life and to not hurt anyone else along the way.

I think I created the ideal because I felt so many people expected too much of me. I became overburdened by wicked, evil demands on my time. But I couldn't do it. I couldn't do whatever it was they all wanted me to do. I was promised that great things would happen to me. I believed lies.

And then, I realized that it wasn't going to happen *to* me. I realized I didn't need an ideal. I didn't need hope. I didn't even need the lottery. I just needed to trust in who I was.

Perhaps I am only selfish. Perhaps, however, my days in Philadelphia were merely a sloughing off of a dry, dead skin that was nothing more than cracked and wrinkled and prone to cancerous doom. I shed the old to give way to the new and arrive at the birth of the self. The self I had always wanted to be but couldn't because too many people wanted too many things and I didn't want to disappoint them.

For the first time in twenty-five years, I have no commitments to a family, to a child, to a lover, or to a friend. There is only me.

Perhaps the ghosts of my past will come crashing down to haunt me, as I know they will. But I think there will always be ghosts. I pray that I do not go crazy listening to their howling voices because I must remain strong enough to run bare foot through the grass at least once a day no matter how green or how brown it may be.

If I get to pick a banana from the banana tree in my back yard and offer it up to Maitresse Erzulie at least a few times this year, things will be O.K.

To Olivia, I offer my love. To Remy, I offer my love. To my parents. To Phoebe. To Oliver. To Gus. And to everyone else I have ever known, I offer my love.

Unfortunately, sometimes I've had to look out for myself. That turns my stomach and makes me ashamed.

But that is why I have come here to the city of my dreams. To find love. To truly be able to love. If necessary, I will accept unrequited love because I still believe it exists in the world. Somewhere, there is selfless love and nowhere else to be, nowhere else to go, no one left to meet. Someday, there will be a time to stop running because I will have borne my self.

I am alive. I breathe. I move. I read. I think. I touch. I see. I drink. I eat. I fuck. I walk. I write.

J. Ward Brennan
5 April, 1999
11:48 PM

www.ingramcontent.com/pod-product-compliance
Lightning Source LLC
Chambersburg PA
CBHW050356260626
47156CB00003B/759